Frederic B. (Frederic Beecher) Perkins

Scrope, or, the Lost Library

A Novel of New York and Hartford

Frederic B. (Frederic Beecher) Perkins

Scrope, or, the Lost Library
A Novel of New York and Hartford

ISBN/EAN: 9783337032838

Printed in Europe, USA, Canada, Australia, Japan

Cover: Foto ©Andreas Hilbeck / pixelio.de

More available books at **www.hansebooks.com**

SCROPE;

OR,

THE LOST LIBRARY.

A NOVEL OF

NEW YORK AND HARTFORD.

BY FREDERIC B. PERKINS.

HÆC FABULA NARRATUR.

BOSTON:
ROBERTS BROTHERS.
1874.

CONTENTS.

4 *Contents.*

CHAPTER I.

"HALF-A-DOLLAR, halfadollarfadollafadollafadollafadollathat's bid now, give more'f ye want it! Half-a-dollar five-eighths three-quarters — Three-quarters I'm bid: — will you say a dollar for this standard work octavo best edition harf morocker extry? Three-quarters I'm bid, three-quarters will ye give any MORE? Three-quarters, threequartthecquartthecquawtthecquawtthecquawt one dollar shall I HAVE?"

Thus vociferated, at a quarter past five o'clock in the afternoon of Tuesday, January 9th, A. D. 186—, with the professional *accelerando* and with a final smart rising inflection, that experienced and successful auctioneer Mr. Howard Ball, a broad-shouldered powerful looking man of middle height, with a large head, full eyes, a bluff look, spectacles and plenty of stiff short irongray hair.

A tall personage, old, gaunt and dry, but apparently strong, with dusty black clothes and a "stove-pipe" hat, pulled down over his eyes, in the front row of seats, a little to one side of Mr. Ball's desk, answered in a grave dry deliberate voice,

"Seven-eighths. But it's damaged."

"No tain't either" sharply answered the auctioneer, "what do ye mean, Chase?"

"Catalogue says so. It says the titlepage is greasy."

Every man at once examined the catalogue he held in his hand, and a laugh arose as one and another detected the mistake that old Chase was jesting about. The printer's proof-reader — as sometimes happens even to proof-readers — had been half learned, and out of the halfness of his learning had substituted "lubricated" which he knew, for "rubricated," which he did not, and the catalogue bore that the book had a lubricated titlepage. Everybody laughed except Chase, whose saturnine features did not change.

"Gentlemen," said Mr. Ball, "pay no attention to Chase's jokes, but go on with the sale. Seven-eighths I am bid. Seven-eighths, sevnatesnatesnatesnatesnate say a dollar, somebody!" implored he in his strong harsh voice. Then he paused a moment and looking around upon his hearers with an earnest expression, he slowly lifted his right hand as if about to make oath before any duly qualified justice of the peace or notary public:

"Going. Will nobody give me one dollar for that valuable and interesting work, octarvo best edition harf morocker extry, cheap at five dollars?"— A pause —"Gone! Chase at seven-eighths."

As he said "Gone," down came his hand with a slap. The hand is in these days often used for the traditional hammer, as a decent dress-coat is instead of the judge's ermine. The following words were his announcement to his book-keeper of the customer's name and the price; and then Mr. Ball, turning again to the audience, observed with a grin and a queer chuckle —"And a good time mister Chase'll have a gittin his money back!"

A young man in a back seat whispered to his neighbor,

"He said Chase. Isn't that Gowans?"

"What's the next line?" sung out Ball at this moment to an assistant at the side opposite to the book-keeper, always behind the long desk or counter which separates the high-priest from the votaries in such temples as this— "What's the next line? Oh yes, number ninety-three, gentlemen. 'Requeel de Divers Voyges.' Something about the pearl fisheries I guess. How much moffered f' th' Requeel, gentlemen? Full of valuable old copperplate illustrations ; rare, catalogue says, — I spose that means tisn't well done (chuckle) — rare and interesting old book "—

"Yes. He always buys by that name," briefly answered the young man's neighbor, looking up a moment from entering "7-8 Chase" in the margin of his catalogue against No. 92.

"Do they all do so?" queried the young man.

"A good many. You see "—

"Shut up there, Sibley !" broke in the strong business voice of the auctioneer. "Order in the ranks! I can't hear myself think, you keep up such a racket !"

The words were sufficiently rough, but the speaker's bluff features wore a jolly smile, and he ended with a short chuckle. He was right, too, in substance, and the person he called Sibley did "shut up," though a kind of sniff and a meaning smile and look at his young companion intimated the dissent of superior breeding as to the manner of the request.

The sale was one which might be classed as "strictly miscellaneous." It is true that a hasty glance at the title-page of the catalogue informed the reader in "full faced display type " that there was a "valuable private library ;" but a closer inspection would show that like those speakers who go

at once from whisper to shout, this deluding inscription leaped from small "lower-case" to a heavy "condensed Gothic," somewhat thus :

"CATALOGUE

of books, including

A VALUABLE PRIVATE LIBRARY,

etc, etc."

No doubt it was "valuable" in a sense. So is dirt. But assuredly no human being having his wits about him, would give shelf-room to such a mess as this was, taking it all together, unless for purposes of commerce. It was one of those sales that are made up once in a while from odds and ends of consignments, with some luckless invoice of better books mingled in, to flavor a little, if it may be, the unpleasant mass. But the plan is sure to fail : poor Tray is judged by his company ; the good books go for the price of poor ones, the poor ones for the price of " paper stock ; " the account-sales ends with a small additional charge over and above receipts against the consignor to meet expenses, cataloguing and auctioneer's commissions ; and the consignor, using indefensible terms of general reproach, goes through the absurd operation of paying money for the loss of his property. The auctioneer's shelves are cleared, at any rate, and ready for replenishment with those gorgeous or rare books which he loves to sell, feeling his commission rising warm in his very pockets, as the emulous calls or nods or delicate wafts of catalogues or tip-ups of fore-fingers flock up to him from every part of the room, and his voice grows round and full as he glances hither and thither, hopping up the numeration table ten dollars at a time.—

How still the room grows, when such a passage-at-purses soars aloft like the spirits of the dead soldiers in Kaulbach's "Battle of the Huns," into that rare and exhausting two-or-three-hundred-dollar atmosphere!

But there was none of that, on this occasion. The number of "lines" or lots, in the catalogue, was only two hundred and eighty-nine, in all. In the New York book-auctions, somewhat more than a hundred lots an hour are commonly despatched; the cheaper the lots the faster they must be run off; and in the present instance a single sitting of two hours or so was deemed an ample allowance. The actual bulk, or weight, or number, whichever category you may prefer, of volumes, however, was very considerable, as the common practice had been pursued of "bunching up" five, ten or twenty of the miserable things, into parcels with a string, and cataloguing them somewhat thus:

245. Tupper's Proverbial Philosophy etc. 5 vols.

246. Patent Reports etc. 10 vols. Some valuable.

247. School-books. 20 vols.

Well: the sale went on, Chase buying an extraordinary number of lots, and a small, short, bushy-bearded and wonderfully dirty Israelite who sat next him, and whom the bluff auctioneer irreverently saluted when he first bid with "Hallo! you there, father Abraham?" buying a very few bundles at two cents or three cents per volume. The securing of one of these small prizes by the dirty man seemed to irritate worthy Mr. Ball; for having offered to the company the succeeding lot, and there being a moment's pause in which no one bid, the auctioneer with much gravity exclaimed,

"Put it down to Chase at five cents!"

"I won't have it!" said the old man.

"Yo *shall* have it — what's the next?" was all the auctioneer replied, with a facetious chuckle and an assumption of great violence, and down it went to Chase, while Mr. Ball, without heeding his remonstrances, went straight on with the next lot. This was a worn looking octavo volume, with what is technically called a "skiver" or "split sheep" back and old-fashioned marbled board sides.

"Number 109," cried the auctioneer; "Reverend Strong's ordination sermon and so forth. Valuable old pamphlets, and what'll you give for IT?" — with a quaint sudden stress on this seldom emphasized pronoun, as if Mr. Ball had meant that the poor neglected thing should find one at least to think it of some weight.

"Ten cents," said old Chase, in his grave dry voice — "what's the book?"

"Twenty-five," said somebody.

"Thirty," called out the young man who had asked about Chase. His voice was eager, and no doubt more than one of the sharp veterans present said to themselves, at that intonation, "Ah, I can put *him* up if I like!" But the sale was dull; as it happened no one did "put him up."

"Thirty cents I'm bid," proceeded Mr. Ball; "Thirty, thirty, thirty. Say thirty-five. Thirty-five shall I HAVE? And gone [slap] for thirty cents WHIZZIT?"

"Cash," was the reply to this inquiry for a name; and the buyer, stepping up to the desk, paid his money and took his book.

"Mark it delivered," resumed the auctioneer; "The next is number 110, Life of Brown. How much will you give for IT? How much for Brown? The celebrated Brown! Come, be quick, gentlemen! I can't stay here all night! One dollar one dollar one dollawundollawundolla why is that too much? What *will* you give then?"

"Two cents" timidly ventured the soiled dove of a Hebrew, who looked as if he had "lain among the pots" ever since the idea of doing so was first started.

"No you don't!" exclaimed the scandalized auctioneer, "I'll give three cents myself. Here, Chase, now I expect you to offer five cents apiece for every book on this catalogue."

"I'll do it," returned the old man promptly; and the humble hopes of the poor Jew were effectually extinguished. He rose and quietly stole out of the room, his head bent forward, with an air of exhaustion, suffering and patient endurance. No wonder; it must have been a burden to carry the real estate and perfumery together that were upon his person.

As he went out, in came Sibley in haste, from the hall outside, and resumed his seat, which nobody in particular had observed him leaving, calling out as he did so,

"What number are you selling?"

"One hundred and ten, Sibley,—five cents is bid, seven and a half will you give?"

"One hundred and ten!" exclaimed Sibley, greatly discomposed—"I wanted one hundred and nine; got an unlimited order; I was only called out for a moment—who's got it?"

"Cash is his name," returned the accommodating auctioneer, chuckling; and a long thin fellow who bought books in the name of Park, and whose quiet, shrewd and rather satirical cast of features denoted much character, added briskly,

—"and cash is his nature. Be on hand next time, Sibley. 'Too late I staid, forgive the crime.'"

But Sibley paid no heed to their chaffing, and the sale went noisily on, while Mr. "Cash" civilly informed his disappointed neighbor that he had bought the book, and at the same time handed it to him for inspection. Sibley took it, and barely glancing at the title page of the first pamphlet in it, returned it with thanks;

"Thank you (then to the auctioneer)—five-eighths! (then to Cash) My customer wanted that first sermon, no doubt (then to Ball) Yes!—quarter (then to Cash) I've got a fresh uncut copy that I'll give him. for the same money (then to Ball) No—let him have it (then to Cash)—much obliged to you all the same."

The young man who had described himself as "Cash" now proceeded to give the volume a vicious wrench open across his knee; took out his knife and cut the twine strings at the back; then, turning the covers back together, as cruel victors pinion their captives' elbows close in behind them, he passed the knifeblade behind a smaller pamphlet bound out of sight, as it were among the full sized octavos that constituted the bulk of the volume, so as to slit it out complete, perhaps bringing with it a film of the sheepskin of the back, held to the pamphlet by the clinging dry old paste. Then he again passed the volume to his neighbor, observing

"There; that's all I wanted; I'm going, and I shall leave the rest of the volume any way; so I'll make you a present of it."

"Well," said Sibley, rather startled —"stay—however, if you say so"—

And he laid the book in his lap, for the young man had risen with sudden quickness and was already out of the room.

CHAPTER II.

THERE is a small oblong upland meadow, of an acre or thereabouts in extent. It is enclosed by a high but ruinous board fence, showing signs of prehistoric paint, and its line reels, as it were, every now and then, sometimes outward and sometimes inward, as if quite too drunk to be steady, but still obstinate in clinging to the general line of duty; a strange cincture for the neglected grass land within, which seems more likely to be shut in by the traditionary post-and-rail or the still more primitive " stake-and-rider " of the farm. This area is uneven, as if it had never since the removal of the first forest growth been once well levelled and cultivated; humpy almost as if irregularly set with old graves; all overgrown with meadow grass, long and fine and thin, like ill kept hair of one now growing old; and looped and tangled here and there in the hollows, in dry wisps and knots, along with a scanty growth of brambles. At distant points there are a few trees. Two or three are ancient apple trees, dry-barked, thin of leafage, unhappy and starved in aspect. There is one solitary Lombardy poplar; an erect shaft, obstinately pointing upwards, though wizened and almost bare, like an energetic old fashioned maiden aunt, good, upright, rigid and homely. The largest group is a clump, or rather a dispersed squad, of weeping willows; unexpected occupants of such high and dry and thirsty earth. Yet there they stand, with the dried, scrawny, half-bald look that pertains to the very earth beneath them, and to every thing that grows out of it; their long sad boughs trailing to the ground, so nearly destitute even of the scanty lanceolate foliage which is proper to them, as to repeat at a little distance the idea of the grass — that of long thin neglected hair.

In the middle of the space around which these dreary trees stand like a picket line, is that which they were doubtless meant to adorn; an old comfortless-looking white wooden house. It is not ruinous, but is ill repaired and will be ruinous very soon; in a year or two more the dingy white will verge into a dingy brown; warping clapboards will have worked loose at one end, and the sloping line of only two or three of them will throw a disreputable shade over the whole front; some furious night-blast will fling those loose bricks that balance on the rim of the large old-fashioned central chimney-shaft, down with an ominous hollow bang, upon the loosened shingles of the roof, and thence to the ground : the shock will dislodge the shingles and admit the rain into the roomy old garret in streams, instead of the slow strings of drops that now make their quiet way here and there in upon the floor. When that point is reached, the destruction goes on more swiftly. Even if small boys do not break many a ready road through every old-fashioned little window-pane, the leakage through the roof itself will not require many years to loosen the faithful old plaster of the ceilings of the second story rooms, to lay it in ruin upon their floors, and to make its steady way onward to the lower floor, by a process not unlike that to which the French were forced, in penetrating the heroic city of Zaragoza.

Even to say where this desolate old house and lot is not, would never suggest where it is. Any one familiar with New England will say, That is like an old family homestead in some ancient Connecticut or Massachusetts town, where all the young people have regularly moved away every year for the last century, and the old people have died, and the old houses are dying too.

True; it is like it. But the old house and lot is not there. It is in the heart of New York City — that is, the ground is there, and the old house too, unless it has been pulled down, which to be sure is likely enough. The place however is on Hudson street, a considerable distance above Canal, and nearly or quite opposite an old church. But the old church may be gone too, by this time. At any rate, so it was at the time of the auction; and the graded level of the four streets around — for this lost-looking spot occupied a whole block — contrasted stiffly with the humps and hollows within. More than one such piece of waste real estate can be found in every great city. Sometimes it is land unimproved, sometimes it is covered with ruinous shabby little hovels standing among great business houses or rich mansions, sometimes it is a costly tenement standing shut and empty year after year. The reason is commonly, either minority of heirs, a lingering law-suit, or a capitalist's whim.

The parlor of this house was a comfortably furnished well-sized room of no very particular appearance, with an open grate and a bright coal fire, a piano, tables, curtains, and "tackle, apparel and furniture complete," as they say in a ship's bill of sale. Something there was however about the room, rather to be felt than seen, and which not every one could perceive at all. This something, when recognized, proved to be a feeling that somebody lived in the room; that it was used; was occupied; was a home. It would be difficult to say what gave this impression. Perhaps it was that the chairs did not all stand on the meridian; that the willow work-basket at one side of the fireplace was a little too far out in the room, as if put there on purpose; and that it overflowed with the gracious little enginery and materials of feminine domestic manufacture; that a book lay carelessly over the edge of the shelf, and several others and some magazines and papers, in no order, on the table; that a curtain hung a little one side, as if some one had looked out of the window and had let the curtain fall, instead of executing a precise re-adjustment of it. The room and its contents seemed as if in process of use; not as if under effort not to use them, nor as if set apart for show, or for consecration. Some would say, no doubt, that this feeling was from the impressions or emanations or atmosphere — the persisting color or flavor or tone, or all together — that had been dispersed about this room and printed upon its whole bounds and contents, by those who dwelt in it.

However this may be, something of this kind there was. The room was rather dusky than light however, for the colors of wall-paper, carpet, curtains, table-cover and furniture alike were chiefly of rather sombre and rusty reds and browns. A little conservatory opened from one window, which was cut down to the floor on purpose. This was filled to overflowing with strongly grown plants, most of them of the ornamental-leaved sorts that have become such favorites within the last ten or fifteen years; and among these glowed the magnificent blooms of some of the brightest and largest flowered pelargoniums and tuberous-rooted fuchsias. There was a small fountain and basin with gold fish, almost buried under their leafage;

and above over it, hung from the roof by scarlet cords, a large brightly colored shell, from which grew a graceful feathery plume of green sprays.

Of ornaments or works of art, there were but very few in this room. The principal one was a large and broadly executed steel engraving, whose white "high lights" shone from its place above the grate in violent contrast to the sombre quiet of the rest of the room. Its subject was simply horrible — one of those powerful literal representations of mere agony that people seem to enjoy, with a vulgar brutal appetite like that which draws a crowd to see a public death. It was called "The Dying Camel." The field of the picture was filled with two broad masses, sky and desert. Below, stretched the flat thirsty stony sand, lifeless, endless, bounded by its one heavy horizon line, and glimmering and trembling in the naked cruel stillness of the insufferable sunbeams that filled the hot white sky above. Close down in the middle of the foreground was the huge dark ungainly mass of the camel, prostrate, exhausted. His dead master lay flat on his face crowded under the shade of the beast's flank, his arms spread out at full length. An empty water flask, just beyond the dead fingers' ends, protruded a mocking round vacant mouth at the spectator. The miserable camel had just strength enough left to lift its long dry neck and grotesque muzzle into the air, and the artist had imparted to the savage hairy face a horrible expression of despair, for the sunken eyes watched the circlings of a wide-winged vulture from moment to moment poising himself close above for the first gripe of claw and stab of beak; and from the extreme distance there came flying low over the sand, with eager necks outstretched before

them a long line of other vultures, already scenting their prey.

At the centre table of this room, on the evening of the day of the book-auction, sat an old man. He was slender and almost frail; tall, dressed in black; with long silvery curls, and a bloodlessly white face, delicately featured, and whose thoughtful spiritual intelligence was saddened by some element of sorrow which might be weakness or disappointment or dissatisfaction or pain, — any or all of them together. His forehead was high, smooth, retreating and narrow ; his attitude upright; and the ease and precision of his movements, and the clearness and brightness of his eyes, although they were sunken deep under the long overgrown eyebrows, showed that he had a good deal of life still left in him. On the table under a drop-light, confused with the books and magazines, were writing materials and a disorderly pile of papers, among which he had been working — or else, as they say in the country — "puttering."

In a wadded arm-chair by the fire sat a girl, easily enough recognized as his daughter; and the next observation likely to be made was, that old as her father was, he would probably outlive her. She was of middle height, very delicately formed, but with that roundness of modelling which makes people look so much lighter than they really are. Her skin was singularly clear and thin and almost as bloodlessly white as her father's; the blue veins here and there showing indicated that the whiteness was not that of opaque tissue, but of deficient circulation and general condition. Her heavy black hair was coiled carelessly at the back of her head, and combed away from her forehead, and from the small white ears, so as to show the wavy line that limited the growth of the hair along the temples, and to display fully the remarkable width and fullness of the forehead. This, indeed, was so marked that the family likeness which was unmistakable upon the two faces of herself and her father, existed there in spite of the contradiction of the foreheads. Her eyes were very large, of a limpid gray, with long black lashes, and with delicate clearly pencilled eyebrows whose line was almost level for a little ways outward from the nose, and then fell on either hand in a more distinct curve. The nose was fine but high, with well opened nostrils and thin, almost translucent tissues, like those of a blood horse; the mouth neither small nor large, the lips rather full than thin, and as well as the chin, beautifully modelled, with that statuesque emphasis and distinctness of cut whose absence is one of the defects of the generic American face — if such generic face there be. But these lips were much too pale for beauty of color; and they were extremely sensitive; so much so as to suggest some excessively wild and timid creature of the woods rather than a human being. And yet this vivid sensitiveness of the lips was contradicted by the serious thoughtful fearlessness of the eyes. The character of ill health so clearly intimated by the dead whiteness of the complexion and the paleness of the lips was greatly strengthened by the dark shades under the eyes, and by an undefinable but unmistakable languor of attitude, movement and of voice. Like her father, she was dressed in black; a heavy rich black silk, cut high in the neck, but with a small square space in front after the pretty fashion called *à la Pompadour*, A narrow border of lace at the neck, and lace cuffs to match, were the only

approach to ornament in the whole costume. There was no ribbon, no bow, no ear-drops, no necklace, no bracelet, no buckle, no brooch, not even a ring. The young girl's singularly elegant figure, the extreme quietness and even impassiveness of her perfectly composed and refined manner, were in some way intensified and set off by this rigid elderly plainness and richness of costume, which, as the French would say, swore furiously at her youth. Thus the whole effect was a contradiction, so harsh, so violent, as to suggest at first the hateful idea of an obtruded modesty. This however quickly gave way, on a little observation, to the correct conclusion, that it was an incongruity only. But there was another effect, which the whole personality of the girl produced; it was, if one might say so, that there radiated from her, or slowly gathered about her wherever she was, not the light and life that should glow from the young, but an atmosphere — or influence — that was dark, and dreary, if not cold; perhaps not dead, but lifeless, — is there not a shade of difference? Lastly: perhaps the strongest — certainly the most obvious mark of family resemblance was a habit of eye common to her and her father. With noticeable frequency their upper eyelids came down so as to veil half the iris, and delayed there. All that this indicated was, reflection, or some other mental effort. Clowns, for the purpose, scratch their heads; philosophers — and people with headaches — rest their foreheads in their hands.

A third personage sat on a sofa at the hither side of the fire — i. e. to your right hand as you came from the door towards the fire — opposite the young girl, so that the three were at the angles of a triangle; and as if the two had been chatting across the hearth while her father was busy among his papers. This third was a young man; rather tall, well made, with a noticeable quickness and liveliness of manner and movement. He was somewhat fair, with merry brown eyes, good white teeth, full lips, a nose decidedly well shaped except that it was too broad and round at the end, and too thick in the wings of the nostrils, as if the maker being in some haste, had carelessly left some surplus material there. Otherwise, the face was perhaps at first sight rather dull than bright; not nearly so sprightly as the expression of the eye and the bearing of the whole figure.

A peculiar look, which might almost be called grotesque, was given to the face, undeniably well-featured as it was, by the management of the hair and beard. The abundant crisp curls of the hair were cut at about two and a half inches in length and trained on a radiating, or what the pomologists call the fan, system. This gave the hair seen in profile the look of a crest, covering the top of the head and jutting in an enterprising manner forward and upward from the upper line of the forehead. The front view was much more glorious; for it showed a thick frizzled halo standing out within an almost circular outline about the upper part of the long oval of the face, like the solid aureoles on ancient pictures of saints; or as if he dressed his hair by giving himself an awful fright every morning. The eyebrows were rather lifted, giving a funny sort of wide-awake look, which the young gentleman was accustomed to veil in some manner, if it might be, with a double eye-glass. Truly, nature having exhausted herself in this magnificent hairy crown of glory, had come short in the matter of beard; for the

chin of our friend was sparingly garnished with hair, that grew in a little thin brush or pencil, spreading outward at the ends, like the pictures of the growth of the bamboo. A like starved growth, as if a few hairs had been cruelly deserted upon some barren shore, struggled stiffly for existence upon his upper lip; and some dim prophetic glimpses of the whiskers of the future could be seen by the eye of faith, between ears and chin.

The ill-made gray suit, and the clumsy thick shoes indicated that he was an Englishman; and if this was not enough, there was a perceptible awkwardness of attitude and of manner also, such as is often seen among Englishmen even of the best social training and experience, but which in an American would be proof positive of want of such experience. Last and most of all, the cockney shibboleth of his speech ever and anon bewrayed him, in spite of the sedulous watchfulness with which he tried to talk good English — a language which exists — orally — only west of the Atlantic. In England there are corrupt dialects of it only; — 1. cockney, and 2. provincial.

CHAPTER III.

"So" — said the old man, smiling indulgently as he spoke, to the younger one, — "so, cousin Scrope, you think one needs a good deal here below, and for a good while?"

"I do so, — I do indeed," replied the young fellow: — "Now, I should say, an ouse here in the city, — yacht, of course, — place at Newport — ah, sweet place Newport, such soft hair, you know! — countwy seat on the Udson — say near Tawwytown — was up there yesterday — lovely countwy, I ashuah you. Went up there with Button — singular name that,

Mr. Van Bwaam — Button, button, who's got the button?"

"Oh, I don't know," returned the old gentleman, (not meaning any ambiguity), — "Monsieur Bouton would seem quite fine, wouldn't it? By the way, I wonder why there has been no Mr. Scissors? But how do you like Button's first name?"

"Weally, I don't know it. T Button Esq., it said — Do you know, now, you ave a monstwous many hesquires in Hamewica?"

"Oh, he might call himself Baron Button of Buttonhole, and sign all instruments, and sue and be sued by that name, if he chose. And he might have any coat of arms he might fancy, — a coat' all over gilt buttons, if he liked — on his seal, and on his carriage too, without being annoyed by the proud minions of the College of Heralds. He may tattoo himself and all his house — and grounds — all over, with any insignia he chooses, for that matter. This is a free country, cousin Scrope!"

There was something satirical in the old man's manner, as if he were half laughing at both Americans and English. He went on however:

"'Tarbox Button, his name is; 'most musical, most melancholy!'"

"Most musical, most jolly, I should say," answered the young man.. "But I can't imagine were e got that name, do you know? Hit's certainly not in my copy of the Squope and Gwosvenor Woll. Bwummagem name I should fancy, Button, at any rate."

"Father," said the young girl, with a shade of grave motherliness and mild reproof in her manner — her mother was dead, and she was both mother and daughter to the old man — "Father, you mustn't be bad, now, and make fun of Mr. Button. He has been too kind to us for that.

What would you have to do, and where should we find so good a home to live in, and where should we visit at all, if it were not for him?"

The voice was very sweet, and was low and clear like her father's; but in place of the slight but perceptible sharpness of intonation which recurred every now and then in his speech, when his sub-acid humor tinged it, hers had a striking liquid fulness like the lowest notes of a full-throated singing-bird. But it was neither sad nor glad; it had a certain indifferent or dreamy quality, almost as if the speech were that of a somnambulist; or perhaps it was an intonation of weariness.

"No harm, Civille," said Mr. Van Braam; "I was observing upon his name, not upon him."

"Vewy well off is Mr. Button, I should say?" queried Scrope.

"Yes," answered the old man. "Here's this vacant piece of ground that this old house stands on, — why, it must be worth a quarter of a million dollars, and he finds it convenient to hold it unimproved and pay our New York taxes on it, until he has time to speculate with it in some way. Meanwhile Civille and I occupy one of the most valuable estates in the city," added the old man, laughing.

"Do you know, now," pursued Scrope, "I never should ave taken Button for one of the family if I'd met im by accident say in Gweenland? E asn't the style, at all."

"Why," said the old gentleman, "I've often thought of it myself. But he had a pretty hard time when he was a boy, like a good many other rich people, and he has made his own way, without any leisure to finish and polish himself. Besides there's a poor strain of blood in that branch of the family; those Gookins that his mother, old Mrs. Button came from were distillers and hard-cases from generation to generation, by the town records ; — rough, violent people, — a kind of natural-born pirates. And his wife's family, although they were decent enough, were narrow and small-minded, somehow. The fact is, that unless you take Button's executive ability as showing Scrope blood, there's only the record to prove that he has it. I don't know any of the rest of them that have so few of the family traits. And perhaps, as we are three Scropes here together, we may take Civille's and my Van Braam blood into our confidence and mention in strict secrecy that cousin Button's immense bragging about his Scrope blood is as near an absolute proof that he hasn't a drop of it, as any one thing could be. All the rest of us like to have it very well, but no other of us would advertise it so extensively."

"Now I should ave fancied," said Mr. Scrope, after having listened to all this with evident and close interest, "that Mr. Button's political hambition was more unnatuwal in one of our connection than is boasting."

"Very justly observed," answered Mr. Van Braam. "A good many of us have refused offices, and I know none of us except my cousin Button who wants them. But so it is ; Mr. Button is proud of his descent, and he is terribly fond of being talked about, of having influence and of holding offices. I fancy he likes all that best of all, moreover, because it is such a capital advertisement of his books. And he is so energetic and shrewd in managing, that, you may say, he ought to have influence and office, particularly as he is reckoned perfectly honest. 'The tools to him that

can use them.' And he is very generous with his money where these two interests of his are concerned, and very sharp and close with it everywhere else. There, cousin Scrope — that is a pretty complete account of Mr. Button. It has only to be filled out with his minor traits ; and those you can see for yourself."

"A vewy good man to ave on your side I should say," observed Mr. Scrope, smiling. "Indeed, he's given me some vewy good advice halweady about horganizing the Squope Association. He knows exactly ow to manage people — exactly. E put me up to hall the dodges about the newspapers, and about cowwespondence, and influence and intwoductions. Do ye know, now, hi fancy I shouldn't ave been able to awange this matter at all without im."

Mr. Van Braam smiled and nodded, as much as to say, The most likely thing in the world. Scrope resumed ;

"This other cousin now, Chester — your cowwespondent about the genealogy, — e's hanother sort of person, I imagine ?"

"Why, yes," answered Mr. Van Braam. "He hasn't any money — that is, nothing except the little old place at Hartford where he and his great-aunt live together, and the income he earns. But an assistant-librarian doesn't have a very large salary, and I don't suppose his other revenues enable him to do much more than live comfortably. I guess Adrian is a pretty clear case of Scrope, though. He doesn't care much for money, he is fond of principles, he isn't afraid, he goes his own road, he has managed, by the help of a capital set of instincts of his own, to make himself a well-educated and accomplished young gentleman, he loves all manner of right thought and sound study, he is fond of fun, he is sweet-tempered, he likes pets and children, and old people, and they like him; and he likes to do things for others."

"Beg pardon," said Scrope of Scrope, "but if hit's a fair question, ow did e get hout of caven?"

All three of the company laughed, and it was the young lady who answered this time: "The sons of God saw the daughters of men, that they were fair," she quoted. "It must have been my cousin Ann Button for whom Adrian came down to us."

"Oh," said Scrope; "then if e mawies her e won't need to twouble himself about money."

"Very true" replied Miss Civille; "and yet it would be a great mistake to suppose that Adrian wanted her money. I knew all about their engagement. Ann was never very much of a favorite with anybody in those days — I don't know that she is very much liked now. But then, she used to be really neglected and lonesome and miserable. Adrian just devoted himself to her because nobody else would; out of pure kindness; and so they fell in love."

Mr. Scrope bowed an acquiescence, but with a queer look, which Civille understood perfectly, and answered;

"Oh, you needn't think it — that was two or three years ago, when we were all younger and didn't think so much of money. Besides, Mr. Button was not nearly so rich then. It was afterwards that he made so much."

"Oh," replied Scrope; — "That does seem like it. But I don't suppose the money will make him like her any the less."

"I don't know about that," said Civille reverting to her dreamy manner, and looking out from great half covered gray eyes as if she was watch-

ing something beyond the walls of the room — "I don't know about that. If I know cousin Adrian, it's the likeliest reason in the world to repel him."

"I shouldn't wonder," observed the old man; — "it would be Scrope all over."

"If you'll allow me," said Scrope, "I'd like to suggest that that would be more suitable to the hold spelling than the new. S, c, ah, o, o, p, they used to spell it — Squoop, not Squope. Now old Colonel Adwian the wegicide was so vewy particular that I say his name gave wise to the vewy term Squooples. He was full of 'em. And if my Yankee cousin is so squoopulous, I don't know but I shall advise him to take the old-fashioned name again, and leave off the Chester entirely."

"I dare say he would like to do so," observed Mr. Van Braam. "I want you to see him to-night, however, if possible, so that you and he may know one another a little before the Association meeting. It may be of service to both. And my old-fashioned ways," added the old gentleman with a good-natured smile, "make me desirous that all those of our kin should know each other. — It's high time he was here, too."

"I can't honestly say I shall miss im," said Scrope, with a gallant look towards the young lady, "if e does not come. No man could be quite appy to see another hadmiwer in Miss Van Bwaam's pwesence; and I know no man can see er without being er hadmiwer."

At this not very elegant compliment one might have seen Mr. Van Braam's eyebrows give a curious lift, and he just glanced at the young man, but without moving what Mr. Scrope would call his ed. As for the young lady herself, she answered in her indifferent voice:

"Oh, thank you very much, Mr. Scrope, I'm sure. But your Yankee cousin will not be in your way. He is engaged already, as we were saying. Indeed, we here are not at all in society; you will be free of rivals, both with my father and myself."

"There, cousin Scrope," said the old man, "That's as much as to say that you may marry us both if you can get us!"

The young Englishman looked rather uneasy; even fewer Englishmen are good at taking jokes, good or bad, than at making them; and he answered quite at random, but as it happened quite well enough for such talk —

"Vewy appy, I'm sure!"

The perfect coolness and speed with which the two Americans carried forward his hint to such remote consequences had terrified him; for he could not be sure whether they spoke in irony or not, their manner was so entirely grave and impassive.

Mr. Van Braam laughed quietly, the daughter just smiled, while the old gentleman remarked,

"Not badly answered, cousin Scrope; but don't be alarmed; we neither of us propose matrimony at present."

The young man was silent for an awkward moment; when there was a ring at the door, a card was handed to Mr. Van Braam, who said "Show the gentleman in," and the absent kinsman entered. It was our young friend Mr. "Cash," of the auction room. As he came in. Mr. Van Braam rose and stepped forward to receive him, with hearty cordiality. Miss Civille and Mr. Scrope arose, as the old gentleman, leading the new comer toward the fire, presented him:

"I want you to be at home here at once, cousin Adrian," he said. "Ci-ville, you knew your cousin better two or three years ago than now, but I hope you'll make up for lost time. Cousin Scrope, I know you and Mr. Chester will be friends, for you are kinsmen, and you have interests in common besides at present, in this estate and association business."

Mr. Adrian Scrope Chester had enough of general resemblance to Mr. Van Braam and his daughter, and indeed to his five or six times removed English cousin, to pass very well for a co-descendant. That is; he was tall, erect, well-formed, quick and easy in movement, and of an intelligent and comely countenance. His brown hair, instead of the cometary horrors of Mr. Scrope's, was brushed in a conventional manner, and curled in large soft curls instead of persisting in the frizzle of the Englishman, and his beard and mustache were thick and fine. His eyes were of a clear dark blue, his lips at once full and sensitive, all his features delicate and yet not small; and whereas Mr. Scrope's bearing and presence gave an impression of good-nature, quickness, levity, fun, Chester's spoke of thorough kindness, instead of mere good nature; of penetration, of insight, instead of quickness; of sense and directness and strength rather than levity; of general intellectual activity, rather than of mirth only. Comparatively speaking, the American seemed to possess large good qualities, of which the Englishman had only somewhat small imitations. And yet the English are very often what people sometimes call "singed cats — better than they look."

The young people tried to do justice to Mr. Van Braam's favorable introduction: but Miss Civille's manner was chilling enough, although she did not mean it to be, and indeed in spite of her intentions; so that Chester, barely touching her hand, which was cold and limp, said to himself, How did she come to dislike me? Mr. Scrope did rather better. He may possibly, in spite of the mild caustic that had just been applied to his demonstrations of jealousy, have felt some slight objection to the second young man in that company, or it may have been his ordinary awkwardness only that was upon him. However, he made his bow, shook hands, expressed his pleasure, and crowned the operation by taking from his pocket a card which he ceremoniously presented to Mr. Chester. Mr. Chester received it with thanks, delivered his own in exchange, as seemed to be expected, and then took time to peruse the legend upon that of Mr. Scrope. The phrase is correct — he took time. The card, a long one, like those sometimes sent on wedding occasions, contained the following composition:

*

BRABAZON AYMAR DE VERE SCROPE OF SCROPE.

And at the point where an asterisk is put, there was moreover a most noble-looking coronet, printed in the three primary colors, very impressive to behold.

"I am sorry my daughter was absent at your recent visits to New York," said Mr. Van Braam, when the four had seated themselves. "You and I agree on so many points that I shall be glad to see you and her contending over them. She is always refuting her father."

But the kind smile and pleasant tone and half-mischievous expression with which the words were said gave them a second meaning directly opposite to their grammatical one.

"I am afraid of controversies with ladies," said the new comer. "They receive things by intuition, instead of groping to them by feeling along chains of reasoning. Reasoning will not induce a woman to agree with you; reasoning with women is like hunting wild ducks with a brass band. It scares them. I should never hope to convince a woman except by making her like me and then unintentionally on purpose letting her see what I thought."

"What treason!" exclaimed Miss Civille, this time with a sufficiently perceptible tone of interest.

"There you go!" exclaimed her father, amused. — "Thirlestane forever!"

"Thirlestane?" queried Mr. Scrope. "How Thirlestane?"

"Why," resumed the old gentleman; "don't you remember their motto? It's in the Lay of the Last Minstrel. 'Ready, aye, ready!'" Civille will always answer the trumpet call when it sounds for battle over Women's Rights!"

"Now father," she remonstrated; "are you going to quote every minute? How can I entertain the gentleman, particularly if you wish me to fight with Mr. Chester, if you open your broadside upon me too, like that miserable Frenchman against John Paul Jones in the Bonhomme Richard?"

"Well, well, my child — I'm dumb — *vox faucibus hæsit!*"

"But permit me to explain," said Chester, with some anxiety: "I had no treason in my soul. I do not mean that men have no intuitions, nor that women have no reason; but only that as between the two, women have most of one, and men of the other. It is just as it is with another couple of faculties — or sets of faculties; I mean executive power and what people call goodness. I believe men have most of the former, and I believe women are better than men; I believe God put them into the world on purpose to be better than men; I do not believe that either of them is destitute of either faculty."

"I don't believe one single word of it," said Miss Civille, with a resolute tone. "If women are inferior to men in any particular or superior to them either, it's because they have been educated into going without their rights, and it's a great shame!"

"Well," rejoined Mr. Chester, pacifically; "Miss Van Braam will pardon me, I am sure, if I venture to act as if I were talking with a man in one particular?"

"I don't know about that," said the young lady, almost alertly — she had plenty of spirit, it would appear, under that cold and languid manner, and the debate appeared not to be at all unwelcome; "what is it?"

"Why, only that really and truly, I do detest arguing and I tell you plainly, and say I'd rather not. I get so angry — or if I don't, I want to, — when I undertake to argue. But there's another reason for my begging off just now" — he looked at the two gentlemen — "I'll let you tread me into the very dust next time, but there are some things that we ought to talk about."

As they all agreed that the apology was real, Miss Civille was graciously pleased to accept it.

"First," said Mr. Van Braam, "when did you come to town? I got your note only this afternoon."

"Yesterday, sir," said Chester. "I should have called last evening, only that I was too tired, and to tell you the honest truth I went to bed and slept all night long."

"The wisest thing you could do.

Next, let us arrange about the Association meeting."

This meeting, however, as quickly appeared, was set for that day week; Scrope, moreover, in reply to their inquiries, showed them that under the experienced guidance of Mr. Button, all things had been put in such readiness that it only remained for the persons concerned to render themselves at the time and place appointed. Both Mr. Van Braam and Mr. Chester congratulated Mr. Scrope upon the thorough manner in which all these preliminaries had been adjusted, when there was once more a ringing at the door-bell, and once more a card was brought to the master of the house, who took it and read it, saddling his eyeglasses with an experienced little *jiggle* on the bridge of his nose, and looked puzzled. Then he read it again, very carefully, half shutting his eyes, cocking his head backwards, and focusing the object with a kind of trombone motion. Then his head dropped, and he looked around him like one who has received an unexpected affusion of cold water.

"Why," he said, rather to himself than to any one else — "what" — and he stopped, and said to the servant, with something of displeasure in his manner,

"Ask him to walk in."

Returning in a moment, the servant reported that the gentleman had only a word to say to Mr. Van Braam, and would trouble him but for a very little.

Still with the same wondering and half displeased look, the old gentleman arose and went out into the hall, leaving the door open. Listening, the three others heard some indistinct murmur of voices only. Then in a few minutes Mr. Van Braam said, speaking from the hall,

"Never mind me for a little while, young people!" and he shut the door. Evidently the business was to take rather more time than he had supposed.

CHAPTER IV.

CHESTER, when the door had closed, proceeded to make some further inquiries about the Scrope Association and its operations. All these were readily answered, becoming quite a debate on ways and means, and greatly enlightening the querist. The Association, it appeared, consisted, or was to consist, of the descendants of Adrian Scrope, son and heir of Colonel Adrian Scrope the Regicide, executed at Tyburn on the 9th or as others say the 17th October, 1660. To these descendants, it appeared, there now of right belonged a certain large sum of money representing property which had devolved to Adrian Scrope the younger after his flight to New England, and which still remained so situated that the heirs could certainly recover it upon making proof of their descent. Scrope of Scrope, being himself a descendant not of the regicide Colonel, but of a younger brother, could not inherit while there were direct heirs; but being fond of genealogical investigations he had come to a knowledge of the facts in this case. He avowed very frankly that he desired to make a profit by means of the affair, but he said that he was also partly actuated by the equally laudable motives of family pride and family liking. It was from these causes that he had come to America with the design of searching out the Scrope heirs, forming them into an Association, becoming their agent, obtaining from them the necessary funds, proving their claim, and receiving as compensation a proper percentage, to be allowed him when the heirs should be actually in receipt of their respective inheritances. This arrangement, of course, effectually prevented any malversation by the agent. In the prosecution of this undertaking, Scrope had first fortified himself with letters and documents, and had then come to the United States, where he had for some time been investigating, advertising and corresponding; and with much labor had advanced so far as to appoint the meeting referred to, in New York, one week from date, of a number of the American heirs.

Miss Civille Van Braam took little part in this discussion between the two young men, listening only, and even this was with the air of pre-occupation or fatigue or almost melancholy which was habitual to her. So, when all at once business matters having been sufficiently debated, Scrope of Scrope suddenly turned to her and asked for some music, she started almost as if from sleep.

"Oh! Excuse me!—What was it?—I beg your pardon!"

The request was repeated, and with an apology for her inattention, the young lady very readily went to the piano, and selecting some music, played, and then sang, with good judgment and good execution, both instrumental and vocal, but without much emotion. The music she chose, apparently, was a graceful melody with lucidly arranged accompaniment, rather than crowded harmonies or technical difficulties; it was sufficiently good music, and at the same time simple enough for mixed society: safe music to play anywhere. There was a certain ease and truth of expression in her fingering and vocalizing however, which seemed to intimate the capacity of doing much more; and the poculiar vibrating fulness of her voice gave the impression of large passionate vehemence existing, though it might be asleep and unconscious of itself.

Having ended, she smilingly asked Mr. Scrope to take his turn, and he very readily complied. He sang one or two English ballads in a clear, not very expressive barytone or rather counter-tenor, and he sang without any embarrassment, sitting quietly on the sofa, simply explaining before he began that he knew no instrument. This style of singing is not very common in America, but it might well be; it requires, and gives, a sort of self-reliance of ear and a peculiar completeness of style, exacted by the absence of accompaniment. The performance, indeed, was much better than any one would have argued from the exterior and general bearing of Scrope of Scrope; and he was applauded accordingly.

Next came Chester, externally much more easy in manner than Scrope, but in reality very much more shy. He would gladly have declined, but with some little effort he came up to the mark like a man, with the allowable apology that he could neither sing without an instrument like Mr. Scrope nor play like Miss Van Braam, and should therefore give them two inferior kinds of music together. So he went to the piano, and sang a little ballad of William Allingham's, whose words and music are sufficiently a specimen of that evening's performance to be worth reproducing.

THE CHILD'S THREE WISHES.

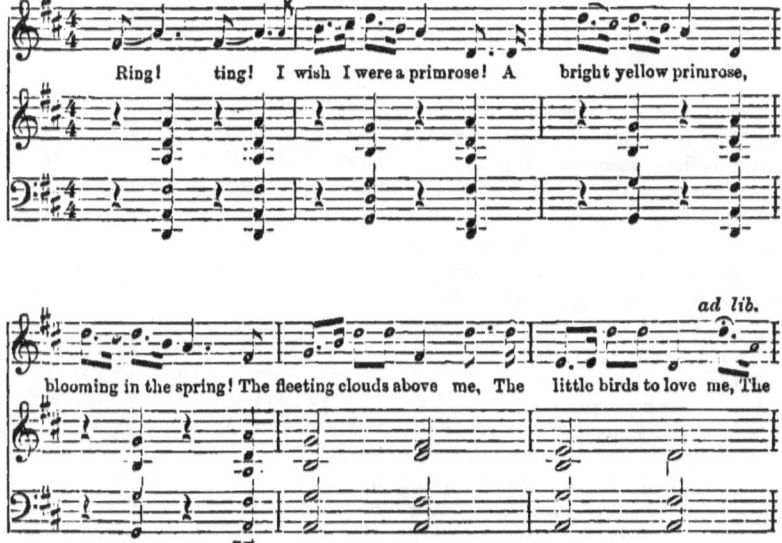

Ring! ting! I wish I were a primrose! A bright yellow primrose, blooming in the spring! The fleeting clouds above me, The little birds to love me, The

fern and moss to creep a-cross, And the   elm-tree for our king!

II.

Oh, no! I wish I were an elm-tree!—
A great royal elm-tree, with green leaves gay:
   The wind would set them dancing;
   The sun and moonbeams glance in;
And birds would house among the boughs,
   And sweetly sing.

III.

Nay, stay; I wish I were a robin!—
A robin or a little wren, everywhere to go,—
   Through forest, field, or garden,
   And ask no leave nor pardon,
Till winter comes with icy thumbs
   To ruffle up our wing.

IV.

Well, tell, whither would you fly to?
Where would you rest,—in forest or in dell?
   Before a day is over,
   Home would come the rover
For mother's kiss,—for sweeter this
   Than any other thing.

Chester was no player, and the air was nothing; but he sang the pretty little ballad, accompanying it by a few chords, with so much truth of intonation, with so much expression, and his voice, not noticeable except for clearness and sweetness, conveyed so much of intelligent sympathetic feeling, that his rendering was more effective than a great deal of the "best" singing, and he was rewarded with genuine praises. Miss Van Braam's were not very enthusiastic, and yet they conveyed an impression of restrained feeling which meant much; and Scrope's, somewhat over-eager and voluble as they were, still had sincerity enough in them to make them agreeable. They pressed him for another song, but he excused himself, saying, as indeed his flushed face, quick movements, and the evident tension of his nerves plainly enough showed, that he was easily excited by music, and adding that being unpractised, his fingers and his voice in such case quickly became uncertain. Nobody would have suspected the tall erect broad-shouldered fellow of being excitable. But he was, and the more so in proportion to the remoteness and spirituality of the exciting cause; that is, more (for instance) by music than he would have been by gambling or by a quarrel.

The conversation, which was now resumed, became lively, Scrope and Chester exchanging puns, jokes and nonsense, and Chester and Miss Van Braam finding that they had preserved in common many reminiscences of their previous acquaintance; so that the young lady after a time, bethinking her of her cool greeting, was a little pained in conscience thereat, and very prettily apologized:

"My health is poor this last year or two, since we came to live here, and my head aches a good deal of the time, cousin Adrian," she said; "I very often hardly know whether I am alive. I am having a severe attack to-night, and if I was rude to you at first, you will not misunderstand it, will you? I could hardly see or stand."

Chester hastened to make the proper answer; and Scrope hastened further to offer a remedy.

"Praps you'd allow me to cure your edache," he obligingly suggested. "I've only to lay my two ands on top of your ed for a few minutes."

Miss Van Braam hesitated a moment. But she reflected, how absurd is that conventional idea that the touch of one human being differs from that of another! And again, she said to herself, why should it be any worse than waltzing — or as bad, for that matter? Still, she did not so much welcome the experiment as force herself to acquiesce by reason; and her manner was a little cold — as often the case with shy and sensitive people — as she replied that she would be greatly obliged to Mr. Scrope if he liked to take so much trouble.

That gentleman however, assuring her that it was no trouble but a privilege ("I should think it was," said Chester to himself contrasting the features and bearing of the Englishman with the pale and spiritual face of the young girl), jumped up, and, stepping briskly to the back of her chair, laid his two hands upon the top of her head.

There was silence for a moment or two. Then Civille, who had been leaning in a tired way against the back of her great stuffed chair, suddenly raised herself, at the same time shaking her head violently, so as to free it from the touch of Mr Scrope's hands, which indeed were almost tossed away in the vivacity of the rejecting movement.

"Oh! I can't! you'll kill me!" she exclaimed. Scrope of Scrope looked excessively displeased, but managed to

say he was "vewy sowy, I'm sure!" and returned to his seat.

Civille suddenly threw her two hands up to her temples, uttering a low cry of intense pain, and resumed her leaning attitude, her head thrown far back.

"Oh!" she repeated, as if quite unable to repress the voice of physical anguish.

To persons of sympathetic temperament, and whose kindness is a genuine instinct, perhaps no emotion is so piercingly painful as to recognize the suffering of another. Both Scrope and Chester had much of this feeling, but Scrope's was a sense of his own personal discomfort and a good-natured readiness to help. Chester, however, at once strong and sensitive, possessed a share very unusual for a man of those spiritual endowments which are so little understood, and which are commonly termed intuitions. At the sight of the young girl's pain, he felt it, with a pang like a knife-thrust; he turned pale; his eyes filled with tears; and in his inexpressible longing to free her from it, without any distinct purpose or in fact consciousness, his left hand, which was nearest her, was held out towards her. With a quickness like the spring of an electric spark, she seized it and held it tight across her forehead. Her slender fingers closed upon it like iron, yet with a quiver that revealed a frightful nervous tension.

"Both hands will be better, cousin Civille," said Chester, after a moment's silence, and rising, he moved to the position that Scrope had occupied, shifting his left hand along upon her forehead, and placing his right hand next it, so that the fingers' ends met above her eyes, the two hands forming as it were a band around the whole front of her head. She sat still, with eyes closed, making no answer, except a sigh.

CHAPTER V.

OLD Mr. Van Braam found standing in his hall a monstrous fat vulgar oily looking red-haired man with a vast face, of which a terrible over-proportion had gravitated into an elaborate apparatus of double chins. The old gentleman, a squeamish and delicate person, was about as much pleased as if he had been visited by a bone-boiling establishment; but he put on as good a face as possible, and said, as civilly as he could,

"Did you wish to see me, sir?"

"Yes sir," promptly answered this whale of a man, speaking in a thick wheezy gobbling voice, as if his larynx operated from under a pile of half melted scrap tallow, and puffing as he spoke. "Sorry to trouble you, sir, but it is necessary." And turning forwards the lapel of his coat he showed beneath it the broad silver badge of the Detective Service. At this corroboration of the professional name on the visitor's card, the old gentleman was more annoyed and mystified than before. The detective's broad impassive countenance did not change, and his head remained motionless; but his small dull grayish eyes just turned from Mr. Van Braam's puzzled face to the end of the hall and back.

"Haven't you some little side room where we could be quite alone for a few moments?" he asked.

Mr. Van Braam, without saying a word, showed the way into a small waiting-room, lit the gas, and handed his visitor a seat. He waddled over to a sofa, however, saying as he did so, in his fat wheezing way,

"Thank ye; but I take sofys ginrally when I can git um. Chairs ain't much 'count for a man o' my build, anyway."

The discomfort of the old gentleman arose to an extreme, as he sat waiting for this vast greasy man to reveal whatever horror there might be. But his conjectures were most wild. His own accounts and papers—he was, through the influence of Mr. Tarbox Button, Secretary of the Splosh Fire Insurance Company—he knew were correct. But had some defalcation been discovered in the office? Had either of his two servant-girls been caught in any evil-doing? Had his solitary old dwelling been marked down by burglars, and was he to be prepared for their coming? He strove in vain to imagine what the mystery might be. In a thousand years, however, strive as he might, the poor old gentleman would never have dreamed of what would be implied in the very first words of the vast fat man, who after divers signs of reluctance, broke out, with a clumsy abruptness where he had meant to begin from afar off—

"Is your daughter's health good?"

Mr. Van Braam started, and looked at the detective with a blank astounded face, whiter, if possible, than usual; his mouth open, without a word. The officer instantly saw that the old man, far more sensitive than he had imagined, had received one of those shocks which for the moment annihilate all consciousness. Discomfited, he could only wait. In a few minutes, his host had somewhat recovered. The detective, rough police officer as he was, was no brute, and he instantly decided upon what he saw was the only possible method with such nervous subjects; for, he reflected, if the old gentleman is this way, what must the young lady be? It was very important, he also remembered that he had been told at head-quarters in Mulberry Street, on account of the very great respectability of the parties interested, that no more annoyance should be caused to any one, than was absolutely unavoidable, and that every thing should be managed in the most quiet possible manner. " I'll take the line of not believing a word of it," said the officer to himself, "and of acting on their side entirely." Accordingly, when he saw that the old man was in a situation to hear what was said to him, he began again :

"Ther ain't no casion to be troubled, Mr. Van Braam. No charges is made, and ther ain't no reason why ther should be. Fact is, I spose I might jest as well a sent the doctor as come myself."

" I'm not very strong," interrupted the old man, faintly, but gaining a desperate angry courage as he went on, "and she's my only child. I can't stand this long. For God Almighty's sake do be quick. Out with it. Why the devil don't you tell me what's the matter without toasting me in hell like that for an hour ? "

" You're right, sir," said the man, without showing any ill humor — and indeed why should he ? — " I will. Certain parties has intimated that Miss Van Braam, bein delicate, and a little out of her head like, had accidentally carried away a small passel o' lace from Jenks and Trainor's yesterday. Now it's very likely she ain't got it. Ef she has, of course she only took it by oversight. And there's no disposition to make trouble. What's wanted is to prevent it. They's some parties that would be very troublesome in sech cases. Jenks and Trainor 've ben plegged to death a'most with this kinder thing now for near onto a year, and they're out of all patience. But all that's necessary is to jest oversee the young lady quietly, and sorter let on in her hearin about some o'these kleptermaniacs bein took up, and it's goin ruther hard with 'em."

The long word which the detective evoked from the domains of modern sentimental criminality — or criminal sentimentality, — and which he flourished with an evident pride, like a strong man whirling a heavy Indian club, to show how easily he can do it, was the first out of all this singularly horrible discourse, that at all enlightened the shocked and confounded auditor. But when it came, it was enough. His anger disappeared as quickly as it had arisen, and an inexpressible sinking pain came in its stead. If any one can comprehend the terror, the agony, of a man who loves, who has but one to love, and who is old; of a father who sees his daughter, his only beloved, and the desire of his eyes, not merely suffering, not merely in sorrow, but in danger of becoming the very scandal and sport of the dirtiest of publics — that of a great city — who sees her certainly ill, possibly monomaniac, and at the parting of the two ways that lead to the mad-house or to the police station — if any one can imagine the sharp deep misery of such a prospect, the hint of it is even too much; and for any one who cannot, a library of detail could not paint it.

But the external signs of the pain that evil news inflicts, are seldom so marked as is often supposed. And persons whose characters are strong by nature, or solidified by hard experiences of life, are more likely to seem impassible even, than to show what they feel. Age, again, often contributes a real insensibility, which is perhaps the unconscious acquirement of the soul from whose relations with material and embodied existence threads are already beginning to unfasten. Mr. Van Braam, as a person of even spiritually delicate organization both physically and mentally, was as easily startled, old man as he had become, as any wild bird. So he would soon have fainted under sharp physical pain. But neither of these weaknesses belonged to his mind, any more than delicate lungs would belong to his mind. Accordingly, although the experienced detective had correctly judged by the physical symptoms, that his suggestion inflicted a fearful shock at first, yet he was surprised at the promptness with which the distress was mastered, and the degree of steadiness with which the trouble was faced, by this white and slender old man.

" Well, Mr. Officer," he said, " you have done right to come to me. It is the first hint I have heard, of course. My daughter's health is not very strong, it is true " —

Here it suddenly struck him that the best thing he could do was to let her condition seem bad rather than good. Evidently if the persons concerned in this demonstration were — as they were said to be — inclined to avoid exposure if the annoyance should cease, the best way to co-operate with them was to promise the supervision suggested, and to acquiesce in the necessity of it. Evidently, also, to talk big and be indignant and threaten, would be to insure a scandal. All this Mr. Van Braam saw, not by wording it over at such length, but at one flash, in the instant's pause as he said " true " — and he went on :

— "and I have been a good deal troubled at some of her symptoms and some of her actions. But it is equally important that a careful watch

should be kept, whether or not she is as badly off as the gentlemen at your office seem to think. I will do my best ; and if you employ some one, so much the better ; only she mustn't know it."

Some consultation now followed as to the sort of arrangement to be made ; it was decided that a quiet and unobtrusive observation should be maintained by the police ; and that some reason or other should be found for discontinuing or at least diminishing, even the very modest actual indulgences of the young lady in what is called "shopping." And the officer further guaranteed that, if as he hoped (he said it with obvious sincerity), there was only a mistake, not another word should be heard about it by Mr. Van Braam or by anybody. And so the fat detective, — a singularly unsuitable person, Mr. Van Braam couldn't help thinking, physically at least, for such a profession — waddled away.

After seeing him to the door, Mr. Van Braam returned to the parlor. His distress was so great, the effort to control it was becoming such a strain, and the irritability that in such temperaments as his always accompanies displeasure, was rising so fast and so strongly within him, that courteous gentleman as he naturally and habitually was, he was strongly tempted to hustle the two young men instantly out of the house on any or no pretence except that they must begone.

He only came quietly in, however, resumed his seat ; and began mechanically to turn over his papers. He said not a word. He did not notice, in the whirl of his perplexed thoughts, the sense of monstrous evil, the violent struggle to control himself, that his daughter seemed to be asleep and that the two young men were sitting as silent as she — for Chester, after a little while, had quietly resumed his seat without any motion or resistance from Miss Van Braam. But they both saw that something was wrong, the moment he entered; and as he still turned and turned his papers mechanically, Chester, seeing what was proper, looked at his watch, exclaimed at the lateness of the hour, and arose to go. Scrope of Scrope, with creditable promptness, followed his example. The old man, arousing himself, gave them a very genuine invitation to call again and as often as they pleased, on the footing, indeed, he said, of well-acquainted cousins.

"Why, Civille," he exclaimed all at once; "are you going to let our friends go without saying a word? — I do believe she's sound asleep!" he continued, as she did not reply. He lifted the shade from the drop-light on the table and stepped over to her. She was perfectly still, her white teeth just showing between her lips, her head resting easily on the back of the chair, and breathing quietly and regularly.

"Why, Civille, my child!" he said, laying his hand on her shoulder; "You do make your cousins very much at home, I think!" And he shook her a little.

Chester spoke.

"Mr. Van Braam," he said, with embarrassment, "I'm afraid it's my fault. I never did such a thing before, but I think I put her asleep. I did not know it either, if it is so."

The old man looked at him in amazement. Chester then told him just what he had done, and that they had been sitting in silence not knowing whether she were awake and in pain or asleep and therefore relieved, but supposing that quiet was kindest in either case.

Still with a confused look, Mr. Van Braam observed, "Asleep? put her asleep?"

"Magnetized," said Chester; "let me make some reversed passes. I've seen them do that; if I did put her asleep, I can awaken her, at any rate."

And holding his hands palms downward and flat, with the fingers towards her chin, he lifted them rapidly past her face, throwing them apart above her forehead as if lifting and flinging back a veil. Half-a-dozen times he repeated the gesture, and paused. "Civille!" called the old man. They saw the pencilled eyebrows lift a little, as if in repeated efforts to open the eyes; a distressed look came over the face: and one finger of the hand that rested uppermost in her lap, moved in an odd restless way.

Again Chester made the "reversed passes," saying at the last one, in a peremptory voice, "There; wake up!"

So she did; opening her great gray eyes wide, with an innocent puzzled look like a child's.

"Why, what is it?" she asked, startled at the three anxious faces gazing so intently at her. "Oh, — Cousin Adrian, you put me asleep, didn't you?"

"It appears so," said the young man, gravely. "But I did not mean to. I wanted to relieve your headache."

"You did. It's all gone. But my head is so sore! It feels as if it had been pounded all over! But that's nothing. Oh, thank you!"

"Ah," said he, with a troubled voice, — "but please don't have any such pain again!"

She smiled quietly. "I shall though, often enough! But I will try not to trouble you with it."

"If I can cure it, cousin Civille, please always trouble me with it!"

As they shook hands at going, Chester drew Mr. Van Braam one side, saying, just loud enough for the others to hear,

"About this meeting," — and then dropping his voice, he quietly slid a card into the old man's hand, adding, below his breath,

"I thought you might perhaps not choose anybody else to see this; I picked it up from the floor."

It was the detective's card; not engraved, but having on it in a sufficiently legible hand-writing, the words, "Amos Olds, Detective."

PART II.

CHAPTER VI.

"No one can know," said Mrs. Tarbox Button with deep feeling, and a suitable separate emphasis on each word — "no one can know what Perfect Happiness is, until they have attended a Female Prayer-Meeting. Of course I shall be there, and Anjesinthy too, Doctor Toomston. I have been there, and still would go, For 'tis a little heaven below."

"And you too then, let me hope, my dear young Female Timothy, my example of the believers. You will accompany your good mother, thy mother Eunice?"

Thus asked further the Reverend Doctor Toomston of Miss Ann Jacintha Button — the "Anjesinthy" of the first speaker above, who always gave her daughter both names. He asked the question, — no, he did not so much ask, or speak, or utter. He uttered this overture — the Doctor was a Presbyterian — with his invariable majestic manner, and with the same forth-putting, roomy articulation as if he had been speaking from what he always called "the sacred desk." He always spoke from the sacred desk, even if he were talking to a baby. He had the sacred desk, in fact, as the slang phrase is, "about his clothes;" indeed, nearer still. He walked abroad in the sacred desk; he slept in it; if he had been stripped to the skin and forced to dance a death-dance by the Modoc Indians, he would have danced it in the sacred desk.

"Oh yes indeed, Doctor," replied the young lady. "I feel it a great privilege."

They have in theatres what they call the Leading Lady. She is the chief actress, who does the heavy heroine business, such as queens' parts. So they have in churches. Mrs. Tarbox Button was the leading lady in the Reverend Doctor Toomston's church.

Churches are in some things a good deal like some other institutions composed of human beings. There are things to be done, people to do them, and people to take charge of doing them. And as in politics, it is very commonly the case that there is an official organization to stand up and look well, and by the side of it or mingled with it, informal powers that do a great part of what is to be done.

In a church, there is the regular course of obligatory religious observances proper, and there is also a semi-official and semi-temporal series closely parallel with this; and there is besides these, — in large cities particularly, — what may be called the optional or volunteer course. The stated preaching of the Gospel is the regular course. Along with it, it is true, goes the Worship of God, which Protestants have been so good as to admit to a place in their religious rites only inferior to that occupied by the Sermon. And the Sunday School belongs in this series. The semi-official and semi-temporal series includes the business meetings of the church; the week-day prayer-meeting; the teachers' meeting; the rehearsal by the choir; and the like. And the optional or volunteer course includes any charity schools, sewing societies, organized helps for the poor or afflicted, picnics and parties for the Sunday School children, donation parties; — in short the charity and amusement department, being pretty much all that gives enjoyment or relieves suffering.

The minister and his officials, — deacons, ruling elder, treasurer of the society, or what not, along with the chief musician and Sunday-school superintendent, — govern for the most part the two former of these three currents of action and influence. The ladies of the church commonly conduct the third, under a more or less definite chieftainship by the Leading Lady, and with whatever recourse they may wish or can obtain to the purses and counsels of their husbands and fathers. Be it understood always, moreover, that according to strength and wisdom, the ladies use more or less of influence in the two other departments of church activity also.

Mr. Tarbox Button was the richest man in Doctor Toomston's church, and the most energetic, practical and efficient also. In fact, he had been the chief agent in bringing this sound conservative divine to the city, and in the whole strenuous and laborious campaign which established the church. He was the Doctor's right hand man, his tower of strength and unfailing resource in every strait. And Mrs. Button, a shrewd, hard-working New England woman, fortified always by the counsels of her experienced spouse, was at once the Doctor's chief stay and support and her husband's powerful and successful auxiliary in all church matters, as she was in all social matters also. The distinction exists, the fact is, in American religious circles, only after the wholly imaginary manner of those estates which lawyers call "one undivided half."

Among all the good works which were so remarkable a feature of this well known metropolitan church (as the newspapers called it), it was of course that one and another should be engineered by one and another chief executive. It will be found that in Sewing Societies, Flower Missions and Companies for Executing Classical Music to the Afflicted, as much as in insurance companies, associations for recovering estates in England, civil governments or war administrations, the successful ones proceed on the principle of having one executive to do things, and a board or chorus or ministry to consult, indorse, help along and keep watch. Thus it was in Doctor Toomston's church. The Doctor was a thoroughly good and kind hearted man, a regular old-fashioned verbal inspirationist and textual preacher, a strict orthodox Calvinist, a well read theologian, and a steady sermonizer, good for ninety honest new sermons every year (deduct two months' summer vacation, and you have left forty-four "Sabbaths" — as he called them, — to which add Fast and Thanksgiving, at one discourse each) ; but he did not know this practical rule so as to state it, nor perhaps did Mr. or Mrs. Button ; but things took that shape simply because these able managers had' that unconscious faculty of complying with the universe which constitutes "tact and sense in getting along."

Mrs. Button, accordingly, was often consulted by the executive ladies of all the beneficent enterprises of the church, and she was wise enough to let them use her advice while she kept out of sight; it was the power that she liked, not the show. She had also her own pet or predilection among these, which she along with her Anjesinthy managed pretty much as they pleased, but always with the same dexterous deferential treatment of the other members of their board. This pet or predilection was called by the pretty fanciful name of The Shadowing Wings. It was a little institution established in a poor quarter of the city, which abounded in tenement houses, surplus sewerage, piles of filth, evil smells, rum-shops, and small dirty children, and not very far from the high-lying and airy cross street on Murray Hill where Mr. Button inhabited a stately undistinguishable slice of a long row of brown stone front houses exactly alike.

The Shadowing Wings included two — wings, so to speak; being indeed the usual number, and as few as the plural will justify. One was for supplying to needy mothers having new born children, what the French call a *layette*. The other was what the French call — really, it seems as if those benighted Romanists had invented some handy names, destitute as they may be of a pure Gospel — what

the French call a *crèche ;* a neat little room or two where mothers too needy to lose their days' works might leave their little babies under competent care during the day-time. The two ladies were on their way to The Shadowing Wings, when they met Doctor Toomston, and answered his inquiry about the female prayer-meeting for the week, as aforementioned. This done, the pastor and the ladies parted, the doctor to go about some clerical errand, the ladies to their ordinary Wednesday's inspection at The Shadowing Wings.

Deftly they went, tiptoeing along as every well-dressed Christian must among the dirt and wet of this world, their neatly gloved hands holding their embroidered white skirts carefully up from contact with the various unclean things by the way. Over the ill-cleaned gutters of the Third Avenue they tripped, and then through a terrible Thermopylæ where the wide double sliding doors of a great livery-stable gaped upon a cobble-stoned break in the sidewalk, and a sloping gulf yawned below, leading to the basement where horses stamped and whinnied. A "bret" and a buggy were paraded before the door, while a red shirted hostler with a pipe in his mouth swashed and squirted Croton water, in utter defiance of the city ordinances, from a hose, over the vehicles and all about them. Close to the street edge of this perilous way were crowded a great red-wheeled furniture van and a truck; and the reek of horses and harnesses and all things horsy, with the mighty incense of the groom's tobacco floating upon it like wreaths upon a river, seethed in the place, a very Phlegethon of smell).

Past this and other equally noble street monuments of American civic civilization, the unterrified ladies proceeded on their errand of mercy, until they reached the humble doors of The Shadowing Wings, which for the time being were outspread in the second floor of a great brick tenement block. It was a most suitable place; for it was one of those localities where in summer time it seems as if the very substance of the immense edifice crawled with children, as cheese does with mites. They are heaps upon heaps, in doorways and entries; they squeal and chatter out of every window; they overflow upon the sidewalk, into the black sloppy filth of the cobble-stoned street itself; the very air is one screeching din of sharp childish voices.

Even now a good many of them were playing about in the chilly wintry sunshine. None of them however paid any attention to the two ladies, except to move — a little — to let them pass. The attention business, and the penny-begging business, had long ago been tried upon them to the uttermost. As soon take Gibraltar by casting cut flowers at it. Both ladies were principled against giving money in the street, and against encouraging street childhood at all; for they were of that healthy and severe New England training, which justly reckons the receipt of charity always a misfortune and commonly a shame, and begging a crime; and they knew that children should be either at home or at school. Still, if they had been very fond of little children some would have run along with them, dirty or not dirty. But they kept them off without the least difficulty, and went upstairs to the rooms.

As they opened the door an infant's screech, coming out, met them, and a voice said, " Give me the dear little thing, doctor. I can quiet it."

" I declare," observed Miss Button to her mother, stopping short with her hand on the door-knob, " I do believe Civille Van Braam lives in these rooms ! Adrian sha'n't see her here, anyhow ! " She spoke in a low voice, and with obvious discomfort or displeasure, over and above the intimation of jealousy — if jealousy it were — as much as to say, I'm sure I don't want to see her !

" Oh, never mind," answered Mrs. Button, adding, with evident reference to some previous consultation or discussion as to something that might be supposed to change their previous relations, " we are to meet her jest the same, you know." Then, as if enforcing a moral lesson from a fact in point, she said, with serious emphasis, " And by the way — remember that, too, Anjesinthy ! 'Tain't right to set in judgment on your neighbor."

" Yes, ma," said the young lady, and they went in.

" Good morning, cousin," said Civille smiling, " and good morning cousin Ann." " And good morning, ladies," said a comfortable looking gentleman in black, with a handsome smiling face a good deal like that of Sir Edwin Landseer in the portrait of him along with two dogs, who was watching with much satisfaction the dexterous manner in which Miss Civille handled a very young child that lay kicking and crowing in her lap while she tickled it and laughed to it and cooed over it, and kissed it. This gentleman was Doctor Codleigh Veroil, Medical Adviser of the Shadowing Wings, family physician at Mr. Tarbox Button's and a regular and punctual and seriously interested attendant upon the stated preaching of the gospel at Dr. Toomston's church, although, to the great grief of the good pastor, the physician was not what he was wont to call "a professor."

Mrs. Button and her daughter responded with affability to these greetings, and the elder lady, as was her custom, went straight to the business in hand. The premises were four rooms, forming a single suite from front to rear of the building.

There is a certain creature of which naturalists tell us, having gregarious habits, and often found to construct for itself a kind of comb, somewhat resembling that of the honey-bee. But the cells of this comb, instead of storerooms, are dwellings, which the ingenious and social occupants inhabit, forming an aggregate not unlike that of the social grosbeak in its great collective nest. The separateness of the cells and the disconnected individual growth of the creatures distinguishes them from the coral insect. The form and arrangement of these cells is commonly either a pile of square tubes somewhat on the caddis-worm principle, laid upon and next each other like sticks in a wood pile, and penetrable from end to end, or else of half-tubes piled in the same way, but shut apart in the middle. The creatures are men and women. The tubes are the four-room tenements that run through a tenement-house from front to rear, the front and back rooms open by windows to the air, the two middle ones dark and airless, except so far as the doorways admit light and ventilation from the end rooms. The half tubes are the two-room or three-room tenements of which twice as many will fill the same space. And these tubes are the homes of tens of thousands in New York City alone. One of these tubes, with its four compartments, was occupied by The Shadowing Wings.

Its back room looked towards the south, though this south was only a great pit or Yosemite Valley with brick sides, full of clothes-lines laden with damp linen. But a little sunshine managed to dodge in now and then, past the flapping wet sheets and shirts, like a spy escaping through the besiegers' lines into a fortress; while the front windows that looked into the street never received any direct light at all.

In this back room were eight or ten cribs, numbered in order, and neatly arranged in two rows. In each of them, all but one, whose tiny tenant was just then in Civille's lap, lay an infant, having at its neck, for fear of mistakes, a printed ticket or "address tag," bearing the number of the crib. Each parent at leaving the child, was accustomed to receive a similar ticket, as much as to say, "On demand we promise to pay One Baby, Value Received. SHADOWING WINGS;" and on the presentation of this duplicate — for after all it was perhaps more like a pawn-broker's duplicate than a note of hand — the mother could obtain her baby again, free from any danger of mistakes in consequence of deficiency in maternal instinct or "unnatural selection." These ticketed mites of humanity were sleeping, or wailing, or lying broad awake with the cloudy looking eyes and deceptive aspect of profound reflection which belong to early infancy. A couple of respectable looking women were in charge, being the official nurses or guardians of the establishment. The front room was occupied by these nurses, and the two inner rooms were storerooms. First of all, Mrs. Button and her daughter marched gravely through from rear to front of the whole tenement, sharply scrutinizing floor, walls, ceilings, shelves, piles of minute garments, every thing. Then they came back, and with the same strict housekeeper's watchfulness, they inspected every cradle, lifting the small bedclothes, peeping into the tiny face of each occupant, and into all sorts of places besides, and viewing, uncorking and smelling with special and peculiar solicitude divers flat glass bottles whereof each was surmounted with a thing capable of easy entrance into the mouth of infancy, and some contained a white fluid. Then Mrs. Button catechised the nurses shrewdly and thoroughly. Every thing was right, every thing clean and sweet and in good order. So in truth it behooved to be, under the rule of that forceful and stringent woman.

Now it so happened that the popularity of The Shadowing Wings had been greatly increasing, and of late the demands upon it were so many that it was obvious that it must enlarge its borders. Upon this very Wednesday, in fact, a meeting of the Board was notified to consider the matter. So, by the time that Mrs. Button's inspection was finished, divers ladies of the Board arrived, and a business meeting was organized in the front room, Civille, whose sole office whether of trust or emolument was a place in this board, going in too, still with her little live plaything in her lap. Doctor Veroil, also by request, attended on this occasion as advising member or *amicus curiæ*.

"The meeting will please to come to order," said Mrs. President Button — and it came. Then the good lady, glancing around with a serious and composed expression, bent her head a little forward, and covered her eyes with her hand. The others gravely followed the example of their fuglewoman, and so remained for the space

of about one and a half minutes, — all except Civille and the doctor. The former was occupied with her pet. As for the doctor, he gave a queer sort of start at this sudden manual exercise, and controlled a desire to laugh. This however shone in his wicked eyes, for when he gave a look at Civille, who was next him, she almost laughed too ; but managed to get off with a blush, a smile, a reproachful glance, and great demonstrations of tenderness over the baby.

When this silent preliminary was over, Civille again looked at the naughty doctor and shook her head in a warning manner.

"I didn't say any thing," answered the cavilling and irreverent man, in a low tone — "it's a good thing. Do well to have the whole proceedings that way, at most meetings."

"Well, ladies," said the president, in her prompt way, "the business before the Board is, to see whether we shall hire more rooms here, or move. If we move, we shall kinder begin over again. I suppose we had better stay if we can get room here, for considering the way things are in this street, we have a very desirable class of infants, and their mothers are very respectable. Isn't that so, Doctor Veroil ?"

"Eminently so, madam," replied the doctor : "Sanitary condition most satisfactory, and popularity and consequent usefulness, as you say, require larger accommodations. This little creature, now" — he pointed to the baby that Civille was holding — "shows how wide a range we already have among the poor. There are some rather interesting questions of a physiological and ethnological nature that I would like to look at a little by comparing a few infants of different races. I hope we may have a

Mongolian child to match our small African here before long."

♦Mrs. Button gazed upon the doctor's handsome and intelligent face, with a reproving look, as much as to say, No rude jests in the sacred precincts of a pious Charity!

"African?" she queried, with decided dryness in her tone. "What do you mean, Doctor?"

"Just what I say, my dear madam," replied Doctor Veroil, pleasantly. "Didn't you know that it's next to impossible to tell a new-born negro child from a new-born white child? Can be done, however. This one's old enough to show very plainly,—aren't you, Sambolet?" apostrophized the good-natured physician, tickling the infant with his forefinger. The little creature grasped the doctor's digit with its tiny hands, and after the fashion of sucklings, strove to carry it to its mouth, which it opened for the purpose.

The Lady President, with a most disinfectant and nose-holding expression of countenance, as if descending into a plague-pit, or resisting the natural effects of a quart of "ipecac" taken internally, approached the immortal soul incarnated in a human being which had occasioned the doctor's little essay on Comparative Ethnology, and scrutinized it in a manner for describing which the term intense is a mere paralysis. Babies are quite as susceptible to the atmosphere of their interlocutors as grown people, although they have to yell and kick instead of using execrations, trespass on the person, assault with intent to kill and murder in the first degree. But if the deed could have been substituted for the will, few and evil indeed would have been the remaining days of Mrs. Tarbox Button in the land! That excellent and charitable

dame had barely time to recognize in the little thing,—either in the scanty hairs, or in the not very aquiline nose, or in the rather pulpy little red lips, or in the soft satiny ruddiness of the delicate skin,—some faint reminiscences from the mysterious continent of Augustine, Tertullian and Cleopatra. Perhaps she smelt the very Original Sin that Augustine used to be troubled with; who knows? But she groaned out, with exactly the tone of voice for the Lady of Shalott when she remarked that the curse had come upon her—

"A Nigger Baby!"

As was observed, she had barely time thus to inspect and thus to observe, when the N. B. aforesaid, experiencing something disagreeable, quickly shut its eyes tight, opened its mouth a great deal more than enough to make up, and gave one yell that almost knocked the lady president flat on her back. She struggled to her seat and looked feebly around her. Doctor Veroil laughed softly, but so heartily that his face turned a bright red in his efforts not to make a noise; and poor Civille, insulted and frightened almost as much as the baby, with one appealing glance at the doctor, burst into tears, and lifting the yell—beg pardon, the baby—in her arms, fled into the back room, where a sympathetic chorus of wails arose, upon which the doors were shut, and quiet gradually fell again upon the infant band, under the skilful ministrations of the nurses.

As soon as Mrs. Button had in some measure recovered from the blow, she exclaimed,

"We must get rid of that child!"

"Oh, nonsense!" exclaimed Doctor Veroil impulsively, but recovering himself he added, "Well, ladies, I must leave you, unless you have some further commands."

The Doctor was unwilling to be present at the human sacrifice which he saw Mrs. Button meant to offer, and as the discussion was turning quite away from the field of his duties, he seized the opportunity to escape, with polite farewells. A debate followed, in which some of the ladies, not sufficiently devoted to principle, intimated that it would do no harm to permit Number Ten — such was the mark on the child's crib-ticket — to remain. But they were speedily enlightened by their presiding officer, who argued with many words and very great power, the following heads of discourse, — for, though it is a great pity, there is not room to report her remarks verbatim :

First: The Shadowing Wings is for the purpose of doing good.

Second: A wise compliance with the weaknesses of others is commanded by Saint Paul, who says that we must not cause our brother to offend; and it is indispensable for practical usefulness.

Third: The poorer classes, among whom we labor, have the weakness of disliking negroes, and if we insist on keeping the two together, we shall cause our brother to offend.

Fourth: Therefore, a wise and scripturally reasoned regard for Christian Expediency ordains that we expel the negro infant, Number Ten, from The Shadowing Wings, in order to do good.

When the vote was taken, it was carried for expulsion by one majority. If Civille had been present there would have been a tie; but she had gone away without returning to the meeting. And accordingly, Mrs. Button, at the close of the session, as she was departing, commanded the nurses to notify the mother of Number Ten that evening, that she could no longer be allowed to leave her infant at The Shadowing Wings.

CHAPTER VII.

On the same morning, and at about the same hour when the great Christian Expediency Baby-Expulsion was being enacted by the high priestess of The Shadowing Wings, there existed (it will not do to say "there might have been seen," for the narrow entry was too dark for that) a small tin sign. This was on the outside of a door up two flights of stairs and deep in the bowels of one of those crowded buzzing buildings crammed with offices of all kinds, divided and subdivided like a new system for the classification of knowledge, of which there are so many in that densely occupied business section of New York to the southeast of the City Hall Park. The particular building in question was on Nassau Street, not far from Fulton. Inside of the door on which was this invisible sign, there was a front office, a desolate room, where a couple of clerks were busily writing. At its further side were folding doors, close shut. Behind these was the private office; a small room, or rather den, uncarpeted and dreary, though not very dirty. It contained a heavy table with a few books on it, two or three desks, a large safe, several heavy wooden chairs, and a small Morning Glory stove. It was lighted by one dusty window, opening into a kind of well with brick sides. If you should look up this well or pit, you would see at the top a little piece of sky; in its sides, were other similar dusty windows of similar dens. Its floor or bottom was a low-pitched glass roof, lighting some back store or stores on the ground floor. A few feet above this glass roof was extended on stout uprights a web or screen of wire net, with coarse meshes, to protect the glass from any deceased cats, old boots, broken bottles, or other meteoric bodies likely to descend from the higher regions.

The lion of this den sat writing at the table — a heavily built man just passing beyond middle age — Mr. Tarbox Button. The legend upon the invisible tin sign was:

"BUTTON : SUBSCRIPTION PUBLISHER."

For it was in this strenuous and ferocious, if not piratical business, that this great man had laid the foundations of his fortune. He still pursued it, waiting either to sell out to some proper successor, or to close it, at entering upon the career of statesmanship for which every American citizen is by law made fit, and which, Mr. Button felt, would be a noble close for the active years of his laborious and successful life. He was expecting Mr. Adrian Scrope Chester, on business, and by appointment, the interview having been before agreed upon, whenever next Chester should be in New York.

Mr. Button, a "self-made man," to use the irreverent slang of biographers, was, as may have been gathered from Mr. Van Braam's remarks about him, strong, shrewd, energetic, prompt, peremptory and coarse. As a wit once remarked of another of his kind, and like most of them, "he was a self-made man, and worshipped his creator."

His energy, his promptness, his vehement will and his unrelaxing enforcement of it, his skill in judging candidates for employment, his shrewd insight into the merits of a speculation, his sagacity in estimating values, had by his long and active use of them,

greatly increased within their range in power and precision, but their range had not increased. His way of life, moreover, had developed his promptness and decision into rough and sometimes even brutal manners, and his success had filled him fuller and fuller of a great pride in what he had done, and in his own individual self as the man that had done it. And being narrow and vulgar in his original mental structure, and having grown very much more so by reason of his having done so well in life with such attainments as he had, he had acquired a habit of pretty thorough contempt for the less money-making qualities, and indeed for any qualities except his own, and a habit of expressing it pretty freely too, — exceptions excepted. These exceptions were the cases where he wanted any thing of anybody. This happened quite often, indeed; and in these cases Mr. Button always used one and often both, of his two regular lines of persuasion, to wit, money and flattery. It was Mr. Button's full belief, as it had been his experience, that these, properly used, were infallible. How could he think otherwise? He knew what would be infallible with himself. It should be added, that like a born economizer as he was, he never used either of these motives where a plain statement of what he wanted and a direct asking for it, would serve the purpose, as in a great many cases it would. Most people like to do what they are asked, other things being equal. So that nothing of what was just above said is to the disadvantage of any of those numerous virtuous persons who have (for instance) given recommendations of Mr. Button's various publications, merely because he asked them.

Lastly : there were now and then

occasions when Mr. Button found his account in stern reproof or even in furious bullying, of which last in particular he was a good master. But when good-natured, he was often jolly enough, and even jocular in a queer random sort of way.

As for Adrian's errand, the proposed interview was in a certain, sense an effort of the two men to come to a satisfactory understanding. Button, like some other people, was not without his little inconsistencies. Excessively vain of his own success in life, he was almost equally vain of his ancient Scrope descent; which was his only reason for assisting Scrope of Scrope, except of course such expectations as he might have from the great Scrope estate, and which had far more to do with his patronage of Mr. Van Braam than even the proud pleasure of being a patron. It was because Adrian was also a Scrope, that he had acquiesced in his daughter's engagement to the young man ; for certainly Adrian had very few of such qualities or acquirements as Mr. Button would desire in a son-in-law. He had no money, or next to none ; no disposition to make any, so far as could be seen, and therefore, it was fair enough to conclude, no ability to do so. Of moral qualities, intelligence and education he had a sufficient share however ; and Mr. Button had conceived the idea of endeavoring to make these qualities the basis of some employment for Adrian in some department of his own business.

There had been before this more or less skirmishing, so to speak, though of a reasonably good-humored kind, between the two men, on the general subject of Adrian's prospects. They had — very naturally — not exchanged their full opinions of each other,

nor of matters and things in general ; but they knew very well how they differed, and they were willing enough to come to some understanding if possible. Mr. Button did not avow, it is true, that once for all this was Adrian's opportunity to accept or refuse a lucrative establishment for life, in his business as well as in his family. Nor did Adrian avow his repugnance for many of the surroundings of his betrothed and of her relatives, nor the sacrifice of inclination and enjoyment which a business career would inflict upon him. They both knew very well however what to-day's meeting was. It was like the Peace of Amiens ; a diplomatically friendly negotiation between powers naturally hostile, for preventing or postponing an open rupture.

Adrian, who as it happened had never visited the office before, after some stumbling and fumbling in the outer darkness, at last deciphered the legend on the tin sign by the aid of a lucifer match, and entering, was shown into the presence. Mr. Button received him in his pleasantest manner, that is, with a nod, a grin, and a shake of the hand, without getting out of his chair.

"Wal, how air ye ? Seddown. Glad to see ye."

Adrian, as he replied, took the chair which the publisher indicated, and the latter continued :

"Seen the wimmen folks to-day ? Heard on ye yesterday afternoon."

"Yes ; I could only run up for a few moments yesterday, but I made quite a call this morning. They sent me off, at last, Mr. Button ; — they had to go to The Shadowing Wings, and Mrs. Button said I had no business with the babies."

"Oh, wal ; every man must git up his own, I spose she meant. Won't stay with us, I spose, this time neither?"

"I can't, really, without turning your house upside down," said Adrian with a smile. "I've so many people to see, and so many places to go to and so many things to do, that it would be nothing but a plague to you; I shouldn't be on hand at meals nor bed time, nor any time."

"All right; all the better for me; I have to be as regular as clockwork of late years; a little thing puts me out, now. Though I shouldn't budge an inch for you, nor nobody else — can't, in fact. But ma's rather funny about her housekeepin', and it's jest as well not to annoy her. You're jest in season here, any way. One o' my clerks is out, and there's a lot o' little things that he usually helps me with, that I ought to see to before I say a word to ye. Now spose you jest take hold with me here a while and close out some on um?"

"With all my heart," said Adrian. It is possible that the clerk had been sent out.

"Wal; the fust thing is, these letters" — he indicated two piles of a dozen or two each — "they're kinder confidential, some on um, and I don't like to put on a new clerk, so it comes jest right to git you instid. I always answer every thing right away. 'Tain't no way to do business, to have a lot o' fag ends hangin round. Sfishunt unto the day is the evil thereof, without havin an extry lot on't cold, left over from yesterday."

With this sound practical exposition of a wise text, the publisher pushed over to Adrian some letter paper and writing materials, took up one of the piles of letters, and began:

"There; these are miscellaneous. I'll read um out, and then tell ye the substance of what to say, or dictate, if's necessary. Leave the signature. I'll put that in myself. Some on um don't require no answer, but I've kep um all, so's you can see how they run, like the three blind mice."

He took up the first letter, and read it aloud. It was dated in the city, and was as follows:

DEAR SIR: — Knowing your Christian character, goodness of heart and interest in the unfortunate, I write to explain to you my sad situation, being fully confident that you will help me. I am a regular attendant at Dr. Toomston's church,

— "that's sad, certain," commented Mr. Button —

but believe there is a greater Spiritual Church in which we are all members. I have been favored with some spiritual gifts among the recent revelations from the spirit world, which I have tried to cultivate, but I have not been favored in the things of this life, as you have, and I am in great poverty and sorrow, not knowing wherewith to procure the means of living, nor clothes to wear, nor a shelter for my head. As I am a stranger to you, I respectfully invite you to investigate my case personally. My present abode is at No. ——, corner Sixth Avenue and —— Street, Room 24, top floor. Do not neglect me, I implore you; for what is to you but one drop out of the bucket will be to me a rescue from the utmost suffering. I am daily in fear of being even thrust out into the street, by an unmerciful landlord. So hoping to receive at once of your charity, I remain in truth and love

Yours sincerely

AMELIA GRIGGS.

"There," said Mr. Button, with a serious face.

"Shall you go?" asked Adrian, who, not being rich, had not found out what a begging letter is, and really felt quite sorry for poor Amelia Griggs.

"Go!" said Mr. Button, with energy, — "not much. No black mail for me, thank you. If that woman could get me up there once, I should have my choice between maintaining her afterwards, or some kind of a scandal. She's a spiritualist too, or she says so; that's rather queer, all by itself."

"But suppose Mrs. Button or Ann should look her up?"—

"Oh pshaw! you're green, Adrian. It's a regular begging letter. I git sometimes a dozen in a day. I kep a lot of um at fust, but I found I should have to have a house on purpose, and I fling um all in the waste-basket now. So much for that."

And he suited the action to the word. But Adrian, not quite able to accept this harsh decree, and at any rate desirous to keep the letter as a curiosity, asked for it.

"Why, certain;" and he gave it to him—"but my boy, don't you git mixed up with no sech critters,—now mind *that!* Once for all, in this city, when you look into cases of charity and particularly when you talk with wimmen, unless you know exactly where you air, either stop before you begin, or have your witnesses with you. Why, I won't talk with no wimmen in this very office, except it should be my own family or so, without openin' them doors wide so's to hev my clerks see what's a goin on."

Adrian opened his eyes as wide as Mr. Button his doors, at discovering a state of things that many a respectable citizen fully understands to his great cost and discomfort.

"Wal," resumed the other, "the next thing on the programme will be something else, as the nigger minstrels say."

So he took up the next letter. It was a request for money for a political purpose. "Note in the upper right hand corner," observed Mr. But-

ton, "yes, politely, with check. The number for filing goes in tother corner. I'll git it back agin, in some shape, one o' these days."

The next was a notice of an insurance premium due; and there followed an invitation to a church fair, a notice to serve on a jury, a letter from a conveyancer about the title to certain real estate, and so on. To most of these a word or two sufficiently indicated the reply; a few required answers dictated in full, which were accordingly executed on the spot.

The extreme difference in the natures of the two men was well illustrated by the contrast in their appearance as they sat at their work at the same table. One was tall, the other only middle-sized; one was singularly light, swift and easy in all his motions, the other not exactly clumsy, but at least deliberate and unelastic. Both were light rather than dark in personal colors, but the young man's fine glossy dark brown hair, clear well opened eyes, and delicate skin announced great fineness of texture throughout, while Mr. Button's thick close-cut hair, strong and coarse, was of a dull indistinct sandy hue, so to speak of no color whatever; and its stubbly growth was somewhat as if he had saved up old scrubbing-brushes to make him a wig of. He was close shaven, while Adrian's beard and mustache, naturally growing shapely and full, were untouched by steel—it is to be observed that now-a-days no man is described until beard and mustache have been accounted for. Thus, Button's square coarse jaws, his rather full and not very shapely lips, and blunt fleshy nose took a complete relief upon his head, which was not very large; and as his neck was thick and short, the back and base of his brain relatively full, and the top of his head shallow, the result was a contracted and little look not at all beautiful, and which the quite respectable development of the lower or perceptive part of his forehead was not of itself able to compensate. Even the long upper lip, so usually held a mark of practical sense, rather increased than diminished the ungainliness of the face. His shoulders and chest were massive, as indeed was the whole frame; so that he gave the impression of a slow rock-like strength, which was doubly striking as contrasted with the grace and ease of the younger man. A last odd finish was given to Mr. Button's face by a fantasy of nature, which had framed his thick sandy eyebrows in two round uplifted arches, giving a rather funny fixed look of astonishment to his face, which was the more ludicrous as it was the exact opposite of his solid, rugged, resolute and firmly poised mental character. The one man lived, so to speak, in coarse heavy bone and muscle; the other, in swift blood and lightning-quick nerve force. It was the contrast in full between the fleshly man, and the spiritual man. When the first pile of letters was despatched, Mr. Button directed Adrian to write out the answers as noted, and drawing the dictated letters to him, read them over, and remarked with evident pleasure, after signing them,

"Fustrate, fustrate. That's what I call par excellence. You write the fastest of any feller I ever see, to write so plain."

Adrian smiled as he replied that he was very glad to suit; he left Mr. Button to suppose that the smile was caused wholly by this pleasure, although it was in fact partly due to the new use made by Mr. Button of two words from the French tongue;

the worthy gentleman no doubt confounding them with their English fac-similes, which indeed furnished a very suitable meaning.

"I've taken pains enough with my hand-writing," he added, "to be entitled to some credit for that. I believe I could run a writing school on a new and original plan of my own, and a good one."

"Could, hay? Plan of your own, hay? What's that, I'd like to know?" asked Mr. Button, with an accent that seemed to intimate something like: Fine plan such a chap as you are is likely to hit on!

"Why," said the young man, "I'd teach just the opposite of the ordinary commercial hand-writing teachers. They try to teach a handsome hand first, then a rapid one, and a legible one last. if it happens so. Now I'd have these three things to do, instead; First, write plain. Second, write fast. Third, write pretty."

"Wal, I declare," said the senior, "Adrian, I didn't know you'd got so much practical sense. You're right, sure as you're alive. You can, really; you can make money on that plan, certain. Wal, we sha'n't git through here by organizin no writin' schools this mornin."

And he turned again to the remaining letters. These were as speedily and satisfactorily despatched, and Mr. Button, as he shoved them aside, observed,

"There; so far so good. Them's all ready to number and file. The answers must be press-copied. John!" he shouted.

One of the clerks entered, and was set to take the copies. Mr. Button looked at his watch.

"I declare it's later than I thought. I've got to run across to Broadway for a while — now these business letters are more particular ; got to dictate most of them " — and he paused.

" Why," said Adrian, " dictating don't take long. I'll take down the answers in short hand. Then you can go, and I'll have them all extended when you come back."

" I want to know ! Can ye ? " exclaimed Mr. Button, once more agreeably surprised. " Wal, we'll try it." And in a very little while the answers were all taken down ready for writing out, and Mr. Button took his hat and coat.

" I had a short-hand feller once for a while," he remarked, " but he wasn't good for nothin' else, and he didn't know his own trade so but what I had to dictate half his work to him over agin. I didn't keep him but two days ; told him I wasn't goin' to have him learn his own business at my expense, and shipt him. Hain't thought much o' short hand sence that. Praps you'll do better."

And off he went, leaving Adrian busy at his writing, which occupied him nearly up to the return of the publisher. The answers were now read over, fully approved, the press copies taken as before, the originals numbered and filed, and the day's correspondence was attended to.

" That last letter there," observed Mr. Button, " that there wasn't no answer to, from that air old Doctor Giddins that said he couldn't do no such thing, — I'll have the old feller's name sure, if he is a Doctor of Divinity. That's jest what I'm a goin to buy of him. But there's two pints to tend to before that. One's about a book, and tother's about a man. The book's here — or at least the plan on't is, and the man's a comin ; or if he ain't it's his resk, for I wrote him ef he wasn't here at half past twelve

exact, I wouldn't have nothin to say to him. He wants to git some territory for my Histry o' the Bible. Tain't likely it's in him, anyhow. Good agents are about as plenty as hen's teeth. But we'll soon find out."

" Territory ? " said Adrian — " what's that ? "

" Why, I own the hull United States," said Mr. Button, adding with a grin, — " for the sale of my publications, I mean. Now ef a feller comes'n wants to git an agency — say the Histry, now — the fust thing is to see 'f he can sell a book."

" Why," said Adrian, " how can you tell that ? "

" I reckon you'll see how I can tell, before you git out o' this office, ef that feller comes as he agreed. I'll open his eyes, unless he's smart, I tell ye — and yourn too, smart's ye be ! — Wal ; spose I find he can sell. Next thing is, is there any territory. This book'll tell ; " — Mr. Button selected a thin folio volume from the pile on the table and opened it — " This is my record of the hull United States, as fur'z I've lotted deestricks out on't to sell the Histry o' the Bible. You see, the agents are my army, and I'm like the centurion in the Bible ; I say unto um to come, and go, and do it, and they do ; and if they don't, they ketch it ! I make every man stand in his lot, and work it thoroughly too, I tell ye ! But about this book : " —

Here Mr. Button took from a drawer a written paper, and read aloud a very long title, beginning with the words " Useful Information," ending with the imprint, viz., " Published by Subscription Only. T. Button. New York ; " and having between the two, after that fashion of subscription books which is so disgusting to practical printers of good taste, what really amounted to a whole table of contents, showing in substance that the work therein described was or was to be a sort of encyclopedic collection of receipts for cooking, recipes for simple medicines, rules for farming affairs, directions for planning and calculating various mechanical processes, arithmetical tables, forms for simple written instruments, — in short a most extensive miscellany of information, necessarily of the greatest convenience provided always it should be trustworthy.

"There," added Mr. Button, as he ended, " my fust name for that was, " Button's Every Thing."

"More striking," commented Adrian.

"Praps so," said the publisher; " but these sensation titles won't do for my way of doin' business, no more'n sensation books. I can't do nothin' without a book that's really right up and down valable. When I've got that, then I can bear on jest as hard as I like, and the more's said about the book the better. That's the way I've made my money, — by givin' right good goods — better'n I agreed, every time, and puttin' on a tre-menjus pressure."

Adrian, who had never closely looked into such matters, was quite man enough to perceive and to admire the real breadth of view, the just sense, and the vast energy, that these statements implied, and he said as much, to the evident gratification of Mr. Button.

"But how do you make people buy the book?" he inquired, — just as one of the clerks' looked in to say that Mr. Jacox, and another gentleman, were present.

"Show um both right in," answered Button, adding, — to Adrian, — "That's jest exactly what I'm a goin' to show ye."

CHAPTER VIII.

Two men came in. One was a tall or rather a long man; oldish, lean, seedy, solemn, with a hollow chest, a long lean face, and an unwholesome dusky unclean complexion. He wore a rusty black suit, and a stock instead of a cravat.

"Mr. Jacox?" asked Button.

"No," said the other man, quickly. "My name's Jacox." He was a brisk little fellow, it might be either thirty-five or forty years old, dry, jerky, with twinkling light-blue eyes, straight whitish hair, whitish eyebrows, a voluble quick utterance, and every appearance of absolute confidence in Mr. Jacox.

Mr. Button looked for a moment at the two men, decided which was worth attending to, and proceeded to eliminate the surd, as the algebraists say.

"Seddown, gentlemen," he said, to begin with; "Glad to see ye."

They saddown, not knowing — nor did Mr. Button either — that this form of the verb "to sit" viz., with a d, is really a close approach to the primeval Aryan root.

"Did you want to see me?" he asked of the desolate long rusty man.

"Yes," replied he in a dejected tone.

"Wal?" barked Button, inquiringly and disapprovingly in a single loud harsh syllable, — "Here I be."

"Uh-uh-uh-m," begån the long man, with a long cough, apparently only a cough of habitual preface; and he added, with a spiritless manner, " I was stopping in the city for a few days, and not having any occupation just at present — I am a member of the ministerial profession, sir — but not being engaged just now, I thought I would confer with you on the subject of undertaking to engage in the sale of some of your publications."

Button moved impatiently in his chair.

"No use, Mr. —— Mr. —— no use. You can't sell my books."

The long man, as if unaccustomed to such direct and uncompromising speech, started perceptibly, and looked aghast for a moment, as if some one had "spatted" him in the face with a cold wet hand.

"Uh-uh-uh-uh-m," he began again; "I trust, sir, that the fact of my being a minister of the gospel " —

"Not the least in the world," interrupted Button — "Nothin' of the kind. You hain't gut the root o' the matter in ye — that's the long and the short on't. You can't sell books. You can't sell nothin'. I hain't no use for ye. A hundred sech fellers as you couldn't sell a baby a tract. It's *jizm* I want. Piety ain't no count in the subscription book business. Nor ministers neither; only men. I'd like to 'commodate ye, my friend, but taint no kind o' use. Good mornin'. I'm very busy. John!" he shouted again to his clerk, who instantly appeared — "Show this gentleman out."

And without paying the least attention to the confounded long man, who coughed again in full, and would have begun another circumlocution, Mr. Button made a sudden half-face, and addressed Jacox.

"Now, Mr. Jacox, your turn. So you want to git some territory to sell my Histry o' the Bible ? "

"Yes," said Jacox. But both he and Adrian wore looks that testified to an uncomfortable sensation in view of the dismissal of the poor broken-down clergyman, who had as it were gradually been extracted from the room in a state of astonished but feeble indignation.

"Hmh !" snuffed the publisher, vigorously. "That chap would have sot there 'n talked all day long 'f I'd a let him. No more go in him than there is in a broken-backed snek. Sell books ! No wonder he hain't got no engagement. What's *he* good for, I'd like to know ? He may be wuth somethin a preachin, for what I know, where they only want a kind o nuss to git um asleep, but I don't believe he can save no souls. Forty sech preachers couldn't convert a rat, let alone a sinner in britches ! All the used up ministers in the world, I blieve, think they can make their everlastin fortins a sellin books. They're the wust and meanest failures on um all. I've lost money enough and time enough with um, I tell ye, before this. I shuck um off mighty quick now."

This was not, perhaps, very charitable, except in that range of charity that begins at home; but the two hearers felt that it was hard sense, and business-like. Button went on :

"Married, Mr. Jacox ? "

"Yes."

"Where's yer famly ? "

"North Denmark, Connecticut."

"References ? "

Jacox had at once begun to be uneasy under this inquisition, probably thinking it only another mode of prefacing a rejection, and being a person of no great patience, and having a good deal of free and independent American citizenship about him, he snatched out a pocket-book and hastily drew forth some bank bills, which he exhibited, saying at the same time, with extreme swiftness of utterance,

"Well, by thunder, I'd about as soon expect to give references to run a gin mill as to run the subscription book business. I can pay my way, and do my work, and do exactly as I agree. References! I snum! Well, by ginger, you can write to Noyes and Skittery of Hartford, if you want to. They don't want me to leave 'em. But I won't give no man no references!"

"Don't kick before you're spurred, Mr. Jacox," placidly observed Mr. Button. "I like your spunk. I think it's possible you and I may agree, and if we do, and you do as I say, you'll make a comfortable independence in a few years. But you say you've bin one of Noyes and Skittery's agents?"

"Yes I do, and right smart men they are. Why, they made not less'n three thousand dollars last year just on outfits they sold to agents."

"Wal," said Mr. Button, weightily, "I don't make no money a sellin one book and a canvassin book apiece to my agents for an outfit. I don't make money off my agents. I can do better. I make money for um. I made last year twenty thousand dollars, not off a nasty little mess of outfits, but off one work I published. And my agents made forty-five thousand."

Jacox opened his eyes.

"I don't say nothin against Noyes and Skittery," resumed the chieftain; "I know um to be good men and smart men. But their system ain't my system, and my agents can't use no system but mine. I hain't no expectation that Noyes and Skittery'll like mine, no more'n I like theirn. But look a here, Mr. Jacox;—the bigger share you git of the **sixty thousand dollars**"—Mr. Button pronounced with an emphasis like one that carves colossal words on a pyramid of granite—"of the **sixty thousand dollars** my agents **shall make, this year**, on my new Histry o' the Bible,—the more you git out,

the better I shall be pleased,—supposin you take a holt."

Adrian himself, not at all inclined nor accustomed to look at things from the pecuniary side, began to feel the influence of this powerful passion for wealth that smouldered so hotly in the strong and large though low nature of Mr. Button. In spite of himself it stimulated him from underneath, as where a mass of coal on fire, burning under ground, heats and drives up an unnatural growth of vegetation on the surface above it, too rank for the cool clear air on the mountain. As for Jacox, a quick-thoughted and vivid creature, and eager for wealth after the genuine sharp-witted Yankee fashion, even if possible more than Button in proportion as he was poorer, he was not merely smouldering. He was white hot already, though with correct business habit he was trying desperately to seem totally indifferent. He could hardly sit still. Adrian fancied that as the little man sat there in his chair, he could hear him fizz and see him thrill in the new-fangled scientific manner,—and he said to himself, "Heat a Mode of Motion."

Mr. Button, indeed, was under a full head of steam. He had seen at once that Jacox would make a capital agent, and he was fully resolved to capture him on the spot. Besides, he wanted to show Adrian how to handle Men. He resumed; as one might say, to change the figure, he re-opened his broadside of hot shot.

"Now, Mr. Jacox, I'll be plain with ye, for that's the best way. I like your looks; and I b'lieve you and I can do fustrate by each other. But you can't sell no books for me not on your plan. I'll jest tell ye a little about mine, and if you don't like, why, there's no harm done. Ef ye do, it's a thing agreed. Now, — sellin' books is like workin' land. It can be done shallow, or deep. Your way — I don't mean no disrespect to nobody, Mr. Jacox, but it's my way of explainin' things — your way's what I call the Skitteryskimmery System. Your firm rakes in a rijiment — I should say a brigade, I reckon, of fellers, anybody they can git — the more the better, because the firm wants to save itself if it can jest by sellin outfits alone. And any man that can lay down the price of an outfit's enlisted. Then they give out territory jest as fast as they can, the faster the better, and they send out their agents jest like them locusts that come up over the land of Egypt, and they skitter and skim over the hull country in about three months or six months, 'n sell what they can, and deliver the books, and the hull thing's over. And the next six months or the next year it's jest so over again with another book, and so on ; and no book don't sell for more'n a year at the outside, and the country gits jammed and choked with trash that ain't fit to be read. Ain't that so, Mr. Jacox ? "

Jacox laughed. "Something of that kind, Mr. Button."

"Wal — my system is the Subsoil System. I don't employ no agent until I've seen him and talked to him and found out what he can do, and shown him how, if he don't know already, for I do know, Mr. Jacox! and the proof on't is the money I've made. And when he's taken territory I make him stay there and sell and report to me and sell and report to me until he's worked every house in his deestrict — every house ! And my books'll sell for ten years, for twenty years, and they're better and better all the time, for I keep improvin on

'em, so's't every subscriber gits all I promise him and a good deal o' the time more too. — Now, Mr. Jacox, do you know how to sell a customer a book ? "

"Why," said the little man, greatly impressed by the intense manner and weighty matter of Mr. Button's address, — "Why, I've been in the habit of thinking so ; and I've sold a good many books ; but I'll say this, Mr. Button — that I'm ready to take your directions."

"Now ye talk like a man o' sense," said Button. "Here," — and taking up a copy of the History of the Bible, he held it out to Mr. Jacox, adding, — "Now sell me that book."

Jacox looked puzzled.

"I mean it. I mean exactly that. Sell me that book ! I don't want it. D—n a book agent anyhow ! Cussed piratical villins ! "

Jacox, without a word, took the volume, and rose from his chair. Button seized a pen, turned to the table, and began to write assiduously.

"Mr. Button, I believe ? " said Jacox, in a prompt and sharp but good natured voice.

Button just glanced up and then down again, saying, gruffly, "Yes. What want?"

Jacox laid the book on the table, open to the title-page.

"There, Mr. Button. You're a man of family. That book will do more to keep your children honest and safe in their morals and their practice, than all the Sunday schools in York State. You've got to own it."

"Get out with your book ! " exclaimed Button, slapping down the cover of the book and giving it a slide so angry and vicious that it flew quite over the edge of the table.

Jacox caught it neatly in the air, laid it right back where it was before,

open just the same, and went straight
on in exactly the same tone, barely
making a semicolon at the interrup-
tion.

"— As I was saying; now for instance; your daughter hears somebody say the Bible's a humbug; she's
a young innocent girl and don't know
good and evil. Or your son, and he
thinks it's smart to be an independent
thinker. But when they come home
and ask you or their mother about it,
you just look up the points in this book
and you set 'em all right, and save a
fine young fellow that you've set your
heart on, from going head first into
infidelity, and all the wickedness that
generally goes along with it."

— "You see," broke off Jacox, all
of a sudden, "this is no fair shakes. I
haven't studied up the book. I don't
know any thing about it at all. I can't
sell a book that I don't understand.
Neither could you; nor anybody. I
can't preach at random."

"You've done very well, Mr. Jacox,"
said Button with a smile — "That's
jest what I was a waitin' to hear ye
say. I was a lookin' to see how long you
could run your mill without any grist
in't. You're the man I want, I guess.
You ain't afraid, and you don't git
upsot, and you don't lose your temper.
And if you'd a had the fax about that
book well in your mind, how long would
you have hung on to me ?"

A full look of bull-dog tenacity settled in the queer light-blue eyes of
the little man as he answered with his
teeth set together,

"Till I had your name down for
one or more copies, unless I died first."

"Wal," said Mr. Button; "that's
extremely satisfactory ; now I must
go ; — can you come in here to-morrow
morning at nine exactly ?"

Jacox said he could.

"Then I'll make an arrangement
with ye that'll suit ye, I guess. I
want to give ye some particklers about
sellin too, that'll be of service to ye.
And see here ; — I wish you'd master
this here " — he took a printed thing
like a sort of hand-bill or broad sheet
off the table and gave it to him —
" and see how full an account on't
you can give me in the mornin'.
Adrian, you take one too — " he
handed him one accordingly — " I
want ye to see how these things are
done. Good day, Mr. Jacox."

And with more cordiality than he
had yet shown, the great man arose
and gave his new agent a hearty
farewell shake of the hand.

When Jacox was gone, Button sat
back in his chair with an air of weariness that rather surprised Adrian, and,
wiping his forehead, he asked the latter,

"What d'ye think o' that ?"

"I didn't know there was so much
generalship in the business," answered the young man.

"There is though — and it uses up
the general, too. Tell ye what 'tis, it
spends a man's life to put force into
things like that. I've got that Jacox,
— but I'm tired. I've grown kinder
shaky, nervous a woman would call it.
I can't stan it as well as I could fifteen
years ago. I feel a queer kind o dizziness every once in a while, and sorter
pains in the back o my neck. I only
wish my son Bill would take to the
business — Really, I'd a bought my
own book o Jacox if 'twould a sot Bill
in the right path," continued Mr. Button, with a queer painful smile — " I
couldn't help a thinkin on't when he
made them pints about a man's children. But it's too late now, I reckon.
He must graduate at the law school,
I spose, and travel, and be somethin
or other — I'm sure I do'no what."

Mr. William Button was the only

and not particularly hopeful son of the capitalist. Among the sufficiently numerous deficiencies of our beloved country is, the want of an Education for the Children of the Rich. Physiological results of ignorance and of consequent mistakes in the use of life — or perhaps instead of mistakes the term should be wrong conditions of society, — in our great business centres, make them often a sort of whirlpools into which good strains of blood are incessantly diving and disappearing. A strong eager resolute worker comes into the city, intent on wealth. He plunges into a career of furious unrelaxing vacationless struggling for money, marries, and he and his wife go straight on in the same road. Even while a young man, even though upright and pure of life, the freshness and cleanly vigor of his youth are soiled, dried, stagnated, enfeebled, by the hot fury of his money-making, the dead air of the city streets, a life without exercise, vacation, or any health-giving constituent; and the children born to him are by a necessary result the physiological embodiments of mistake, unbalance, imperfection. They are born ill-constructed; their very marrow and pith has weak streaks in it; they are ships whose timbers had dry rot in them when they were framed.

Now, of all the distinctions of man, the highest is, his infinite power of amendment, of reparation, of recovery, of improvement. Even for the strengthless sprouts of these unlucky city stocks, neither physiologist nor educator — scientific as we pretend to be — knows how great a measure of redemption might be secured by a proper education of mind and body. For our poor, our schools and our life afford it. In other countries, much is accomplished by the aid of wise and just sentiments as to the responsibility of inheritors of wealth. But with us, physiological ignorance prevents any remedy for the congenital weaknesses of money-makers' children, and social and moral ignorance prevents any remedy for the peculiar temptations around the helpless little fools as they grow up. So the impartial self-limitations of nature are left to do their cold unerring work, and in the second or third generation the abused race is extinct, by a vital *reductio ad absurdum*. But Mr. Button, though profoundly displeased at many things concerning his two children, and particularly his son, — who was, in short, rather foolish and more than rather fast — could not imagine any reason for it. So like a practical man as he was, he said but little about it and did the best he could.

People who are largely and instinctively kindly and desirous to help, often attract the confidences of others, without any purposes or advances of their own. Women are most often called to such lovely offices; but there are a few men who without having less of the masculine forces, have as it were superadded something of the feminine emotional and sympathetic endowment. Such was Adrian, and he had often met with experiences accordingly. He was the established confidant, *ex officio*, of all his friends. A stranger sitting by his side in the rail car would confess to him his disappointments in life, his sorrows and even — sometimes — his ill deeds; for until a late stage of the case-hardening of evil-doing, sin in most people is more or less consciously a sickness, a pain, and almost everybody longs for sympathy in sickness or pain. Even lost children and lost old women at the street corners always floated up to Adrian by this unconscious attraction, to ask him the way ; a stray dog, or a poor mewing outcast kitten infallibly trotted at his heels. And here was this big bull of a capitalist confessing griefs that he would hardly admit to himself, to the young man that he habitually looked on as a " kind o' Nimshi " — as is the funny Yankee term for a shiftless person ; apparently from some fancied fitness of sound, rather than from any actual inefficiency recorded as belonging to the ancient Hebrew gentleman and progenitor of Jehu.

Adrian, whose opinion of Mr. Button junior was certainly not higher than the father's, found no adequate consolation to offer, but he argued as well as he could that there was plenty of time yet ; and that many men had waited and doubted a long time before choosing their occupation ; and that perhaps it was good fortune that the young man could afford to wait. But the shrewd publisher shook his head.

" I do' know — we'll hope for the best. — But there's no use a talkin about it, anyhow. Now, as to my Useful Information. There's a lot o work to be done on't yet, and a General Introduction to be writ, and I'd thought o makin on ye an offer to take holt on't. I've got an old feller to daddy it, as I call it — I can have any I want out of a dozen, — with a D.D. to his name, that'll let me put his name on the title-page. Nothin like havin handles to the author's name ; if he has as many as one o these big steamboat engines, a stickin out everywhere, all the better. D.D. stands for Daddy, I reckon. Well, as I was a sayin, there's room in this office for a smart man, and there's money too. One thing leads to another, ye know. Who knows what might come on't ? "

In truth, the promptness and neatness with which Adrian had turned off his work as secretary, had greatly surprised and impressed Mr. Button, and had decided him almost on the instant to make somewhat such a proposition to the young man as he had thought of a hundred times. But he had always been held back by a notion that Adrian " couldn't do nothin," as he would have phrased it, and still more by his not understanding him. Natures like Button's, whose morality is decently good, but whose highest aspirations are filled full by authority and by wealth, are perhaps the best that can be really happy in this world ; for happiness is the successful exertion of the best of our faculties. But the range of life that lies above, in thought ; — all that can be lived by seeing and feeling and producing beauty or truth or love — all the higher grades of activity are unknown to these merely materialist and executive minds. They are strongly built basements ; they have no sunny upper rooms nor oratories with skylights. Accordingly Mr. Button was conscious that forceful as he knew himself, his weapons would not bite upon Adrian, and he was divided between displeasure which he was inclined to think just contempt, and another feeling which he would perhaps have called dislike ; but it had a tinge of apprehension in it. There is always some fear toward a superior organization. It is as belonging to a higher — a more spiritual — range of being, that we are afraid of a ghost. To Button, Adrian was a kind of ghost — unpractical, intangible, useless, scareful.

Adrian in reply expressed a very honest surprise ; for he, understanding Button pretty well, was conscious of his sentiments, and had smiled to himself more than once at the idea of their yoking together in business — for he had naturally thought of it, having thoughts active, discursive and many. But, he said, not having expected it, he could not at once decide; and furthermore, he was to be so much occupied with divers affairs that in any event he would have to postpone a reply for some weeks. To this Mr. Button agreed, with the cautious remark "there ain't nothin bindin in sejestions." And thereupon the two left the office, Mr. Button to assault and carry the defences of the Reverend Doctor Giddings, and Adrian to undertake a hunt in Gowans' antiquarian or rather second-hand book store, only a few blocks away in Nassau Street.

CHAPTER IX.

THE visit of Adrian Scrope Chester to New York was for several purposes. The first of these, of course, was to enjoy some of those hours, — such as are always so blissful and so brief — in the permitted happiness of Miss Button's society. Another was, to be present at the approaching meeting of the Scrope Association. Another was, to obtain the relief of a vacation, or at least of a change of activities, from the steady tediousness of his drudging duty as Assistant Librarian. By passing this interval in New York, he was certain of the stimulus always offered by the swift and motley variety of experiences which the great city is forever offering to the sojourner from without it — the said sojourner being for the most part, as the citizens know very well, the only person decently informed about what is going on in the city. And besides all these errands, there was still another; a purpose which was in fact a secret of his own; in which he had already

been eagerly interested for several years. How eagerly, none can very well understand, except those who have themselves been possessed by that keen and absorbing sort of passion which belongs to pursuits intrinsically not important, as if the trifling nature of the occupation itself were to be made up for by the correspondingly greater zeal it inspires. In the particular taste in question, Adrian was however only exhibiting one of the traits which belonged to the Scrope race, and exhibiting it in the pronounced manner natural to the manifestations of that strong blood.

The Scrope descendants generally, not exclusively Mr. Van Braam, Mr. Button, Adrian, and Scrope of Scrope, but a very respectable army of kinsfolk scattered by this time as is so commonly the case with New England families, into all manner of positions in life, and all over the United States, retained more or less of the vivid sentiment of kinship and the pride of good descent, as well as the sturdy moral quality, the mental activity and the liking for good literature, which belonged to their best known Puritan ancestors. Indeed, even a special trait of the literary tendency of the race — the taste for collecting and recording — remained often distinct and recognizable, as hereditary in this race of Yankee yeomen and men of business, as the like in the old French family of De Thou or the noble English house of Spencer.

Thus it came to pass that there were in existence a score at least, and very likely thrice as many, manuscript copies of the document which was connected with Adrian's visit to the famous establishment of Mr. William Gowans in Nassau Street, if not a cause of it; and of which he had in fact at the time of that visit one such copy safely bestowed in his pocket-book. This document was all that was left of the will of Adrian Scroope the Refugee; and this will,—a holograph, as the collectors call it, viz., a document written throughout by its maker or author, instead of being written by some one else in order to be signed by him,—and two signatures, were in fact all the existing record evidence of his personal presence in America, so far as had hitherto become known to antiquaries. There were reports, suspicions, and traditions in abundance, and of very great circumstantial weight; but, as Mr. Van Braam very well knew, and had explained to young Scrope, this was the extent of the certainties. Exactly this dearth of information it was, which obviously enough was going to be the great difficulty in the way of establishing any American claim by inheritance upon the very large sum which was represented as ready to be delivered to whomsoever should prove his right as heir to the regicide colonel, Adrian Scroope.

The will in question had been proved in Hartford, in 1728, and was executed the year before, as appeared from that half of the attestation to that effect, which remained. This date indicated that the maker of the will had attained to a full measure of that long life which was an almost invariable possession of such Scroope descendants as were strongly marked with either the physical or mental traits of the race. For, Adrian Scroope the Refugee, having fled to New England after his father's execution in 1660, was then a man grown, according to the current tradition, and according to reason. If he were twenty years old in 1660, he would of course be eighty-seven in 1727, the year of the execution of the will.

The original will was drawn upon a page of foolscap paper, and the portion remaining was such a strip as would be torn out of a bound book by some one snatching at a leaf in haste. It was the outer half, torn roughly down the middle of the leaf from top to bottom; and—if this theory about a book was true, for there was no evidence on the subject—it had been on the left hand page as you open the book, for it was the left hand half of the lines which had been preserved. As antiquaries know very well, paper was used economically in the early days of New England, as if a costly thing, and this will was, accordingly, though verbose in style, written in a small, crowded, though clear and clerkly hand, wonderfully firm and steady for so old a writer; so that the whole instrument, signatures, attestations and all, was easily contained upon the single page.

The original half was in the hands of a well known antiquarian and collector, Philetus Stanley of East Hartford,— and should naturally be there still, as he is himself, like Adrian Scrope Chester, a descendant from the Deidamia named in the will. What was left upon this mutilated page throws various lights upon hereditary Scrope traits, and is not without interest as a specimen of the wordy style of its period, as well as of the thorough manner in which it was then usual to imbue business documents with a formal piety. It is not meant that this piety was insincere, but that it was superfluous. Many an old deed of those days begins, not "To all persons to whom these presents shall concern," but "To all CHRISTIAN people to whom" &c.—as if faith need not be kept with the heathen. In like manner was it, that the most dishonest of merchants as much as the most honest, would in old times put "Laus Deo" at the head of a new set of books. The same notion is to-day alive in those who are striving for a law to enforce the acknowledgment of God in all constitutions, laws, conveyances of real estate, notes of hand and bills for groceries.

The body of the existing portion of the so-called Scrope Will was as follows, omitting the witnesses' names and the attestation of proof. The testator's signature was lost, all except the first two letters.

20th of y⁰ second m⁰ called April, 1727.   I Ad
at present sojourning in Hartford on the C
being at this tyme sick and weake in body, yett
and mercy of the Lord retaining my full unde
icular my purposes often heretofore expressed, doe d
my last will and testament as Followeth :

My miserable and sinfull bodie to be bur
with y⁰ leaste cost and pomp y¹ decently may
testimony against y⁰ heathen custome of vaine show
beseech to be regarded. And my soul I comitt un
in full faith and trust in his kindness to me a worm
fied that my state be whatsoever he chooseth.

And whereas I am of right entitled to all
personall which was or should have been that of Ad
ther within y⁰ realme of England, and Whereas I
nall lyfe of others and myselfe than for the thinges of
temporall in New England is therefore but small :

And whereas my daughter Adriana hath disob
things, and especially in marrying Philipp Van Booraem,
my deare daughter Deidamia hath been loving & ob
and in particular hath been the staffe of my old age, N
of my aforesaid purposes already often expressed,
queath all my temporall estate both real and person
soever, lands, tenements and hereditaments, whether
wrongfully or otherwise withheld from me, whether sit
bookes in y⁰ chest with name and armes of Scroope
and all goods, chattels and choses in action of every
and that without prejudice or unkindness to my deare son
of said Hartford, presently contracted in
To my said deare daughter Deidamia and her he
fullest and amplest estate therein that may be.

Ad

Many careful and repeated studies had been made upon this mutilated record ; for it was a chief centre of interest to a somewhat numerous family connection, and it presented a less fascinating though yet very attractive problem to the local antiquaries of Connecticut — a persistent, hard-headed, and sharp-witted tribe of close reasoners, shrewd investigators and determined searchers, though not numerous.

"Oh few and small their numbers were,
A handful of *sharp* men."

The conclusions drawn from the Will are not very difficult to discern, however. Some of them of course, were reckoned certain, and others uncertain. Thus: it was considered clear that the testator was a person of deep piety, after the type of his period; strong and enduring in resentment, yet disinterested and beneficent; that he was of original and decided ways of thinking, as was shown by his unconventional notions about funerals; that he believed himself entitled to property of some kind in England; that whatever he could give was given exclusively to his daughter Deidamia, — undoubtedly that Deidamia Throop who is well known to have married John Chester of Windsor; that he had a son, whom he had probably provided for as is often the case, by what are called "advancements" or gifts during his life, and who therefore took nothing by this will; that although no express words of disinheriting were used, nothing whatever was given to the disobedient daughter Adriana, married to the Dutchman Philipp Van Booraem or Van Braam. The tenacious character of the Scropes was evidenced in such minor matters as the language and handwriting, which were rather that of the Commonwealth, when the writer was a boy at school, than of the period of Swift and Addison, at which the instrument was executed. It was clear enough also that a chest carved with the Scrope name and arms, and containing books, had been given to Deidamia.

But — however weighty the presumptions in the case might be, and although the testator's given name began with the two letters "Ad"— and although both the body of the will and these two letters, especially the very characteristic and strikingly designed capital A were admitted to be in the same handwriting with the two existing signatures of Adrian Scroope, and although no other reasonable hypothesis would account for a daughter of the uncommon name of Adriana, and although it was specified that the chest with the "bookes" bore the name and arms of Scroope — in spite of all these cumulative circumstances, they were circumstantial evidence only, and the more cautious authorities hesitated to affirm positively that the will was absolutely that of Adrian Scroope, son and heir of Colonel Adrian Scroope the Regicide Judge. It may, they reasoned, be that of the Reverend Adeodatus Throop, minister of a small society in New London County, afterwards known as New Concord, and by law incorporated as the town of Bozrah in May 1786; — and whose son or grandson Benjamin Throop, succeeding him in his spiritual charge, having graduated at Yale College in 1734, was ordained Jan. 3, 1739, and became his successor in his spiritual office, living to a great age and dying, still after the good old fashion the settled minister at New Concord or Bozrah, in 1785.

It is very true, however, that another family tradition identified the two, Adrian Scroope and Adeodatus Throop. This tradition was a constant and unvarying one, and had become an unquestioned article of faith among the Scrope descendants. It was, that Adrian Scroope had been hunted for by the officers of the crown at the same time with his father, viz. in 1660, and had indeed only escaped from them by great presence of mind and a shrewd deceit. The party of officers had, it would appear, even made their way into the house where young Scroope was. They did not know his person however; and with a ready coolness remarkable in a young fellow, he perceived this, and adroitly mingled with them, pretending to aid them in their search. Finally, looking out at a window, and affecting to see the man they wanted he cried out "There goes Scroope!" flung himself out as if in pursuit, and so got off. He remained, apparently, in hiding, and crossed secretly to New England; though the time as well as the manner of his doing so are purely matters of conjecture. He may have crossed in the same ship with the regicides Goffe and Whalley, who landed at Boston in July 1660. There is not however the remotest trace of his presence in New England, either, until the year 1666, when he must have been living at Hartford under his own name, for the signature at the end of this chapter, and which is a fac-simile furnished by the kindness of that accomplished historical scholar C. J. Hoadly Esq., State librarian of Connecticut, is upon a document dated March 11, of that year, and he is there described as "of Hartford."

The other of his two known signatures is of about the same time. He had therefore then passed safely through the time of the first pursuit of Goffe and Whalley, in the fall and winter of 1660–61, and had thought it safe to appear in his own name. Whatever was the immediate occasion of his adopting that of Throop instead (taking it for granted that he did so, according to this distinct and positive family tradition), the reason must necessarily have been fear of legal proceedings by the crown. Reason enough; for those were the days when no counsel was allowed to a prisoner on a criminal charge; and when if the king and his ministers so required, a crown prosecution for high treason was all but certain death. And the same consideration continued almost or quite as powerful not only under that hog and murderer Chief Justice Jeffries in the reign of James II., but even for almost a century later. It was barely over a century ago that a storm blew down the last skull from Temple Bar, in 1772, — four years before our own Declaration of Independence. It is no wonder, then, if the imperilled refugee remained quietly in the safe concealment of an assumed name, (a concealment rendered peculiarly safe by the fact that near by, in the town of Lebanon, there was actually established a well known family of the name of Throop), and in an obscure Connecticut village, to the end of his days. One of more ambitious, vain or greedy temper might have risked attempting to regain the wealth and high position that justly belonged to him in England. But the Scropes were proud, not vain; nor did they greatly feel the want of either riches or honor; and there is reason enough to believe that the obscure and silent life which he lived was filled with good works and contented studies and meditations, such as would afford at least as much real enjoyment as such a character could find in any higher position.

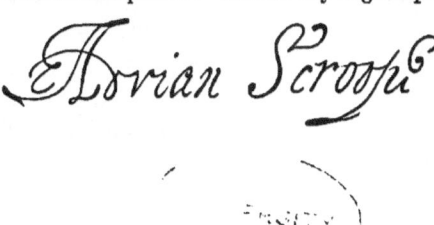

PART III

CHAPTER X.

"Gowans'," was only a few steps from Mr. Button's office. Adrian had only to go a block or two northward, and to enter the door of a roomy establishment on the western side of Nassau Street between Ann and Beekman — being in fact at present the southernmost of the three partitions of the ground-floor occupied by the American News Company — and he had arrived. The street front was filled by two immense windows with the door between. Both windows were extremely dusty, and upon the space close behind the glass, where in a dry goods shop would have been displayed some artistic array — or dishevelment — of glossy fabrics, were arranged — or rather flung — a few dozen books or sets. Close in front of each window, outside, was a large board or rough tray on trestles, filled each with a heap of weather worn books, and bearing the enticing legend, on a square of " straw board," " Ten cents each." Within the opening of the doorway, and bestriding the threshold at an informal angle, was a smaller similar tray, holding books a grade more valuable — or rather less worthless, — whose price was Fifteen Cents. Adrian, with the genuine book-collector's instinct, stopped and examined all three of these trays, and the contents of the window-seats too, closely watched the while by the guardian angel of the spot, a *genius loculi* or Nassau Street cherub of about twelve years old, whose face was sharp enough and his garments ragged and dirty enough to suggest that he was an embodiment or efflorescence of all the mind in Mr. Gowans' establishment and of all its dirt too — the offspring, so to speak, of a marriage between the old gentleman's literature and his litter. But carefully as Adrian turned over the trays-full of small volumes and scrutinized one by one the titles of the books in the windows, not one did he find that was worth money to him, or even shelf-room ; and remembering the auction sale of the day before, he said to himself that it was no wonder the Hebrew bidder restricted himself to two cents. But truly, what fearful stuff it was ! Old weather-beaten copies of school arithmetics and spelling-books, thickly arabesqued with the ingenuous devices of artistic childhood ; odd volumes of G. P. R. James' novels ; poor thin books of verses published thirty years ago at the author's expense, and falling into an instantaneous oblivion — infants too weak to bear even the effort of birth ; one or two Annual Reports of the Smithsonian Institution ; a .mishmash of books perfectly unknown, perfectly valueless except by avoirdupois weight, very dead cats of books except that they keep better, and yet, many of them intrinsically every whit as desirable as some "excessively rare" volumes famous in catalogues. Indeed they would be excessively rare themselves if anybody would only want them.

The books in the windows were pretty much a repetition of the same story, a few grades higher in the scale. There was a set of Rees' Cyclopædia ; one of the *seventh* edition of the Encyclopædia Britannica; an awful clean new set of the Horæ Homileticæ, or sermons, of the Reverend Charles Simeon, in twenty-one volumes octavo, as enticing as a row of twenty-one clean new skulls, and above them on a placard, the following recommendation, copied out of Bohn's General Catalogue, page 1778:

"A monument of pastoral labor and piety, with much judgment on doctrinal subjects, and useful practical application." BICKERSTETH.

A monument, indeed! and over a whole cemetery of dead sermons at once, reflected Adrian; and — for he was a thoughtful observer of words — he reflected further, What a circumspect commendation! It implies that the "labor and piety" are dead and buried; it doesn't say the "judgment" is good. How could he have said less? It's a real model for recommendations! Next to this impressive "monument" was a pirated Brussels copy of the third edition of Brunet's *Manuel du Libraire*, and a good looking Paris copy of the fourth edition; but no signs of the fifth. And so on, and so on; but Mr. Gowans' collection of books was that day the largest collection of published works on the continent of America, reaching about two hundred and fifty thousand volumes. Adrian cannot go through them all at this rate, unless he has a number of years to spare; he must go in.

He went in. The sudden change at entering from even a Nassau Street daylight into this vast cavern made its gloom doubly obscure. He penetrated along a narrow alley at one side of a broad table, that stood in all the front of the great store, heaped full and high with books, finding hardly room to walk between its tableland and superincumbent book-Cor-

dilleras and the crowded shelves on the wall, while his feet, as he stepped, grazed or caught against piles and piles of books or pamphlets, stacked along on both sides in the angles at the floor. Working thus some twenty or thirty feet back, the gloom always growing darker as he went, he found a small open space back of the mighty table or platform just mentioned, and in the middle of the breadth of the great room. In this space was a great rusty old cylinder stove, with a cool sort of fire burning away down in the inside, so that you could feel it if you reached a good way in. Against the north side of the room, abreast of this stove, was a small desk, with a dirty litter of pamphlets, and scraps of paper, a dried-up looking inkstand, and one or two old quill pens. Enthroned upon a broken backed wooden chair before this desk sat Mr. Gowans himself, the Pluto of this Orcus, with his back to the desk however, his long legs distributed before him, his old stove-pipe hat on his head and pulled down over his eyes just as it was at the auction, and his hands clasped together behind the back of his neck, fingers interwoven and thumbs down, so that his elbows projected at either side like frame-bones for wings. In this restful and philosophic attitude, he was conversing with a customer, and did not so much as turn his head at Adrian's approach.

"Have you a copy of Caulfield's History of the High Court of Justice?" asked Adrian.

"No," said the old man, promptly, and gruffly, shaking his head at the same time, like Jove, by way of ratification.

"A copy of the Reverend Mr. Lee's Connecticut Election Sermon?"

"No. Haven't got it."

Here the person who had been talking with Mr. Gowans interrupted, asking with good natured and courteous jocularity,

" Didn't you know that Mr. Gowans has no books at all ? "

" Why, no," said Adrian, amused; " I knew no better than to suppose it was precisely his business to have them."

" Well, I've dealt with Mr. Gowans for twenty years, and I've never heard him acknowledge to a chance customer that he had a book."

" I don't quite understand," said Adrian.

" Why, it's perfectly easy.   It's cheaper for him to say No and be done with it, than to hunt for a week through two hundred and fifty thousand volumes and not find the book after all."

Here the speaker interrupted himself suddenly, to give a scrutinizing look at the young man, and exclaimed,

" Well, I declare, if you're not the very person I was praying for.   Was it not you who was so good as to give me a volume of pamphlets at Ball's yesterday ? "

Adrian, looking closely in his turn, and recognizing the person called Sibley, — a dark complexioned middle-sized man he was, with a pleasant intelligent face and voice, a lively manner and very bright eyes, answered, Yes.

" Couldn't see you at all, at first, in this old sepulchre," continued he. " Well, you're exactly the man I wanted to see.   And — by your leave, Mr. Gowans," he interjected, —

" Oh, yes ! " carelessly returned the monarch of the cavern, at the same time turning round and beginning to make entries on a loose sheet of paper on his little old desk, by a dim gaslight.   The speaker continued,—

" Well then, I know enough more about Mr. Gowans' stock than he does himself, and if you'll tell me what you want I'll show it with pleasure.   I have to hunt here very often."

" Why," returned Adrian, a certain ridiculous habit of quoting coming upon him, " then to use the words of the poet, you have ' pu'd the Gowans fine,' no doubt, — all of them I'm afraid I stand but little chance. What can the man do that cometh after the King ? "

The other looked a little unhappy at the quotation — it might be at the abominableness of the pun, it might be only the discomfort of one who don't know exactly what to make of what is said to him; but he passed it over, and not without some satisfaction at the compliment that followed, he answered,

" Well, I don't say but that I know what I'm about.   Twenty years of close work ought to give me some knowledge of the book business.   But I don't want every thing, — indeed I don't want any thing in the book line, except for trade.   Perhaps I can make some money by you."

" Well, — as to Caulfield, then, and that election sermon ? "

" You will hardly find Caulfield short of London; it's the merest chance if there's a copy for sale on this side ; it's not a common book.   As for Mr. Gowans' collection of Election Sermons, I'll show you those, and you can look them through yourself.   Come this way."

He turned and plunged into another narrow alley, between two lofty and interminable looking ranges of crowded and over-crowded shelves, still with other piles on piles of books stacked all along upon the floor, that led back still further into the dark depths of the great room, and Adrian followed. An assistant or two was at work cataloguing. niched in some obscure nook; a step-ladder, hardly more silent, leaned near one of them; and one or two customers were quietly hunting along the shelves, a small boy haunting each of them, by way of watchdog. Like the worthy Roman gentlemen so handsomely complimented by Mark Antony, these book-hunters are all honorable men, and of course for that very reason can have no objection to be watched!

On a shelf in a corner almost at the furthest extremity of the room, and very dimly lit by a window opening on that narrow and ill-flavored streetlet, of old running past the rear of the Park Theatre and thence named Theatre Alley, — a window half shut in by piles of books, and almost crusted within and without with immemorial dirt, — Sibley pointed out the desired collection; a row perhaps four feet long, of mingled volumes and pamphlets, some upright, some leaning over, some piled sideways, all dirty. Adrian and his guide both inspected the array, item by item, without finding the Reverend Mr. Lee's Election Sermon.

"It isn't here," said Adrian. "One more proof that if you know exactly what you want, you can't find it. Jonathan Lee's election sermon, 1766, I have; it is Andrew Lee's, 1795, that I want."

"Andrew Lee" — repeated Sibley. "I sold a copy of his sermon at the funeral of Reverend Benjamin Throop, 1785. the other day."

"Did you?" asked Adrian with interest, — "to whom? I know very well there's such a sermon, and I want it."

"I guess you can get it," said Sibley, significantly.

"What will it cost?"

"Why, — the fact is," said Sibley, not without hesitation, — "it's a pretty good customer of mine who bought it, and he don't care about money. He's a collector. You are too, aren't you?"

"Oh no," said Adrian frankly; "I have worked a little at genealogy. But I've neither the money nor the knowledge nor the time for collecting. I'd like to have, though, Mr. Sibley."

"Oh," said the other, laughing, "Sibley's only my buying name at the auctions, like Chase for Gowans. I am Andrew Purvis, very much at your service. — Didn't mean to rhyme, either."

"It's a capital name for politeness, Mr. Purvis," replied Adrian laughing with him at the unintended jingle — "I know the name very well as connected with the book business, and I'm very much obliged to you; and what would tempt your customer, if money won't?"

"Why," said Mr. Purvis, "my man won't part with any thing he has, if he can help it; he'd rather buy more. It appears he happens to want the very pamphlet that you took out of the volume you bought yesterday. I thought it as well to just take you one side rather than talk about it before Gowans. Now, — what will you take for it? If you are working at genealogy, though, you will want it?"

"What will he give?" asked Adrian in reply. — Scrope is not a trading name, to be sure; but when you are in trade you must do as the tradesmen do.

"Well," rejoined the book-dealer, "I suppose Five Dollars is a very high price for a pamphlet?"

Adrian smiled: "I won't deny," he said, "that I know what a great prize I happened upon. I was ready to go up to thirty dollars for it yesterday — every cent I had in the world just then. It is the unique Scrope Genealogy, that everybody has thought was lost, and that I had no more idea of finding then and there, than of finding the lost decades of Livy."

Mr. Purvis looked rather caught, but made the best of the situation. "You are right," said he; "I beg your pardon. I ought not to have offered you five dollars. But I can't help my trading habits, I suppose. I had an unlimited order for that volume; though I don't think I should have dared go over fifty dollars. I ought not to have been out of the room."

"I'm glad you were, for my part," said Adrian. "But I'll tell you what 'tis, Mr. Purvis, I don't wish to part with the pamphlet just now, and besides, I am very busy over it to-day and to-morrow in particular. If I should be willing, I'll give you the refusal of it, and in a few days I'll send you an address; there is a possibility of my changing it, or I would give it now. And if I won't sell my pamphlet, I suppose your man won't sell his Throop sermon?"

"I'm afraid not; but if you like I'll try to find you another copy. That's not unique, at any rate."

Adrian thanked the obliging dealer, whose manner had in it something so agreeable and sincerely friendly that it greatly attracted the young man. It is possible that the liking was mutual; for either from some such reason or perhaps only with a view to establish a new customer, or possibly merely because business was not very pressing, Mr. Purvis was in no haste to go, and rather encouraged the questions which Adrian was ready enough to put, about the vast collection of Mr. Gowans, about the old gentleman himself, and about books,

collecting and collectors. He explained to Adrian among other things the curious phenomenon of the haunting boys already referred to, telling him plainly that it was an indispensable compliance with the weakness of human nature.

"Kleptomania," said Purvis, "I suppose they'd call it in court if a minister was caught at it, as I caught a minister the other day in my own shop."

"But did you let him off?"

"Oh yes. I couldn't spend the time and trouble to have him punished. I told him however that if he ever came into the place again I'd put him in jail."

As they talked, they were looking along the shelves in a desultory way, and just at the account of the minister's delinquency, Adrian espied a copy of the curious gossipy "Historiettes" of Tallemant de Réaux.

"Did you ever see the anecdote of the old painter Du Moustier and Monsignor Pamphilio?" he asked.

"No." said Purvis.

"Well, let me read it to you," said Adrian; "it's a case exactly in point;" and taking down the volume he read aloud in extempore English the queer old story, which is in substance as follows (see p. 166 of vol. 4 of the edition of Brussels, 1834, by Monmerqué and others): Du Moustier, in his day a famous portrait painter of Paris, and who was born about 1550, was a dear lover of books, rude in speech and quick of hand. As a celebrated painter, he had many visitors; and under his bookshelves, by way of a delicate precautionary hint, he had painted the words "The Devil take book-borrowers." But in particular; one day the Cardinal Barberini, the Pope's legate to France, visited Du Moustier and inspected his collections. Monsignor Pamphilio, afterwards Innocent X., was at the head of the cardinal's suite, and finding on Du Moustier's table a fine copy of the superb London edition of the History of the Council of Trent, he said to himself, " Truly, a fine thing for such a fellow to have such a rare book as that ! " And he quietly took the book and slid it under his gown. But the little man (says Tallemant), who had been on the lookout, flew into a rage, and telling the legate that ' he was greatly obliged for the honor of the visit, but that it was shameful for him to have thieves in his company ; " he forthwith seized Pamphilio, snatched the book away from him, and calling him by a very unpleasant name indeed, he fairly flung him by the shoulders out of his door.

" That's excellent," said the amused dealer ; "and perfectly in character — I know a dozen worthy gentlemen that couldn't be trusted alone in the dark with a rare book. Let me see a moment, please, — oh, — why, can you translate off hand as neatly as that ? "

" I've read the story before," said Adrian ; "and French is pretty easy to tell stories from."

" Very good, very good indeed," repeated the friendly Mr. Purvis ; " I declare I believe I'll make you an offer to translate that book for publication. But as I was saying, there's my customer that wanted this Scrope Genealogy. And by the way, how the mischief did you come to know that it was in that volume ? "

" Pure chance," said Adrian — " pure chance. One of those coincidences that are happening every day in fact, and that it would not do to put into a novel because everybody would say it was altogether too improbable. I went in there a little before the sale and found the books laid out for examination, and I just looked through a lot of them and found this. I remember thinking I must be rather a suspicious looking chap, for there was a big Irish porter or watchman or something on guard, and I couldn't have stolen a pin, he followed me up so. I guess they know about collectors in that office too ! "

" Indeed they do," said Purvis ; " and in spite of them there's hardly a sale of any importance where they don't lose some valuable books off the show-tables, in spite of that sharp old Irish watch-dog of theirs ! "

" Well, how did your customer know about the pamphlet ? " said Adrian.

" Why," replied Mr. Purvis, laughing, " he was in the city himself the day before, and he was nosing about in there too, and he found the pamphlet just as you did, and moreover, he tried as hard as he could to steal it. He told me all about it in a letter that I got only this morning. You don't know who 'tis, so it won't do any harm for me to tell that much. He was in a terrible excitement about it. He wiggled round there for more than half an hour, and the fact is he actually would have carried the volume off if Pat hadn't fairly seized him very much as your old Frenchman did his thief and actually twisted the book out of his hands. As it happened none of the partners were in the place, or he would have seen them and got it, I'm sure. There was a regular string of coincidences in your favor ; for he would have come back again after it the same afternoon, but he found a despatch at his hotel that forced him to hurry home out of town on some business. He telegraphed to me instantly from Hartford, and wrote by the first mail, and he feels dreadfully over losing it, you may be sure."

"How do you suppose that pamphlet came to be in that lot of books?" asked Adrian, by a very natural transition of interest.

"A good many of those books belonged to old Doctor Gideon Bulkley of Middlefield; and, you know,—or you don't know—his collection had been in the family for four generations, and neither the old man nor his father would ever let one human being see what was in it. They never wrote or made any mark on a book, either of them; so that it's difficult to trace with accuracy; but I have no doubt whatever in my own mind that the pamphlet was an early copy direct from the author to the Bulkley of the day, and so escaped the fire that burned the edition, and remained unknown all this time until Bulkley's death, when it was sent for sale."

"That's a good idea, not to mark one's books," commented Adrian; "I knew an excellent old gentleman, a lawyer, who never wrote his name in his law-books, and whenever he found a law-book in any of his friends' offices with no name in it, he always carried it off as his own. He had a valuable law-library at his death."

"Now," said Purvis—"by the way, I beg your pardon, but by what name may I call you?"

"Chester."

—"Mr. Chester, you have never been in Gowans' place before?"

"No."

"Well; as you are an appreciative person, you must see the catacombs. I'll take you round once, and then you can come in and hunt whenever you like. Gowans never will look for a book, and nobody can get any thing of him except by finding it one's self and bringing it to him.

Unless, that is, one of his clerks happens to know about it, or unless some particularly good-natured moment or some special reason prevails with the old man. But come down stairs."

And pausing at the head of a wide stairway, hidden under another great platform heaped high with books, he took up a small lamp, that stood ready, lit it with a match, and descended, marshalling Adrian downwards into a darkness as of the *oubliettes* of Vincennes.

The store, Adrian thought, was the dreariest place he had ever seen; but it was a bright and homelike abode in comparison with the basement which they now entered. This was a cellar as large, and nearly as high, as the store above it. It had absolutely no window light, and the feeble oil lamp which Mr. Purvis carried served only to show how thick the darkness was. But the dealer, with an assured step, briskly descended the dirty old staircase, cumbered on either side with heaps of books piled on each stair. As they reached the bottom, a great stack of books, heaped indiscriminately like the fallen bricks of the Birs Nimroud upon another broad platform, and rising almost to the ceiling, confronted them. But Purvis turned short to the right, crossed to the side of the room, and engaging himself intrepidly in an alley if possible still narrower than that which skirted the up-stairs store, passed on, close along by the southern wall, Adrian following. Ever and anon the guide held up his lamp at one side or the other, showing only the same interminable shelf after shelf, shelf after shelf, each double-ranked, piled, crammed, wedged, with books, numberless, useless, worthless. As up-stairs, not only were the shelves at either hand intolerably full clear up to the ceiling, but a *talus*, as the geologists call it, or steep slope as if of fragments fallen from the precipice at either hand, lined each side of the path. Adrian, an imaginative fellow, remembered the awful stories of men lost in the catacombs of Paris and found dead and rat-eaten weeks after in some corner among the bones; and the stifling accounts of travellers of their scratching and crawling and wriggling along endless passages through the masses of mummies in the vast subterranean pits of Egypt, eyes and mouth and nose and lungs insufferably choked with the floating dust of corpses three thousand years old; and he asked, making a joke of it,

"Would they ever find us if the light should go out?"

"Dear me, no," was the consoling reply, "not unless it was by mere accident. Nobody would come to look for us. I could live here ten years, I believe, for all anybody's looking after me. There's a dozen dried book-hunters lying dead in the corners down here for what I know."

There was a grave-like chill in the air, and a faint flavor of dry cold dust, very dreary. "This is the Catacomb, the Potter's Field, the bone-yard, of literature," observed Mr. Purvis. "There is nothing beyond except Stockwell's old paper shop and then the paper-mill."

"The auction may stand for a slaughter-house," observed Adrian; "then comes the graveyard, and after that, the resurrection into clean new white paper. But wait a moment, please — here's something I want."

The flitting gleam of the lamp had shone for an instant on the gilt backs of four goodly quartos, where Adrian's quick eye had read the name of Behmen. He took down the first volume and opened it, and then examined the others. It was a good clean copy of the Reverend William Law's translation (London, 1774–1781) of the writings of "the Teutonick Theosopher," as he calls the mystical old German, complete, with all the strange overlaid engravings and cabalistical diagrams.

"There," said Adrian, "I'm going to have that. I want to give it to somebody I know, who will enjoy it like a honeymoon."

"One volume a week will just cover his month," observed Purvis. "Well, lug it up-stairs. I don't think Gowans 'll want much for it."

So Adrian took the set on his arm, and having now nearly completed the circuit of the front or Nassau-street half of the cave, they got back to the stairway by the cross alley into which it opened.

"The back half is only the front half over again," said Purvis, as he blew out the lamp in going up the stairs. They returned to the old desk where Mr. Gowans was still scratching away at his scraps of paper, and Adrian, laying down his four volumes, asked what he should pay for them.

"Five dollars," said the old man, carelessly, glancing at the title of Vol. 1. — "I've had 'em ten years, and glad to get 'em out of the way."

Adrian paid him; and at Mr. Gowans' summons, a clerk proceeded to tie up the books.

"Well," said Purvis, "I didn't interfere with your bargain, Mr. Chester, but I'll double your money with pleasure, if you want to speculate."

"I would," said Adrian, "certainly, if I hadn't more than five dollars' worth of enjoyment to expect from my old friend's pleasure over the books."

At this moment there came stumbling along, from the street door, very much as Adrian had done, an elderly man, who could be discerned by the three, but who could not see them or indeed much of any thing. He was plainly and coarsely dressed, like a farmer or old fashioned country tradesman, a good deal bent, though strongly made; carried his hands in a peculiar spread-out attitude, palms down; and as he came into the feeble circle of light where they stood, they could see that his face was browned, rugged and homely, but kindly and sensible.

"Why," said Adrian, "it's my old friend Adam Welles of Manchester. Mr. Welles, how do you do?" And he held out his hand to the old man, who peered at him for a moment before he could see who it was, but at last recognized him with evident pleasure.

"Mr. Chester, I'm delighted to find you," he said, speaking a little slowly, and with something of that deliberate primness or rather solicitude in articulation and in choice of words, frequently seen in those whose culture has not been equal to their aspirations. "I expected to see you at the Scrope Association meeting, next week; but this is an additional delight. What a paradise of books!" continued the old man, looking about him with the air of a humble saint just admitted into the New Jerusalem. "Oh, I could be happy here for a hundred years!"

Adrian laughed. "I knew that you were a lover of old books, Mr. Welles," he said, "but according to what I have noticed, fifty years would do for this collection if you throw out the odd volumes."

"Odd volumes?" exclaimed Mr. Welles — "then I can fill up some of my broken sets! If I can only get the third volume of Winterbotham's Historical View of the United States, with the maps!" —

Mr. Purvis was looking on, well pleased. Adrian now introduced Mr. Welles to him, and the good-natured dealer at once pointed out to the eager old countryman a set of shelves containing some hundreds of all manner of odd volumes, which the old man set himself to inspect one by one, like a miser weighing pieces of gold. And Adrian, having ascertained the old man's city address, and given him his own, at an uptown boarding house, along with injunctions to make him, Adrian, of any service that should be required, left him, going with Mr. Purvis.

"That old man is foreman of a large paper-mill at Manchester," said Adrian, as they reached the street door. "He is a distant cousin of mine, and I believe he is ten times as much of a bibliomaniac."

"Biblioidiot, I should be afraid," said Purvis, "to be so anxious over that foolish old Winterbotham. Why, 'tisn't worth over seven-eighths or a dollar a volume at auction. But I like to see the old man so eager, and I'll help him if I can."

"It isn't because it's Winterbotham," said Adrian : it's because it's a broken set. That old fellow has I guess a thousand volumes in an old attic at Manchester, and I don't believe there's a complete set in the whole. He's been thirty years picking odd volumes and things out of all the paper stock that came into the mill, and he doesn't have many coincidences. You never saw such a lot in your life. There were a few valuable things, but I reckon Stanley's got most of them — he's paid him what the old man thought a good deal of money, first and last."

"What Stanley," asked Purvis, seeming a little startled.

"East Hartford — the book man," said Adrian.

"Oh, — you know him, do you!"

"Why, yes; I'm from Hartford myself, and he's a cousin of mine, as well as old Mr. Welles."

"Whew!" whistled Mr. Purvis, as if somewhat astonished.

"Why?" asked Adrian.

"Oh — nothing. Only it rather surprised me to find you knew each other."

Adrian mused a moment, and then looked up with a smile.

"It was Stanley that" —

"Hush, — not a word," interrupted Purvis, laughing; "I can see that you are a man to be trusted, or else I should be annoyed. I should lose a good deal, one way and another, if he knew I had let it out. He's as secret as death, you know."

Adrian nodded.

"Well; now that we have gone so far, let's make a clean thing of it. Do you know any thing of the lost Scrope Library?"

"I've been watching and searching for it this ten years," said Adrian frankly. "Mr. Stanley has been after it for twenty years. He wants it to complete his collection of early American books, and I want it for my collection of family books and relics. I guess he knows I want it as well as I know he does; but we have never spoken of it."

"Shouldn't wonder if you were hunting for it here?"

"Yes, I was. I have never tried New York before, but I remember that old Scrope Chest and the books in it wherever I see two books together. It wasn't much of a library — probably twenty books."

"If there were twenty and each equal to a clean copy of Eliot's Indian Bible, I should call it a good deal of a library," said Purvis. "But I really believe if any of those books had got in here I should have found them, or else he would. He never comes here without having a hunt."

"He has money and time," said Adrian, with a shade of regret in his voice. "I don't grudge them to him, but I don't break the tenth commandment, do I, by wishing I had the duplicate of something that is my neighbor's?"

"Why, no; I don't see how you can make that out covetousness."

"Well, — he must find them if he can. But I shall keep looking just the same. I've had the best luck about the Scrope Genealogy, anyhow; but perhaps it will be his turn for the next — Well, I must go and present my gift. Good day, Mr. Purvis."

"Good day, Mr. Chester. Come and see me at my store," said the good-natured book dealer, and he handed Adrian a business card as they parted.

CHAPTER XI.

As Adrian that evening approached Mr. Van Braam's, carrying his heavy parcel stoutly on his shoulder — for he was not "in the best society," and need not therefore depend on others when it was more convenient to wait on himself — it suddenly popped into his mind that perhaps he had done wrong in avowing to Mr. Purvis the fact that he was engaged in the Quest — as the romances of the Holy Grail would have called it — of the Lost Library. This doubt was for a moment even painful; for Adrian, like the rest of his kin, was strongly secretive. He was sometimes frank also — for the two traits are not at all inconsistent. His secretiveness was not a mere dog-in-the-manger instinct, such as some collectors have, leading him not only to acquire for himself, but to prevent others from acquiring or even knowing. Perhaps a case of this exaggerated type among Adrian's own relatives might be cited. But in Adrian, it was simply either an instinctive reluctance to speak of his own thoughts, or a precaution against failure in his own designs.

However; after a few moments of doubt whether the revealing of his secret would interfere with the purpose that he had so long entertained, he concluded that probably no harm was done. Mr. Stanley and Mr. Purvis had ransacked their fill in the vast repository of Mr. Gowans, long ago, and with a thousand times his opportunities and advantages. So they had, of course, in scores of other places in the great city; and, for what he knew, they had secured half those old books already. Stanley, he knew, would never say so if he had — it would be a great deal more like the ways of collectors for him to flatly deny it. All is fair in war and collecting. Purvis' inquiries about the lost books proved nothing; he might have had one of them in his pocket all the time, and he could not honestly reveal his customer's secret. Thus reflecting, and comforting himself with the sage conclusion that even if any mischief had been done, it was too late to prevent it, he reached the old white house in the city meadow, and was shown once more into the dusky red-brown parlor where Mr. Van Braam sat as usual at the table, "puttering" in a disorderly heap of papers and memoranda.

At Adrian's entrance, the old gentleman arose with his usual courtly kindness and welcomed him. Adrian answered with equal heartiness, and

if it was with less elegance of manner, perhaps there was natural gracefulness enough to indicate that he would become a courtly old gentleman if he lived as long. But the first thing he added to his salutations came as it were of involuntary impulse, and had it not been between good friends and kinsmen, it might have been uncivil. But placing his parcel on the table, Adrian peered about him into the dim corners of the room, — for the shaded drop-light made an exclusive little circle close round it, — and sniffed, lifting his nose, and peering or pointing about, to tell the truth, somewhat as a dog does who suspects the presence of edibles.

" Do you know," he said, " it's very close in here ? "

" Pooh !" said Mr. Van Braam. " Nonsense, my boy. Come, what is there in your parcel ? "

" Well, but really," persisted Adrian, " it would make me sick to live in such a place a week. And then all those plants, in the night-time too, in the same room. Won't you let me open the window a little ? "

" Oh pshaw !" said the old man. " I'm more than seventy years old, and I've always avoided ventilation. Fresh air and all that stuff kills people. They've invented fresh air, Adrian, within about thirty years, to kill people with. I avoid it, and I'm over seventy. So did all my ancestors, as far as I know. My grandmother Adriana did, and she died at ninety. My father did, and he died at ninety-five. I do, and I mean to die at a hundred. Civille shall, and I don't mean her to die until she's a hundred and five."

But although the old man finished his half joking half earnest assertion of the old fashioned disregards of which with genuine Scrope tenacity, he preserved so many, yet as he named his daughter a shadow came over his face, and he paused, with an obvious strong effort of self-control.

"I don't care," said Adrian, not observing his emotion. "You'd be a hundred now if you had always been careful to be in fresh air, and then you would live to be a hundred and thirty. But really and truly, Mr. Van Braam, I perceived the same sort of lifelessness in the air here last evening, and there's something more, too; I don't think the drains are right. I wish I hadn't that sort of keen scent, but I have," —

"Stuff, stuff, stuff!" said the old gentleman, a little impatiently. "I won't change my old fashioned ways for anybody. Now there's that picture" — for Adrian, who had stepped over to the mantle-piece, had looked for a moment at the horrid engraving of The Dying Camel — "I don't know but that's enough to make anybody sick."

"Well, I think so. How can you live with such an awful thing before your eyes? I would about as soon have a beast butchered in the parlor every evening for my amusement."

"Why," said the old gentleman, "the fact is, Mr. Button made us a present of it with so much ceremony, and thought it was so fine, that I really haven't the heart to — Why, — Adrian, my dear boy, — have you cut you? — How did you do that?"

For a sharp crackling crash mingled with a tearing sound had interrupted the old man's explanation, as Adrian, stepping along across the hearthrug, half-fell suddenly against the mantle-piece and his elbow went smash through glass, dying camel and all, rending that suffering quadruped into several pieces, whose irregular

lines of section converged in the very middle of his abdomen.

"I thought I'd put your old camel out of his pain," said Adrian, looking with pretended gravity straight at his host. "'Tisn't right to have him so long a-dying. I'd rather have it done quietly than to go and tell Bergh and make a scandal. But I'll bring another picture tomorrow. Let me choose, this time, won't you?"

"You scamp," said Mr. Van Braam, "you did it on purpose, then? Well, I'm sorry our cousin's gift is spoiled. Just tear out some of the blackest of that camel, won't you, and put it in the fire so that it can't be mended." — Adrian did so. — "The frame will do perfectly well," continued the old gentleman. — "Yes, you may have another picture put in, and if anybody ever finds it out, we'll charge the whole to you."

"All right," answered Adrian; "and now you must see if you will take what I've brought for you." And drawing up a chair, he took his parcel on his lap, cut the strings, and selecting Volume First, he handed it to his host.

Mr. Van Braam received it in silence, and after the manner of a book-lover, he first poised it to feel its specific gravity; then inspected the binding; then read the title on the back; then opened it and read the title-page; and barely glancing at the copper-plate which represents the intelligent, thoughtful, and yet somewhat conceited face of the famous mysticist, he laid down the book and looked at Adrian with a countenance in which pleasure was mingled with apprehension.

Mr. Van Braam, descended from an intensely puritan stock, was by a legitimate though not invariable law of spiritual inheritance, a mysticist.

To be a mysticist, one need not possess any great share of either mind or morals. What must be present is, a good deal of the instinct for worshipping, and a good deal of the appetite for the wonderful. Given these two, and perhaps any great share of intellect would be as much in the way of a successful compound as the water in Father Tom's punch: "'Put in the sperits first,' says his Riv'rence, 'and then put in the sugar; and remember, every dhrop ov wather you put in afther that spoils the punch.'"

Add conscience, spirituality, imagination and intellect to your worshipping and wondering instincts, and you have Thomas à Kempis; with variations in the mental endowment and a different culture, you have Keble. Mr. Van Braam had not poetical gifts nor creative imagination nor instinct for expression. Deduct from him the instinct for the marvellous, and intensify his reasoning faculties, and his executive abilities; and with his conscientiousness and indifference to prosperities of all kinds, he would have made a model missionary, martyr, or Calvinistic clergyman. As it was, he had not much energy — although, like a woman, he had great power of endurance; so that he remained, lifted by his conscientiousness and culture above the dangers which beset vulgar and non-moral mystics, but none the less a constitutional and genuine worshipper and wonderer — for that is what Mystic means, — except just west of Stonington.

The apprehension which alloyed Mr. Van Braam's pleasure was simply a natural dislike of ridicule. This Adrian saw, and with instinctive good sense he said at once,

"My dear sir, I don't believe in Behmen or in any of the mystics; but as long as so many pure and sweet hearted people have been mystics, I certainly can't object to their belief. I thought you would like the book."

"I do," said the old gentleman, relieved; "I don't know what would have pleased me more; I was half afraid you would laugh at me, but a difference of opinion does no harm." And he looked through volume after volume, lifting the curious reduplicated layers on the fantastic illustrations, reading here and there a paragraph, fully as pleased as Adrian could have imagined, and the young man enjoyed the pleasantest experience possible in this world, or in any other, for that matter — the pleasure of giving pleasure.

And yet what stuff it is! Adrian had transcribed a few sentences, before bringing the book, out of mere curiosity; and here are two or three of them; almost all the book is of the like sort:

"But when the Dawning or Morning Redness shall shine from the East to the West, or from the Rising to the Setting, then assuredly Time will be no more; but the SUN of the Heart of God rises or springs forth, and, R.A. R.A. R. P. will be pressed in the Wine-press without the City, and therewith to R.P." *Aurora,* p. 266.

"Now to speak in a creaturely way, *Sulphur, Mercurius,* and *Sal,* are understood to be thus. SUL is the Soul or the Spirit that is risen up, or in a Similitude [it is] God: PHUR is the *Prima Materia,* or first Matter out of which the Spirit is generated, but especially the Harshness: *Mercurius* has a fourfold Form in it, viz. Harshness, Bitterness, Fire, and Water. *Sal* is the Child that is generated from these four, and is harsh, eager, and a Cause of the Comprehensibility" *The Three Principles of the Divine Essence,* p. 10.

"Each Letter in this Name (Jehova) intimates to us a peculiar virtue and working, that is, a Form in the working Power.

For I is the Effluence of the Eternal indivisible Unity, or the sweet grace and fulness of the ground of the Divine Power of becoming something. E is a threefold I, where the Trinity shuts itself up in the Unity, for the I goes into E, and joineth I E, which is an outbreathing of the Unity in itself. H is the Word, or breathing of the Trinity of God. O is the Circumference, or the Son of God, through which the I E, and the H, or breathing, speaks forth from the compressed delight of the Power and Virtue. V is the joyful Effluence from the breathing, that is, the proceeding Spirit of God. A is that which is proceeded from the power and virtue, *viz.*, the wisdom; a Subject of the Trinity; wherein the Trinity works, and wherein the Trinity is also manifest. This Name is nothing else but a speaking forth, or expression of the Threefold working of the Holy Trinity in the Unity of God." *The Clavis*, p. 7.

Adrian had also transcribed the threatening puns which the irate Theosopher had wreaked upon Gregorius Richter, the persecuting Superintendent of Gorlitz; and divers other equally profitable passages. But of this disrespectful proceeding he was careful not to say one word to his good old relative, who shortly selected a passage, and spoke.

"Well, Adrian, no doubt there are plenty of passages that can be laughed at. But I don't know that it is any worse in Behmen than in the Bible, to be without the modern scientific discoveries. I know it's the fashion to scoff at him. But Coleridge did not; he confessed that he owed great obligations to the 'illuminated cobler of Gorlitz.' And now let me read you the four first answers of the Master, in the conference 'Of the Supersensual Life,' to the Scholar who is inquiring how he 'may see God, and hear him speak.' "

And the old gentleman read from p. 75 of "The Way to Christ," as follows:

"When thou canst throw thyself but for a Moment into that where no Creature dwelleth, then thou hearest what God speaketh. . . . It is in thee, and if thou canst for a while cease from all thy thinking and willing, thou shalt hear unspeakable Words of God. . . . When thou standest still from the thinking and willing of Self, then the Eternal Hearing, Seeing, and Speaking, will be revealed in thee; and so God heareth and seeth through thee: Thine own Hearing, Willing, and Seeing, hindereth thee, that thou dost not see nor hear God. . . . When thou art quiet or silent, then thou art that which God was before Nature and Creature, and whereof he made thy Nature and Creature: Then thou hearest and seest with that wherewith God saw and heard in thee, before thy own Willing, Seeing, and Hearing began."

Mr. Van Braam read well. That is, he spoke well, and he read so that if the hearer's eyes were shut, it would not appear but that he was speaking. And he read these profound and simple thoughts with a depth of sympathy that might have prevailed with a scoffer, much more with a kindly nature like Adrian's; and the young man, who had not lighted on this passage, was greatly impressed.

"That is very spiritual," he observed, when the reader paused; — "and it is broad enough to permit a Protestant, a Romanist, a Jew, a Mohammedan, a Buddhist, and a Brahminist all to worship together. I did not know that Behmen could think or say any thing so deep."

"My boy," said Mr. Van Braam, "if you watch for what is good you find it. No fair judgment is possible except a charitable one. Justice *is* mercy. — However, I'm talking to the average opinion about old Behmen rather than to yours."

"I guess it would be a good rule for all critics — and for all opinions too," said Adrian; "But I've got still another thing to show you, — something better than Behmen."

"Better than Behmen?" repeated Mr. Van Braam, with a smile — "what can that be?"

Chester drew from his breast pocket a long letter envelope; took out of it a flat brownish looking thing of paper, ragged-edged, and with an appearance generally of having been rescued from the very sepulchres of waste paper. This he carefully opened and laid it on the table before Mr. Van Braam. Excited by the solemn air of the young man, Mr. Van Braam picked up his eye-glasses, which had fallen from their precarious perch on his nose, looked at the title-page, which lay open before him, and jumped out of his chair.

"Why, Adrian Chester," he cried, "it's the lost Scrope Genealogy!"

Adrian smiled and nodded.

"Absolutely unique!" continued the old man, in a rapture of mingled genealogical and bibliographical bliss — "absolutely unique — been sought for eagerly this fifty years — first genealogy printed in this country — half a century before that silly Stebbins affair! — Why, — they talk about weight in gold — it would be throwing this away to give it for five times its weight in gold! — Adrian, you're quite right; I wouldn't give it for a ship-load of Behmens! But where — how on earth did you come by this, my boy?"

Adrian repeated the circumstances, and ended by saying, "I would readily have given a hundred dollars for it if I had been able; but nobody bid against me, and I got it for thirty "—

"Dirt-cheap!" broke in Mr. Van Braam —

"Cents," added Adrian.

Mr. Van Braam gave a kind of groan, and sat down suddenly as if something had hit him in the stomach. No collector of mortal mould could have endured to hear of such a thing befalling another without some emotion. There is something disagreeable to the best of us — says, or might have said, some villain or other — in the good fortune of our friends. It is to be feared that this is in some small measure true of book-collectors at least. And besides, the cheapness of the rate at which the other man got it! No rare book can be perfectly enjoyed by one who has paid for it all it is worth. The delight of ownership increases not only inversely as the cost, but inversely as the square of the cost. For example: Full value one, cost one, delight one. But full value one, cost one-half, delight four! So that here was the case of a beatitude raised to the nth power (for surely the real value of this unique pamphlet divided by thirty cents would equal n at least), and of the acquisition of the inestimable treasure by another person superadded — a terrible temptation even to a disciple of Behmen! But he bore the ordeal bravely, though it cost him a struggle.

"Well, well," he said at last, "if anybody on earth was to have such an extraordinary piece of luck, next to myself I would choose you. It isn't human to go further, is it?"

"I couldn't go further, certainly," said Chester gayly; "and I reciprocate the sentiment exactly. But are you remembering, my dear sir, all this time, that this pamphlet tells us what became of Adrian Scroope? I looked into it and found the facts, though they are put in a singular way."

"Of course I remember," said the

old man eagerly "and that this fills in the great blank in the American genealogy." And absorbed by this mighty consideration, he plunged into an intense and exhaustive scrutiny with full written memoranda of the bibliography, and the genealogical and other contents of this not merely rare, nor even Very Rare, but *absolutely* UNIQUE work. His memoranda were to form the basis of a paper which might or might not be offered for publication; indeed, which might or might not be made ready to offer; for the good gentleman was a terrible maker of memoranda and beginner of papers, and had in his archives some bushels of the same;—such mere heaps of scraps and strips cannot be stated unless by measure or by weight —you may say if you like fifty pounds avoirdupois weight instead of so many bushels dry measure;—after the fashion of the French biographer who reports that an author named Dingé. ("very unknown," he says) died leaving behind him autograph manuscripts of the weight of 880 pounds avoirdupois (400 kilograms).

Being (theoretically) a strict and systematical bibliographer, even to intolerance, Mr. Van Braam began with a tremendous quantity of care. He first copied the title-page, with the professional dashes or what-you-may-call-ems (isn't that the name?) to show the lines of the display; Mr. Stevens G M B his method of photographing all the pages of books in small — or is it part of them only ?— and then making a string of the photographs and calling it a catalogue of the books had not then been invented. Somewhat on the following wise was his transcript; it may be verified by any one who will find this very copy of the pamphlet itself in the Historical Society's Library at Hartford and compare it with even this printed reproduction;

SCROOPE, Adrian.

The | Family of SCROOPE | Retrac'd from these Present | or at the least the Later | Unhappy Times | to its Originall. | Litera Scripta manet. | I have been yong, and am olde ; yet I saw never | the righteous forsaken, nor his seed begging bread. Psalms xxxvii. 25. | By Mr. Adrian Scroope,| (sometime of Hartford in *Conecticott.*) [*No imprint.*]

— And so on, and so forth. Then came a description of the pamphlet, executed with entomological minuteness, to wit; Size of type-page, so many inches so many tenths, in width; so many in height; catchwords; folios; character of letter; style of setting, spacing, justifying; display of titlepage; width of margin; kind of paper; watermark; method of arranging the families and individuals in their genealogical order;—But to fully set forth this piece of solicitous and affectionate labor would require to repeat it word for word; and there is no room. The curious matters however upon the *verso* or back of the title-page may be here transcribed as they stand, except two written signatures at the lower left hand of the printed part, written to all appearance by the same person at the same time. One was a close repetition of the very characteristic signature of "Adrian Scroope," and the other, written just below it, and in absolutely the same handwriting, was "Adeodatus Throop." As for the printed words, they were as follows:

See, here I raise a Monvmente in hast
Charg'd to protect old Names, old Fames,
from Waste.
That is laid off, its Hist'rie here is told.
Here I take up new Name, old Life to hold.

Read in this Verse the Truth, the Cause, the
Hope.
Old Faith now Fame shall found ; farewell to
Scroope.
Old Fame, farewell! Old Faith, live in new
Fame!
Pray God, though Life be short, I scape from
shame:
Earth first, and Heaven at last, shall give me
a new name.

Non hæc, sed me.

E $\left\{ \begin{array}{l} \text{King's church.} \\ \text{Church's king} \end{array} \right\}$ ibam
1670

[The two signatures]

Adrian sat meanwhile quietly enjoying the old gentleman's pleasure.
All at once an idea occurred to Mr.
Van Braam, and he looked up suddenly —

"Adrian, why didn't you show this
to our cousin Scrope last evening?"

Chester smiled, but considered a
moment before replying, and even then
a sort of friendly sport came before
the real answer.

"Why, my dear sir; does anybody
of the Scrope blood tell secrets or
speak of his successes?"

"Very true, my boy; nobody except Mr. Button; — and now, why was
it?"

"I'll tell you, but it must be in
confidence. — Do you entirely believe
in our English cousin and his estate
in England?"

Mr. Van Braam was startled. He
and Adrian, as is natural among kinsmen, were exactly unlike in some
things, as they were exactly alike in
others. Thus, as to matters of conscience and matters of taste, they felt
as alike as twins. On the point of
credulity however, they were as opposite as the magnetic poles. To the
old man, belief was the satisfaction
of a hunger; and subject to the not
very strict or narrow limitations that
experience had succeeded in enforcing

upon him, the more marvellous an
account, the more flavorsome its taste,
and the more eager his reception of
it. To such natures a narrative is
credible in proportion as it is incredible. This paradox only states the
mode of operation of the instinct of
"marvellousness" as the phrenolo-
gists with correct analysis but miserable terminology, have called it. It
is the faculty to which the argument
from miracles is addressed ; that which
has ruled in so many religions, and
whose acme is in Tertullian's famous
"*Certum est, quia impossibile est.*"
So, just as he had enjoyed his Ploti-
nus and his Behmen, and if the truth
be told perhaps wished he might
accept along with Mr. Taylor all the
gods of Olympus — mainly however
for the sake of the deeper mysteries
of the elder gods — the Titans and
the Cabiri — in like manner Mr. Van
Braam had fastened upon the belief
in the complete traditional account of
the two Adrian Scroopes, and upon
the whole of the statement about the
great Scrope estate in England. And
Adrian's question was disagreeable,
for it forced the old gentleman to consult a guide that he did not love,
though he had been obliged to inquire at his mouth more than once —
to wit, his judgment. It was with
visible unwillingness that he answered;

"Entirely? Why, — no more
than is reasonable. Don't you believe in them?"

"The fact is," answered Adrian, "I
can't say I either do or do not. I am
simply waiting to see. I shall believe
whatever I find is true."

"Well, I have examined all the
young man's papers. He certainly is
the person he represents himself to
be."

This was not the point, and Adrian

hinted as much; but with natural tact, he slid away from the distasteful consideration, since there was no need of annoying his host.

"Oh, well, you and I are perfectly safe, as long as we have only paid our five dollars to join the Scrope Association. But that is not answering your question about showing the pamphlet. As to Scrope, he does not quite suit me, I confess, and it was the impression he made on me that kept me from telling him. And you won't tell him either, will you, please? I intend to offer such evidence as it furnishes, at the meeting. Scrope is evidently kind hearted — or rather good natured, but to tell you the truth I shouldn't like to be in his power, and I want to see what sort of a case he will make out alone. Did you notice how flat and low the top part of his head is in spite of that hairbush that he grows on top of it? There's plenty of intellect, but I don't think he knows there's any difference between right and wrong. I should not be afraid to deal with him in plain sight; but he's not a person that I would trust."

"Fiddlesticks, Adrian! There you go with your bumps again! If that's all you have against him I don't greatly relish your prejudice."

The young man quietly evaded once more a point on which they disagreed and tried a weaker place for attack with considerable skill.

"It isn't a matter of bumps, my dear sir; I know very well you don't believe in them. But you believe as much as I do in the perception of spiritual atmospheres. He makes such an impression on me that I feel rather inclined to watch him. However, I like him, in spite of my notion, for he's very jolly; and I promise you I will own up like a man if he comes

out all right. And I'll tell you what — if Civille puts faith in him, I will. Her intuitions are far better than mine."

At this mention of his daughter, the old man's countenance fell as it had done before; but this time Adrian perceived it and asked if she were ill. And now Mr. Van Braam suddenly unburdened his poor old heart, and confided to his strong and healthy young relative the interview with the detective, which he had been carrying silently about with him, as one who has taken poison but has not yet found the right person to tell of it. It was an impulse, and even while he spoke he more than once expressed almost as much horror of speaking, as of the horrible thing itself. But the impulse was a correct one; for Adrian's strong cheerfulness, and his perfect faith in Civille, aside from the natural sympathetic kindness of the young man, were cordials to the extreme pain of the distressed father, which seemed to have been the bitterer, now that it was expressed in words, from the very fact of having been endured in silence, even for a few hours.

"Civille?" exclaimed Adrian in utter astonishment — "Why, he might as well try to make me think it is darkness that comes from the sun! What a fool! But how should those fellows recognize human beings? They live amongst corruption, and they lose the power of distinguishing what is clean. But we must be quiet about it, of course. Just have patience for a few days, and I'll find out something for you. We shall discover exactly what the rascality is, you may be sure. — Why, I should as soon believe that there was no God!"

"One thing that frightens me,"

said the old gentleman, "is, the chance of some — some kind of ailment " — he spoke with difficulty, and stopped short. Adrian himself remembered the young girl's habitual and acute headaches; her excessive paleness; her weary look: and for a few moments he was at a stand. Mr. Van Braam went on:

"She has certainly lost color and flesh since we came here, now eighteen months ago. But then, again, there's something else that the officer knows about, I dare say, but you don't — her going about alone so much, and to such places."

Adrian looked astonished again.

"She has very few friends, poor thing," said the old man. "We have lived so much alone ever since her mother died — and always, for that matter. She has had no escort. How could she? I have not been able to go with her. And she has been interested in so much of the recent psychology and sociology — And the poor child's life is so empty! — And I never could refuse her any thing — nor could I anybody, if I had it to give," — the old gentleman smiled pitifully enough — " I'm an old fool, if that's being one."

" But pray where did she go? " asked Adrian, a good deal startled and puzzled. He was relieved however when he was told that besides some charitable offices regularly performed in connection with Dr. Toomston's church, she had resorted to no place worse than — the old gentleman rather hesitated but at last came out with it — divers spiritualist " circles," and the meetings in public and private of a certain so-called *Solidarité de l'Avenir,* or of the members of the same.

" What's that? " asked Adrian, a little vexed, for he had a strong prejudice in favor of using English words whenever they would do. — " What's that ? — a French Red Republican club ? "

" Oh no," replied Mr. Van Braam, somewhat embarrassed; " they are advanced reformers, irrespective of nationality or creed or politics."

Adrian, if he had done exactly as he wanted to, would now have pronounced a vigorous invective against sundry doctrines and practices. But as was observed, he had a good deal of natural tact, and he felt that if he could serve his relatives in this matter, it must be not as an opposer, but as a sympathizer. Besides, he reflected in a moment, that these people might be very deserving people, after all. And a plan of campaign occurred to him, simple enough, and effective if it should appear that any thing at all could be done. It was simply to take the position of an interested inquirer into what Mr. Van Braam thought proper to call " psychology and sociology," to stay in the city as long as he could, and to watch over Civille as closely as possible without offence, in the character of an escort and fellow votary in these profound researches of hers, and to see in the meanwhile what could have occasioned the abominable imputation that had been cast upon her.

To Mr. Van Braam, however, he put the matter as one of cousinly kindness; and the sweet and disinterested nature of the good old gentleman receiving such a motive in another as a most reasonable and competent one, the scheme was agreed on.

" But Ann," suggested Mr. Van Braam — " might she not be annoyed ? "—

" Oh no," said Adrian with perfect confidence. " I shall tell her all

about it of course. And she is too
fond of Civille not to be right glad I
can be of service. And she is too
good for any misunderstanding on
such a point. I shall be careful not
to let Civille know, but I shall tell
Ann the first time I see her — to-
morrow, I presume."

"I don't know but you're right,"
said the poor old gentleman, "but I
declare it seems to me as if my girl
was being shown up all over" — he
almost cried, and had to stop.

"Well, Ann shall not know," said
Adrian at once. "She may suppose
I am only interested in the reform
movement. I *am* interested in reforms, and so is she. She is bound
to be, as a church member. And we
shall both be glad to have her go
with us. And I can answer for it
that she shall have faith in both of
us."

It was so decided ; and Adrian proceeded to make a number of desultory
inquiries about the Solidarité and its
associated interests, partly for information, partly with a view to instil
into Mr. Van Braam's mind, by way
of precaution, the same belief which
Civille was to entertain, viz., that
Adrian was a genuine catechumen.
The old gentleman, who was really a
good deal cheered and comforted by
Adrian's energetic and whole hearted
sympathy and help, gave what account he could of these reforms, but
he knew only what his daughter had
told him, and furnished nothing but
indistinct hints. While he was in
the midst of them, there was a ring
at the door, and in came Scrope of
Scrope, accompanied by a stranger,
whom he introduced as " my fwiend
Mr. Bird, a gentleman connected with
the pwess," further explaining that he
had taken the liberty of bringing him
as he himself could not resist the

temptation to call, and having to go
elsewhere with Mr. Bird, had ventured
thus much ; which excuse was graciously received by Mr. Van Braam.

Mr. Bird was a rather slender
young man with a dark complexion,
fine gray eyes, wavy black hair, lively expressive features and a sufficiently good manner ; and being politely
received, the company entered upon
that brief and amicable discussion of
the weather which was the formal
introduction to all conversation until
General Myer took out all its interest by eliminating the speculative
element and reducing it to a mere
prophecy. What comfort or advantage is there in saying "Good morning, Brown. Cautionary signals are
ordered at Pumpanopeague, Squank
and Bung Head," and in answering
"Yes ; but the area of low barome-
ter has passed from Idaho to Arkan-
sas, and variable weather is indicated
in the Gulf States."

No wonder one of the sages of the
"metropolitan press" remarked the
other day that the art of conversation
is lost. General Myer has destroyed
the very beginning of it.

Mr. Scrope, after a few minutes,
gallantly inquired after the health of
his cousin, Miss Van Braam, upon
which her father rang and sent for
her, and in a few moments she entered.

The new comer was duly presented,
and Civille placed herself in her usual
nest, as she was accustomed to call it,
the wadded arm-chair, which almost
always stood in the same place at
your left hand as you face the fire,
and with the little two-story wicker
work-basket close to it. As she sat
down there was one of those silences
which happens every now and then
in any company, and Civille, who
had gazed indifferently into the fire,

after a moment looked up with a start : —

"What are you all looking at me for?" she said. — And they were.

The extreme natural sensitiveness of her temperament, was in truth at present carried somewhat beyond the limit of healthy activity, and her mind was beginning to receive impressions through any of the nervous extremities, without regard to the regular channels of the five senses. That is, she was beginning to be a "clairvoyant." But supposing her to be at all susceptible to the gaze of others, her consciousness of it was not so strange either, for all four of the men had really been looking at her with positive, and two of them with intense emotion.

The precise phenomenon which had been the centre of crystallization for all their looks, was a rare and lovely one, though very simple. It was only, while Civille entered the room, came forward, received the visitors, turned aside and sat down, — the spiritually perfect grace and ease of her movements.

Beauty of feature is almost common, in America; refinement and intelligence of feature absolutely so. But gracefulness is very rare. Among men, — why, the idea is superfluous; no matter about it either way. But among women, whose business is beauty ; — a man who knows say a hundred ladies well enough to recollect distinctly the traits and manner of each, can perhaps select one, possibly two, but very likely none, — who possess that supreme and divine grace of beautiful motion. Even to be able to recognize and admire it, if not due to unusual natural keenness of perception, is in itself an elegant culture. What most people call beauty is of the forms and colors of the face only.

The person of a woman is most often taken for granted, or ignored. But there may be real beauty, — which by the way is of the whole person, from the crown of the head to the tips of the toes — without gracefulness. What does give gracefulness — beauty of motion — is unknown. It is something of the body, and something of the soul. But whatever it is, Civille had it. As for her father, he never thought of that perfection alone; for him, she was all that is lovely. He would have silently contemned any suggestion that she had not that attraction, or any other; but his sense of all her sweetnesses was drowned in his own extreme emotion of love, and as she glided in, he thought neither that she was lovely nor pale nor good, but only, "My darling, my darling!" As for the three young men, the case was otherwise, as was natural and right. For each of them, the invisible, unconscious, universal, unfailing enchantment was upon him. They did not either of them say, or think, or know, that he was to marry Civille, or that he could, or that he wished to, or that he would under any circumstances. Yet, humanly speaking, it was a possibility; and distant and absolutely unremembered as it was, or as was even the idea of so much as venturing to kiss her hand, this it was which lent a faintest rose-color to their regards.

The uncompromising directness of her question startled them all in their turn.

"I always look at you, my dear," said the old man, simply.

"I was hoping you had had no more trouble with your head," said Adrian, — and so he was; but his thoughts had been almost impassioned even in the moment of his looks, for he had felt an even painful sense of her helplessness, unconscious and pure as he knew her to be, innocent as a baby, and with a charge of vulgar street theft lying in wait for her, and there followed instantly an intense shock as it were of resolve that he would keep not only the danger, but the very knowledge of it, away from her. He had moreover perceived — and for the first time, this wonderful loveliness in her steps and gestures, — and he felt it.

" I was admiring to see how gwacefully you moved," said Scrope, bluntly. Like most Englishmen, —not that it is wholly wrong either — he saw women and horses with eyes a good deal the same; but he was the only one of the three who told the whole story, after all.

As for Mr. Bird, what did *he* tell? He began with just such an assertion as has prefaced many a special lie —

" *To tell you the truth*," he said, " I was wondering particularly how that fine engraving on the mantlepiece came to be so damaged."

This dexterous or at least apposite diversion turned the conversation; the story of the picture was told, there was an animated inquiry about the substitute to be chosen. Civille was glad the camel was at last dead; it made her faint to look at it, she said; she hated agony pictures as much as Adrian.

" Then Saint Sebastian won't do," remarked Scrope, " nor Isaiah being sawn asunder; nor the Crucifixion of St. Peter ? "

" Oh, don't! " exclaimed the young lady, with a shudder. " I always feel as if the arrows had been fired into my own shoulder! I believe I am growing more and more nervous. But it's no wonder to-day, for I got such a fright this morning! "

" What was it, my dear ? " quickly asked the old gentleman.

" Oh, it can't have been any thing, of course. But I thought there was some one following me. While I was in at Jenks and Trainor's, there was a man buying something near me, and I saw him twice afterwards — once I am sure it was he, just as I came out of another store ; and I thought I saw him on the platform after I got into the street car. I have always despised women that I have heard speak of being annoyed in that way, but I sha'n't any more. It was excessively unpleasant."

All the gentleman, as men are pretty likely to do in such a case, made rather elaborate representations intended to dissipate Civille's disagreeable impression. Perhaps they were too elaborate; for although she thanked them, she did not seem relieved. It is true that Scrope, according to his fashion, performed what he meant for a compliment; a not very elegantly worded intimation that the unknown showed good taste in his selection.

" Thank you sir," answered Miss Van Braam — as has been hinted she had abundance of spirit sometimes — " I can't see the compliment of his taking me for a person willing to be followed by a perfect stranger."

And the Englishman was snubbed; for even he felt that he should only make the matter worse by explaining what he had meant. A compliment to a lady, like a vote in congress, should never need explanation. But Adrian seized his opportunity :

" Cousin Civille, your father has been telling me something about your interest in some reformers and their discussions. I find I am to be in New York rather longer than I thought. A visitor, you know, is always more eager to see the sights than a New Yorker; and I want you to let me escort you about a little; will you?"

She looked at him a moment, with her half-hidden look of distant dreaming; it gave him an impression that she was looking into his motives. It was only her way however. "I beg pardon," she said, recollecting herself, — "I was considering — Yes, I should like it very much."

And three appointments were made on the spot, covering Civille's operations as a reformer and sociologist for the current week. One was to attend a spiritual "séance" the next (viz. Thursday) evening; one to attend the weekly meeting of the *Solidarité de l'Avenir* on Friday; and one, to visit the chief philosopher, or President, or whatever his title may be, of the said *Solidarité*, at his house, when it should be convenient, for a deep conference upon "The Readjustment of Things in General," which readjustment, as it would seem, Mr. President had kindly proposed to conduct, and which he had already got so far advanced that a centre of operations to be called The Germ, as being the Nucleus of the New Universe, was actually to be organized within a few months and perhaps weeks.

Messrs. Scrope and Bird, who likewise proceeded to profess a profound interest in these matters, being a little behind-hand with their zeal, received only permission to attend the meeting of the *Solidarité;* where, Miss Civille informed them, was the centre of activity of the great network of new agencies which was swiftly leavening the age, and where they would find all the requisite opportunities for aiding in the great work to any extent whatever.

Mr. Scrope now rose to take leave, explaining that Mr. Bird, who knew all about New York, had agreed to pilot him to an entertaining exhibition appointed that evening, of what Mr. Scrope thought proper to call "The Manly Game of Billiards." Adrian, himself an amateur in a small way, at once asked permission to accompany them, which was readily given, and the three young men went off together, Adrian leaving his treasured pamphlet for the time in the charge of Mr. Van Braam.

CHAPTER XII.

As the young men left the old house together, Adrian quoted from a certain ancient anthology:

> "We're three brethren out of Spain,
> Come to court your daughter Jane."

"Jane's no fool, either," commented Scrope; "she might ave answered for herself as the old lady did:

> 'My daughter Jane is yet too young,
> To be snared by your false flattering tongue.'

Hay, Bird? — We couldn't secure invitations."

"I'm going to the meeting Friday evening though," observed Mr. Bird, in his quiet evasive way; "I'd like to see what those people are about."

"Now for my part," said Scrope, "I'd far rather sit in one of their dark circles. Hit's very funny, I assure you. Great chance for the finer feelinks."

Adrian had perceived in the very first words of the young man, — more perhaps in tone and air than in their positive meaning, something very disagreeable. It was as if being now with men, and young men, only, Mr. Scrope felt that some restraints of some kind were removed. There was something not of freedom only but of recklessness, in his talk, in his voice, and Adrian fancied, in his step. Adrian, who was free enough, but who was clean, had already felt, as he had intimated to Mr. Van Braam, something opposed to himself in this young person, and had defined it as an ignorance of the difference between right and wrong.

"Smoke?" said Scrope, drawing forth a well filled cigar-case and offering it to his companions. Adrian declined, and Bird accepted. There was a halt while the two smokers "fired up;" and Scrope said, pleasantly enough,

"Hope it's not disagreeable to you, Mr. Chester?"

"Oh, I don't object," said Adrian; "and by the way, as everybody smokes in the street here, and so I can ask as a mere matter of curiosity, without being rude, please to tell me if it is the etiquette in London too?"

"Wy, not exactly the ticket anywere, I should say," answered Scrope; "but wot's the odds, as long as you're appy?"

"Very little odds," said Adrian; "but I'm luckier than you two gentlemen, for I haven't got tired of God's fresh air yet. When I do I shall be ready for smells. If I had to live in Mr. Van Braam's parlor I think I should learn to smoke though."

"Yes," assented Bird — "As the mountaineer remarked the first time he tasted a codfish-ball, 'Something dead in there!' That can't be a healthy house to live in."

"The fact is," said Adrian, "I perceive a good deal of that same deadness in the air all over this city."

"By the way, Chester," said Scrope — familiarly, as Adrian thought — "a neat thing that of yours last evening about women being

good. Vewy telling compliment indeed."

"All the better for being true," said Adrian, not entirely pleased.

"Oh, — beg pardon," said Scrope, "if I wan against an opinion — I never mean to do that."

"Why, you can't help it sometimes," said Adrian.

"If you have any of your own," remarked Mr. Bird.

"Oh, I haven't," said Scrope, with every appearance of sincerity. "There's no choice of opinions. I'd like to do some things, and I want people to help me; but I entertain all their views just as they come. Vewy convenient indeed."

"Wouldn't do for a missionary," observed Bird —

"But" said Scrope, with an unexpected readiness of Scriptural quotation, "St. Paul says we may be all things to all men if we are only trying to save them."

"Ah," retorted Bird, "but he doesn't say you may *say* all things."

"And besides," joined in Adrian, "a fair interpretation makes it necessary to understand 'all *good* things.'"

"Sure enough," assented Scrope, who at once showed "the courage of his *non*-opinions," — "sure enough, — you're quite wight."

Thus chatting amicably they walked a few blocks up town until they reached a point on the cross-town Bleecker Street line of horse-cars, where they got aboard, and disembarked at the corner of Broadway and Bleecker Street.

Piloted by Mr. Bird, the three friends turned northward, taking the eastern side of Broadway; but they had hardly gone half a block when Scrope, stopping suddenly at the opening of a wide flight of steps leading down into a basement, said,

"Will it do to go down here? I've never seen one of these places."

"Oh yes," acquiesced Bird — "there's time to just look in and have a single glass of beer."

It is no wonder that the young man was attracted, not by the beauty, but by the glare, of even this cellar stairway; for a broad sheet of light seemed actually to flame up, as if from some intense subterranean conflagration. This light came from a profuse supply of gas-jets, of which one powerful combination, placed over the doorway, — that is, just below the level of the sidewalk, blazoned forth the letters of the words "THE PARADISE." Gaudy transparencies to the same effect were also adjusted at the sides of the stairway, also even with the sidewalk. As you looked down, a great screen, placed just within the open door, all bathed in the same blazing blinding glare of gas-light, shut off the mysteries within from casual peeps, and at the same time displayed what might be supposed the picture of one of the Peris of the place — but she was far from being the disconsolate one of the poet. It was a painting in distemper, in glaring color, all red and white, of some kind of princess or other reclining in state, with a crown of roses, a laconic costume, extremely developed contours, and sporting in unconscious glee with a tremendous birdling, which might be either a vast parrot or a green owl; for the creature had been very broadly generalized by the artist, who may have been representing a Bird of Paradise of a new sort; or he was perhaps offering a pre-historic type; possibly his own private notion of an archæopteryx. And moreover, there thrilled up the rather dirty stairway, mingling as it were with this flood of light, an indistinct murmur of voices, and a flood of music, to wit, the enrapturing strains of "Champagne Charley" — which noble composition had then just come across the Atlantic Ocean.

"Then you'll be a Bird of Paradise for the time being," said Mr. Scrope to the "member of the Press," as they went down the stairs, Adrian following with curiosity, yet with distinct repugnance. For as he stepped down, his senses were offended by a strong gush of warm and almost hot air rushing out from the interior, infamously defiled with odors not of paradise, but of pandemonium; rank tobacco, bad liquor, undrained cellarage, coarse edibles, foul breaths, dirty persons — a hideous swash that made him feel as if he were drowning in putrefaction. But he was unwilling to interfere with the wishes of his companions, and he had a certain curiosity to see the place, particularly as they were not to stay long. He could not have staid long, indeed, with his cleanly and fresh-air habits. But they did not stay even as long as they had intended.

This Paradise was one of the thousands of doorways to hell which the respectable citizens of New York maintain along the chief thoroughfare of their city, to rot young men and women; — a "concert saloon." The three young men, submerging themselves in the fetid atmosphere of the place, passed behind the great daub of the bare-legged Peri. The interior was no doubt familiar to the newspaper man; to Scrope it was very likely only a variety of what he had seen in London or Paris; but to Adrian it was quite new. It was a rather low but roomy and very long apartment, strongly lighted throughout, the walls and ceiling whitewashed, the floor sanded and thickly set with plain round wooden tables. Half way down one side was a platform on which the orchestra were established — a jangling old piano, two fiddles, a key-bugle, a clarinet and a bass-viol were the instruments. At nearly all the tables were customers, all wearing their hats, most of them smoking, all with liquors of some kind, some with plates of Schweizer-kase and mustard, or with slices of Bologna sausage also. The waiters who supplied these customers were almost equally numerous. They were young girls, dressed in a coarse high colored kind of uniform, vulgar and dirty, on the pattern of the Peri; some flitting hither and thither with small waiters containing glasses and plates, some sitting in familiar conversation with the drinkers, and a group gathered before the bar, which was at one side just within the door, giving orders, returning empty glasses and receiving full ones, and all the time chattering, laughing, singing or scolding; while the bar-keeper, with two assistants, was exerting a preternatural activity in serving out the commodities of the place.

Bird led the way straight through this noisy crowd of girls. Adrian's ear was inexpressibly shocked by the rasping harshness of their tones, whether they spoke or sang or laughed. It was in sound, what you may sometimes see in color where an old picture has been abused by the cleaner, and all the delicacy and goodness of the coloring removed, leaving glaring harsh masses of ground tint. He had never before heard that awful voice — for ineffably awful it is — the undertone of ruin. A grotesque similitude arose in his mind; he thought of the dry clashing and clattering of potsherds. As they passed on, Bird accidentally jostled one of the girls, whose mug of beer was spilled. She

had been chanting along with the music; but turning short with a furious face, she uttered an elaborate curse. That also, perhaps the most completely fiendish sound on earth, the cursing and swearing of women, Adrian had never heard before; and he wished he was out. Bird begged her pardon, paid for the beer, and with perfect good humor handed her a further sum, saying.

"Never mind, sis; there's half-a-dollar for yourself besides." Her face cleared as quickly as it had flushed. and she laughed loudly, saying, "All right, my dear. You're a gentleman and a scholar."

Making their way to one of the tables, they sat down. One of the girls came and took their orders for three glasses of beer.

"What for me, gentlemen?" she said.

"Oh, any thing you like," replied Bird.

"Sherry wine, then," was the answer, and she went off to get the liquors.

"Pray do they drink all the evening?" asked Adrian, astonished.

"Oh, they make everybody order something for them, if they can," explained Bird, "for the good of the house. She said wine because it costs more. Then she brings it to drink with us — but it's colored water, and the price of wine goes into the till."

She returned with the glasses. Scrope, who had been singing "Champagne Charley" along with the *blarting* key-bugle, stinted in his song, and touched glasses with the girl, and they drank. Adrian barely touched the stuff to his lips. It had the sharp poisonous bitter flavor of cheap beer.

"Worst liquors in New York city, in this hole," said Bird.

At this moment a tall young fellow, in a seedy black frock-coat and black felt hat, came unsteadily along, holding by chairs and tables, and balanced himself right opposite Adrian, next whom the girl had sat down while Mr. Bird made change. Adrian had been noting the coarse texture and very dirty condition of the cheap red and white stuff of her dress, the paint on her cheeks, and he noticed moreover that her face as well as her arms and neck were very thin; and she coughed.

"I'm afraid you're not very well," he said, naturally enough, in his sympathetic way. The girl felt the kindness in his voice, and shook her head in silence, but as if recollecting herself, she laughed in the loud rattling manner of the place and said in her dry, harsh voice.

"Well as a fish, my dear. Say, give us a dollar, will you?"

The drunken young man spoke suddenly, with the indistinct utterance of intoxication, and the thick husky tone of habitual intoxication:

"Look here you!—Goin home with that gal?"

Adrian looked up at the abominable dark red face, the swimming bleared half-shut eyes, dim yet vicious, the flabby, almost hanging, thick lips. It was as if the very genius of the den was accosting him. The first impression was that of nauseating disgust; the next was anger; for Adrian had not learned the topers' conventionality that a drunken man is to be humored; and he answered,

"None of your business!"

Without a word, the young man lifted a chair by which he was holding and raising it over his head with both hands, aimed a blow full at Adrian; but he was so drunk that he could not handle himself, and the chair fell short, coming down with a crash on the table, breaking a glass or two; and the brute, pitching forward, saved himself with his hands as well as he could; but they both slopped into the spilled beer, one was cut on a piece of broken glass and bled freely, and his head meeting the chair, his felt hat was shoved awry. Recovering himself somewhat, he unsteadily raised himself again, looked muddily about, muttered some oath, drew his wet and bleeding hand across his face, leaving a track of beer and blood, and would have made his way round the table towards Adrian.

But Adrian and his companions all sprang up; the girl herself quickly stepped round to the drunken fellow, and without showing any signs of fear, disgust, or indeed any other emotion, put her arms round him and said quietly,

"It's all right, Jim. Sit down; I'll get you a drink."

"No danger, gentlemen," added one of the men from the bar, who had hurried up as soon as he saw that there was a scuffle.

"I shouldn't think there was," said Bird coolly; "that scoundrel's too drunk. You've no business to let him come in here at all in that state. I've a great mind to have your place pulled. I've only got to see Captain Wallace to have it done, as you know very well."

"We don't mean to have any trouble," answered the man, abashed and disconcerted at Bird's steady tone. "Hope you won't do it. Make it all right with you, with pleasure, sir," he insinuated.

"Well, never mind this time," was the reply. "We were only stopping a moment, anyhow. Come, gentlemen." And they went out, amidst a brief silence that came down upon all the noisy talk, while everybody looked to see what the disturbance was, and the toneless jangling bang and toot of the poor little orchestra, sounding alone in the place for the moment, served as a kind of Rogue's March, Adrian could not but think, as it were to drum them out of this devil's camp. But all the noises, — gruff talk, loud orders, tipsy singing, harsh laughter, curses and all, began again before they had reached the door. And as Adrian stepped out on the sidewalk, he felt filthy, defiled through and through, unfit for decent society — as one might feel who has been soaked and all but drowned in a cess-pool, barely escaping alive.

"Well, 'that's enough,'" he exclaimed, as he drew a long breath — "why, that even makes a New York street seem clean! But Mr. Bird, what did he mean by saying that he would make it right with you?"

"Rather hand me fifty dollars than run the risk of having his place broken up."

"But how did he know you could do it?"

"Oh, anybody could do it, almost — he has to submit to some such extortion every little while. But he makes so much out of the business that he can afford to bribe pretty heavily."

And they passed on up Broadway.

PART IV.

CHAPTER XIII.

"AND yet there are a great deal worse places than that in New York," said Bird, reflectively, as they passed up Broadway, beyond Bond Street and Great Jones Street.

"What ones?" said Scrope at once, and with perceptible eagerness. And Adrian, sickened as he was, and though he said nothing, also wanted to know. Ever since the Tree of Knowledge of Good was also the Tree of Knowledge of Evil, man's instinct to understand has asked after both. As God joined the two knowledges together, it is no wonder that man has not yet succeeded in putting them asunder. And still, there was a great difference between the animal eagerness of Scrope and the intellectual instinct for knowing that stirred in Adrian, and which he distrusted while he felt it.

"Well, gentlemen," replied Bird, "police reporting is one of the roughest pursuits in the world, I suppose. It is in that line that I have seen things — Perhaps I'll tell you about them some day. But I really can't, now — it's too bad. Besides, some of the best citizens are interested in some of the worst of them."

"How do you mean?" asked Adrian.

"Why, — now there's that Paradise, for instance," replied the police reporter, — for such his words implied that he was — "do you know who owns that building?"

"No, — who?"

"It's one of the very worst holes on Broadway. There's been two murders there that I know of already. They break all the ten commandments as much as once every ten minutes, almost all night. And it belongs to one of these eminent capitalist fellows that are so respectable and subscribe to all sorts of things. Button, his name is."

"I don't believe it," said Adrian, shocked, and impulsively — "I beg your pardon, what I mean is that you must be mistaken. I know Mr. Button."

"Then I beg *your* pardon, if he is a friend of yours. But there's no mistake about the fact. You may go with me to the register of disreputable tenements which the Police keep at the Mulberry Street Headquarters, with the names of the owners, and I'll show it to you written out in full, and then you may go and search the records of land at the City Hall and find the deed to Mr. Button all recorded at length."

"But why don't they print that whole list of names?"

"Reason enough: it would show that the respectability of New York gives houseroom to the crime of New York and so maintains it for money."

"But it isn't possible," persisted Adrian. "He don't know it, of course. Or he has let the place to some one who is misusing it or underletting it against his will."

"All right," said Bird — "that's just the way they talk. As if a man like him would own a building on Broadway and not know what is done with it! And as for the misuse against his will, — do you suppose he don't know that the Paradise is a law-breaking concern every night of the year, and that he can have it shut now, late as it is, before midnight, if he chooses?"

Adrian was silent; for the truth had hit him very hard. Bird resumed:

"Of course there's underletting; there's an agent, and a tenant, and one or two undertenants. Such places pay two or three times as much rent as any respectable business could pay; but I don't insinuate that *that* has any thing to do with it. Dear me, no!"

Adrian said no more, but like a straight-forward and clean-hearted young fellow as he was, he silently resolved that at his first meeting with Mr. Button he would reveal to him the outrage which he was suffering in this matter. "I'll have the pleasure of shutting up one hell-hole," he said to himself, as they walked along.

In a few moments they reached the scene of the proposed exhibition: a billiard saloon known as "Jack's," nearly opposite the New York Hotel. They entered through a sort of fancy grocery store, and turning short and passing through a side door at the back, came into the billiard room itself, a large square apartment, immediately under "Hope Chapel," and of course belonging to the same owner. A magnificent bar stretched all the way across one side; nine full-sized tables — none of your trifling three-quarters affairs — were orderly disposed in three ranks upon the ample floor, each strongly illuminated with its own shaded gas-lights, the wires with the wooden beads for marking the game strung upon them, hanging across above in their long catenary

curves, and the armory-like racks of cues standing stiffly back against the wall. The bar-keeper, a far more magnificent creature than his guild-brother of the Paradise (particularly as to his curled and shiny hair; — there must be some mysterious real connection corresponding to the coincident first syllables of bar-ber and bar-tender —) was, however, no less assiduous, and was swiftly ministering juleps and other rivers of delight — "sweet fields arrayed in living green (i.e. the juleps) and rivers of delight," to divers persons who stood before his shrine. Two of these, nearest the new-comers, were in a muzzy state, talkative and disputatious, but imbecilely good humored, and were at the moment discussing a weighty point in orthoepy, perhaps none the less interesting to Adrian, who was close to them, from the fact that of the two methods of spelling the word in dispute which they severally asserted, neither agreed with his own.

"No 'tain't," said one — "it's J, e, r, m, y, e, r."

"Why no tisn't," said the other, articulating with the most painstaking distinctness, — "it's G, u, r, m, i, a, r."

"Less arsh thish genlmn," was the reply, and they began to submit the question of the grand old Hebrew mourner-poet-prophet's name to Adrian, who briefly assured them with a bow that he didn't know how to spell at all, and pushed forward to get away from their drunkenness, to the front rank of the spectators. These were already intently beholding the Billiard Tournament, which was in progress upon a carom table, the deep green of whose cloth testified that it had been newly caparisoned, doubtless for this very occasion.

The game was what is technically called the French game, played with one red ball and two white ones, and is about as much superior to the "full" or "American four-ball game" as chess is to draughts. The two heroes who were contending for "a purse of $500, and the championship," were a couple of serious looking youths, very business-like and thoughtful of aspect, both trim-built, alert, and well-made, and with a professional deftness of execution very pleasant to see. There was nothing so very remarkable about their play, which was only for the State Championship, and not for the vaster supremacy of the continent : the whole boundless continent was not theirs on the present occasion, but a pent-up New York contracted their powers. As in this game the nerves are at least as important as they were to Mrs. Wititterly, applause or disapproval is as stringently forbidden as it would be at a funeral, and the silence that prevailed was almost oppressive. Perhaps a hundred connoisseurs and amateurs were present. From one or two distant tables where dullards incapable of a worthy admiration were pursuing their own selfish amusement, the click of the balls, or some quiet remark, echoed faintly now and then ; or some silly babble from a toper at the bar sounded over the heads of the crowd ; but they themselves were impassible as Amphictyons. Once or twice, when some brilliant shot round the table restored a desperate run, or when the figures from some delicately prolonged process of "nursing" accumulated high, an irrepressible murmur of excitement just breathed around ; but only to be hushed under the warning glance or the quiet gesture of the umpire.

Adrian watched with much enjoyment the graceful and accurate movements and manipulations of the two players, and the almost intelligent obedience of the clean ivory balls, that travelled about on their geometrical errands over the green level of the table, touching a cushion at one point, giving a delicate tap to one ball in a far corner, coming straight back home to tap the other ball, then trundling off a little way and waiting to receive the next message. At last the game was up ; the winner, with one or two hardy and perilous "shots round the table" and one brilliant and desperate "draw," completed a run of thirty, and the breathless marker, standing mace in hand, called out "Game !" Then the ring broke up, the prize was adjudged; the assembly broke out into a loud buzz of conversation and debate ; there was prompt application at the bar for many drinks; and groups of two, three or four at once occupied all the tables.

"Come," said Scrope promptly, "let's have a game ;" and stepping swiftly across to a table still vacant, with the quick dexterity of familiar custom, he laid his hand on the table, just in time to prevent two others from reaching it.

"Here's a table," he exclaimed. The two strangers, discomfited, turned away with some surly muttering, but the etiquette of the billiard saloon is as the law of the Medes and Persians, which altereth not : — "First come first served," it saith, — and they did not resist. The three friends, nothing loath, took off their coats; each man selected his cue from the rack ; a bullet-headed, short-haired person of Irish-American appearance, brought them the billiard balls, and they set to work at a three-handed game.

Neither of the three was particularly skilful, but as their unskilfulness was about equal they matched very well; and playing for amusement only, they had a very jolly time of it. Scrope's play was reckless, Bird's cautious and safe, Adrian's well calculated and in a certain sense scientific because he always played with a definite purpose; but from lack of practice his execution was far below his ideal. After a while Scrope, who had been noticing Adrian "lay out" good shots and then miss them, observed upon it:

"Vewy ably missed!" he exclaimed, as Adrian's cue ball, a little too delicately touched, stopped about two inches short of the deep red on which it should have caromed for three, and left a run of thirty or forty on the two reds for Bird: — "Vewy ably missed. I never saw anybody make so many ansome misses in my life. An ole boarding-school of them."

"Yes," said Adrian merrily, "it's because I am too scientific and sacrifice every thing to principle. I don't envy you your scratches, either. 'Tis better to have aimed and missed than never to have aimed at all! And here's our worldly friend Mr. Bird, who has been picking up our crumbs, and is ahead of both your luck and my science, just by practical sense and industry."

It was quite true; it is as true in billiards as in trade or in politics, that steady attention to business, hard work and careful good sense are the best means of accumulation. In many other ways also, however, are the moralities of this beautiful game, — moralities hitherto never developed — illustrative of the affairs of life. A man's shots, for instance, show his character. One player is forever putting on a twist, or making draw shots, and counts in the most unexpected manner, forcing the tormented balls in every direction by cunning under-

handed strokes. Another, by sheer straight forward force, drives his ball far round the table, with long-sighted powerful combinations. Another prefers "follow shots;" softly and delicately he coaxes the hard ivory balls, who quietly do what he wants, but don't know that they are coaxed. Another still, the cunningest of all, a silent monopolizer, gets a corner on the balls. He gets the two reds "jawed," and stepping back and forth round the corner pocket, counts and counts to the paralysis and infuriation of the helpless excluded adversary, who longs to whack him over the head with the butt of his cue. And the vicissitudes of the game, moreover, prove and exhibit the characters of the players like those of life.

However: — the three young men played away, and after a time Adrian missed one or two easy shots. Now, men who would bear a colossal misfortune with equanimity may get quite excited over a game. And in billiards, there is a very curious but undeniable relation between the player's state of mind and his success. Virgil has stated the point as if he had been inspired with a motto on purpose for this game:

"Possunt quia posse videntur."

"They can, just because they believe it." And *vice versa* too. The first miss was, you may say, pure accident, but it damaged Adrian's *morale;* the second shot *he did not have faith that he would make,* and so he did not make it. "I guess I sha'n't count any more," he said, in a sort of half serious discouragement.

"Take three fingers of Old Burbon straight, Ad!" uttered a voice in an oracular tone; "that'll set you up again, just like a fly."

All three of the players looked to

see who was the oracle. It was the taller of two young men who had approached without being noticed by the players, and who had been looking on in silence for a few moments. The shorter was a very dark complexioned young fellow, natty of costume, adorned with jewels of price, and very flashy in bearing. The other, who had spoken, was big and fat, even noticeably so ; and — delicately be it intimated — his substance was distributed after such a manner that the circumference of his waistband bore to that of his trousers' leg, too great a ratio for the best sculpturesque effect. He also was well dressed — in the pretentious sense, — being majestic in fine black broadcloth, a glossy new hat, gloves, a showy lavender-colored waistcoat, a white under-waistcoat, a speckled shirt, a bright red cravat, a diamond pin, and a slender cane whose ivory head was carved in the similitude of a plump human leg bent at the knee. His face was round and full and almost puffy : his dark hair was coarse and straight ; his rather thin mustache was elegantly waxed into two sticky-looking little horizontal tips, in that fashion that always suggests that they are agglutinated with the remainder-grease of the last meal. His lips were not very thick, but had a sort of over-full look ; and they were slightly varnished, and their red color thus brought out, by the dewy moisture of a perceptible exudation of tobacco-spit. His eyes were dark, rather small, but quick enough, and the black eyebrows were rather thin, like the mustache.

Before Adrian had time to speak, this splendid youth resumed, with a jovial haw-haw which exhibited a row of tobacco-stained teeth that otherwise would have been white and regular enough —

" Why, by — Ad, you d—d rascal, what the" —but really, the oaths must be omitted, although it cuts " a monstrous cantle out " of the speaker's observations, and deprives us of something like half the utterances of his great mind, leaving them insipid, like a dish of eggs with the yolks all picked out. But, as the showman says in the burlesque, " the Public Heye must and shall be regarded ; " in one sentence parenthesized blanks may indicate the habitual proportion of this speaker's appeals to his Maker, and afterwards — as Lord Timothy Dexter said about the stops in his style of composition, people must " pepper and solt it to suit themselves."

" Why ( ) " said the big fat young man, " Ad, you ( ) rascal, what the ( ) are you doing here, ( ) you ? Is Saul also among the prophets ? "

" How do you do, Cousin William." said Adrian, good humoredly, and it must be confessed not without some little feeling that he was out of place. But where can you play billiards in New York — on a decent public table — without having rum, tobacco, gambling, profanity and vulgarity in the room ? — " How do you do ? — More like a prophet among the Sauls, I guess, isn't it ? "

" Ha ! ha ! ha ! " laughed the other, with so voluble an effusion of glee, and with eyes so swimming and such a swaying of his heavy figure, that Adrian instantly perceived that he was at least half tipsy ; but even while he laughed, he administered a mighty slap between Adrian's shoulders, and then taking his cue out of his hand, gave three resounding bangs upon the floor. A boy hurried up, in obedience to the well-known billiard-room summons ; and the summoner continued,

"What's yours, gentlemen?"— looking to Bird and Scrope—"Introduce me, Adrian," he interrupted; "can't drink with an entire stranger —against my principles."

"Mr. Scrope," said Adrian, thus appealed to, and making a considerable effort to seem proud and happy; "My cousin Mr. William Button. Yours too: I suppose you missed finding him at home. Mr. Bird, a member of the press;" and so on. Then Mr. Button in his turn introduced his short and swarthy companion to them all as Mr. Oppenheimer; and therewith he vouched for him amidst a perfect storm of oaths, as "the sharpest sport in this city— can't beat me though—hay, Op?" And the whole bowed and shook hands all round and round. They all attempted to decline drinking, but young Button began to be vociferous; enlarging with much vigor on the happy occasion of his meeting a new cousin, as one most proper for hospitality; the players at the adjoining tables began to look with obvious displeasure at the big noisy fellow who was disturbing their game, and Bird, touching Adrian's elbow, nodded, as much as to say, "We had better do it," and they all consented, and jointly remitted to the entertainer the choice of liquors.

"Five Old Burbon straight," said Mr. Button, — but Oppenheimer, amending, ordered for himself a "soda cocktail" instead, saying "You know, Bill, my head ain't so strong as yours. I can't carry any more."

The liquors came and were drank, and Adrian, though like most persons of clean descent and pure health he unfeignedly abhorred the abominable rank sharp scalding-hot flavor of the whiskey, which he swigged down pure in obedience to the exhortation of his cousin, found to his surprise that the sort of stir it produced through every fibre of his frame, although he felt in his brain the beginning of something like a loosening of his usual clear perfect command of all his wits, somewhat as if a thin hot mist or cloud was just beginning to gather among them, yet did really appear to have re-enforced his billiard faculties, whatever those are, in some way; for he proceeded to make some unusually good runs, and in fact came out first, Mr. Bird's economy carrying him through a good second, while Scrope had the game to pay for.

Very likely, according to that wise ordinance of our Maker under which the more we lose the more we want to keep on and get it back, Scrope would have insisted on another game; but he was really good-natured; and, as soon as Bird had completed his hundred, Mr. Button, not being quite clear in his intellectuals, and not having the most correct instincts in the world to make up for his lack of good training, called out,

"There you go, Mister Scrope. All gone up in a kite! Now see me wipe out Brother Oppenheimer. Come, Op!"

And he pulled off his coat and proceeded to pick out a cue. The "sport," sharper as he was, looked rather confused at the invitation, but the others, laughing, acquiesced, and sat down to look on. The game which now followed puzzled Adrian for a time. Button, though at least half drunk, played a very fair game indeed. As for Oppenheimer, Adrian observed at once how perfectly cool and clear-headed he was; then he noticed the extreme neatness of his style of play. He used exactly the force required, and no more; the cue ball, like a trusty middle-aged servant with errands, trundled deliberately off, called at a cushion or left the duplicate message of a carom, and moved just a few steps further to a place convenient for setting out on the next errand. It was an instructive exhibition to Adrian of that judicious play which always considers *the next* shot. But at the same time he was struck by the easy shots which Oppenheimer missed; once a plain short carom ; once a fair shot round the table ; and Adrian was sure that as the "sport" made these misses, he as it were relaxed muscles and attention together, — striking, one might say, with his eyes shut. Whenever he had done so, he muttered some short exclamation of disgust, or gave a vexed sort of whirl round on his heels ; while Mr. Button exulted over him with effusive, self-exalting and half-tipsy glee. Adrian cautiously intimated to Mr. Bird something of these observations.

"Oh yes," said that gentleman, in his quiet intelligent way ; "that Oppenheimer is just playing him off. I know him. He sleeps on a billiard table every night, — unless sometimes it's a faro table for a change. He can give points to either of those champions we saw over there. He's a first class billiard sharp. You may play with him if you want to, and you'll win any small bets, if he thinks he can coax you into a large one. But don't bet a cent more than you are willing to lose."

"I never risked a cent on chances yet in my life," said Adrian, quietly, "and I don't want to. He'll never make any thing out of me."

"You're a lucky man," said Bird with a smile.

As the game proceeded, Adrian noticed over and over the same set of phenomena he had thus observed, and every time he saw the contrast of fine play and intentional failure, he wondered more that Button did not see it. But conceit and tippling together are a very thick cloud, and the big foolish youth was fully convinced that it was his own skill that kept him just behind or just in the lead of his cool and steady opponent. Towards the close, Button grew more and more noisy, laughing and bawling out slang observations with every shot whether he counted or not. At last there remained as it happened only one single point for Mr. Button to make, while Oppenheimer had let himself fall behind twenty-five points ; and the uproar of the triumphant Button was becoming tremendous. The balls were left, moreover, in one of those technically troublesome positions which look so desperate to an ordinary player, the cue ball being "frozen" to one of the others, while the rest were behind that one and close together, so that all four lay in a short straight row. Of course, Oppenheimer could not count if he moved the ball which the cue ball touched ; and for a moment he seemed to study the position with some little care. As for Button, he exulted. Bending over the balls, and shading them with his hand so as to keep off the reflections of the gas-light, he peered intently at the focus of interest, where the "spot ball" — which was Oppenheimer's — lay just touching the deep red. "Frozen, by —— " he exclaimed at last. "Tight as Greenland. Doctor Kane himself couldn't get out of it. *Now* count. Oppy! Gentlemen, see Oppy count now !"

"You've got me, William, that's a fact," remarked Mr. Oppenheimer, with a discouraged air. "No use playing against you and luck together. However, I'll play away from the other balls, at any rate." So saying, he stepped around to the further side from his cue ball, and quickly and almost carelessly placed his left hand as a "bridge," in the high way necessary for playing over other balls; touching the table with three fingers only, instead of with the lower rim of the palm also, and Adrian, watching closely, noticed not only the delicate moulding of his projecting thumb, and the almond shape of his clean pink nails, but the coquettish *perk* of his little finger sticking out as a fanciful lady's does when she lifts a teacup to her lips, and the sparkle of a small bright diamond in a plain gold ring on the same little finger. In a moment, almost as it seemed without looking at the balls, the "sport" administered a delicate little dig to the cue-ball; a short stroke, directed from above downward almost upon the very top of the ball, and that did not seem to follow the ball an inch. Button, watching his closest to see that the "frozen" ball did not move, was baffled, but said, "No harm, I guess."

But there was harm. The spot ball had received one of those mysterious "twists" somewhat such as are given in what are called "macé" shots, which seem to inform the white ivory with the knowledge of a complete campaign. Slowly, as if reluctantly, but almost whizzing on its own perpendicular axis, the spot ball crept a few inches to the cushion — then leaped suddenly away as if it was there that its errand was given it, but at an unexpectedly wide angle across a corner, then taking a second cushion, rebounded accurately upon the two balls that had been so snugly sheltered behind the deep red one; and Oppenheimer had counted two.

"I declare!" exclaimed Adrian, softly, but in great admiration, — and watching the "sport," who stood near him, he saw, to his surprise, a swift subtle smile that just glimmered as it were for an instant upon his dark face, and was instantly repressed. Oppenheimer had counted on purpose. As for Button, his oaths would have terrified a custom-house.

"What for did you want to scratch exactly then, I want to know?" he asked.

"I *didn't* want to scratch, Bill," said Oppenheimer, with a neat double meaning — "you can't always make the balls do what you expect, you know!" — And he played on.

"Two, five, eight, ten," enumerated Adrian to himself, as the sport counted and counted towards his twenty-five, playing always with the same swift apparently careless precision — and so on up; — "twenty — twenty-two — twenty-four — twenty-No! A miss, upon my word!"

"Sold again — and I've got the money," bawled Button quite beside himself, for a miss counts one for the opposite party, and Oppenheimer had thus *beaten himself;* and Button gave three such bangs on the floor with the butt of his cue as if he had meant to plant it in the hard Carolina pine, as the old Saxon bishop Wulstan of Worcester planted his crosier in the marble of Saint Edward the Confessor's tomb, rather than yield it to the Norman primate Lanfranc.

"Five more Burbon!" he vociferated, as the boy ran up for the order. Everybody refused however. But Button, whose views on the subject of "treating" were to the full those of the foolish, vulgar, rich, rowdy, young American — and that drunk — almost foamed at the mouth at such a reception of his hospitality, and swore by a great many more things than there are in the universe that if they wouldn't drink with him in honor of this victory, he'd drink all five glasses himself. He was the more obstinate, as he grew more excited; and they were fain to yield once more at least in form, even Oppenheimer not insisting on his harmless alkaline beverage.

The five drinks came, each flanked with its attendant tumbler of ice and water for mixing; every man took his glass; Adrian prepared to endure another half hour of uncomfortable stir within him and of unclean flavor in his mouth.

Mr. Button lifted his glass with an air of triumph; "Gentlemen," he said, "I give you on this occasion" —

The glass dropped on the floor and smashed into bits among the slop of whiskey. The young man's tongue failed him at the same moment with his fingers; so did all his muscles at once, and instantaneously he toppled over against the billiard table and then upon the floor. Adrian and Oppenheimer, who were nearest, instantly seized him by the shoulders to lift him up. Adrian saw that his face was very red; his eyes were shut, a little thick foam discolored with the juice of the tobacco that was visibly lodged in one cheek to make room for swigging and speaking, was working out from between his lips. The lips and the whole face were thrilling and working as if with shocks of nervous pain; the same thrills vibrated through the arm and back under both of Adrian's hands, and seemed to pass out through the helpless fingers, which clutched and wavered.

"Put him in a chair here by the window," said Oppenheimer, and they did so. Then he quickly opened the window, and the cold air of the win-

try night fell in upon them like a block of ice, so solid and pure and cold was it, as it broke into the heated and gas-lit and perceptibly smoke and drink-flavored atmosphere of the room.

Adrian had never been so close to such a sight; "What a horror it is!" he was saying to himself, thinking of drunkenness, when Oppenheimer, taking up one of the glasses of ice-water, poured some into his right hand and slopped it upon Button's forehead. It trickled all over his face and down upon his shirt-front. Nobody paid much attention; a drunken man in a billiard saloon is not a black swan, nor a black sheep either, for that matter.

"He'll come out of it in a few minutes," said the gambler.

Bird was looking on in his quiet attentive way: "It's a fit, isn't it!" he said coolly, not questioning, but asserting with slight surprise; then, to the gambler, — "Has he had many of them?"

"No — not more than half-a-dozen," said the other, — "'Tisn't much more than a dizziness."

"Just hold those bits of ice on his forehead," suggested Bird. The gambler did so; and sure enough, in a moment or two Button's face and whole frame became quiet; he seemed to go into a sleep, breathing softly and regularly; the dark flush began to pass from his face; and in perhaps five minutes he opened his eyes in a sleepy sort of way and looked round as if puzzled to know how he came there.

"What is it?" he asked — "Guess I had another little spasm, didn't I?"

"Yes; but you're all right now," said Oppenheimer, and he closed the window. Button sat still a few moments, with a dazed sort of look, somewhat like one awaked before he has slept enough. The rest chatted about indifferent matters for a few minutes; and then the big youth, with an effort, laid his hands on the arms of his chair and hoisted himself up, saying,

" Come ; let's trot out."

" Best thing you can do is to get a good long sleep, Bill," said Oppenheimer, very sensibly. But that, as it would appear, was no part of Mr. Button's plan. He " scorned delights, and lived laborious days " and nights too ; with a double-Milton power of labor, for the time being; though what would have been an intolerable slavery to the pure and lofty old poet and scholar, Mr. William Button believed to be the strenuous pursuit of manly pleasures befitting a free and independent American citizen. Nor can anybody, even though as heavy, not to say strong, as Mr. Button, over-draw on his vital revenues, without finding sooner or later that when the current dividends are exhausted, his checks have been honored out of his capital. He usually finds it out sooner rather than later, and always too soon. It was not yet too late for the foolish Mr. William Button, if he had only known it; but it was pretty nearly too late.

" Sleep —!" was the irritated reply; though the future state (or place) to which the speaker relegated the idea of repose was precisely that where it is commonly least believed to exist. Oppenheimer looked a little surprised. " Just as you like," he said however, with a kind of indifferent acquiescence, such as one uses with a feeble or sick person who is querulous about trifles; "just as you like, about sleeping there or going there; it's all one to me ! "

" Well, — let's go up stairs, Opp ; Ad's a stranger ; want to show him the elephant."

The gambler gave a swift suspicious look, not at Button, but at the three others. Scrope answered, this time.

" I guess e means the tiger, wather than the helephant, don't e ? Weckon we've all visited the animal ? " — and he looked inquiringly at Bird and Adrian. The police reporter only smiled and nodded; Adrian said he believed he knew what the beast was, but had never seen him. Button at once insisted on going, and was quite nervous and fussy about it.

" Well, come on," said Oppenheimer, adding, "Never saw you so fretful before, William — what's the matter with you lately ? " If Mr. Oppenheimer had been familiar with epilepsy, he would have recognized this fretfulness as a common symptom ; but neither he nor young Button himself knew this; indeed, the attack he had just had was his first clearly pronounced one. The disease was just taking a good hold ; or rather was just showing the good hold it had already taken ; — for the degeneracy of brain and nerve tissue which seems to be the proximate vehicle of epilepsy works a good while in secret, like an engineer approaching by mines and getting a good many of them placed and loaded before any explode.

CHAPTER XIV.

THE party, now consisting of five, came out from the house that Jack kept, and stepping round to the same recess in which was the outer entrance to Hope Chapel, Oppenheimer entered one of the side doors, led the way up two flights of stairs, and ushered the rest into a middle-sized room, fronting on Broadway. Here they found a dozen persons, gathered round a table about the size of a common dining table for six, and which was covered with green cloth. On a platform a few inches high occupying most of its surface, was displayed an array of playing cards, faces uppermost. On or among these there lay here and there little piles of ivory disks an inch or more in diameter, some white, some red. Back of the table sat a tall and sedate looking personage, who solemnly drew out other cards from a neat little German silver case at his right hand. At every third card, as he turned it and showed it, there was some little stir among the company: one shifted one of the little piles of ivory disks from one card or interval to another; another placed more disks on his pile; another drew some of them to himself; or the presiding genius took some of them; and a watchful person with a little frame something like what they call or used to call in primary schools an arithmeticon, moved backward and forward small pips strung on wires.

Adrian, who had read divers accounts of the splendid fittings of gambling establishments, of their noble hospitalities, such as game suppers, champagne and the like, felt rather cheated; however, he quietly asked Bird if this was a faro table. Bird said it was.

The five stood watching for a few moments. Then young Button, taking a seat at the table, began to manipulate disks, which he seemed to purchase of the president. Mr. Bird with much gravity drew forth in his turn a bank note and deposited it upon the little platform among the cards. The president — if that was

his title — in a moment or two with perhaps even more gravity put forth his hand and took the same into his own possession. Indeed, the card part is almost superfluous in this transparent and equitable diversion, which could be made still simpler and of course more beautiful if reduced to the plain and brief transaction of handing successive five dollar bills across a table by one person, to be received by another, who should place them in his trousers' pocket. This would save time, and also the whole expense of " lay-out," dealing-box, and checks; and ivory in particular, as the best authorities both on natural history and on commerce inform us, grows scarcer and more costly every day.

"Is that all there is to it?" whispered Adrian to Bird.

"Pretty much," was the reply, — "once in a while the money comes back the other way."

"I don't see much fun in it," rejoined Adrian.

"Ever play, sir?" joined in Oppenheimer suddenly, apparently having overheard.

"No," said Adrian; "never did such a thing in my life."

"Didn't?" said Oppenheimer with obvious eagerness. "Well, try your luck. Come on."

"Why," said Adrian, civilly, "I don't care the least about it; — besides, I can't afford it. I'm as poor as a rat."

"Never mind that," said the gambler. " Here " — and he pulled some notes out of his pocket — "Give me great pleasure to furnish you twenty dollars to begin with — We'll go in cahoot: — fifty if you want."

But Adrian's healthy nature was clean physically and morally " by sixteen descents " — and more too; for he was of almost unmingled blood, of the ancient English Puritan type. He was as ready for fun as anybody; and he was eager to see, and for increase of knowledge was willing to undergo even the stink of tobacco and the almost equally foul fumes of liquor and dirtiness. But it was only the wish to know that impelled him; the instinct of an active mind, inquiring after all truth, and analyzing sewerage, if necessary, to get at the portion of truth which may be peculiar to sewerage; not the instinct of the hog, which will eat it and wallow in it. He did feel an impulse, not to accept the unaccountable offer of Mr. Oppenheimer, but to take some of his own money and play it away if only to ascertain for himself what the sensation was — if there was any sensation. But he was strongly dissuaded by the repulsive something which quietly but steadily impressed him, as a subtle evil quality in an infected air comes to weigh upon one's senses. He could not see that either Scrope, who had been betting a little, Button, who was playing away in an eager manner, or Bird, who after losing his five dollars had looked on with his usual quiet air, felt any thing of this repulsion. The furniture and fittings of the room were meagre and soiled. Perhaps the foot-worn old Brussels carpet, the faded grease-spotted wallpaper with its awkward bunchy pink roses, the frowsy old maroon colored window-curtains, may have helped this feeling. But most of it was from the vulgar and evil bearing and atmosphere of the familiars of the place. There was no princely personage; no haughty young aristocrat; not even a solid banker, infuriated with a species of excitement even more hot and hellish than stock-gambling. Not even the likeness of Mr. Bret Harte's self-

sacrificing scoundrel of an Oakhurst could Adrian discern. All the faces were not only hard and greedy and unfeeling.and also violent and lowering in expression, but of a small, mean, vulgar type; so that Adrian remembered what he had read somewhere of some criminal class or population, that they would cut anybody's throat to get an old pair of trousers.

And he steadily declined the pressing and not particularly elegant officiousness of Mr. Oppenheimer. This gentleman's insinuating smile, after a few minutes, suddenly deserted him, and he darted a very ugly look at Adrian, muttering something about "beats," and then looking across at the president of the bank, he made some sign or other.

There was an immediate stir among the company, who arose as with one consent, president and all, leaving Button alone at the table. Several very elaborate oaths were sworn, which somehow seemed to Adrian not improper, but, like weeds on a dunghill, simply the natural product of the place. Three or four of the men stepped to the door and stood there as if to prevent exit; the others, turning, and with murmurs more or less indistinct, bent scowling countenances upon the visitors. The chief or dealer, nearly opposite to whom, a little to the left, Adrian had been standing, was stepping around that end of the table, apparently with some vengeful intent. Adrian, startled and uncomfortable, watching all this movement, heard the dealer say something about "playing any d—d games on a party of gentlemen about their private business." As he uttered these words in a most growling and inauspicious manner, he was moving close past Bird, who stood at Adrian's left. Adrian heard his companion say in a low tone something of which he only caught the words — " On the square — quit it, Jimmy " — and he made some very quick gesture or other, as if to button his coat or reach after some weapon or other article in or under the breast of the same. Whatever it was that was done or said, its operation upon the indignation of the dealer was as instantaneous as the touch of oil to water in which a bit of camphor is travelling. In an instant, the fellow was perfectly motionless. Then he turned, and saying "Beg pardon — all right, gentlemen," resumed his place, and the whole trouble, whatever it was, fell instantly to the previous dead calm.

Mr. Bird, now looking at his watch, said aloud, " Well, boys, I must go ; — will you come ? "

Adrian assented ; so did Scrope ; as for Button, he swore he wouldn't until he'd got that last twenty-five dollars back. Bird looked at the dealer — at least Adrian thought so — At any rate that worthy promptly laid down the cards he had taken up, and said in a very peremptory tone,

" Bank's closed, gentlemen."

Button still grumbled ; but the dealer coolly seized the pile of white checks before the young gentleman, gave him some bank-notes, which he counted out as if constituting an understood equivalent, and without paying the least attention to his irritated reclamations, arose and turned off the gas from the large burners which illuminated the faro table, leaving it in the comparatively dim light of the rest of the room. Again there was a general movement ; but this time only of dispersion ; and Bird, Scrope, Adrian and Button went down stairs, Mr. Oppenheimer remaining. Adrian had politely testified to the last gentleman, his obligations for guidance as

well as for proffered financial aid, but the gambler was quite curt and ungenial in his reply.

From the outer door they all went together up Broadway to Union Square. Button, after divers murmurs and complaints, admitted that he was tired out. Indeed, they were all pretty tired, and Adrian not the least so ; for he had been on his feet since early in the morning ; and travelling in the iron-bound streets of New York is peculiarly exhausting to those unaccustomed to the unyielding footing of the stone.

As they went, Adrian, questioning with interest about the scene they had left, found that it was one of those minor haunts of gamblers which the police call a " skin game ; " i.e., where the object is to (metaphorically) skin the visitors ; that the company they had found there were "ropers-in " or "cappers," to wit mere decoys.

" The fact is," said Bird, "if it hadn't been that Jimmy Dexter the dealer knew I was in with the police authorities, they might have made it a little awkward for you. They get mad very easily, if they see any reason for it. Your refusing to play vexed friend Oppenheimer."

" I don't see why," said Adrian ; "and what on earth made him offer me money ? I never heard of such a thing."

" Don't you know ? " said Bird, " Many gamblers believe a man is sure to win the first time he plays. He was going in cahoot, you know — to have half the winnings ; and he looks on it that you have kept him out of so much money."

At Fourteenth Street they parted, all four going different ways ; Button on a Fourth Avenue car, Scrope on a Broadway car, Bird on a down town car — having, he said, to go to one of the newspaper offices, late as it was; while Adrian though weary, preferred to walk at least part of the way to his quarters, for the sake of refreshing himself with a little out-door air after his triple seething in the hot close filth of concert-saloon, billiard-room and gambling-hole.

As he went, he meditated, the series of his thoughts running somewhat as follows :

" Lucky it isn't William that I'm engaged to ! — Rather undesirable brother-in-law ! — However, no danger that Ann will let him infest her household much ! — Hope Mr. Button doesn't own Hope Chapel building too ! — Wonder if I could get a copy of that police list of New York good men that own bad houses ? — Shouldn't like to have a quarrel with Mr. Button over that concert saloon tenement ! — What a defiling evening ! Makes one feel unclean through and through ! Touch pitch — I don't envy this Mr. Bird his other experiences that he wouldn't tell — Sha'n't ask him either; I've dived deep enough for my purposes ! — No use to try to do any thing for William, I'm afraid — Fit, too ; — I've heard that epilepsy never lets go if it once gets hold — Fitzwilliam, I suppose Scrope will be calling him — Sorry for his father " —

And so on, his mind rambling round and round amongst the particular web of circumstances closest to him at the time, until he reached his boarding-house, on one of the cross streets near the since disused Twenty-Seventh Street Railroad Station. Here, after a good deal of trouble, he was admitted, and with profuse apologies he retired to the small " hall bedroom" which was his

lair for the time being, and at once went to bed.

He fell asleep instantly ; but some broken and disjected members of his waking thoughts still haunted him in his dreams. Their fantastic and unwelcome nature may have been partly caused by a still remaining evil effect of the nasty liquors of which he had twice partaken that evening. Perhaps some additional unpleasantness may have accrued from the endemic co-tenants of his bed ; for nothing in the experiences of his own home, cleanliest of the cleanly homes of old Hartford, had prepared him for these blood-sucking vexations. To inquire whether or no any prophetic force or quality was concerned or contained in these dreams, would be to raise questions even deeper than those of entomology or hygiene.

Whatever the causes, however, it is certain that at some time in that night he dreamed a grotesque and disagreeable dream, one of those peculiarly distinct and truthful-seeming ones that occasionally come to us, and which leave in the mind the memory as of a real past experience. It appeared to him that he was with difficulty making his way westward along the sidewalk on the north side of Pearl Street, Hartford, between Main and Trumbull Streets. The walk was one unbroken sheet of " glare ice," and the weather was bitter cold. As he slid and tottered unsteadily along, he suddenly, — but with a horror singularly in the reverse of what must have been his waking feelings at an appeal from that voice, — heard himself called by name, but in a jeering and most ill-natured manner, by his own lady-love — Miss Ann Jacintha Button. " Here, here, you fool ! " she scolded, in a sharp high tone — " why don't you

wait for me! Wait, I tell you!"
But scared most unreasonably by the
call, he seemed to redouble what became a frantic effort to escape instead
of a more unstable but decorous progress along the street; and looking
behind in his fright, he saw Miss Button skating, — as it were, — with terrific velocity upon his traces, her arms
outstretched as if to seize him, with
something of the fell and fatal per-
tinacity of Death after the Youth in
the New England Primer —

> " *Youth* forward slips —
> Death soonest nips."

With horribly inefficient increase
of effort, he scrambled onward, thinking " I'll get round the corner of Trumbull Street in a minute, and then I'll
run ! " — though why he should not
have adopted this unutterably base
and cowardly expedient at once, he
could not have told, — unless because he must have tumbled down.
Still he strove forward, while the calls
and jeers and reproaches of the pursuing maiden grew as voluble and furious as the magical voices that in the
Arabian tale beset persons ascending
the hill on their road to the Talking
Bird, the Singing Tree and the Yellow
Water. Persons met him and passed
him, looking with open contempt
upon his flight; and ever and anon
Miss Button threw in a sarcastic request to them to "see that fool trying to run away ! " The icy sidewalk of the single block from the Pearl
Street Church to the Town Clerk's
Office seemed to stretch into a perspective as hopeless as the whole
Great Arctic Floe; and just as his
fright, his vexation at not getting
forward, and his mortification at
making such an exhibition in public,
began to be further complicated by
fantastic doubts as to the topographi-
cal possibilities of what he was ac-

tually about, he woke, with an incredible sense of relief, and before he fell
asleep again, he puzzled himself for
a long time, trying to decide whether
there was any rational element in the
vision. Possibly the fact of his making the inquiry may have been evidence for the affirmative; but if so,
it was without any consciousness or
assent on his part.

CHAPTER XV.

THE proposed " see-ance " (that is
what most of them call it, with accent
on the first syllable, doubtless supposing it to mean a session of seers) of
the next day being postponed for
some reason or other, Adrian passed
his Thursday and Friday in sight-
seeing and other varied occupations,
taking care to find pretexts for calling
two or three times at Mr. Van Braam's
and once or twice at Mr. Button's, as
was right and proper. He also met
more than once Mr. Scrope and Mr.
Scrope's new friend Bird the police
reporter, with whom the free and
easy young Englishman seemed to
have struck up a friendship almost
as prompt and absorbing as that of
the soulful maiden in "The Rovers,
or, The Double Arrangement," who,
after two minutes' converse with
another soulful maiden that she has
never met before, exclaims, "A sudden thought strikes me — let us
swear an eternal friendship!"

Mr. Bird was, however, in fact a
"very nice fellow." He was quiet,
silent rather than talkative, but had a
way of knowing every thing — within a certain range, that is, — giving
a clear and sufficient account of it
if applied to, in a perfectly unpre-
tending manner; and there was an
air of steadiness and coolness that
somehow made him comfortable to be
with. Besides, he was willing to go

anywhere, provided his professional duties, which were somewhat irregular, allowed, and as his knowledge of the evil side of city life appeared — so far at least — to be peculiarly complete, he was just the guide, philosopher and friend that the scatter-brained Scrope wanted. Indeed, Scrope urged Adrian to go with him and Bird on more than one voyage of inquiry during these same two days; but the young man had had quite enough for the present of the subsoiling investigations that seemed so delightful to the Englishman ; and the more mysterious and enthusiastic Scrope became in his descriptions and anticipations, the less did Adrian relish either the pursuit or the pursuer. Bird seemed totally indifferent as to these expeditions themselves, and to be actuated only by a pleasant goodnatured willingness to obtain for the eager young foreigner any knowledge or experience whatever that he might desire, without raising any question about good or evil.

On the evening of Friday, however, Adrian and Civille made their appearance in due season at the little hall which was the usual gathering-place of the *Solidarité de l'Avenir ;* a rather close and fusty upper room in a public building in the neighborhood of Stuyvesant Place. It is a discouraging fact that reforming assemblies are usually almost as ill ventilated as primary meetings. If the founders of the New Patent Future don't provide clean fresh atmospheric air to begin with, they need not expect they can bring about a clean fresh social atmosphere. A dirty philosopher may perhaps by possible exception teach a clean philosophy. So may a frail and crooked-looking person possess a good deal of strength ; but it is not probable.

Adrian and Civille accommodated themselves with seats pretty near the desk, somewhat at one side, and which, by virtue of a curve in the line of the seats, gave a view both of the little stage and of all the auditors. They had hardly settled themselves in their places, before Messrs. Scrope and Bird — who, it will be remembered, had received from Miss Civille, permission to be present, — and Mr. William Button along with them, who had not received any such permission, — walked gravely in, and espying the young people, came and ensconced themselves, after salutation due, behind them ; Bird behind Civille, Scrope behind Adrian, next to the right and Button at Scrope's right, so as to be furthest from Civille ; a diagram apparently laid down by pure chance, but which very neatly represented the spiritual relations of the five ; Civille and Adrian (for instance) perhaps not very far from the same line, but Civille at the left or heart side ; Bird very decidedly behind her ; Scrope at least as much further from her as the hypothenuse of a right angled triangle is longer than a side ; and Button at a trapezoidal distance. The room rapidly filled up with men and women, a good many of the latter coming without masculine escort ; it was not long before every seat was full, and a number of later comers were forced to stand in a row next the walls. A grave and tall old man with long thick iron-gray hair combed smoothly back over his head and behind his ears, arose from one of the side seats and took the chair. There was a sort of expectant interval of a few minutes, and a buzz of whispering talk like a thin acoustic cloud floating at the level of the people's heads. To this our quintette of friends quietly contributed.

"How d'ye like the looks of the Solidarity de Lavenoo?" asked Mr. William Button, among the others, in Adrian's right ear. A spirituous incense on his breath floated round at the same time to his hearer's nose.

"All very nice, so far," replied Adrian, smiling at the young gentleman's joke.

"Queer crowd," pursued Button — "like boarding-house butter — more hair than fat."

This, though inelegant in point of rhetoric, was a very just observation in substance, as Adrian perceived to his great amusement as he glanced around the room. In truth, he thought to himself that Button alone was probably possessed of more fat than all the rest of the assembly. They were terribly skinny, indeed, almost all of them, with hollow eyes, lank cheeks, and frames as spare as if the assembly was a congress of clothes-horses. Adrian fancied they had all been desiccated in some hot dry air, and he had a feeling as if it was still playing about among them. Sensitive to impressions and atmospheres, he seemed almost to feel that his own lips and his eyes were beginning to parch a little; that he was beginning to dry up in the heat that seemed to quiver in the crowded room. In truth he had entered into a new world; the thin ghostly windy over-heated oven-dried world of Talking Reform Enthusiasts, that he had so often heard of, but had never really touched and felt; that strange un-real buzz, of mere good intention with so little morality or religion mingling in it, so little positive constructive intellect, above all so infinitely less of real power — of common sense. A fantastic realm is theirs, situated, like the Nephelococcygia, the cloud-bird-land, of Aristophanes,

between the heavens and the earth. Here they flit, with no footing on the one, and no reach into the other, yet with a feeling that like the Birds of the witty Greek dramatist they are managing both. But they have no hold. Like the ghosts that flocked about Ulysses at the entrance to Hades, their own unsubstantiality repels them when they try to grasp. A curious further detail or two of analogy might be traced between those melancholy Odyssean shades and our Talking Enthusiasts of to-day. They are querulous; there is something remote and thin in all their utterances; they gibber; and some of them at least — such as the extreme Red Republicans for instance, make their nearest approach to a substantial and efficient life by drinking warm blood.

The present occasion, too, although Adrian had not been told of it, was a grand field day or General Muster, such as should take place for every army from time to time, to serve as roll-call, to enable the force to encourage itself by the sight of its whole proud self all together and by the consciousness of its power in unison; and to maintain habits of associated activity and concerted effort. The hosts of progress — or rather Progress, — were here in presence. Hosts is the word; for each of those skinny middle-aged women, each of those lank long-haired, dried-eyed men, is a host in h{lm}{er}self — if you will accept the host's own word for it.

Another trait in this assembly was very striking to Adrian. This was the exceptional forms of the heads. In a State legislature, in the representative deliberative assembly of a powerful religious sect, the large average size of the heads may be noticeable, or their average height

—and sometimes their average baldness; but they are almost all heads that do not greatly vary from a usual form. But the *Solidarité* looked in this particular like the head-maker's lumber-room for bad jobs. Some of the people had over-large brains on thin weak necks; some of the heads were small and over-intense; some were oddly high and narrow; some bulged upward and forward; some were cut short off in a perpendicular line close behind the ears; some shot out in a shelving slope over the eyes; some poked up and back into a peak at the crown.

Adrian, studying this grotesque assortment of exteriors, and musing upon the spirit of the assembly, strove to apprehend some element in it which might seem a reasonable point of sympathy for attracting such a finely and sensitively organized person as Civille. The best conclusion he could reach was, however, that there must be in her an appreciation of their good intentions, and a loving charity, together large and strong enough to silence any repugnance that she might feel from the side of taste, or any jeers from the mirthful side of her nature. *A priori*, most certainly, one would judge that a fastidious and delicately cultured lady could only have laughed, or looked the other way. As it was, she seemed to him almost like a solitary Sister of Charity in a hospital full of harmless lunatics.

—The gray haired old chairman rapped thrice upon the desk:

—"The *Solidarité* will please come to order!"

—"Don Rodrigo Scipio de Nada, of Cuba, will address the friends, on the Progress of the Physical Sciences."

Don Rodrigo, a short slight little man, very gentlemanly in dress and bearing, with black eyes and hair, a dark complexion, a pleasant face, a smiling and courtly manner, on this stepped forward from one of the front seats and opened the business of the evening. Nobody could possibly have surmised what the graceful little gentleman was going to say. He began with a well worded apology for his English, — which did not need it, — and then went on somewhat thus:

"One of the Physical Sciences recently investigated with the most active interest is Optics. — If we admit a beam of the sun's light through a small hole into a dark room, and cause it to fall upon a smooth white surface after passing through a triangular piece of glass called a prism, there will be seen upon the white surface not a spot of white light, but a bar composed of successive portions of different colors. This is called the Solar Spectrum."

And so on; being the merest rudiments of the subject, as given in any school philosophy. Poor little Don Rodrigo! His notions about the average attainments of a probable audience in that community were based on the condition of common schools in Cuba. He was importing coals into Newcastle as fast as he could; you may say of the bituminous variety too, by the spontaneously combustible tendency which was quickly developed. For a few moments the hearers were mannerly and quiet enough; then they began to whisper and giggle; to grow restless and stir about in their seats. An odd looking bald man, very dusty of aspect, in a brown coat, hopped up at the further side of the room and opened his mouth, with the obvious purpose of interrupting, but was expeditiously pulled down again by a more forbearing companion, which enterprise caused a ripple of laughter, and Don Rodrigo paused a moment in innocent wonder. In a few moments more the bald man made another vain attempt to hop up. Almost at the same time, another queer looking person with a sharp wrinkled face and dyed hair and beard, — though really queerness in that assembly consisted in not being queer — with the same jerkiness of action as the bald man's, also hopped up, and being either less fortunate in a companion or more powerful in resolution or in physique, he completed his nefarious, or at least discourteous, design. "Mr. Chairman," he snapped out in a high sharp key, speaking very fast and fidgety, and growing madder as he went on, "Mr. Chairman, I think the gentleman had better stop right here. I didn't come here to-night to be told a lot of stuff that I learned when I was a little boy at school. He's wasting the time of this meeting, when it ought to be occupied in promoting the greatest interest of the human race."

A strange cracked feminine voice a little behind Adrian squealed out,

"I think the brother's quite right."

Don Rodrigo, altogether dismayed, surrendered at once, and crept humbly back from the stage to his place, where he sat immovable and distraught, all the rest of the evening, gazing at the toes of his neat little boots, as unconscious of the collision of majestic intellects that was going on around him as one of the corpses in Kaulbach's great picture, of the furious warrior-wraiths contending in the air above.

The cracked squealing voice resumed;

"Mr. Chairman!" —

The chairman gave an uneasy look around him, like one who seeks shelter from an impending shower. Civille whispered to Adrian, who was with extreme difficulty preserving a grave countenance,

"It's Mrs. Gloriana Babbles the Inspirational Speaking Medium. She's a little troublesome sometimes, for the spirits that control her have many things to say."

Adrian turned and gazed at Mrs. Babbles with a good deal of interest, for it was his first close view of one of the prophetesses of the period, and she was only three seats away. She was, it is needless to say, skinny; but in a superlative degree: so that the idea occurred to Adrian's naughty mind, whether in such a case the cuticle might not admit of gores being cut out at the sides or elsewhere, as they treat over-full garments, the slits thus formed to be neatly sewed together, thus restoring a smooth fit. Otherwise, the good lady, like Mrs. Gamp, had "the remains of a fine woman" about her. She had once possessed a quite comely face, and a good figure. But little beside the bones was left to show it; her blue eyes were faded and sunken in deep sockets; the lips, thin and pale, were a little crowded by the artificial teeth; the whole face had a dried look; the long stringy curls that dangled at either side of her head looked wispy and fatigued; and her voice, besides being cracked and high and thin, was curiously nasal withal; a falsetto-soprano squeal through the nose.

"Mister Chairman," she began, "I am impressed this evening with the greatness of the work before us. Brethren and sisters," — Adrian, looking back to the chairman, saw that the old gentleman's face had assumed a grotesque expression of rueful endurance, and he drew a very long breath to the same effect — But at the moment up jumped again the guardian angel with dyed hair,

— "A shadow like an angel, with bright hair
• Dabbled in *dye*," —

snapped out that he rose to a point of order, and therewithal he moved that all speeches be limited to five minutes. This was seconded, Adrian thought, by almost everybody in the room, and was carried by an enormous majority, the cracked voice of Mrs. Babbles being prominent among the few negatives.

"Dear friends," resumed the medium, waving about in a sort of rhythmic motion, "I sorrow that such narrow limitations should be laid upon the spirit-utterance. Yet the loss is yours. I am impressed to reveal to you the sure approach of the glorious day of spiritual enlargement. I see, in the immediate future, bright traces of the wondrous sunrise of spirit freedom, of spirit love, of spirit happiness" —

And so on. At the end of five minutes sharp, rap rap rap! went the old chairman's gavel with most emphatic good will; and Mrs. Babbles succumbed at once.

Then succeeded a number of speakers, some on one subject and some on another, some of whom were in the most shameless and partial manner allowed to transgress the wholesome five-minute rule. Mrs. Babbles murmured audibly at this more than once, but in vain. A spirit of oppression was present, and she could not resist it. Adrian listened, in wonder at the immense range of views which were presented — from the extremest intolerant Calvinist piety to the most utter denial of any thing superhuman or of a distinction between right and wrong; from absolute materialism to absolute spiritism; from a servile obedience to organized legality, to the jumpingest individual freedom.

Equally was he struck with the fantastic nature of the suggestions thrown out, at their astounding disconnectedness, and at the wonderful tolerance of the speakers, which was very genuine, and very funny; for it consisted, not so much in giving hospitality to other people's views, as in being patient while other people snubbed your own. They snapped and snarled, as if ready to bite one another's heads off; the mordant dusty dyed man getting full as many nips as he gave, and though everybody spoke as irritably as if they all had neuralgia, yet nobody resented it. They were no more civil, and no more resentful, than so many members of the Peace Society; which indeed a good many of them were.

But the jumble was terrific. There was a neat little brown-eyed woman who solemnly told in an absorbed manner and with a sweet voice how her prayers had already slain the Pope of Rome, and how the Scarlet Lady was in consequence on or before the seventh day of the seventh month of the seventh year from that, to be finally dislodged from her sevenfold seat. There was Mr. Jobraker the Linguist with his new Universal Language, in which he delivered a short address, after explaining that as this language was based on the principles of the universe, all those who were in the right relations to the universe would understand every syllable. The alternative was obvious, and Adrian had to conclude that his relations were not right — if Mr. Jobraker was; for he could hear in the new language only a hash of uncouth noises. Then arose a woman who developed a theory that only women have souls; men having none, but only enough of a sort of animal intelligence to fit them for waiting on the ladies. This was received with a good deal of applause, in which the oppressed Mrs. Babbles was particularly vehement. There was a man whose view was that only the Old Testament should be regarded as the authoritative scriptures, for the reason that neither Christ nor any New Testament writer had commanded or recommended any such book or writing except the Old Testament; there was a person, with the puzzled and weary look of one that labors among thoughts too heavy for him, and whose eyes gleamed with incipient madness, who delivered an incoherent discourse, stuffed with Latin and Greek references, upon the coming renewal of all things, which, he said, was in English, the Period of Cosmopolitics; but should more properly be called by the name (well adapted to convey a hint of the confounding of all relations together) — The Epikataparastasis. Upon this poor fellow the five-minute rule was ruthlessly enforced. There was a gentleman who was just returned from a great city in the interior of Africa, accompanied by a native chieftain therefrom; — the names, as nearly as Adrian could get at them were, the city of Ofoofoo, the chief Woojubleevit; who looked like any other decent person of color respectably dressed; and the traveller announced that a subscription was open at the desk to educate Mr. W—— nobody subscribing. Then there was Professor Yellitt Strong, who wanted to advocate his great project of an Elocutionary College for Brakemen, to prevent the misery which arises from so many people's not understanding where they are to get off the cars; and Professor Strong gave some very impressive illustrations of the inarticulate howls now in vogue on railroad trains, and then contrasted these with the clear and resounding shouts that ought to be, and with which the professor almost hoisted the assembly bodily off their seats.

Perhaps the most interesting of all however was a lady — skinny, of course, — elderly, as it happened, — who presented herself as a delegate from a band of sisters claiming to be far in advance of any other reformers. At this audacious statement the *Solidarité* fairly gasped. No wonder. In advance of us! Why, they thought, we have gone to the very extreme — and then jumped off, — how is it possible to float any further out into Chaos! But the delegate proceeded to read the resolutions of her constituent body. Were they in earnest, or not? Adrian, dizzy with the whirling phantoms of the place, beset and buffeted like an intellectual Saint Anthony by a whole pandemonium of monstrous visions, was ready for almost any thing.

"Resolutions," read this fearless champion of her sex, and who by the way had visibly possessed herself by some means or other of no mean portion of the badge of nobility which she vindicated for her down-trodden sex—

"Resolutions of the society for HIRSUTE EMANCIPATION.

" *Whereas* there is every reason to believe that the effeminate beardlessness which distinguishes most women is an ingeniously contrived badge of slavery imposed upon them by the Tyrant Man; and

" *Whereas* there is equal reason to believe that one bold, united and persevering effort will free us from this or any other physiological mark of the degradation of our sex, therefore

" *Resolved :* that we hereby organize for the glorious and noble purpose of Securing Beards to Women, as the first step in the great progress of the age towards the Equality of the Sexes.

"*Resolved :* that we will take the remaining steps as soon as we have achieved the first.

"*Resolved :* That all who are not wholly recreant to the cause of their sister men, degraded below the least comprehension of the Spirit of the Age, and lost to every sense of justice, are called upon to rally round our banner."

Having read this declaration, the lady informed the *Solidarité* that Mr. Darwin's doctrine of the beauty of hairlessness was no other than a cunning attempt to ward off in advance this very movement by the women. She developed also a long and unanswerable historic argument constructed on the principle of those that show how all the good things in the Christian religion were pretty universally known long before Christianity was invented ; which argument began with that striking passage from the Old Edda, which describes how, in order to bind Fenrir the Wolf, the child of Loki and Angurbodi,

"Al-father sent Skirnir the messenger of Frey into the country of the Dark Elves or Svartalfaheim (swart-elf-home) to engage certain dwarfs to make the fetter called Gleipnir. It was fashioned out of six things ; to wit, the noise made by the foot-fall of a cat, THE BEARDS OF WOMEN, the roots of stones, the sinews of tears, the breath of fish and the spittle of birds." Coming hence down the long tract of ages, the speaker ended with a triumphant presentation of the case of Signora Julia Pastrana, the Cele-

brated Bearded Lady, who, she said, is a living proof of the truth of the new principles, — and The President of the Society. The Treasurer, she continued, is Mrs. Jackman of Wilmington, Illinois — and here the speaker read from a Western newspaper,

"Wilmington, Ill., has a bearded lady, who is 27 years old, born in the State of Maine, has shaved for 18 years, and weighs 150 pounds. She is short in stature, and is married to a Mr. Jackman. She wears a beautiful mustache and chin whiskers black as a coal. Mrs. Jackman is a very intelligent woman, and is not at all ashamed of her whiskers."

There was also a Physiological and Medical Director — Doctor Beard : —

"Patron Saint, the Old Hairy," thought Adrian ; but he did not dare say it.

In such addresses the evening sped excitingly away. Adrian, always a student of character, was singularly interested in this astonishing collection of exceptional types, and felt the same interest, with a distinct sense of pain superadded, in considering the question, What business has my pure and delicate cousin Civille in this rout ? She is like the Lady amongst the beasts in "Comus" — how can I get her out ? Perplexed and pondering, — but reserving his conclusion with an instinctive use of what is called "the judicial mind," until he should have got in all the evidence, he resolved to wait before making up his mind, until he should have attended the other proposed sittings, namely at the medium's, and at "The Germ." So he escorted his cousin home, — their talk consisting of his inquiries about the personages of the *Solidarité* and their objects, — and left her.

PART V.

CHAPTER XVI.

THE see-ance to which Adrian was to escort Civille was appointed for early Saturday evening, and the visit to The Germ was to follow it; so Adrian waited on his cousin accordingly, in good season. As they left the door, Civille asked Adrian who Mr. Bird was.

" A reporter, I believe," said Adrian, — " why ? "

" He called this morning," was the young lady's answer; " — rather an odd thing, I thought."

" Odd? How ? "

" Well — I never saw him except the other evening when Mr. Scrope brought him, and once more at the *Solidarité*."

" But if he has been properly introduced, he may call again and try to establish an acquaintance, may he not ? "

" Yes —— I guess the thing that puzzled me was, his taking such an interest in all of us. I didn't think of it until he had gone, but he had got me to talk about almost everybody I know; father, Mr. Button, Ann, her mother — even their hired girls; Mr. Scrope, yourself, the *Solidarité*, Mrs. Babbles, Miss Griggs " —

" Griggs ! " — repeated Adrian, a little startled —. " What Griggs ? "

" Amelia Griggs the medium. Why ? "

" Oh," said Adrian, with an evasion which was upon a perfectly true pretext, — " it's a rather odd name. You know there's an old saying, ' as merry as grigs.' A medium, is she ? " He remembered the allusion to spiritual endowments in the letter Mr. Button had given him.

" Yes. She's miserably poor, but she is an excellent test medium. We shall see her to-night."

" But now, cousin Civille, what did you tell Mr. Bird? About me, first of all, of course ? "

An innocent young woman has just the same sweet helpless beautiful gravity that is so inexpressibly touching in a little child; not an affectation, but only a perfect seriousness and earnestness of direct purpose. The transparent purity of intention makes up a million-fold for the funny ignorance and — not foolishness, but — inexperience, that is exhibited. Adrian was not remarkably aged, neither was he wise enough to do any harm; but he had lived more "amongst folks" as they say in the country, and the solemn satisfaction with which his cousin now went on to tell the unwise things she had done caused in him a curious mixture of emotions and reflections, which however with a reserve partly natural and partly acquired he did not utter in words.

" Oh," observed Civille, her sweet heartfelt low-pitched full-toned voice giving a wonderful additional intensity of attractiveness even to the baby-like simplicity of her confession, " Oh, you know I go by intuitions. Mr. Bird is good. I wanted him to know all about my friends. I gave you a very nice character indeed, cousin Adrian. I told him how unselfish you are, and how you don't care about money, and how you are not calculated to succeed in this world, unless you should find some missionary work that would call out all your energies."

"All that, Civille?" said Adrian, laughing,—"it's more good than I know of myself, at any rate." And he thought in his own mind, "A nice recommendation for a business man! But Bird will see what it amounts to, of course!"

"Many thanks for the favorable diagnosis," he resumed aloud,—"now tell me all you said of the rest."

So she did; she had, so to speak, opened her mental photograph-album to her visitor, and confided to him her whole private collection of portraits. What she had told was not very much; the innocent observation and judgments of a very intuitively acting mind, exalted, moreover, in degree and intensity of action by the very nature of the state of physical ailment or feebleness or susceptibility which was for the time at least fastened upon her; but without much real knowledge of good, and with none of evil. Adrian, somewhat astonished as he was at their unreserve, was startled by the truthfulness of some of the points, while he was sure that some others were quite mistakes. However, he made very little comment, but when she ended asked what she had said about herself?

"Myself?—nothing."

"And yet," said Adrian, "was it not you that he wanted to know about?"

"Perhaps it was—he called on me."

"Well,—don't encourage him and then pretend to be astonished at his taking encouragement."

"That would be flirting," decreed Civille with much majesty. "I am sure you would not say so to me in earnest."

Adrian hastened to disclaim. But still, he took the liberty of intimating to his cousin that she was quite attractive enough to make Mr. Bird, or anybody else, in love with her. This idea the young lady put aside with a great deal of decision, and when Adrian would have persisted, she told him plainly that she didn't want to hear any more such nonsense. So he held his peace; but he was none the less and very naturally, of opinion that Bird's interest in her was the sole, as it was a sufficient, reason of his visit. Adrian was right, too. And he added in his own thoughts another comment, no less just: that she was a person of much too ethereal make to be a suitable companion for the police reporter, good fellow and man of sense though he was.

Civille, after an interval of silence, spoke first, as if she had in the meanwhile been pursuing a train of thought by herself—like the River Arethusa coming up again after going underground:

"I shall never marry."

The solemn tone of absolute conviction would have been funny enough if Civille had been a bag of a hundred. Being a singularly attractive young woman, it was very much more so, and Adrian, who was quick enough to see the ludicrous side of things, had to pull very hard to pull a long face. He wished, moreover, to quote signior Benedick; "When I said I would die a bachelor I did not know I should live to be married." But he held in with all his might, and succeeded in coming down to a tone of grave and cousinly counsel.

"My dear cousin," said he; "every young woman who is worth marrying at all, has exactly that conviction some time or other, just as, they say, any one who can become an orator has the awfullest frights lest he cannot. It may be true of yourself; but you are so good and so nice and I like you so much that I promise you when you do fall in love I won't bring up your promise against you."

"Don't talk so, cousin Adrian! 'Fall in love!' If you could understand how disagreeable the phrase is. I can see how a woman might sacrifice herself to make another person happy. But to risk a whole life — and other lives too — on the chance of an emotion! I don't think I am in much danger of it!"

"I don't think so either," said Adrian. "But an intuition may be both emotional and correct. And a self-sacrifice such as you speak of might be as much of a blunder as gambling on emotions. The truth is, there is no blinder emotion than self-sacrifice. It is as sightless as anger."

An immense deal of comfort is taken by young persons of about as few years and as little experience as this couple, in comparing their profound maxims and reflections. The conversation of the present occasion was thus felt. It continued until they reached the place of the see-ance, with no result in particular for Civille, who only spoke whatever came into her innocent fearless mind, and whose ignorance of things and people in general was only exceeded by her ignorance of herself. Adrian, on his part, was a little older and wiser — but he was talking with a purpose. For the first time in his life he was talking and watching in order to form a deliberate judgment on the nature and condition of a human soul.

But he could not feel that he discovered much, and as he put questions or suggested distinctions or listened to replies, he kept thinking over and over again of that vast spring of living

water in the wild Florida woods, where the visitor looking over the edge of the boat is frightened, because the water is so absolutely transparent that he sees no water. "Is her soul so shallow? Is her soul so deep? Is it only utterly transparent?" he kept asking and asking, — and his interest in her as a fellow-being in peril, as a relative who might be endangering the reputation and happiness of a large circle of friends, began to take the special additional interest — to him excessively attractive, — of a living and new problem in practical psychology. Was she really such a solitary-hearted thing? It might be. The suspicious pointed at Civille had not made the least lodgement in the honest young fellow's clear mind; and this being so, he now began to feel that they were to be interpreted as the reaction of low souls against another too high for them; that perhaps she was really too good to live happily amongst human beings. He instinctively reverenced women; he had not seen so very much of Civille, it is true; but all that he had seen was most lovely; and he was almost ready even now to conclude that in good faith she ought always to live single, because nobody would ever be fit to possess her.

While they talked, and he considered, they had — on foot or by street-car — reached that dreary block of houses on the south side of Bleecker Street between Thompson and Sullivan some distance west of Broadway, called Depau Row. This block, in times gone by, was a centre of magnificence, having a paved archway piercing the building between each two tenements by way of *porte cochère;* separate wings in the rear for offices and servants' rooms; immense big parlors and chambers with heavy old fashioned plaster cornices and great floriated dabs of the same in the middle of the ceilings around the gas chandeliers, as if piercing the ceiling had made a very bad plaster of Paris sore with granulations; faded fresco work in abundance; and the like remainders of departed glory. The great merchants of past ages — for the grandeur of these houses belongs to a remote New York City antiquity of at least twenty-five and perhaps thirty years ago ! — whose households once enlivened these abodes, are dead, or are inhabiting far more gorgeous abodes on Murray Hill or Fifth Avenue ; for the city builds itself northward, and its rich people evacuate place after place, leaving each locality deserted, as the inhabitant of the nautilus does the successive chambers of his shell. Thus the great Depau Row houses are rented to boarding-house-keepers or to tenants of single rooms. The lofty comfortless caverns are depressing and horrid; it is like living in a deserted city of giants ; one is tempted to suppose that rich men a quarter of a century ago were all twelve feet high. The dismayed tenant tries in vain to secrete himself in a corner of the room like Ulysses in the cave of Polyphemus; he feels as if some mighty ghost would stride forth upon him in the night and eat him; and he soon flees away to seek a smaller and snugger abode, terrified into the non-payment of even the insignificant rent which is all that such ill-adapted premises will bring.

Such mystical and ghostly associations however, it is obvious, make such quarters fittest of all for the necromantic marvel-shop of the Medium. It stands to reason that to this spectral person, a real ghost would be a real godsend — that is, supposing the Medium not to be frightened.

There are different kinds of mediums as there are of spirit communications. But they are almost all alike in one thing — they sell their revelations for fifty cents apiece. There is the Healing Medium, whose office is to discern diseases and to cure them; the different kinds of Test Mediums whose message from the spirit land may always be stated thus: "I show you a puzzle. If you can't say how it was done, then it follows that it was by a spirit. Price fifty cents." There is the Psychometrist, who reveals character from inspecting a toe-nail or a lock of hair. There is the Spirit Artist, who paints or draws or photographs spirit-portraits. There is the Inspirational Medium or Trance Speaker; the Consulting Business Medium, and so on.

The meeting of this evening at Mrs. Babbles' room, was however not of any of these sorts, although mediums of more than one of these established varieties were present. It was of still another kind, comparing with the others somewhat as a theological seminary or medical school compares with the settled clergyman's or the established physician's operations. It was a sort of school of the prophets, or College de Propaganda Fide; and the technical spiritist name for it is, "a developing circle." Like all activities, the spiritist phenomena depend for fulness and readiness of manifestation a good deal upon practice and habit. Moreover, Spiritism, as thus far practised, has a good deal of the vampire in it. This is because it has worked on and through the nervous system, which of all the human systems draws most directly from life-sources. Whatever acts by excitement of the nerves, sucks close from the very spring-heads of life. This is the reason why so many spiritists dry up so and grow skinny. Let the nerve-excitement cease, and they will become as fat as Christians.

New mediums must be found, of course, from time to time, to preserve the apostolical succession and to spread the true doctrine. An approved mode for this purpose is, to set up a "developing circle," presided over by persons of experience, and in a series of sessions to try all comers, and as good subjects shall appear, to train them in the manifestations and work them gradually into the regular professional order.

Civille, even in perfect health, was naturally as sensitive as a healthy human being could possibly be, from mere purity of temperament, and fineness of fibre and organization. Unhealthy conditions of life — want of exercise, of sunlight, of fresh air, for instance — had recently caused her to drift beyond the line of healthy susceptibility, both in mind and in body, and the quick wits of her spiritist friends had with considerable delight recognized in her the qualities for a medium of rare and perhaps unequalled powers. Experienced as they were in managing their affairs, they had said nothing directly to her of any ulterior purpose, but had with much shrewdness confined themselves to discussions and explanations of the subject generally and of such phenomena as she had herself undergone or witnessed ; the proper method being, so to arrange that the novice shall seem to acquire by her own seeking and her own finding, the mysterious powers or knowledges which are to fascinate her into a professor. Acquirements thus made are most treasured ; convictions thus reached are as nearly impregnable as human convictions can be.

Adrian and Civille, passing under one of the archways, stopped at a door midway in one side of it, that looked very dark and mysterious in the deep shadow of the place. Opening this door, they entered a roomy and deserted-looking hall, ascended a broad staircase along one of the walls, and after one or two turns in corridors, knocked at the door of a rear room and were admitted. The room was one of the great empty gloomy chambers proper to the place and the occasion. Its floor was matted instead of carpeted, though it was winter. The furniture, which would have been sufficiently abundant and comfortable for a small room, seemed like a few forlorn sticks of things neglected in a vast lumber-garret. Only one light was burning ; not a gas-light either, but one of those very ingenious patent solar somethings that burn petroleum or an extract of it, that always smell bad, and smell the worse as you turn them down. This one was burning very dim indeed, and consequently "smelt like fury," as Adrian couldn't help saying to himself. He was desperately tempted to ask Civille if it was a spirit that he smelt. Indeed, in this investigation of his, one of his worst terrors was, the constant recurrence of things that were ridiculous, and that kept distressing him with stifled laughs and jokes. But he watched his thoughts as closely as Christian in passing through the Valley of the Shadow of Death ; for one jeering question or observation would have hopelessly destroyed his whole enterprise. Of course the funnier it was, the harder it was to be grave, and the graver he was, the funnier things became ; and the poor fellow passed through some awful struggles accordingly.

Several men and women were sitting in silence round a table at the further side of the dim room. The woman who had admitted them, recognized Civille, greeted her in a quiet half-whisper, and looked at Adrian.

"My cousin, Mr. Chester," explained Civille, also in a low tone; "he is much interested in our inquiries. Adrian, this is Mrs. Babbles."

Adrian fell readily into the solemn manner and almost soundless utterance which he recognized as the conventional fashion of the place. How could he without impoliteness do otherwise ? So he briefly expressed his assent, and his expectations of enlightenment.

"Come and be seated," said Mrs. Babbles. She led them towards the table, and made room for Civille between two men and for Adrian a little way off between two women. Was this a precaution against any possible conspiracy ? It is the invariable rule to divide companies in this way at these meetings, at any rate.

The company, eight or ten in number, were sitting round the table, each with the right hand lying on the table, the left being superimposed on the right hand of the next neighbor.

The session occupied about an hour. Most of this time was occupied in gravely and earnestly sitting perfectly still very hard in the dark. Once or twice the people sang some verses, of an indeterminate hortatory kind, about loving and so on, to such old tunes as Balerma and Golden Hill. From time to time, Mrs. Babbles, who seemed to be the ruler of the feast, would ask in a low tone,

"Is any spirit present ?" "Does any spirit wish to communicate with us ?"

Adrian could not sing, as he did not know the words used; but he could hear Civille's clear sweet full voice amidst the nasal head tones that all the rest of them used. Ever and anon, in the dimness, one or another of the patient sitters drew a long breath, or changed posture. The noises of the street came only muffled and dulled, to the remote room, in such a way as almost to show off and heighten the silence. Adrian, not expecting any thing in particular, and not very credulous, was however imaginative and impressible. The darkness and silence, the mysterious expectancy of the rest, seemed to intensify his senses. More than once, at Mrs Babbles' questions, he fancied he heard some faint knocks or snaps in the table before him, or in the floor beneath; but he held his peace; no one else seemed to hear them; he judged that it was his own excited fancy.

All at once Adrian was aware that there was a commotion within the breast of his left-hand neighbor, a woman. She gave three or four deep and vigorous sighs, almost groans. Then she withdrew her hand for a moment from under Adrian's, and smote her breast therewith repeatedly. Then she turned to Adrian and spoke with awful solemnity, but in the low voice which was the rule :

"I have a communication for you."

"It will give me great pleasure to receive it," murmured the favored youth, with equal gravity.

"I am impressed," continued the fair speaker, "that you are in near relations with the lady who came with you."

"That's very extraordinary," answered Adrian, throwing into his voice a tone of as much astonishment as he could assume — "very extraordinary, indeed. We are cousins — not very near though, and we like each other very much."

This was a sufficiently presumptuous claim, no doubt, in its assertion as to Civille's sentiments; but the

artful young man had on the moment
conceived the wicked idea of furnishing the medium a hint for more revelations, just to see how it would
work.

"Yes," resumed the medium, with
a self-satisfied manner, "all communications from the spirit-land through
me have always been perfectly relia-
ble. I have great power of discerning truth. You would try in vain to
conceal it from me. I am impressed
that you are to be very happy with
your chosen companion."

"That is a very pleasant message,'
observed Adrian, gravely, but amused
at the success of his little trick. He
did not notify the seeress that his
chosen companion was Miss Ann
Button.

As no further messages or manifestations could be coaxed from the spirit-
land, the chief priestess after a time
suggested that as the conditions were
in that respect apparently unfavora-
ble, the exercises of the occasion
should be varied.

"Many lovely things" observed
Mrs. Babbles, with seriousness, "have
already come to us through inspiration
in the trance state. It has been strongly impressed upon me, to-day, that
such revelations are now about us, and
are awaiting a suitable medium. Perhaps our dear friend Miss Van Braam,
will consent to permit any communications which may be offered through
her? Professor Pawson Clawson said
Miss Van Braam was a seer already.
I am sure she will not refuse to help
forward the great cause?"

Civille, slowly, and, Adrian thought
reluctantly, arose from her place at the
table, and took an arm-chair which
Mrs. Babbles placed for her, and a
little more light was now turned on.
One of the two men between whom
Civille had been sitting, a big fellow

with a red face and straight hair, got
up, somewhat as if it were a matter of
course; placed a chair before Civille,
and seating himself in it, would have
taken her hands. She however looked
to Mrs. Babbles and then toward Adrian, saying,

"I prefer my cousin, Mrs. Babbles."

The big man rose up readily enough.
Adrian had experienced a pretty sharp
shock of anger at the idea of this rather greasy-looking person touching Civille, and he was extremely pleased to
find that she felt the same prejudice.
It did not occur to him that he himself took a liberty in touching her.
Few people reason in that way. The
definition of right and wrong which
the Bushman chief gave to his cate-
chising spiritual father the missionary
—not result of many anxious lessons
—is more or less the rule for most of
us — "It is wrong for another man to
take away my wives; it is right for me
to take away his."

Adrian sat down, and under the
instructions of the experienced Mrs.
Babbles, first made a few magnetic
passes from Civille's forehead, down
her arms; and then took her hands in
his, crossing arms however, so that
right held right and left left. The
grasp which he was shown is peculiar;
thumb is laid against thumb, and the
fingers of each hand clasped over the
other, lying across its back, so that
the palms are firmly pressed together,
as magnetic surfaces.

"What am I to do?" asked Adrian; "do I make no motions?"

"No; sit still, and be perfectly
calm," said Mrs. Babbles; "let your
thoughts be concentrated upon the
subject, and your will be firm and steady that she shall pass under your control, and sleep. Look steadily at the
point between her eyebrows. And let

your thoughts be kind and well wishing; and be open to all good influences from any spirits that may be near you; in a peaceful harmony with the universe around."

Adrian did so. It was easy enough to wish well to the spiritual and lovely girl who reclined before him. As if any human being could wish her otherwise than well! he said to himself.

So he collected his consciousness, and substituted for the ordinary swift successions of his thoughts, one single quiet, but steady and concentrated volition. "Sleep, Civille!" he continuously willed.

The others sat around in silence, or with a few scarcely audible words, now and then. Adrian, although he projected — so to speak — much of his conscious life in the effort of will which he directed toward his lovely cousin, yet had abundance of consciousness left to consider the situation in which for the first time in his life, he found himself: close to a singularly attractive young woman, in actual contact with her person, and aware that she was deliberately surrendering herself to him, to receive his commands, to do his will, to obey him. For a few moments, the large soft pathetic deep gray eyes looked straight into the strong clear blue ones. Then, while Adrian looked, very slowly, very steadily, under his gaze the translucent white lids floated downward over iris and eye, and were sealed shut. Civille smiled faintly, and with a little sigh and a nestling movement laid her head upon the back of the chair; she whispered, "I'm *so* sleepy!" and was silent: and then her breathing became regular, like a pulse, and with the smile still on her lips, she was asleep.

Is this magnetizing? Adrian asked himself — it is more like being magnetized! — for a feeling utterly new to him — such as he had never dreamed could exist in any one, or for any thing, — a warm living breath, as it seemed, but it was a deep throb of emotion too, swept over him or around him, as if from some infinite depth; or it was as if he felt that in those moments his own life budded and bloomed as a flower before his eyes, into its perfect opening. "What excess of sweetness," the feeling was — for it could not reach words, nor be contained in them — "What excess of sweetness, to be permitted so near to one so lovely!" Nor was that all; for even while he felt this ineffable influx, as it seemed to him, from some unheard-of spiritual Eden, from a yet farther distance, from a depth infinitely within that other depth, a still profounder throb, a still more moving emotion, a still lovelier consciousness opened and bloomed and arose upon or around or within him — "We are one!" was this thought. And for the time being, it was assuredly so. The magnetic union is even mystically perfect. It required a nature as intuitional as Adrian's, however, to feel it so instantly and so fully.

But it was not his office to experience emotions or delight himself in dreams of his own; and with a resolute effort he directed his mind as wholly as he could to the beautiful passive girl before him, and away from his own consciousnesses. Perhaps ten minutes passed in this silence, the soft pulses of the joined hands throbbing against each other until Adrian fancied that streams of vital force intermingled and exchanged through the magic ring of their arms almost as perceptibly as running water.

"Ask her if she is asleep," said Mrs. Babbles, softly.

" Are you asleep, Civille ? "

There was an effort to speak; but the delicate lips framed no distinct word. In a few moments more however, repeating the question, enforced with a special volition and command to reply, an articulate " Yes " was given, and the sensitive was fully *en rapport* with the magnetizer; surprisingly fully, considering the short time and extent of their magnetic relation. A number of questions were suggested by the company, put by Adrian, and answered with more or less coherence by Civille. They were sufficiently commonplace ; — Were there any spirits about ? What sphere had she got into ? What is old Mr. Brown doing now, at No. 666 Eleventh Avenue ? Can you go to Europe ? to the North Pole ? What are the prospects of the Cause ? Adrian couldn't help thinking that his charming victim — for the feeling that she was helpless, a victim, kept coming up in his mind, — showed excellent good sense in her replies; for they were little, except " I can't see ; it is all cloudy; there is somebody, that I don't recognize ; it is cold ;" and so on ; for, he said to himself, I should have said just about the same ! But the company were still more edified; for, Mrs. Babbles said, it was beyond all expectation that in ˙so short a time any one should become so strongly clairvoyant; and the subject, she observed, would obviously very soon become an independent clairvoyant investigator.

" Independent how ? " asked Adrian.

" Can go into the trance state by herself, whenever she wishes," was the reply. " You are so good a magnetizer, and your magnetism is so congenial, that you will carry her forward very rapidly."

Now while these vague or merely curious questions were being put, some others all at once occurred to Adrian, which he proceeded to put for himself, and to which he received answers unexpectedly definite. It was reasonable to suppose, Adrian however reflected, that these questions, being put with a vivid actual interest of the asker's own, may have carried a great deal more power with them for that reason, and thus may have evoked a corresponding exertion of mind in the clairvoyant. Still, the replies, though remarkably pat and terse in wording, were articulated in a slow difficult way, as if the speaker were impeded or weighed down or held back.

" A business offer has been made to me," asked Adrian. " Shall I accept it ? "

" No."

" I am interested about another business matter, involving much money abroad. Will it succeed ? "

" No money will come."

Then the thought occurred to Adrian — if he could veil his questions so as to be safe before these strangers, to ask his prophetess about matters of far other importance than even the great Mr. Button's publication business, or the vast Scrope Estate in England.

" There is still another matter in which I am interested, along with a person who is concerned with both those other affairs. That person I dreamed about, Wednesday night."

" *Can't catch you !* "

At this reply, which was not so much an answer to any thing at the moment in Adrian's conscious thoughts, as it was a solution to the excessively disagreeable problem of his dream about being chased by Miss Button, Adrian was much startled. But he asked again, with a distinct sense of running a risk:

"Some one has been stealing. Who is it?"

"*The other one.*"

Adrian could make nothing out of this; the very clerk who had denounced her, it might mean — or the very detective who was shadowing her. But in spite of him these four answers delivered in the slow calm way, and with the delaying articulation of the magnetic sleep, impressed him exceedingly. He could not help a conviction that they might, whether or not they actually did, convey knowledge from some source or by some channel other than the ordinary ones. But he judged it not best to venture any further; and so he let go of his cousin's hands, and after leaving her alone for a few moments, summoned her out of her sleep by the usual mode of reversed passes. After congratulations from the company, Adrian and Civille took leave, as they had still to visit the Philosopher of the Germ, and devote another hour to investigating the New Universe. Does a truly philosophic mind require more than an hour to investigate a universe?

They reached the abode of the great and philosophic being whom they were to meet, without difficulty, Civille, to Adrian's pleasure, and somewhat to his surprise, saying in reply to an inquiry, that she was not only not fatigued, but refreshed rather, by her excursion into dreamland. And she inquired in turn if he were not tired in consequence of sending her thither. No, not at all.

CHAPTER XVII.

GREAT and exceptional souls naturally gather into great and exceptional communities. Where vast numbers of human beings are crowded, heaped, rammed together as the enormous forces of human passions and pursuits drive and compress them in great cities, there are stirring the immense powers that great administrative minds love to wield, there are living the inquiring and waiting souls that great teachers yearn to instruct, there are heaped and heaping treasures such as the ambitious merchant longs to amass, which the ambitious thief or gambler or stock-speculator longs to get away from somebody else. Napoleon, Cuvier, Laffitte, Cartouche, each could not but come to Paris. Rothschild, Carlyle, Miller, Zadkiel, could not but reside in London. And Astor and Stewart, or Jacob Little and James Fisk, Horace Greeley or Bill Tweed, Doctor Brandreth or Mr. Vanderbilt, Mr. Barnum or Mr. Tarbox Button, or that great and profound genius S. P. Quinby Anketell, A.M., the Elucidator of the New Universe, could not but live in New York. The vaster the ambition, the loftier or more strange the doctrine, in like proportion is it more indispensable that it come to the great city. If your teachings can be received by only one soul in a thousand, then in a whole state of a million of population you could have but a thousand followers, and you can neither find them nor assemble them. But in a city of a million, they can all meet you any evening. Mr. Anketell was therefore most of all impelled to come to New York; for his views were — if there is any truth in arithmetic — one hundred times as vast as any just referred to. For the Anketellicalists were at the time of Adrian's visit not over about ten in number. New York is reckoned — suburbs and all — at a million souls. Hence, it is obvious, Mr. Anketell could find but one mind in a hundred thousand, instead of one in a thousand, that was

able to receive his doctrine ; he was
accordingly exactly a hundred-fold
the more pressed and driven into New
York. Could reasoning be more conclusive ?

Mr. Anketell's residence was a re-
spectable-looking house on a cross
street, not very far from Madison
Square, and between Madison and
Fourth Avenues. It was what is called
an "English basement" house, having
a door only one step above the sidewalk
instead of at the top of a long flight
of steps, and having within this door
a small sitting-room at the front,
while the hall led past it back to the
stairs, and past them to a larger room
filling the rear half of the ground
floor. This was occupied at present
as a dining-room and sitting-room
both ; for the exigencies of the cause
to which Mr. Anketell was devoting
his life had at the moment somewhat
crowded the establishment. To tell
the truth, besides the philosopher's
own family, he was at present presiding over the whole band of his
declared followers, assembled within
his household.

"S. P. Quinby Anketell," read
Adrian as they reached the door —
"S. P. Q. A. — Senatus Populus Que
Americanus. Not a bad set of initials
for the leader of such a movement as
this." — And between the ringing of
the bell and the opening of the door
he told Civille of a sign he remembered to have seen at a silversmith's
in Fulton Street. Its four initials,
the mighty ancient quaternion of S.
P. Q. R. had attracted him ; but on
approaching, instead of the sonorous
"Senatus Populus Que Romanus,"
he found the practical business announcement " Silver Plate Quickly
Repaired." " It was like the dust of
Alexander stopping a beer-barrel," he
said. But after his fashion, he irrev-

erently figured to himself another
meaning for Mr. Anketell's initials,
but which he did not think proper to
repeat to his companion, nor, — he
hoped — must she necessarily be referred to in the same. This was,
" Silly People Quickly Attracted."

While he moralized, they were
shown into the waiting-room, and
asked to sit for a few minutes.
Adrian improved the occasion to ask
Civille about the position of Mr.
Anketell's doctrines as related to those
of Spiritism.

" Anketellicalism," answered the
young lady, with the exceeding funny
gravity of a young lady's metaphysi-
cal utterances, " neither asserts nor
denies. It includes and reconciles all
other beliefs. Its roots are so much
deeper than any, that from it they
can all be traced, and by it can all
be explained and combined."

" Then it goes yet deeper," commented Adrian, " than the famous
preacher's statement that ' every great
truth is composed of two incompatible
extremes ' ? "

" I never heard that thought," said
Civille. " But it is Mr. Anketell's.
All truth is his."

" Well," said Adrian, " yes. All
truth is every man's. In that wealth,
monopoly is not to be feared ; we
may all amass our utmost. So that
even Napoleon's saying of ' The tools
to him that can use them,' loses its
bad meaning if truths are the tools.
Then one can believe in the spirit
doctrines and in Mr. Anketell's too ? "

" Why, of course," said the young
lady ; " but they are truths — facts
— not doctrines. But let him tell
you himself," she added, for steps
approached, and a tall man entered
from the rear room.

" My dearest child," he said, in a
solemn clear voice, " welcome. The

spirit of the place lacked you." And taking her hand, he pressed it; and held it, as Adrian observed, longer than was absolutely necessary.

Civille introduced Adrian, as her cousin, and a sincere inquirer after new truth.

"Most rejoiced to receive you," said Mr. Anketell, in the same solemn clear voice. "But, my child," — he turned to Civille, "there is no new truth. All truth is eternal; without beginning or end."

"But," suggested Adrian, "until our existence becomes unconditional, we must use conditioned words, must we not? Is it not practically correct, therefore, to have a word 'new'? It means, as to truths, not truths just manufactured, but truths just found; — New to me, if I never found them before?"

While Adrian spoke, he and Mr. Anketell looked straight into each other's eyes. The great Reformer was a tall and rather slender person, decently enough clad in black, fair, with light blue watchful eyes, a bloodless face, a sharp high projecting forehead, thin features, intelligent enough, marked with thought, and with a look of preternatural gravity. Adrian, summing him up in his swift intuitional way, felt, rather than thought, that he disliked him. But this may have been because the Reformer was so very paternal with Civille. However, the watchful face smiled as Adrian ended, and the great thinker condescended to approve.

"Ah!" he said, "this is a singularly acute mind. A just distinction. But the New Language — which Mr. Jobraker is advocating in my behalf, will obviate such questions. My new categories of thought and speech will forever prevent any confusion between the absolute and the relative.

One word per thought, — one thought per word."

"Ah," said Adrian, "Then the new language is yours?"

"Yes," assented Mr. Anketell, with visible unobtrusiveness — "merely one of the departments of the New Universe. But, my young friends, The Germ was upon development when you rang. Come in and take part in our little conference. I was just setting forth the sum of the New Universe, as it reached me this morning at half past ten precisely. I have improved two epithets and a definition since last week."

And while Adrian considered briefly within himself, how deep and broad a Universe that could be which two epithets and a definition could improve, Mr. Anketell showed them into the dining room, where, around the extension table — now only set with a common red damask cover on which lay a few papers and writing materials — sat the whole strength of the company, so to speak : a whole New Universe in one dingy back room. Such is the concentrative might of Mind!

The little band who were here incubating, — if one may say so — upon the Egg of the Future, seemed to Adrian, glancing round the room as he took his seat, like a rarefied extract of the *Solidarité de l'Avenir.* Indeed, most if not all of them were members of that extremely respectable body. The chief difference between the two assemblages was in their spirit; for while the units of the *Solidarité* were even ludicrously centrifugal in their tendency, there was evident here an equally predominant spirit of perfectly unconditional acquiescent discipleship. The two conditions may just as well co-exist in the same mind as the uproar of the boys in recess, along with their stillness in school-hours.

Mr. Anketell took a chair at one end of the table.

"Perhaps," he said, with his grave manner and clear articulation "Mr. Morue will read my summary once more from the beginning. We have a new friend on this occasion; and it is well that Miss Van Braam should receive the new statement as completed. Great things depend upon it, and upon her."

Mr. Morue, a good looking young fellow with a sweet expression and fine soft dark eyes, bowed and complied. The statements which he read contained very much that was — but is it not impertinent to assume to praise such things? Let a few sentences suffice; and write for circular containing summary of the New Universe, to S. P. Quinby Anketell, New York City, enclosing Fifty cents.

MR. MORUE'S READING.

All that exists is either Action or Result.

This is true throughout the Universe.

Therefore it is true in symbol as well as in fact.

Voice is a symbol of fact.

In Voice the sound is Action; it terminates in Result.

Therefore all Language falls into these two :

1. Sound.   2. Stop.

The first, because the easiest of all possible Sounds is the open Ah ! — when the mouth opens, and we vocalize. The first of all possible stops is 'm ! — when the mouth shuts and we are silent.

We have therefore the One Eternal Word :

AHM !

(This the speaker vocalized with much power, giving a good broad long Ah ! and bringing his lips together with almost a slap at the end.)

As a single instance corroborative, take the Sacred Syllable of the plurality of worshipping humanity, the Buddhists'— Om !

All the rest of Real Language must of necessity be developed from this one word, by modifications. These are of course only such as the vocal organs can supply.

Here the reader gave a carefully arranged series of modifications, such as :

1. Of the Vowel : ee'm ! au'm ! oo'm !

2. Of the Consonant : ah'p ! ah'f ! ah'g !

3. Of the Effort : ahbabah'm ! ahgagah'g !

And he briefly showed the infinite number of combinations — that is, of words, deducible from this single syllable ; which must include not only all the existing words of the present languages — collectively termed the Scatterary or Inartistic — but that inexhaustible remainder of vocables on which the New Universal Language can draw at sight and without end for expression of the whole New Universe of Ideas.

The Name of the New Language is that which could not but arise in the rightly constituted mind. It embodies beginning, sound, end, thus :

M'AH'M.

And for instance corroborative of the justness of the choice, observe that this name embodies the first call of the human being to its mother, and the accepted expression of the man's reverence for the woman.

———

With like reasonings and illustrations did the exposition proceed. As the first part, that relating to language, drew to a close, Mr. Anketell spoke a few words aside to Civille, and both, arising, disappeared into the small ante-room. Mr. Morue went on, explaining that the only emendations had now been read, and that the Teacher was not required for the rest, which he should however repeat "chiefly" he said, "for inculcation."

This was however if any thing still more interesting to our neophyte Adrian than what had preceded it; for it contained the explanation of the development, not merely of sound or language, but successively of Matter, Life, Thought, Society, and Perfection. This whole system, thus set forth, constituted the New Universe. No considerations but those of Space and Time prevent their being here given in full. At present (the statement went on), men are scarcely advanced beyond that base and sordid condition of scattered life in disjunct item, which the pre-Anketellical but only half-enlightened Fourier so well designated by calling them " miserable civilizees." Even in the dawn of our New Universe, even in the first unfolding of The Germ, must we make allowances for the weakness, for the slavishness of mind, so long locked down upon the ages : even the New Universe itself must not clash too violently with the recognized forms of thought and feeling. The old religions, as well as the old political and social conditions, will swiftly fade as our dawn opens into the coming day. Yet the wise Teacher ordains not to diverge too far, and he chooses for the present name of the New System, one which shall express his Greatest Discovery, the Identity of All Forces by the marriage of the Material with the Divine.

I have thus revealed to you the Elements, — the reader ended, — of the New Universe : Let its Spirit receive the New Baptism : what Anketell teaches — what the Anketellicalists believe and propagate, let them, until the New Language shall afford its full and real and mysteriously significant name, mention and proclaim abroad as

ELECTRO–CHRISTIANITY !

At this magnificent climax there was quite a sound of delighted applause, and some offered thanks to Mr. Morue, while others eagerly entered into discussions on the many questions that every one can see arising from these immensely fruitful propositions. In the midst of this happy excitement, Adrian, who was sitting with his back towards the door where they had come in, heard a quick step, a rustle of garments ; a hand was laid on his shoulder, and Civille, in a gasping whisper, said in his ear,

"O Adrian, take me away quick ! "

Astonished beyond measure, the young man sprang up and turned to look at his cousin. Such a frozen white horrified face! It was fright, grief, indignation, all awful pain in one. Without another word, she stepped to the door leading not to the ante-room, but to the hall, and so towards the outer door. Adrian, with an indistinct feeling as if murder had been done, but without a word, hurried after her. So swift were their motions that they were both out of the room before the stream of chattering congratulatory talk could fairly subside. As Adrian got into the hall, Civille had already reached the front door, and was hurriedly endeavoring to open it. At this moment, the great Mr. Anketell appeared from the hall-door of the little ante-room, looking, as nearly as Adrian could see in the rather weak gas-light, somewhat flustered for a philosophic teacher. He went straight to Civille, without observing Adrian, and promptly putting one arm round her waist, said,

"You mistake entirely. Come back a moment."

"No!" she said vigorously, "I don't mistake! Let go!" And she gave him a push. Adrian gave him something more effectual — a tremendous straight right-hand hit under the left ear, that lifted him with a bang against the door, and then dropped him in a limp heap on the carpet. With one jerk the angry fellow slung the Great Teacher backward into the hall, just as one or two startled disciples opened the door of the dining room.

"Pick up that dirty dog!" he said: and opening the front door, he hurried his cousin out. She had kept on her bonnet, and he had as it happened kept his hat with him, so that they made no unconventional display in the street.

The night was bright and cold, and patches of a slight snow that had fallen in the morning, were still pure and white in corners along the sidewalk. Adrian felt Civille grow heavy on his arm.

"Don't faint," he said, and snatching up a handful of clean snow, laid it promptly on her forehead. The shock, along with her own keen resolute will, helped her.

"I won't," said she, with her teeth set tight — and she didn't. But it was a pretty near thing. An empty hack drove by, and Adrian, hailing it, took Civille directly home. She sat silent the whole way, leaning back as if exhausted, and Adrian, though he

thought industriously, said not a word.

When they reached the old shabby white house it was quite late, and no light was visible except a dim one through the front door fanlight. The door however, as it appeared on trying it, was to their surprise not fast. They entered the hall together; — for Adrian thought best to see that nothing was wrong. A female form arose from a chair at one side of the hall and came forward, bearing a bundle.

"Who's that?" said Civille, startled.

"It's me, 'm," said a sharp voice.

"Why, Katy, what are you up for?"

"Yis'm, I think as much," was the reply, with obvious wrath. — "Misther Van Braw he says he was tired out, and I was to set up for yez, and he's gone to bed sure, and I've done it, haven't I?"

"You have, I should think," said Civille, gravely.

"An good night to yez, 'm. I didn't hire out for a watchman at all, so I didn't!"

And the enraged Irishwoman made for the front door, with the energy — and reason — of one million Fenians.

"Why," said Civille, "you only came this noon. My father's old; he didn't know."

"And sure he'll know next time thin!"

"Hold on," interposed Adrian sternly; "let's see what you're carrying off there!"

"An it's a woman's duds, sorr. There; will ye plaze examine!" With fingers that shook in an extraordinary access of fury, she untied her bundle and spread it out on the hall table.

"Oh, tie it up and go," said Civille. "Don't stop her, Adrian. You can have one day's wages, Katy, if you choose."

"No, thank ye 'm. And thank ye sorr," returned the furious serving woman. "An it's moighty little there's to stale in this house any way."

"You've looked, have you?" broke in Adrian, coolly.

"And the curse o Crom'll on sich naygurs!" went on the fury, not finding a perfectly handy parry to this hit; and out she bounced and off she went, a long stream of scolding dying away as she passed down the street.

"Sit down a few moments," said Adrian: "rest you a little; then we'll look round the house and see that every thing is safe; it will do no harm, and you'll sleep better."

So they went into the parlor, lit the gas, and Civille took her own chair by the fire-place. After a few moments Adrian said,

"Cousin Civille, please to tell me if you think proper, what happened at Anketell's."

She started; "Oh no!" Then she considered a moment, and then — reconsidered. "Yet why not? It was very considerate of you, Cousin Adrian, not to ask me before. Thank you. And perhaps you ought to know. But what did you do to him, Adrian?"

"Broke his jaw, I hope; I know I lamed my knuckles," replied the young man, examining his right hand, which was in fact scarified a little as will happen when one strikes very straight and hard on a sharp bone. "I can't write for a week, to judge from the sensation."

Civille was about to run for arnica, but Adrian wouldn't let her, and she then proceeded to describe her interview with the philosophic Mr. Anketell. He had asked her into the ante-room, she said, on pretence of wishing to consult her about a fur-

ther and still more mysterious doctrine upon which, he said, his soul had been deeply pondering for a long time. The statement had begun with some rhapsodies about the ancient idea of an outer and an inner doctrine; about Civille's wonderful qualities; about the Platonic theory of souls made in two halves, which belonged to each other by the very fact itself if they happened to meet, and so on. Then he went into a theory of right and wrong as applied to himself, which ended with a series of propositions in substance somewhat like these: "A truly organized life would be immortal in this body. The society of our other half soul is the one first greatest requisite for this immortality. No law can be paramount to such a truth as that. And moreover, the New Universe is developing so swiftly that my laws will very soon be received all over the earth. This earth is the brain of the Universe; I am the brain of this earth. In less than one year, you will sit at my feet and worship me as a God. In three years I shall be ruling all this earth from the eternal centre of earthly power in Rome. And," concluded Civille, with a great effort, — "he insisted upon it that I was his Queen; that the right way for me to learn his doctrine was to be his; and — ugh! — before I could get away he kissed me!"

In spite of his anger, Adrian could not help laughing at her disgust; for at the recollection, she gave her cheek and her mouth a terrible scrubbing with her handkerchief.

"Augh!" she repeated, — "and he's as cold and damp as a toad!"

"So you just ran away?" queried Adrian.

"Yes: I told him to ask Mrs. Anketell about it, however."

"Mrs. Anketell! Is the old scoundrel married!"

"Why yes; long ago. He said something about his wife being perfectly willing; but I ran out."

"Good riddance," commented Adrian. He was on the point of adding the dangerous suggestion that he hoped she might escape as well from the rest of her psychological investigations; but he stopped just in time. He recommended instead that nothing should be said to her father about the adventure, as it would only distress him, to which she agreed, — not knowing however, poor girl, how much distress she had already occasioned him: and now they made a hasty inspection of doors and windows, which were found all safe; and Civille, as they came round again to the front door, shyly invited Adrian to occupy their "spare bedroom" and breakfast with them in the morning. He however excused himself, in part because he suspected what was indeed true, that Civille would have to get breakfast herself, and ought not to have the additional bother of a visitor; and partly because he had promised to spend the next day — Sunday to wit — with Mr. Button's family, and somehow he preferred to go thither from his lodgings. As Civille came in with him, in readiness to lock the door, he turned and said,

"Good night."

"Good night," she responded, with sleep already drooping cloudily over her lovely gray eyes, and a smile at her own fatigue. Some impulse — a wholly inscrutable one, — was it the example of the philosophic Mr. Anketell? — suddenly sprang up in the young man's mind. So quickly that she could not resist, he had one arm round her waist, the other round her neck, and had pressed a long hearty kiss upon her flower-soft lips. They trembled under his.

"Go quick," she said. He could not understand whether there was sorrow or displeasure in her voice; there was something. But without a word he opened the door and departed; and all the way to his boarding house he was saying to himself

"I wonder what I did that for?"

PART VI.

CHAPTER XVIII.

ADRIAN, with the unconscious good fortune of youth, slept as he usually did, one deep, refreshing sleep, all night long, and awoke, as one should awake; not with sticky eyes, a sense of having been slowly boiled, a sluggish, unwilling recognition of returning, conscious thought, and under an after-night or spiritual darkness of ill-nature, but altogether clean; as one rises promptly from a piece of work handsomely done and finished; bright; jolly.

Not that he sprang instantly out of bed, as the exemplars do — confound them! Is there anything so hateful or so impudent as a good example? The Duke of Wellington used to say, "When it's time to turn over it's time to turn out." N. B. He's dead. Adrian had more sense; he knew enough to lie still a little while and be comfortable. The moments between healthy waking and judicious arising are the honey-moon of the day; in them we welcome the sunlight and its life; rejoice with it before settling down to those sober, conventional utilities of the day's work which begin with clothes and breakfast. The soul is calm and happy; and the thoughts are either quiescent, while a mere sense of sufficient well-being, of sweetness and light, fills the consciousness, or they brood, with that spontaneous, lucid, unconscious evolution which belongs to the highest activities of the mind, over any subject that is present. Genius is simply the action of the mind, as in lying awake in bed before getting up to breakfast. Not that there are not other climaxes of genius. Perhaps it would be more accurate to turn the statement end for end. The action of the mind in bed while we lie awake in the morning before getting up to breakfast, is of the nature of genius. That is, sometimes.

What Adrian considered was, however, a very practical question: What is to be done about Civille? And his statement of the case to himself and his reasonings upon it ran somewhat thus: —

Civille herself, just now, is a spirit not quite sufficiently embodied. It is a case of extreme fineness of organization physically, and extreme spirituality mentally. The risk, therefore, is of over-activity and over-excitement, and of views and actions unpractical, visionary, but not selfish nor materialized; just the contrary, indeed; much too unselfish, much too disregardful of established opinions, of friends, of her own comfort.

Second, the influences around Civille. There is that sunless, ill-aired, ill-drained old house. Her wiry old father may not feel it, but it is steadily lowering the tone of her vitality; thinning down the outer wall, as it were, of her frame, so frail already that it is translucent (translucent to my will, thought the young man, with a distinct thrill as he

thought it); so that all of a sudden the soul will quite slip out and escape us, if we are not careful. There are the doctrines and atmosphere of the *Solidarité*. But what are they? Only a clatter. Nothing there can attract Civille except what she believes to exist there, whether it does or not — an earnest wish for the good of humanity. Then the spirits. For her, this sort of thing is unsuitable. It is a tippling of the soul; as peculiarly dangerous for her high-wrought and already over-spiritual personality as the tippling of liquor for the already over-vivid life of Edgar A. Poe. Also, the Anketellical Universe. That's eliminated from the problem, thanks to the creator of it himself. Civille never will want to see *him* again. And this may help wean her from the *Solidarité*, too. Last of all, the detective, Amos Olds — the charge of theft — the men that Civille has repeatedly seen, or thought she has seen, following her, — doubtless on the part of Olds. This is the worst matter of all, because it is so dangerous to handle. With whom shall I advise about it? Jenks and Trainor? Olds himself? The central police authorities? Mr. Button? None of them seemed a welcome or even a safe counsellor; and the quiet and ready intelligence of Mr. Bird, the reporter, suggested itself to Adrian. So did the long and stiff figure of Doctor Toomston, — ungenial, conventional, conservative, but said to be kind-hearted and sensible.

Below or behind all Adrian's thoughts and purposes was a doubt, — obscure, not perhaps fully recognized — too painful to be fully recognized — by the young man himself, and which he certainly would not have hinted to another; such a doubt as comes into minds that reach after all the possibilities of a case; the doubt of a judge, not of an advocate · such a doubt as has tormented many a friend to some "good man struggling with the storms of fate," under specific slander or general evil repute ; a doubt based, perhaps, upon a humble sense of the doubter's own weakness, or upon a profound apprehension of the weaknesses of humanity at large. It was simply this : Suppose Civille has done it ?

Who has not felt such a question lurking, as it were, in the dark corner of his soul, when some near and dear friend has been accused? It is not suspicion ; it is not wickedness. It is knowledge waiting for more knowledge. It is colorless of feeling meanwhile, and neither chilled by evil passion, nor warmed by that which is kindly. Not that the truth of the charge would have diminished one whit Adrian's regard for Civille ; his was not a nature to forsake the unhappy. Indeed, the fact would have proved her, to him, not bad, but simply ill ; more unfortunate, more unhappy, than she was already. For in spite of her ordinary calm and sweet and kindly composure of manner, and earnest seriousness of occupation, the whole impression which she had made upon Adrian was of profound sadness. If she were really under the dominion of the odious mania of which she was suspected, could she be in a greater misfortune? And did she not all the more need friends and help, poor lonely thing, the more unfortunate she was? The fact is, that to such a nature as Adrian's, and at his time of life, an actual demonstration of her systematic thieving at Jenks and Trainor's would have riveted his sympathy, his helpful affection, it may almost be said,

more than any good fortune or good qualities in the world. Youth, for lofty natures, is knighthood. Adrian was riding abroad in his first knight-errantry. His shield was yet white ; he was unconsciously longing to do some noble deed that might entitle him to an honorable escutcheon. And of all the incitements of chivalry, the sweetest and loftiest is that of a lovely maiden in distress ; and again and again there floated across Adrian's mind, always full of associated ideas, always making pictures, the wondrous imaginations of Una in the forest, and of the gentle lady in Comus. It was this last, however, with whom he most naturally identified Civille ; for all the vulgar surroundings and impositions that beset her — suspicious policemen, crack-brained reformers, low-bred visionaries, sensual, knavish delusionists — were singularly well represented by the bestial rout, — " a rout of monsters, headed like sundry sorts of wild beasts, but otherwise like men and women," — that persecuted the Lady. As for Comus himself, the part was right aptly filled by the great S. P. Quinby Anketell, whose arguments, indeed, fitted not ill with the sophistries which John Milton has put into the mouth of the son of Circe.

So Adrian thought and thought, and could resolve on nothing satisfactory. He reached one partial conclusion which was sound enough, namely : that for directly influencing Civille herself, the appeal must be made to her own strongest motive qualities, being indeed the same that were now carrying her wrong, if she were in fact going wrong, — the same longing for better things, the same keen desire for higher knowledge and clearer light, the same sweet, unselfish wish for the happiness of others, which were impelling her in her researches into what she believed reforms, and in her work about the charities connected with Dr. Toomston's church. If she was to be induced of herself to discontinue any line of conduct, and to adopt a different one, it must be by showing her that she would, by so doing, save suffering and afford happiness to others.

"If I could fill her mind full of some other and more real occupation," the young man thought, "that is the best thing I could do — that would bring her right. Just as they shake a rattle before babies that cry. I guess there's a good deal of baby in unconscious natures." But he could think of no such occupation, and he knew how difficult it is in this age to find good employment for a single young woman.

Whether anything could be done by the usual means of bringing to bear upon her the influence of friends, that is, a pressure of opinion, seemed very doubtful. But Adrian, with natural good sense, resolved to consult whomsoever should seem safest. He felt himself able to influence Mr. Van Braam, who, kindly and pure and visionary, had no "initiative," and could at most recognize and follow good counsel, but certainly would never suggest any. He finally resolved, as he was to pass the day with the Buttons, to try some hints upon the capitalist himself, whose coarse and rough nature did not necessarily prevent him from being an excellent adviser. Adrian was, however, displeased with himself for the reluctance he could not help feeling to speak to Mr. Button on the subject. He retained his resolution, however; it was a mannish resolution, formed from the conclusions of the reasoning faculties, against the wish of the intuitions

With this unsatisfying but definite purpose in his mind, Adrian arose, and after breakfast set out for Mr. Button's residence, as his day there must needs begin in good season, since it was mostly to be spent elsewhere. This paradox only requires that we take "house" in the antique sense of family. Thus: as for Mr. Button and his house, they served the Lord, to the very best of their abilities, and with a special exclusiveness on Sundays, — or Sabbaths, as they called them, — both they and the stranger within their gates; and much more, then, the near relative and intended member who might sojourn with them. Divine service in the morning, Sunday-school in the afternoon, divine service in the evening — such was the invariable programme, and at all three Mr. Button and his family were strictly holden to appear, "armed and equipped as the law directs," to use an ancient formula for notifying militia gatherings, and, therefore, one not unsuitable for the church militant.

Musing sometimes, sometimes looking about him, Adrian strolled along street and avenue, savoring with full breath the clear, bright, vitalized winter air; when, as he drew near the Buttonian regions, in a street of that peculiarly dreary and gloomy grandeur which belongs to the "brown stone front," — a street that looked indeed about as much like a deep cut through a quarry of old red sandstone as like a double row of human habitations, — as he wandered gazing along beneath the towering precipices of one side of this freestone Petra, he espied on an unobtrusive little tin sign over a basement window the words, "Dr

Codleigh Veroil." With an intuitional flash of vision, Adrian saw at once that the doctor was his right adviser about Civille, whose usual medical attendant he knew him to be, and that of Mr. Button's family also. He had seen the doctor once or twice, and remembered perfectly his handsome, intelligent, kindly face. "A physician is my man, of course," he said to himself, as he unhesitatingly turned in under the "high stoop" and rang the office bell; "the Protestant father confessor, now that soul and body are so much confounded together." And with his thoughts running upon the parallel or contrast between ancient religions and modern ones, he was shown into the office, where Doctor Veroil in a few moments joined him. Without waiting to be embarrassed, Adrian spoke: —

" I must beg your pardon, first of all, doctor, for troubling you so early, and on Sunday; and perhaps it is not a strictly professional errand, either."

The doctor bowed and smiled in his pleasant way, — whose manners are as comfortable and agreeable as those of a polite and successful physician? And Dr. Veroil's handsome, pleasant face, his singularly sympathetic manner, were unmatched even among doctors. Certainly they had made his fortune, for he was already rich. Not that his abilities were not great: they were: he was a trained and scientific practitioner of the very best order; a man of much breadth and strength of thought, and of high accomplishments. besides all his natural gifts. But his manners had secured his abilities a chance; for everybody that looked at him liked him, and nobody who employed him could like any other doctor so well.

His practice might be acceptable or not; successful or not; at the death of a patient, the family of the deceased, as sometimes happens, might dismiss the doctor, as if he had killed their friend. They never think of dismissing their God, and trying another! But even in such a case, the man was surely regretted, though the physician might be changed; and he was usually recalled after one experiment elsewhere.

Adrian, encouraged by Dr. Veroil's good nature, proceeded to introduce himself.

"Very glad to see you, indeed," responded the genial doctor, shaking hands; "I remember perfectly — met you at Mr Button's. Entirely at your service. What can I do for you?"

Adrian hereupon explained that he had ventured to call, for the reason that the doctor was family physician as aforesaid. He fancied that the doctor became very attentive after Mr. Button was mentioned. Valuable patrons, no doubt, he thought. He went on, however, to state as succinctly as he could the substance of his morning's reflections, about the character of Civille, the influences at present operating upon her, and in particular the motives — as he suspected — of some of those around her, namely: to make her a lovely mystic high-priestess of abominations, or at least of delusions.

" Now it seems to me, doctor," he observed at last, " all this amounts, not necessarily to an organization originally bad or ill-proportioned, but to one too good, if anything, and liable to manifestations not of organic defect, but of perversions temporary, I suppose at first; from external causes, and admitting of complete cure."

" Very justly reasoned," assented the doctor, — " very well put ; not a bad diagnosis."

" Well, the real question, the real trouble, is one that all these physical sensibilities and mental excitements lead up to." — The young man paused, moved his seat nearer to the doctor's, and glanced apprehensively round the room

" Not a soul on this whole floor except ourselves," said Dr. Veroil, kindly. Adrian went on, his voice dropping of itself almost to a whisper, —

" The real question is, Can any positive mental disorder have supervened already? For, doctor, the police are actually watching her, on a suspicion — a charge, almost, of kleptomania — of theft from Jenks & Trainor's. And the question is : Is it possible? And if so, is there any remedy?"

It is not easy to startle an experienced physician. But Doctor Veroil positively turned white for a moment.

" Good God ! " he said, below his breath ; " then" — he stopped short. Something in his manner gave Adrian a horrible pain, and his heart stood still. " He knows about it," he thought ; " he believes it ! "

" Let me understand," said Doctor Veroil, as if doubtful whether he had not been on a wrong track ; " whom did you say the police were watching?"

" Why, my cousin — Civille Van Braam."

" Ah — O — yes, — to be sure, but, I thought — beg pardon — you were engaged to Miss Button?"

" I am, doctor," said Adrian, surprised ; " why?"

" Well," said the other, with some hesitation, " I believe I was for the moment confounding the two young ladies in my mind. They are cousins, and both patients of mine." He reflected a moment, and continued, more to himself than to Adrian, " I wish I could have her married, and with a baby of her own to take care of, within just twenty minutes from now ; then she 'd be all right. That 's what balances a woman. She 's very fond of children, too." Then he continued, to Adrian, " You 'd think so, if you 'd seen her cuddle that nigger baby, as Mrs. Button called it, the other day, at the Shadowing Wings. Pretty little thing ! They kicked it out, too, I 'm told ! God Almighty ! " exclaimed the physician, angered at the recollection. Upon Adrian's inquiry, Dr. Veroil told him about the Christian Expediency Infant Expulsion business ; and if sympathy was of any use to him, he should have been much benefited ; for Adrian, younger and less hardened, if not naturally more emotional, quite overflowed with pity and rage : —

" Why, doctor," he said, " that 's the same kind of doctrine that says hell is paved with infants' skulls ! I tell you what : folks that believe such things, or do 'em either, will have a chance to find out for themselves whether it 's paved so or not, it 's my opinion ! "

" Tut, tut, young man ! let them do their own damning, — they 're ready enough. Besides, minds that are ignorant and essentially vulgar are always brutalizing the theories of their betters. Calvinism is n't necessarily so bad as that. The practice of it is n't, at least. Dr. Toomston is about the stiffest Calvinist left in New York, they say. But he 's a good old fellow ; he would n't do one unkind thing to a baby to keep his own soul out of hell, even if he believed God had predestined every baby in the world to eternal damnation."

Breaking off for a moment, he resumed : —

"But all that's none of my business, though theology was always interesting to me. It's a kind of intellectual translation of religion ; there's something wonderful as well as melancholy in seeing great minds exhaust themselves in trying to express in the narrowest sort of human limitations, in stiff, verbal phrases, not merely emotions, which are all exactly the things that words cannot ever touch, — but exactly the highest, the grandest, the remotest, the vastest of all the emotions, — those that lift towards God ! As a jackass undertaking to bray out the soliloquy in Hamlet, so, only infinitely more so, is a doctor of divinity undertaking to define and enunciate religion in sentences. But all that's none of my business — professionally. I'm a doctor of medicine. I'm glad you called, Mr. Chester ; all the parties concerned are good friends of mine, besides being my patients. I will see Miss Van Braam, and advise you and assist you to the best of my ability."

"Thank you very much, doctor ; you relieve me greatly. But there's one further idea of mine that I must ask you about. It is — "

Here the office bell was violently rung, and in a moment the servant brought in and handed the doctor a soiled scrap of paper. Glancing at it, he ordered his carriage instantly, adding, —

"Put in the bay — he's the quickest. Now jump ! " and the man shot out of the door, electrified by the doctor's energy.

"Excuse me, Mr. Chester — business, you know." As he spoke, he took from the table a small case of instruments and another of medicines, slid each into a pocket in a heavy overcoat, and then slid the garment upon himself. Hardly had he done so when the impatient tramp of a horse and the pounding of heavy wheels smote sharply on the ear, as the equipage rattled round to the front door and halted.

"Come along," continued the doctor, smiling and peremptory ; "you shall tell me the rest in the carriage ; it won't put you ten minutes out of your way, and no matter if it does."

Adrian followed without a word. The two men entered the carriage ; the doctor, reading a moment from his scrap of paper, gave his driver a number in one of the dirtier parts of the Eighth Ward, to wit, in Greene Street, below Houston ; and the strong, high-fed bay horse sprang off at a speedy trot.

"I declare," said Adrian, who knew the difference between a clothes-horse and a trotting horse, — "I declare, how square he trots, and how he does get over the ground ! "

"Yes indeed," said Doctor Veroil. "Very tough beast, too ; take me two years to use him up, I expect. A man whose time is worth ten dollars an hour can't spare horse-flesh."

"But shall you kill him in two years ? " said Adrian, startled.

"O, no ; but pounding over these stone pavements will stiffen him up by that time so that he can't do my work."

"Ten dollars an hour," repeated Adrian ; "but I didn't know the people in Greene Street could pay such prices."

"This one can't — nor any price, I expect, poor thing ! She has been a patient of mine before ; about used up, I guess. Physicians have to do a good deal of gratuitous work, you know. We make the rich folks pay for the poor, in part. I send a young friend of mine to a good many such cases, — capital practice they are, — but I know this poor girl depends on seeing *me*. I believe she thinks I could raise her from the dead." Adrian was surprised at the matter-of-fact and unmistakably genuine kind-heartedness of the busy, professional man — he did not know how full of it the medical profession is. But without waiting for compliment or explanation, Doctor Veroil went on:

" Well, now, about your idea?"

" I had a notion, as I am obliged to go back home in a day or two, to put my trust in one other man, who can help us, I think, in dealing with the police. To expose my cousin in either court or newspapers would certainly kill her father, besides inflicting inexpressible distress on herself, and others too."

" Is n't Mr. Button the best man to do that?"

" I had meant to consult him," said Adrian; " but " — he paused. Dr. Veroil smiled.

" I understand," he said. " Rather a heavy touch, his is. Well; I 'll try him, perhaps. I think I know how to argue the case to him. But who is your man?"

" I 'm afraid it looks absurd ; 'but he seems to me remarkably shrewd, and I am pretty sure he knows how to do it. A good-hearted fellow, too. He is a police reporter. Bird, his name is."

" A police reporter," repeated the doctor, with some surprise. " Exactly the wrong sort. Stay — Bird, you said?"

" Yes."

" Well, that alters the case. I know him. Patient of mine. Quite a character. Yes, you may do it.

And I 'll tell you how. Send him to me ; he and I will keep everything safe, at least until we reach the truth in the matter, and find out exactly where we are. And for the present, don't say a word to any one else."

CHAPTER XIX.

The doctor's coupé, jumping vehemently along the rough pavement,

" Without stop or stay, down the rocky way,"

halted with a jerk, and the doctor sprang out. Turning back, he said, as the thought struck him, —

" Come along. You can pass for my student. It's worth while to see one of these Greene Street tenement houses for once."

Adrian followed instantly, observing, as he stepped across the sidewalk, that another carriage stood close by, among a number of drays, furniture vans, and tradesmen's wagons ; and he also had time to glance at the front of the house they were entering : it was a lofty brick building, painted of a dark, dull, blueish color, of about thirty feet front, having its door in the middle, with one window at each side, and the floors were low " between joints," showing an unusual number of rather small windows all over the front. Following the doctor, Adrian passed into a very narrow hall or alley that led straight through the house from front to rear ; midway, in the darkness, the staircase to the next floor could be dimly seen. Doctor Veroil hurried past this, however, out through the back door, across a narrow, gloomy, paved space, into the " rear building," as they call a favorite device of New York real-estate owners, for the slow murder of poor people ; half-way through just

such another dark narrow hall, smelling very close and nasty; up just
such another stairway, but still more
dimly seen; into the second-floor
dark alley, and up another stairway;
into the third floor, and up another;
into the fourth floor, and up another.
On the fifth floor Dr. Veroil, turning
towards the area or pit between the
buildings, stepped to a small grimy
window, and once more closely scrutinized his bit of paper. As he did
so, Adrian, who had with some difficulty followed close at his heels,
heard a voice that he recognized, — a
woman's voice, sharp, strong, practical, and decided.

" Never experienced a hope ? "

Adrian's quick ear distinguished a
very feeble rustle, as of one silently
moving one's head on a pillow in
reply. The practical decided voice
went straight on : —

" My erring sister, it is my plain
duty as a Christian woman to warn
you that your time is short, and that
you should in this awful hour repent
of your sins, give yourself to God,
and prepare at once to meet your
Saviour and your Judge. The doors
of hell are gaping for you; it is evident that you cannot live more than
an hour or two — "

" Where's Billy ? I want to see — "

The weak, frightened, longing
cry — a faint, faint cry — ended in
an awful choking gurgle; Dr. Veroil
rushed into the room — it was that
which he was looking for, though he
had naturally enough hesitated a
moment before interrupting; and
Adrian followed.

It is without any special volition
that keen perceptions take in the least
as well as the chiefest details of a picture. Accordingly, the whole of this
painful scene smote upon Adrian's
consciousness, and impressed upon

his memory things both small and
great, as instantly as a die with one
stroke smites every detail of its impress upon the metal beneath it.
Heterogeneous accessories and awful
central figure flashed altogether upon
him, and the whole picture, keyed,
like so many paintings, upon its one
strong red spot, was indelibly printed
in his mind. The small, hot, close
room, with its dusky light; the sickly,
medicinal odor; the dirty little
flat-topped, black cooking-stove, its
front in a dull, red glow from neglected draft; the poor array of feminine gear hanging on pegs at one
side of the room; the scanty, worn-
out, old ingrain carpet; the rickety,
painted furniture; the two or three
cheap, gaudy pictures, and a photograph or two, on the wall; the stiff,
erect form of Mrs. Button, the frightened face of her daughter Ann at the
other side of the bed; the frowsy figure of a young woman in attendance
on the patient, and who was uselessly
holding her head; and in the midst
of all these the ghastly figure, with
its wasted, chalky face, propped up
against a pillow or two; the bright-
red blood actually still flowing from
the mouth; and in which Adrian at
once recognized the poor girl who
had waited on him at the concert saloon: all this seen so suddenly, made
up of such unexpected constituents,
and forming a group so grim, was
felt by Adrian almost like something
burnt in upon him with a red-hot iron.

As the two men entered, the women, startled, uttered a cry, and Mrs.
Button and Ann looked at Adrian,
quite confounded. Adrian stopped
short, horrified. The physician
stepped promptly forward, felt the
pulse of the patient, dropped it.

" Dead ! — and you 've killed
her, you " — he continued, quite be-

side himself, turning short upon Mrs. Button, who was too much astounded to feel insulted. The doctor, turning once more to the bed, tried the pulse, the heart, the mouth. But life was gone, and he laid the poor, wasted phantom back tenderly upon the pillow.

"It may be the poor thing would n't have lived long," he said; "but you finished her off suddenly with your infamous hell. Why could n't you let her die quietly?"

With a great struggle, the resolute woman manned herself — if one may say so — against the wrath of the doctor, and, fighting against her own agitation also, she made answer: —

"I only told her the truth. I did my duty in striving to save an imperilled immortal soul at the eleventh hour."

"Eleventh nonsense!" cried the doctor, in a fury. "Told her the truth!" repeated he, with angry scorn. "If you only knew it, it would have been a Christian deed to tell her a hundred thousand lies if they would have kept her alive. How came you here, anyhow, madam?"

"She sent for me," said Mrs. Button, quite cowed by the furious, disregardful anger of the doctor, all the more appalling from its contrast with his usual genial and pleasant manner.

"I don't believe a word of it," said Doctor Veroil, bluntly. The frowzy girl who had been crying quietly at the foot of the bed, here arose, and snuffling and drawing the back of her dirty hand across her eyes, drew the doctor one side and said something to him under her breath. As she was doing so, Adrian espied a photograph on the little mantel-piece, which to his surprise he thought he recognized, and step-

ping across to it, he saw that it was indeed a picture of his cousin Mr. William Button. He quietly slipped it into his pocket, with a feeling that the ladies had better not see it there, just as the doctor, in answer to the girl, nodded his head, saying: —

"Yes, that must have been the way, — I know all about it" Then he turned to Mrs. Button again, and fairly ordered her and her daughter off the premises.

"It's no place for you," he said, brusquely; "all the harm's done that can be, and I shall see to the rest myself."

The two frightened ladies retreated without resistance, and indeed why should they stay any longer? Nor did they recognize Adrian, except by one or two more half-conscious looks that only testified to further astonishment. And the swiftness of the small though distressing panorama gave no time for forms.

"Now," said the doctor, kindly, to the volunteer nurse, "you call in somebody to sit with you a little while. You're a good girl for staying with that poor child. I'll send the undertaker right away, and have everything attended to."

She obeyed, and upon her return in a few moments with a companion, Dr. Veroil and Adrian departed. Stopping at the first undertaker's they could find, the kind-hearted doctor arranged for all the business and ceremonial formalities of the occasion, telling the necropomp to send him the bill.

On their way home Adrian told the doctor about the picture he had secured.

"Yes," was the answer; "you heard the poor child ask for Billy? Her very last words. It was a strange enough coincidence, that after the son had ruined her, the mother should kill her! Yet it came very naturally, too; a mere mistake about delivering the message. Women must have — at least, a good many of them must — somebody to love. If they have nobody, they make one. That poor child, now, loved that miserable young beast — beg your pardon, Mr. Chester, but it's true — with all her heart. Never saw a lovelier little thing in all my life — a little sewing-girl she was — than she was four years ago, when she first came crying to me to help her in her shame. I would n't do what she wanted, but I tried to help her. She went desperate, however, as the sensitive ones are likely to. I could n't do anything for her. There was some pretty rough villany of some kind, for her health broke down at the same time, just as she jumped overboard into the street. My God! I wish such a man could inflict nothing except what he had to endure himself!" And the benevolent physician groaned in mingled anger and pity. Adrian quietly took the picture out of his pocket, and tearing it into small bits, sprinkled it out into the street.

When they had returned to Dr. Veroil's office, Adrian took his leave, and once more set out for Mr. Button's, now, indeed, only one or two blocks away. But whether for fear of being questioned by the ladies about his presence with Dr. Veroil, or for some other reason, he certainly sought excuses in his own mind for not going directly thither. As excuses are not as scarce as diamonds, any more than they are as valuable, it was not long before he remembered that Mrs. and Miss Button would have none too much time to get ready for church; and he accordingly turned

his steps with deliberation towards the Reverend Mr. Toomston's church, purposing to attend divine service there, and then to go home with his friends to dinner.

The church in question was one of those shrewd real-estate investments whose success may be supposed to have furnished to the operators that contentment without which, the apostle seems to imply, godliness is not much of a gain (I Tim. vi, 6). Its site had been judiciously made so large as to include one or two even lots by way of churchyard, over and above both the church itself and the adjoining parsonage. Thus the rise in real estate in that very aristocratic part of the city was certain, whenever the time of removal should come (really it would be a great saving if they would build New York churches on wheels), to secure to the society, which of course paid no taxes on its real estate, another excellent building lot, and probably plenty of money besides to put up a new church and also to establish a church fund. The edifice, as becomes a Calvinistic organization of the stricter sort, was a very elaborate and magnificent structure of white marble. Church interiors are nowadays mostly on one of three plans: the jail plan, very gloomy and cold; the town-hall plan, like a barn with benches; or the parlor plan, a comfortable room with seats for listening to a friend's discourse. Doctor Toomston's church was a parlor, a little jailed. That is, it was splendidly upholstered, painted, and decorated, as a ritualist -- beg pardon, a strictly Calvinist — church is directed in the New Testament to be; but the rich, dark, stained glass windows, very heavily mullioned and deeply set in the thick walls, and the dark colors which prevailed in all the interior finishing, greatly obscured what would have been the effect if the large and well-proportioned room had been finished, say, in white and gray, or white and lavender, with a very few high lights, and a very few dark lines, and with plain glass windows.

Adrian, entering, was accosted by a white waistcoat and accoutrements, with a trig yet serious young man inside of it, who, by one of those irresistible improprieties that sometimes torment the most devout, reminded the visitor of the undertaker at a fashionable funeral, but who, on request, politely escorted him through the gloom of the great building to Mr. Button's pew (the fifth from the front, middle aisle, right hand as you go up). It was just in time, as it happened; and Mr. Button himself, sitting next the pew door, looked round as the usher touched his shoulder; arose, bowed silently and gravely, motioned Adrian to enter, and then resumed his own place. Mrs. Button was already at her post, the inner end of the pew; Mr. William Button was next, and Miss Ann Jacintha Button next, so that the happy Adrian was between his intended spouse and his intended father-in-law. Short of heaven, few positions can be imagined more delightful.

The service was the usual one: two psalms or hymns, short prayer and long prayer, and a sermon. "A sermon," says some scoffer, "is that part of divine service which does *not* consist of the worship of God." How can it, indeed? Worship goes up, sermons come down. The worship of God must be addressed to God; sermons are addressed to men.

"My text, on the present occasion," said good Doctor Toomston, erecting his long and bony figure in the sacred desk, after the second singing, — it was Watts's version of the First Psalm, — "will be found in the Second Epistle of Paul to the Corinthians, sixth chapter, part of the fourteenth verse: 'Be ye not unequally yoked together with unbelievers.'"

It is a great pity that there is not room for a full verbatim report of this sound and seasonable discourse. But as there is not, a very few hints must suffice. The main point argued by the doctor was, the incompatibility of the objects in life — and in death — of the Christian and of the sinner; and from this he concluded that the psalmist and the apostle to the Gentiles both taught, agreeably, moreover, to common-sense, that there should be a distinct wall of separation between them. This wall, of course, was church membership. The practical application was an urgent appeal to those already in the church, to let their walk and conversation show their heavenly calling; so that "men should take knowledge of them," quoted the preacher, "that they had been with Jesus."

The discourse, as a whole, seemed to Adrian, from the very beginning, conventional, monotonous, and unimpressive. But he reflected that he had heard just such sermons twice a day on nearly every Sunday since he could remember; and with a natural instinct for complete judgments, he set himself to find the good of it also. This was easy to find; the sermon was translucent with sincere and unconditional piety, faith, and love. Merit enough, said Adrian to himself. How can it be so lifeless to me? Am I a vessel of wrath, fitted to destruction, — created on purpose to be damned for the glory of God? "Ah, I have found it," he said in a moment; "these good qualities are the doctor's own, and they 'shine up' his theology. Let me read that sermon in print," — and in spite of him, the irreverent comparison of Doctor Veroil popped into his mind, about putting religion into theological expressions.

There were, moreover, divers matters connected with the sermon which had for Adrian much interest. As he listened to one dry conventional phrase after another, he kept admiring the parallelism between the perfectly sufficient sense, clearness, and even noticeable strength and cogency of the statements, all, nevertheless, utterly without grace, eloquence, or proportion, and the personal appearance and bearing of the speaker: strong, homely, manly enough, but perfect in a long and wooden ungracefulness, which, if it had been conscious, would have been awkwardness even to agony. Then, he observed how exclusively the sermon was addressed to Christians; insomuch that he caught himself repeating a variation on a text — "This is a faithful saying, and worthy of all acceptation, that Christ Jesus came into the world to save *Christians* — of whom *we* are chief;" and again, "For I am not come to call *sinners*, but the *righteous*, to repentance." This sentiment occasioned him, however, an astonishment all at once, when, at the very end of his discourse, the good old doctor, as if he had suddenly remembered that there was a sinner or two left, seemed to throw over a buoy into the dark waves of their guilt for them to catch if they could, while he sailed triumphantly away to glory with his shipful of Christians. He diverged, to speak without figures, into a brief appeal to sinners, by way of appendix or vermiform process; beginning with the words, "And

now, a few words to you, my impenitent hearers, if any such be present," — and proceeding in sentences of admonition and warning, that, like a good deal of the previous discourse, seemed to have been used over and over before, as they build secondhand bricks into a new wall. Still more observable was an indescribable tone or sentiment or something, which seemed to Adrian as if the doctor was saying to himself, "It won't do a bit of good — you'll be damned anyhow, but it's proper and usual to say something of this kind, so, here!" Adrian's own reflection was, that Christ used to *begin* with these same poor fellows, the sinners.

Less excusable were the observations which Adrian made upon the gestures of the preacher. It was not that the divine seemed out of place. Quite otherwise; he always seemed out of place anywhere else. What it was could not easily have been stated in words; but there was certainly something, in spite of all his homeliness and woodenness of motion, that impressed the hearer with the feeling that the sacred desk was the only proper place for him; one might even fancy that he lived there, like an artificial man in his show-box. But his gestures were so original, so queer, so unexpected. In vain would you search for them in any book, or watch for them in any concourse or resort of orators. Indeed, certain of these manœuvres were almost contortions, as if the worthy doctor were wrestling desperately with some great thought, in his intense desire to body it forth through motion; insomuch that Adrian secretly indulged in a few hasty sketches of two or three of them on a fly-leaf of the hymn-book. Two shall be given here. Perhaps they may be the beginning of a wholly new school of pulpit gesture and expression — who knows? Toomston is as good a name as Delsarte, any day. The first of these (see Fig. 1) illustrated a striking comparison used by the doctor in the course of his appeal for the Christian life. He was enlarging upon the trifling and transitory nature of this life, and the uncertainty and blindness in which we poor human beings flit as it were to and fro in dark and purposeless ways; and wound up a period with the words, "We glide vainly hither and thither, like little fishes within the Stream of Time." At these words, holding forth his large and bony hands in the very fish-like attitude of Fig. 1, he brandished them back and forth from the shoulder, past each other, with an indescribable furious angularity, which the cut cannot show at all, but even more wonderfully opposed to the flexible, swift ease of a

Fig. 1. LITTLE FISHES.

fish's movements, than were the rugged outlines of the hands themselves, to the subtle, sinuous grace of a fish's form. Again, in setting forth, by way of contrast to this vain and unprofitable activity, the steady progress of the consistent Christian, from one grade of spiritual attainment to another, he enforced the assertion of the final splendor of the believer's glory, at the end of the laborious ascent, in the words "until at last he attains unto the stature of perfect uprightness," which uprightness he at the

same time pictured forth with the following noble manual diagram (see Fig. 2), but dancing the two fingers thus daintily conjoined up and down at arms' end, before the audience, in a manner that greatly strengthened the impression, and which, as before, the cut, most unfortunately, cannot give.

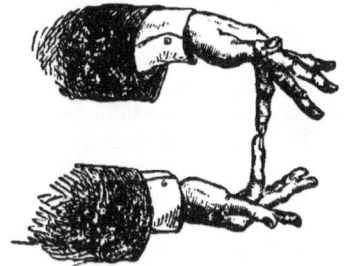

Fig. 2. PERFECT UPRIGHTNESS.

A third almost equally stirring appeal, was that in the afterthought to impenitent friends, where he cried out to the young men that were rushing to destruction, displaying at the same time a full front elevation of both hands as if to push the foolish fellows back again, "Pause, young men, pause!" A laugh that rises in church is always awfully hard to stifle; Adrian had to pretend to cough, and covered his mouth with one hand, and managed not to be openly indecent; he heard Mr. William Button snigger at the same moment.

Instead of filing slowly out along with ordinary people when the service was over and the benediction pronounced, Mr. Button and his family sat still until all that part of the church was almost empty. Then Dr. Toomston came gravely down from the sacred desk, and greeted several persons who had lingered near out of friendship or on some Sunday errand. Then Mr. Button arose, he and all his house, and stood in a group in the aisle, and the doctor came and talked with them.

PART VII.

CHAPTER XX.

EVERY first-class New York capitalist keeps a tame minister. Mr. Button, who meant to rank as high as he could in his vocation, had with judicious foresight, provided this amongst his other apparatus. Dr. Toomston, it is true, did not see the matter in this light. How should he? All that he, or anybody else unfamiliar with financiering, could have seen, was, the shrewd, energetic, successful conduct of Mr. Button in organizing and maintaining the church. Further than this, the doctor was only the beloved pastor; petted, waited on, endowed with many gifts, regularly carried home to dinner every Sunday to hear his sermon and himself and his church and all their doings talked over and praised. None the less was the good old doctor an instrument of the long-headed business man. For Mr. Button, besides his love of money, nourished another ambition. He wanted fame and office, and within some ten or fifteen years he meant to have them, too; and he knew full well that next to being an eminent Sunday-school superintendent, nothing whatever is a better basis for great enterprises, either in money or in politics, than being the premier member of a church.

The house of Button never rode on the Sabbath. Not to be superstitious in extreme observance, however, the affectation of a cold-meat dinner was not practised; indeed, the meal was commonly a little bit of a feast. Mr. Button had a good deal of that sort of hospitality which often goes with a vigorous digestion, a full pocket, and an ambition of popularity. He almost always fed his tame minister at his Sunday dinner, as they feed the wild beasts on public days; and he kept out a standing invitation to Mr. Van Braam and Civille and to Dr. Veroil. The former two came quite often, the doctor very seldom. To-day they were all present; the physician, perhaps, proposing to do something or to see something which might serve him in whatever he proposed in behalf of Civille.

With small delay — for this household was well ordered — the dinner was served. It was a bounteous and toothsome meal, and well garnished and supplemented by conversation; for the Americans are neither like those old beasts of classic heroes, who, like so many Esquimaux, with blubber pared off even with their lips, could not speak until "the sacred rage of hunger was appeased," nor like a boa-constrictor, who, after eating, cannot say a word until he has digested the goat he has gorged. There was plenty of talk, and it meant something. And it was a noticeable company, and pretty curiously assorted, too, both mentally and physically. Mr. Button himself sat at the head of the table and his spouse at the foot. Mrs. Button and her daughter were alike enough for their relationship, and different enough for the difference in their blood. The mother was a tall person, somewhat bony and wooden-looking, swarthy of skin, with harsh, large features, great, cold, strong black eyes, under strong black brows, and abundant and rather coarse hair, erst coal-black, now fast turning gray. Despising dyes, she disposed of this, in part, in three rolls, or horizontal curls, of a cast-iron appearance, — for they were iron-gray of color and iron-hard of look, — at either side of her face. The rest was decently covered by a plain cap. Her forehead was rather low and narrow, but full in the lower centre, as much as to say: I am quick-witted, unimaginative, practical, and not kind-hearted; if I do any charity, for instance, it is on business principles. But the chief emphasis of the face was laid upon the nose, which was big, too thick at the tip, and pinched and lifted inward at the wings of the nostrils, as if by a final jerk with thumb and finger by the sculptor of the face; so that two strong marks or creases were left diverging downwards past the ends of the mouth.

As the good lady was of the Gookin family, she had, along with their other qualities, their well-known persistency of character: a kind of perseverance of the saints, in that sense which means incapacity for receiving new impressions. This appeared, for instance, equally in two very dissimilar things: her theology and her manners. Both remained without perceptible modification from what they had been in the rustic home of her father, old Gookin the distiller, in the ancient town of Windsor in Connecticut. The manners were those of the Gookins, — no more need be said. The theology may be described by a chemical metaphor, as Gookinate of Calvinism. It had the uncompromising rigidity of the stern old minister of her youth, who, if possible more unchangeable still, represented almost as a mirror an extreme Edwardeanism. This, stiffened by his own iron will, had stiffened still more in the mind of Miss Gookin, which, with still less breadth than the old pastor's, had also even less capacity, if possible, for growth or change.

Ann and Civille sat together. They had come down-stairs together from the parlor to the basement dining-room, walking next before Adrian and Dr. Veroil, their arms round each other's waists, according to the loving ways of young girls sometimes, whether they love each other or not. Adrian had been watching them, without meaning to, — as is the natural action of intense perceivers; and as his mind was of that class that instinctively sees things by couples or groups, and discerns resemblances and differences, he had noticed the difference in their figures and movements. Civille's shoulders were sloping; Ann's were no broader, perhaps narrower, but square. Among a hundred square-shouldered women there will be found more who are coarse-grained and vulgar than among a hundred with sloping shoulders. Civille's form was round, Ann's flat. Civille's step was undulating, easy; the volitional, gliding motion of a goddess. Ann's was a hitch; she walked like a saw-horse. But all the same, — Adrian noticed this also, — *they moved their inside feet together.* This is a great mystery. Why is it that two women almost always keep step in that way? Two men walking together put out the two left feet together, and then the two right; but two women put out the two inside feet, then the two outside. Why is it?

"Why is it?" asked Adrian, softly, of the doctor.

"For the same reason that makes them always step on or off a street car with the wrong foot," replied the physician, "and take hold with the wrong hand at the same time. They are never taught to handle themselves. It's one of women's wrongs."

They sat down at table. The faces of the two young women, as they sat together opposite Adrian, formed even a more striking contrast than their figures and motions. Civille's face — so pale and clear-hued; so quiet, refined, and sweet; lighted by the large, soft, thoughtful gray eyes — suggested to Adrian, by some hidden train of associations, a distant night-view he had once seen of a lofty white marble building illuminated. The light, whatever it was, was a little rosy, and throbbed and glimmered; and at the distance, as he well remembered, the effect was, not as of stone lighted from without, but as of a mysterious living thing, all instinct and pulsing with a fulness of silent, gleaming light from within itself, — a living; white light, rose-tinted.

It was his betrothed who sat next Civille, and nearly opposite him. No matter: he could not, for all that, help it, that as he looked at them the thought came into his mind — "Light and Darkness." Miss Button's face was low-browed, the forehead being modelled after her mother's; not low-browed like the lovely Clytie, because abundant hair grew low upon the head, but because the brain-pan was shallow and flat above. It was narrower, too, than her mother's; so that, with about the same quickness and sharpness of mere perceptive intellect, the daughter had even less indication of the combining and reflecting mental faculties. Of the still higher range which phrenology so beautifully describes as towering above even the philosophic part of the intellect, — of ideality, and its related spiritual powers at either hand, with benevolence for the keystone in the midst above, — of this Ann's front head was almost as destitute as if the layers of brain had been shaved off. Adrian was a believer, not only in the mental analysis which belongs to phrenology, and which has quietly become accepted even by its opponents, solely because it is so true, but also to a considerable extent in the corresponding doctrine of regions of the brain; and, indeed, he habitually used this doctrine to aid him in judgments of character. The contrast between the two girls flashed upon him all at once after years in which he might have seen it, as is often the case with even the most striking of contrasts, and to the quickest of perceivers. Probably, it is true, they had never been displayed to him so closely together. Certainly, he had never been placed near the couple with such a close and living sense of having a relation with each of them. The contrast between the soft glowing light and life, the spiritual sweetness of the one expression, and the close and almost sullen look of the other, shone upon the young man's mind, sensitive beyond the common average to impressions, already stirred and stimulated by the morning's experiences beyond its own usual vividness of perception; this consciousness shone or rather flashed upon him with a stroke so sharp that he absolutely started and shut his eyes, as if smitten by a too sudden sunlight. He looked again, discerning the forms and colors and the characters they denoted, too, in this intensity of perceiving, with such a power of seeing that he almost felt as if he ought not to look. Civille, indeed, in a moment, felt him; and lifted her eyes and looked at him with a surprised glance, and then with a smile, as much as to say: "What — you are looking at me, are you! Well, look: man, and God, may see all my thoughts." But Ann did not feel nor know what Adrian was about.

So he beheld with a sense of displeasure, which made him feel very wicked at experiencing it, the traits of his chosen. Her narrow forehead seemed to grow narrower; her complexion and her black hair looked so coarse beside the exceptional silky and satiny texture of Civille's hair and cheek; her black eyes, sharp and beady and rather sunken, almost went out of sight beside those of Civille, large, limpid, and so clear that they seemed full of a light of their own; her nose, always short and small, — it had missed both the largeness of her mother's, and the goodly solidity of her father's, — became a positive snub before him; her lips, rather thin, and with a positive set in them, seemed to grip; her black brows frowned. Both the young women were too thin in flesh. Adrian was not reasoning, while thus experiencing spontaneous intuition, and therefore he did not conclude with his judgment, although it impressed him, that while Civille only needed good health to become singularly perfect in form, Ann, on the other side, had already lost even the measure of

youthful roundness which she had possessed, had even now begun what must, with her, be a long and unbroken declension through degrees of skinniness.

Not with repulsion, but with a feeling of guilt for being capable of seeing her defects, did Adrian thus behold. And as he saw upon Miss Button's finger the plain gold ring he had given her a year or two before, he felt for the first time that he was *held*. Losing recollection for a moment, he said aloud, in an unconscious way, —

"Ah! Number Eleven!"

Ann started, blushed, and looked across at her lover with distinct displeasure. He, recovering himself, begged a thousand pardons; but she did not look satisfied. He had offended one of her deepest instincts — that of concealing. On the inside of her ring, when he gave it to her, Adrian had caused to be engraved a fanciful, perhaps even fantastic, device, being no other than the four words of the last clause but one in the twentieth verse of the twenty-first chapter of the Revelation: "The eleventh, A. Jacinth." This he had never told except to her; she loved secrets; he had frequently called her his number eleven, besides pretty things about her being his own special jewelled way to heaven, and the like. And in this inopportune moment he had so nearly told the whole to this company! It was a deeper offence than he knew; and hers was not a mind to forget offences.

In this company were curious oppositions and agreements. Dr. Toomston represented an old-fashioned, trained, somewhat scholarly Calvinist theology. Mrs. Button and Ann the same, but with prejudice and ignorance, and natural hardness and obstinacy, in place of a sincerely convinced reason. In Civille was a spiritual religion, but without sect, undervaluing and neglecting form, and tending to unmeasured avowal and unreasoning and unconditional self-sacrifice. Her father's religion was as hers, but colored by his mysticist tendency, and usually hidden under natural habits of silent meditation and shy concealment of the deepest thoughts, and under the further cover that the experience of an undervalued soul had taught him to use a cover of half-sarcastic, half-paradoxical quasi denials and queries. Adrian's religion had neither Civille's unmeasured demonstrativeness, nor her father's inverted, sad secretiveness. It was, perhaps, as thorough-going and as deep; but the strength and activity of his vivid health and youth made it his proper office at present to pursue after and accomplish things to be done, more than to experience sentiments or express views. All these six may be reckoned Christians, after some fashion. As for the rest, hardly. Mr. Button was a man of business. Dr. Veroil was a doctor. Mr. William Button, ——. Not that the conditions in life of these three were necessarily inconsistent with the Christian profession or practice; only, as a matter of fact, they had them not.

They talked, beginning thus: —

MR. BUTTON. (*Rapping thrice, solemnly, with his knife-handle upon the table.*) "Doctor, will you ask a blessing?"

DR. TOOMSTON. (*Closing his eyes, and stretching forth his right hand to a great distance among the dishes, as if feeling for something to be thankful for, and holding it with the thumb erect and fingers extended.*) "Our.

Father who art in Heaven, bless unto us, we beseech thee, and consecrate unto thy glory all that we have and do, and in an especial manner this thy holy day, and bless and sanctify unto us at this time the provisions which thy bounty spreadeth here before us, and may the same and all thy other loving-kindnesses unto us be improved to thy honor and glory. Amen."

MR. BUTTON. (*Carving and distributing the turkey with skill and judgment.*) "Mother, give Dr. Toomston plenty of gravy. Dr. Veroil, you like the second jint. You're a surgeon, so I'll let you git that side-bone off yourself, — rather you'd be a-cuttin' off the turkey's legs than mine, any day. Adrian, what part 'll you have?"

ADRIAN. (*Preoccupied.*) "I've no choice."

MR. BUTTON. "Wal, then here's the neck. Ollers choose somethin' yourself, young man, or somebody'll make a wuss choice for ye. Ha, ha! But I'll allow ye a good slice of the breast to make out with."

It is impracticable, however, to report the conversation in full at this time, interesting as it was. It began, after the distributive introduction, with observations on the discourse of the morning, and diverged variously from the main theme of Christian separatism, sometimes to topics having a distinctly secular character. At such times, however, if no one else returned to the order of the day, Mrs. Button did, charging straight "across lots," if necessary; and once with the plain remark, in reply to certain words of Adrian's, in which she apprehended a mirthful quality, —

"There, there! This is frivolous. We can occupy ourselves, I trust, with more serious thoughts on this sacred day."

"But, my dear madam," responded Adrian, "mirthfulness is not necessarily frivolous. And we are ordered to rejoice before the Lord, and to be noisy about it, too ; to make a loud noise, and rejoice, and sing praise."

"I fear, my young friend, that you are in danger of being, not merely frivolous, but irreverent," said Doctor Toomston, from very high up in the sacred desk.

Mr. Van Braam replied, — rather to the surprise of the company, — and interrupting Adrian, who was about to speak : —

"Stop, Adrian — I 'm older than Doctor Toomston, and he may couple me with you if he wants to. God made kittens and monkeys on purpose to be funny. They are God's laughter. God made mirthful young people too. Laughter is in God as much as weeping, and I believe a great deal more. I have heard that Professor Agassiz has notes for a book, to be called 'God as a joker.'"

Here an awful groan from Mrs. Button, and ungodly mirth — as it seemed to the horrified lady — from the doctor of medicine. But the doctor of divinity was not at all dismayed, replying with awful gravity : —

"I have no intention of condescending to argue in support of the serious observance of the Sabbath day, or of a decent respect for either the ordinances or the ministers of God."

This was pretty terrible, and something like a thunder-cloud settled over the dinner-table for a few moments, in the midst of which Doctor Veroil, with the eye next Mr. Button, but farthest from Mrs. Button, winked upon Adrian. But

he "caught it" in his turn, and once more from an unexpected quarter. It was Mr. William Button this time who spoke, saying : —

"'A naughty person, a wicked man, walketh with a froward mouth. *He winketh with his eyes,* he speaketh with his feet, he teacheth with his fingers.'"

"What do you mean by that, William?" said his mother, severely. "I wish you would practise the precepts of the Scriptures, instead of repeating them. 'This people draweth nigh to me with their mouth,'—you have been trained enough in them, I 'm sure."

Then Dr. Veroil said, —

"That walking with your mouth is rather like an octopus, is n't it? And if it 's so naughty to teach with your fingers, where have good Mr. Gallaudet and Dr. Peet gone to, now that they are dead?"

"Come, come," ordered Mr. Button, with good-natured peremptoriness ; "none o' this scufflin'. I ain't a-goin' to have Dr. Toomston talked back to in my house any more 'n if he stood in his own pulpit. There 's plenty o' things ye can all agree on, and now agree on some on em !"

So they did, and explanations were made and accepted all round. But the host himself came near getting into trouble a little afterwards, when they were talking again of the theory of the church's relation to sinners ; for he thus adventured himself in the china-shop of polemic theology in an attempt to sum up :—

"Seems to me, as you 're a-puttin' it, the hull thing comes down to this, don't it? — the church is either a trap, or a safe. Either it 's a trap to ketch sinners in and convert 'em afterwards, jest as they ketch a rat and then drownd him in a pail o' water at their leisure; or else it's a fire-proof safe, to shet up the members after you've got 'em converted, jest like so many convertible securities, so to speak, all indorsed and payable to bearer, so's to have 'em all snug where thieves and sinners can't get no chance at 'em at all to spile 'em nor steal 'em?"

Dr. Toomston shook his head, in grave doubts as to such figures of speech. Mrs. Button, with more decision, warned her spouse that while he might not injure his own beliefs by such worldly comparisons, they would assuredly not be used to edification by younger and less firmly settled minds. He should rather, she added, exhort the young men to be sober-minded, and thus be an example to the believers. This wholesome counsel was received by Dr. Toomston with a smile and an approving nod, and by Mr. Button with silence and with acquiescence due; for he felt that he had probably a little erred.

A number of other important topics came up in the course of the conversation, on all of which there were visible two parties or sets of beliefs among the company. These parties may perhaps be called the Faith party and the Reason party. The latter urged that their reasoning method led directly to all the useful conclusion which the Faith party asserted; that they did not weaken faith, but directly and powerfully reinforced it; that, for instance, the exercise of prayer, the use of the Bible, the belief in an overruling providence, the acknowledgment and the love of a Redeemer, were no less faithful and consoling and elevating, if the believer in them found himself able to receive them with the intellect as well as with the heart.

They even suggested that the progress of humanity was and must be, and could not but be other than intellectual, at least as much as emotional and instinctive; and that therefore it agreed with history that reason should be added to faith just as fast as mankind became wiser and better. But the Faith party would not hear. Figuratively, they cast the reasoners out of the synagogue, declaring that their reasoning was unsanctified, unregenerate, and sinful; an unholy intrusion of the natural man into the office and place set apart for the children of the kingdom; that those who presumed to support the ark of God must risk the fate of Uzzah. So iron and obstinate and uncompromising was the stiffness of these denunciations, particularly by the two ladies of that part, most of all by Mrs. Button, that they seemed excessive in their strictness, even to the mind of Mr. Button himself, not very keen nor discriminating in such spiritual matters, however much it might be so where the mammon of unrighteousness was to be propitiated. He accordingly intervened more than once against the followers of his pastor rather than against the pastor himself, observing, finally, to the excommunicated: —

"Now, you hold your tongues! Don't you see that argument slides off them women like rain off a duck's back? I do' no as I foller ye altogether; but I can see there's some reason on your side as well as theirn; but don't you see that the more you beat 'em the less they'll know it and the madder they'll git? Mother'll be a-cuttin' your throats with a case-knife if you don't look out; and now, I won't hear one single word more of theology; not one word; jest shet right up, the hull on ye! Dr. Toomston, what's the subject of your talk to the Sunday-school children this afternoon?"

This judicious diversion cut a pretty hard knot. The proposed lecture, it seemed, was to be on the Canaanite campaigns of Chedorlaomer; and the good doctor developed some very valuable views — for Sunday-school children — about the extremely horrid wickedness of those pagans of the vale of Siddim and thereabouts, about B. C. 2,000, and the justice of their consequent subjugation by another pagan, perhaps as horridly wicked.

The remainder of the Sunday was passed by Adrian in improving conversation with his friends, or in attendance along with them upon the stated preaching of the gospel, and (during the afternoon) within the precincts of the Sunday school. Here the good doctor's views on Chedorlaomer were duly set forth by way of a dessert or confectionery, after the solid or scholastic part of the exercises was over. Thus it came to pass, that when Adrian went home to his bed he was pretty well tired.

CHAPTER XXI.

THE Sabbath — the rest — may be on Sunday as well as on Saturday. For schoolboys, the real rest is Saturday afternoon. The minister's Sabbath is on Monday; Monday is his rest. If he is a wise minister, by the way, he will be sure to devote it with a peculiar exclusiveness to secular things. He will find a singular renewing and strengthening to come from this resolute wrenching of himself away, for one day in each week, from his professional labors. Whether Dr. Toomston would have stated this

rule exactly in this way, may be doubted. He acted on it, however, and accordingly he readily accepted Mr. Button's invitation to attend with him on the next day, Monday, the meeting of the proposed Scrope Association, which was held in a sufficient hired apartment, in the latter part of the forenoon. Present: Mr. Button and his family, and Dr. Toomston; Mr. and Miss Van Braam; Adrian; Scrope of Scrope, and his friend Mr. Bird, the police reporter; Mr. Adam Welles; Mr. Stanley, the East Hartford antiquarian and collector, and his friend Mr. Purvis, the book-dealer; and some score or more of other persons, mostly of a rustic exterior, who were, or supposed themselves, Scrope descendants, and who had been drummed up by the indefatigable advertising and correspondence of Mr. Scrope.

When the company was seated, there was a kind of pause for a moment; and then Mr. Scrope arose, and just as if he had been a ward politician all his life, moved that Tarbox Button, Esq., of New York, take the chair; put the motion, and had the capitalist presiding within five seconds. Being then in turn called upon by the chairman, Mr. Scrope, without nearly as much of the haw-haw style as might have been apprehended, opened to the meeting the matters for which it had been called together, in a business-like speech, some portions of which have been already stated, in substance, as follows :—

Colonel Adrian Scroope the Regicide was executed in the year 1660. He left a son and two younger brothers. The son came to America, where he changed his name to Throop, and became the ancestor of a considerable number of descendants, all through female lines, however, so that his name was extinct, although his blood survived. Now, whatever estate Colonel Scroope possessed, was confiscated. But the large family estate in Buckinghamshire was still at his death in the possession of his father, a very old man, who at his death left a considerable portion of it vested in trust for the use of his grandson in America. This, the speaker was advised, was still within the reach of the heirs-general of Adrian Scroope of Hartford, if they chose to pursue the proper legal measures. The rest of this Buckinghamshire estate was left by the will of its aged owner in equal shares to his two younger sons. Of these two, the elder left heirs, and the estate had remained in the same family until some thirty-five years ago, or a little more, when its last possessor of the Scroope blood died intestate.

The speaker himself, Scrope of Scrope, was, he said, descended from the younger of these two brothers, the youngest of the three, who was as staunch a loyalist as the colonel was a republican. And, he observed here, he would proceed to recite to them a well-established tradition which they might not all of them have heard, and which would still further interest them in the steadfast and lofty character of Colonel Adrian the Regicide. It may, perhaps, he continued, be considered less creditable to my own ancestor. Colonel Adrian's loyalist nephew; but after all it only implies loyalty at the worst, and surely loyalty is not altogether vile at this day in the eyes of the citizens of the North. (Applause.) The story, continued the speaker, is told in Caulfield's "High Court of Justice," in the bio-

graphical account of Colonel Adrian the Regicide, and is as follows: —

"Colonel Scroop's nephew, visiting him in his dungeon the night before he suffered, said to him, 'Uncle, I am sorry to see you in this condition, and would desire you to repent of the fact for which you are brought hither, and stand to the king's mercy,' and more words to the same effect. Whereupon, Colonel Scroop put forth his hand and thrust him away, using these words: 'Avoid, Satan!'"

This, as you know, said Scrope of Scrope, meant the same with our Saviour's words to the tempter: "Get thee behind me"; and they prove a fearless composure and impregnable uprightness most worthy of the ancestor of so many good Puritans and respectable American citizens. (Applause.)

Having thus very neatly complimented the audience into good humor on the principle which theologians call imputation, the speaker went on to develop more fully the practical part of the subject. The property, which might otherwise have descended to himself, as the representative of the younger of the three Scrope brethren, had been expended two centuries ago in the cause of the king. That of Colonel Adrian could not fall to him (the speaker) except by failure of the lineage of Adrian; and neither could the property of the intestate representative of the second brother. His object, he would frankly avow, was in part to obtain some money; if he should turn out to be the lawful heir of the two separate unclaimed Scrope estates, to get possession of them; if not, as he really believed was the case, then to earn something by acting as agent to secure the property for those who were its heirs, whom, he believed, he now saw (in part) before him. (Applause.)

What he, therefore, wished to do, was, to form an association, by the signing of the names of the audience, and others entitled, to a proper instrument. Such signature should be attended with a small cash subscription to be paid to him as the authorized agent of the association; and which would thus place him in a position to prosecute the necessary researches, and set on foot the requisite legal proceedings in England; and each person thus signing was to receive a corresponding share of the proceeds of the estate whenever secured.

Mr. Scrope then read from one of a handful of pamphlets the form of an association such as he desired to suggest, and exhibited a blank manuscript copy of the same, ready for signing; and he added, that the story of that very pamphlet, issued by the "Jennings Association," in the year 1863, and still more strikingly, the story of the "Wilson Association" (which he also displayed from the parcel of similar pamphlets in his hands), proved — yes, it might safely be said, *proved* — that investigations of a similar nature in behalf of American heirs of English estates, had been more than once pushed to an extent, and with prospects, that had occasioned such proceedings in England as showed a great deal of terror and some very strange proceedings, to say the least, among the holders of vast estates there.

If it should be the pleasure of the assembly to form such an association, and to authorize and enable him to manage their enterprise, he concluded it would gratify at once his desire to earn a livelihood, his natural love of seeing the right prevail, and his powerful instinct of family pride; and, he might be permitted to add, as he looked upon the intelligent faces of these his worthy kinsmen and kinswomen of three thousand miles and five or six degrees of distance, — but, he trusted, of no such distance in natural affection, — as he looked upon these intelligent faces, he could not help adding, that that ancient English family pride was strengthened every moment by his contact with these relatives in the New World!

This rather skilfully arranged discourse, with its *ad captandum* peroration, was very well received, the applause at the close being quite enthusiastic.

Mr. Scrope sat down; and after a moment Mr. Button, after the usual manner, asked what was the further pleasure of the meeting; adding that he presumed their young friend and kinsman would be pleased to answer any questions. Here Mr. Scrope bowed, in sign of assent. For his own part, the chairman confessed that he had been greatly interested and favorably impressed by the statements they had just heard.

Mr. Adam Welles arose, and in his slow, deliberate, awkward, or rather homely, and yet intelligent manner, said: —

"I move you, sir, that we now proceed to the formation of the Scrope Association, in manner and form as just suggested by the gentleman from foreign parts." This motion was seconded, and Mr. Button was on the point of putting it to vote, when a spare, pale, gentlemanly person, with a precise look, a roomy forehead, a clean-shaved face, a sharp, thin nose, and a narrow chin, rose up, and in a dry, sharpish voice and prim manner, observed that if it were in order he would like to make one or two inquiries of his young friend,

Mr. Scrope, before the question should be, as he pronounced it, "putt."

"Mr. Stanley, of East Hartford," said the chairman. It was indeed that eminent antiquarian and collector. Old Mr. Van Braam, who sat next Adrian, gave a kind of uneasy, dissatisfied hitch in his seat, as much as to say, "Now, he means to make trouble!" Sure enough, he did.

"I would like to inquire," said Mr. Stanley, "whether Mr. Scrope is in a position to assure us positively that the English laws respecting real estate and inheritance will entitle the persons present to take possession of the estate left by Colonel Adrian Scrope's father, if the descent of these persons from the colonel himself can be made out?"

To this query Mr. Scrope made answer, that he could not reply with an absolute affirmative; because legal proceedings are always doubtful, peculiarly so in cases of real estate, and most of all in cases of remote descents; but that he wished to be understood to assert, most positively, that the prospect was such as to render the attempt most hopeful.

"Where the reality is least, there we must use the most of hope instead, I suppose," rejoined Mr. Stanley, with a dry, cold smile, which had no mirth in it, but only a kind of bite; "in that sense, I fully believe my young friend to be correct. And I presume he would repeat these assurances with still more confidence in the case of the second estate, — that of the intestate representative of the elder of Colonel Adrian's two brothers?"

"Yes," said Mr. Scrope, "he would; and in this part of the undertaking, he was happy to inform the gentleman that a very positive opinion had been given by eminent London counsel, learned in the law, in favor of the title of the American heirs."

"Provided they can be found," continued the implacable Mr. Stanley, with another mirthless jack-frost grin. "There have been several associations, to my own knowledge, like that which the young gentleman wishes us to form. I have myself the pamphlet reports of the Jennings Association, the Wilson Association, the Booth Association, the Gibson Association, and the Brown Association. I expect any day to get those of the Jones Association and the Smith Association, unless the whole of them conclude, as I should advise them to do, that they had better unite in one name and call the whole the Brown Association. For look you, Mr. Chairman, every one of these printed reports ends with a confession of entire failure. Perhaps Green would be the best name to begin with, but Brown would be the best to come out with. They are all done Brown so far — very brown, indeed. But I must trouble my young friend with one more inquiry: Where does he find, I will not say legal proof, but the least evidence, *first*, that a son of Colonel Adrian Scroope the Regicide fled to New England in 1660? *Second*, that it was this son who signed himself 'Adrian Scroope' at Hartford in 1666? *Third*, that any single one of the persons in this room is descended from the person so signing?"

There is something peculiarly cold-blooded and horrible in applying the unfeeling test of legal rules, or historical rules, of evidence to the glowing emotional happiness of speculative future wealth. The revulsion leaves, as it were, a clammy paste, as when you throw cold water on hot buckwheat cakes. The deliberate, chilly, rasping manner of Mr. Stanley's remarks was about as irritating as any manner could be; and moreover, it had an air of positiveness and superior knowledge about it which was very imposing. So, while it was calculated to annoy Mr. Scrope to the utmost, it was at the same time just the manner to tell on a company of Yankee folks, who were being asked to pay down ready cash to a person they had never seen before, and knew nothing about, for the privilege of sending him to hunt up rights, two hundred years old, to property they had never seen at all, and three thousand miles off. The remarks did tell accordingly. The stout intelligence even of the chairman was visibly disturbed. Mr. Scrope, while his usual affable smile continued, could be seen to grow somewhat pale. A dead silence fell upon the assembly.

Mr. Scrope, whatever his feelings, rose at once to reply; for in such a case any hesitation is surely fatal. It must be confessed that although he struggled gallantly, he was at this moment effectually beaten. He alleged the constant tradition of the Scrope descent; the circumstantial evidence of the well-known will; and the identity of character between the Puritan Scropes and the family of the Throops of Bozrah, from whom, he said, the descent of several of those in the room was proved by absolute record evidence. He enlarged with an air of triumph upon this last consideration. But it was obvious enough that he was dwelling on his strongest point and slurring over his weakest. Was a Yankee audience likely to overlook that? If he could prove that Adrian Scroope

and Adeodatus Throop were one and the same person, or if he could even show that there was a chance to prove it, he might succeed in organizing the association and becoming its agent. But if the question had been taken immediately after his reply to Mr. Stanley, it would have been lost.

The audience were muttering discontentedly to each other. Mr. Stanley rose again, and in the same cold, rasping manner and voice, and with the same mirthless smile, said : —

"Mr. Chairman, I move that this meeting do now adjourn *sine die.*"

This was sudden death which he so obligingly offered. Adrian sprang up, and without an instant in which anybody could say, "Second the motion," exclaimed, —

"One moment, Mr. Chairman!"

"Mr. Adrian Chester," said Mr. Button.

"Before anybody seconds Mr. Stanley's motion," continued Adrian, "just a word, and then I will not oppose its being put." Mr. Stanley, looking perhaps no sourer than usual, but with a stiffish bow, sat down. Adrian continued, while Mr. Button looked towards him with interest, and Mr. Scrope with doubt. He began by saying that he should not speak of English estates or English law, but that he should confine himself to the third question which had been put to Mr. Scrope, to wit : the question of the descent of those present, through Adrian Scroope of Hartford, from Adrian Scroope the Regicide.

At this, Mr. Stanley pricked up his ears, for he knew that Adrian possessed the lost Scrope Genealogy, and he rightly judged that the same was to be cited. Except Purvis and Mr. Van Braam, not another soul in the room knew it; not even Scrope of Scrope, who, however, at hearing this line of argument proposed, showed even a keener interest than the East Hartford antiquarian.

First, proceeded Adrian, he would barely refer to the well-known Scrope will, which, as Mr Scrope had observed, afforded some presumptive evidence. But that was known to them all; and he believed that this pamphlet — here he drew it forth and held it up — did in fact furnish, not the legal proof that had been asked for, but the circumstantial evidence that had been asked for: evidence of so convincing a nature as to completely justify the formation of the proposed association and the contribution of all the money required, or several times as much, for the sake of fully investigating the subject.

By this time everybody in the room was, as they say in the country, "all in a twitter"; and a funny assortment of intensely attentive faces was concentred upon Adrian, about half of them with their mouths wide open. As for Mr. Scrope, his flushed cheeks, as he leaned forward towards Adrian, sufficiently showed his excitement.

"This pamphlet," continued Adrian, "which I discovered, by great good fortune, only a week ago, is the celebrated, though long-lost, unique Scrope Genealogy — " Here a kind of catching of the breath ran through the audience, and Mr. Scrope gave a perceptible start, and gazed upon the orator with unspeakable doubt and astonishment. "Its pages consist of a genealogical account, very much after the usual fashion, and ending with the writer, whose name, Adrian Scroope, is so printed on the title-page. But the evidence to which

I wish to call your attention is on the back of the title-page. It contains five different items, from which I argue that Adrian Scroope was the son of Colonel Adrian Scroope the Regicide, and that, moreover, he and Adeodatus Throop were one and the same person.

"*First.* Both names are signed on this page, in precisely the same handwriting, and that is, by the way, the handwriting of the Scrope will.

"*Second.* The words *non hœc, sed me*, printed below the verses here, which verses I will read in a moment, were the motto of the Buckinghamshire Scroopes, to which family Colonel Adrian belonged. They are a noble motto, though it is impossible to English them in so few words: 'Not the goods of this life, but my own soul's good,' will give their meaning.

"*Third.* There is a rough but distinct pen-and-ink sketch, properly blazoned, of the arms of Colonel Adrian Scroope, — azure a bend or, — at the side of this motto.

"*Fourth.* There is a sort of puzzle of half Latin and half English, bracketed together under this motto." Adrian read it —

E } King's Church } ibam
   Church's King }

"Now, this device has, to begin with, a plain meaning suited to the case of the Puritan refugee who printed them there, viz.: 'I went out from the church-and-state condition;' that is, evidently, 'I fled from England.' But, moreover, these letters have a secret meaning. Omitting either one of the duplicates within the brackets, the device is a perfect anagram of the word 'Buckinghamshire,' the county of Adrian Scroope's family."

By this time the excitement had

fully possessed every person in the room; and indeed, whatever the interest of such obsolete conundrums to the general public, it would have been quite impossible to find any theme more entrancing to old Adam Welles, to Purvis the dealer in rare books, to Philetus Stanley the professional antiquary, to Mr. Van Braam the genealogist and lover of secret things generally, or to Scrope of Scrope, who saw his enterprise thus rising out of actual death into a vitality and hopefulness far beyond any which he could himself have inspired into it; not to speak of the perhaps less special but vivid enough curiosity of all the rest of the marvel-mongers. They had all gathered close around the speaker, who continued : —

" *Fifth.* The verses printed here have a similar double meaning," — Adrian read them; there is no harm in repeating them here, for the clearer illustration of the young man's line of argument : —

See, here I raise a Monvmente in hast
Charg'd to protect old Names, old Fames,
from Waste.
That is laid off, its Hist'rie here is told.
Here I take up new Name, old Life to hold.
Read in this Verse the Truth, the Cause, the
Hope.
Old Faith new Fame shall found ; farewell
to Scroope.
Old Fame, farewell! Old Faith, live in new
Fame!
Pray God, though Life be short, I scape from
shame:
Earth first, and Heaven at last, shall give me
a new name.

" Now," he proceeded, " not only these lines can be construed as an intimation that the writer is exchanging his name of Scroope for another in order to escape danger, but they cannot easily be construed to mean anything else. This is their first or obvious meaning. The second, or hidden meaning, is a conceit of the

same sort with the anagram; and such conceits, I need not remind you, were common in those days. It shows, I think, that the writer meant it to contain a statement of what the name was that he was laying off, and what that was which he was assuming instead. It consists in the fact that the verses are an acrostic. The first letters of the lines are *S. C. T. H. R. O. O. P. E.*: a combination, as you see, that includes the names of Scroope and Throop.

" Now," concluded Adrian, " when you consider the character of the Puritan Scroopes, their danger under Charles II, the amount of other evidence that an Adrian Scroope fled to New England, the elaborate nature of all this concealment, the consistency and preciseness of its meaning when thus interpreted, and its perfect senselessness for any other purpose, I do not see how you can help believing that Adrian Scroope of Hartford was the son of Colonel Adrian Scroope the Regicide, and was the same as the Rev. Adeodatus Throop of Bozrah. And I, for my part, can prove to the satisfaction of any court, that I am descended from the daughter named in the so-called Scrope will, which, if I am right, is the same, whether it be a Scrope will or a Throop will. And now, Mr. Chairman, I submit to your personal examination, and to that of the present company, the document on which my reasoning is founded : a document which, for my part, I confess, I would rather own than to own any other one manuscript or printed thing on this continent. And if any one likes to second my friend Mr. Stanley's resolution for adjournment, I will interrupt no further."

And Adrian handed up the precious pamphlet to Mr. Button, amidst a quantity of applause which, from so small a company, was simply amazing. They stamped and clapped and laughed aloud; and old Adam Welles, when he could make himself heard, absolutely proposed three cheers for Adrian Scrope Chester, the resurrectionist of the Scrope Association of America! — and he got them, too — three rousing ones. Mr. Stanley, on his part, made haste to ask leave to withdraw his motion, and got that. Mr. Button, after a brief inspection of the pamphlet, passed it over to the dazed Mr. Scrope, saying at the same time, "Hand out your articles; now is your time." Scrope did so; and as fast as the signatures could be set down, every descendant in the room was enrolled and the proper amount of money — it was $5.00 apiece — paid down. Last but one, Mr. Stanley signed, and with a very good grace, considering how ungracious a person he was; for he shook hands with Mr. Scrope, and complimented him on the prospects of his enterprise, and as he put down his name, he entered against it the pleasing words, "Ten Shares," laying down therewith a clean fifty-dollar bill. Last of all came Mr. Button, who quietly wrote "One Hundred Shares"; and taking the corresponding amount from a substantial roll of bills, he handed it to Mr. Scrope, and added, —

"There. And, cousin Scrope, I will furnish as much more as is necessary. I'll see this thing clean through to the end, and now shake hands on it." This Mr. Scrope was very willing to do.

At the further suggestion of the chairman, officers were now formally chosen for the Scrope Association, to wit: Tarbox Button, Esq., of New York, President; Adrian Scrope Chester, Esq., of Hartford, Secretary; and A. B. D. V. Scrope of Scrope, Esq., Agent. The agent was authorized to enlist further members, and to push the objects of the association, by and with the advice and consent of the president and secretary; and the meeting then adjourned in a most agreeable state of mind.

After much informal exchange of congratulations, the members dispersed; not, however, until Mr. Button had requested most of those present to attend a little celebration which he proposed to organize on the evening of the next day at his own home, to commemorate this agreeable occasion.

PART VIII.

CHAPTER XXII.

NEXT morning, Adrian went to call on Mr. Scrope at the latter gentleman's place of business. Adrian was going to Hartford, and Mr. Scrope to England; and it was desirable that they should arrange their joint plan of operations in the matter of the Scrope estate.

The place of business in question was in Amity Street, a little off Broadway to the west, in a row of two-story red brick houses, which were respectable dwelling-houses a generation ago, but now degraded — or elevated — to business occupancy. The tenement where the agency of the Scrope Association was established was recognized by Adrian before he saw the number on the door, from a gay water-color drawing in the window, in bright blue, with gold-leaf and silver-leaf liberally laid on, representing a lion of the heraldic variety, surrounded by the other splendid adornments of a coat-of-arms, with crest, supporters, and motto complete, and having underneath the mystic formula: —

"BY THE NAME OF FERGUSON."

"Ferguson," repeated Adrian; "the Ferguson Arms! Mr. Mark Twain, I believe, met a member of that family — or installed one — in Italy." Reading further, upon a wonderfully resplendent sign hanging beside the Ferguson Arms, all white and gold, the announcement "College of Heralds, by Doctor Adelbert O'Rourke," he walked straight in, and entered the room designated by these gorgeous and aristocratic belongings. It was a dingy little place, of old a front parlor, with a few books on the mantel-piece, and two small office desks. On one of these lay a fat, red-covered royal octavo, which Adrian recognized as Burke's Encyclopædia of Heraldry; and at it sat a fat, red man, with moist, full eyes, no less obviously the King-at-Arms, so to speak, of the College. At the other desk sat Mr. Scrope, busily at work with papers and letters. He welcomed Adrian with a very genuine interest.

"Aw, ow do you do! The vewy man I wanted to see. Ave a chair."

"I want to congratulate you on making so good a speech yesterday," said Adrian, sitting down. "Most of you Englishmen hitch dreadfully in speaking."

"Aw, yes; you 're vewy kind, I'm sure. But Bird's entitled to alf the credit, hat least. E coached me twemendously. Vewy clevah fellah, Bird, d' ye know, now?"

Adrian agreed that it was so, but could not help intimating that so much of the missionary spirit was not common among police reporters.

"No? Well, — fact is, e and I ave become vewy fwiendly, — quite pals, in fact."

"Hallo, Brab! how are you?" sung out a clear voice, the singer at the same time coming suddenly in at the door.

"Aw, ow de do?" said Scrope, evidently acknowledging this compendious appellation. "Take a seat. Mr. Chester, Mr. Bird."

It was indeed the reporter who had thus profaned the majestic name of Brabazon. Adrian and he shook hands, and Adrian could not help laughing.

"Wat is it?" asked Scrope.

"Why," said Adrian, "I beg your pardon; but if you let yourself be called Brab, you'll surely be supposed Barabbas, — not Brabazon."

"'Now Bawabbas was a wobber, you know," commented Scrope; "that would n't do at all. Must twouble you to say it in full, I'm afwaid, Bird?"

"Very good," said Bird; "or I'll say Scrope; but there's something grand about Brab; I like it. However, we're in the paper. You saw it, I suppose?"

"No," said Scrope, eagerly; "show me."

So Bird drew forth a morning paper, and opening it, pointed out to the young Englishman a paragraph in the gossip department, giving a brief account of the meeting of the Scrope Association.

"Capital! capital!" exclaimed Scrope, reading it aloud; "could n't be better! Iinfinitely obliged, Bird. Don't know ow I'm hevah going to weturn hall your goodness, I'm sure! Now, Mr. Chester, his n't that good?"

"Very good indeed," assented Adrian, politely. "Excellent advertisement, I should say. But do you know, the first thing I think of when I see gossipy things in the papers, is Mr. Thackeray's maxim?"

"Wat's that?" said Scrope.

Adrian quoted: "Infamation is infamation, and it does n't matter where the infamy comes from." And Scrope looked rather puzzled. Why should n't he? He did not understand such squeamishness.

Bird laughed, and said, "O, he wanted it in, so I put it in for him."

"Can you keep things out as easily?" asked Adrian.

"Not so easily. But it can be done. Pretty important for police purposes, every now and then, to keep things out of print."

"Well," returned Adrian, "I shall ask leave to apply to you if I ever want either of them done, as you are so influential with the papers."

Bird very civilly said he was at Mr. Chester's service, and then congratulated Adrian on the prompt and able manner in which he had intervened at the critical moment to decide the opinions of the assembly the day before.

"Yes," assented Scrope. "By Jove, do you know, now, the ole thing was dead as Julius Cæsar! It was just like a scene in a play! But now, my dear fellah, watever made you keep so vewy dark about that pamphlet?"

"Yes," said Bird, "I've been thinking of that."

"Why," said Adrian, "I did n't keep so very dark. There were four people in the room yesterday who knew I had it. Besides, I had had it only a very few days. And how much stronger it made the effect. It's a great deal more astonishing to make a dead man appear, than a live one."

This was good reasoning, and the two young men assented, though they still felt that it did not fully explain Adrian's keeping the knowledge of his secret from the one man of all most interested in it, viz. Mr. Scrope himself. It would not have been quite elegant to explain, for the chief reason was this: Adrian's opinion — or rather feeling — about Mr. Scrope was, that though he might be a good fellow enough, it was better to be in a position to manage him than to be managed by him. This feeling, indeed, was so distinct, that Adrian even found himself concluding that in Scrope's hands, the financial part of their undertaking was pretty likely not to amount to much, even should it turn out that there was any money to be recovered. In truth, however, Adrian was little concerned about the money. His only real expectation was that all this stir and excitement might lead to the discovery of new information respecting the curious family history of the refugee, and of the Scrope family in general, and — a far more interesting point to him — that it might in some way or other put him on the trace of the Scrope collection of books, the Lost Library ; and he was about as unwilling to state in full these motives, as he was his estimate of the personal character of Mr. Scrope. He had no doubt, moreover, in his own mind that these same motives — viz. the hope of discovering some genealogy and the Lost Library— had decided Mr. Philetus Stanley to join so heartily in the movement as he did, when he found he could not prevent it. It was the most natural thing in the world for a shrewd, sly, cool man to try joining the Association, with a view to manage it and get the benefit of it, as soon as he was sure he could not shut it off from the investigation which he would have preferred to monopolize.

Adrian, perceiving how intimate a friendship had been contracted between Bird and Scrope, judiciously accepted the situation, congratulating himself doubly upon not having made Scrope a confidant, as, he saw, Bird would have been his confidant too ; and he believed, with shrewd old Gilbert Stuart the painter, that a secret known to III persons is too often known, not to three, but to a hundred

and eleven. As, however, the doings of the Scrope Association could neither reveal his own interest in any secrets, or be much of a secret themselves, he proceeded at once, without any reserve on account of Mr. Bird, to discuss, as secretary, with Scrope as agent, the line of operations to be adopted. Half an hour's talk served to arrange this, and several shrewd practical suggestions from Mr. Bird were of a good deal of use, insomuch that Adrian suggested that he should be appointed a " brevet Scrope," by way of acknowledgment. The plan was simple ; it was first to enlist as many more members as possible in the association, during the short remaining period of Mr. Scrope's stay in America, and to prepare full and legally authenticated transcripts of all documents and evidence that could be mustered of all Scrope descents on this side the water, with a view to opening the legal campaign in England This campaign, which was to be the practical and decisive test of the enterprise, was only to be set on foot after the fullest possible preparation, and upon express authority, to be sent from the officers of the association in America, who were expected to furnish most of the means, and had a right to this control.

All this having been adjusted, Mr. Scrope now insisted that the three should step out and celebrate the happy beginning of his authentic official labors by a drink ; " especially," he added, as it was time for his " bitters." Bird assented, and Adrian, reluctant to seem churlish, went with them. There are few blocks on that part of Broadway without half a dozen bars, and a shrine for the proposed libation was not far to seek. It was, indeed, evidently a regular haunt of Mr. Scrope's ; for at his entrance the splendid creature behind the bar nodded familiarly, and said, —

"Your friend was just in — he's coming right back." And he added, "The same?"

"Yes," said Scrope ; "two of ' em, as usual."

"What for you, gents?" continued the affable high-priest.

"O, I 'll drink with them," said Bird.

"What is it?" asked Adrian.

"Absinthe," said Scrope. "Try it."

"Why, I 'd like to know how it tastes," said Adrian, " but I hate liquor I 'll do it if you 'll let me off in case I don't like it. Besides, I can't carry any liquor ; it muddles my head very disagreeably."

"All right," said Bird ; "he *won't* like it. Give him a soda cocktail, too ; then he can go through the motions, at any rate."

Adrian readily permitted the discreet Mr. Bird to adjust the ceremonial, asking only what a soda cocktail might be, and well pleased to learn how very slightly it differed from a glass of soda-water ; and the barkeeper proceeded to the somewhat elaborate and scientific-looking process. of mixing three glasses of the most infamous and fatal poison ever dispensed as a drink, — that liquid idiocy, the scoundrelly French invention of absinthe. The oily-looking, pale-green wormwood-juice was yet dropping and spreading cloudily in the last goblet, when the expected " friend," Mr. William Button, arrived, and boisterously greeting the company, signified his content with the order which had been given on his behalf, adding, with oaths, to Scrope, —

" You taught me to drink it, by ( ), and by ( ), it 's fair to suppose I 'll stick to it as long as you do, by ( )."

We may charitably believe that in commending such a deadly cup to the lips of the unfortunate young man whose very brain and spine were already dissolving in the same frightful disease which this fiend's potion so powerfully promotes, the scatter-brained Englishman was ignorant at once of the double power of strong drink in the stimulating climate of America ; of the peculiar hateful influence of absinthe in causing or accelerating ailments that involve the brain and spinal marrow, and of the fact that such a disease was already rapidly establishing itself in Mr. William Button's frame

However, the three others sipped off the stuff, and smacked their lips approvingly. As for Adrian, he tasted it, it is true ; and at the contortion of his visage, and the abhorrent haste with which he spat forth the nauseous bitter filth and thrust away the glass, they laughed until they cried. Mr. Button rallied him a little on his inexperience ; but Adrian said, —

" I 'll tell you what, Cousin William, there 's only one thing that I should wonder at more than at seeing decent fellows act as if they enjoyed that hell-broth."

"What 's that, by ( )?" inquired Mr. Button, with interest.

"Why, I should wonder more to see anybody, except a natural fool, who should be afraid to say he abominated it, or who should be joked into even smelling at it a second time. Phew ! Give me that other thing, please, Mr. Barkeeper."

It was done, and the quartette drank a solemn toast to the health and prosperity of the Scrope Association, and of Mr. Agent Scrope in particular. And Mr. Button, who had evidently been drinking before, proceeded to bawl out that ancient chorus, —

"For he's a jolly good fellow,"

with a rather uncertain modulation, and to tack on to the end of it the next song that happened to come into his head, having a curious refrain of —

"Skittyittyittyittykadink, a dink, a dink a dido,"

quite too curious and elaborate, in fact, for his fuddled tongue ; for he both broke down in the attempt to execute the swift quadruplicate repetition of its first half, and smashed all to pieces the glass he held in his hand, in trying to beat time with it on the counter. He then proceeded to order " four more, by ( )," in his usual roaring, peremptory way, on which Mr. Bird, winking at Adrian, said, —

" All right — go on, boys, we'll be right back — Mr. Chester and I want to just look in a moment over the way."

And rising, he nodded at Adrian, who took the hint and followed him out.

" I wanted to say a word to you, Mr. Chester," he said, " and I reckon you are willing to get away from those fellows anyhow."

" Yes, I am," said Adrian, very sincerely.

" Well, just walk up a block or two, and we'll cross over to Washington Square."

They did so, and as they were well wrapped up, found it no hardship to sit a while on one of the seats in the snowy open square.

" There," said Bird, " we'll settle about running away next time we see them. What I wanted was to say

to you that I had a note from Doctor Veroil about some matters that you are interested in ; and that I will certainly do all I can to arrange the affair comfortably all round."

Mr. Bird's quiet, steady manner in any business of importance, his composed bearing, that indescribable texture of expressions which belonged to his calm, intelligent face, — " good sense," we say it indicates ; nobody has described what it is in a face that makes us ascribe " good sense " to it, but we know it if we see it ; — all this operated on Adrian just as Adrian's own ready kindliness and swift penetrating, sympathetic intelligence did on others ; and he fell into an unreserved discussion of Civille's affairs far more easily than he could have imagined to be possible. After a good deal of consultation they agreed that she was undoubtedly quite beyond any suspicion, except so far as any very delicate and sensitive woman whatever may be capable of falling into insanity ; that the real question was, not whether Civille had stolen, but who had stolen ; and that the proper line of operations was, to keep perfectly silent, and try to trap the real thief.

" There's so much shop-lifting, however," Bird said at last, " and so many of these respectable thieves — they've got up a long name on purpose for 'em," he commented, — " anybody must be pretty well off to be able to afford such a long name as kleptomaniac — that it's a pretty difficult job to catch the right one. And there's one very disagreeable circumstance you don't know of — it don't prove anything to me, not yet at least, but it would make trouble if it were known — "

He hesitated a moment, but continued, looking very steadily into

Adrian's eyes, "I'm sure you'll understand me, Mr. Chester, I mean just that ; *it don't prove anything.* I have seen Olds since I heard from Dr. Veroil, and that's how I came to know it. And it won't be mentioned, you need n't be afraid of that, but some of Jenks and Trainor's stolen goods, some laces, were certainly found in Miss Van Braam's possession."

Adrian was a very steady and strong young fellow, but at this plain assertion, a deep sinking pain at the heart turned him so white that Bird looked almost alarmed, and repeated his assurances.

" I know so much about such matters," he reiterated, " that the fact is to me only a fact. My theory is, that the real thief put the goods where they were found."

But Adrian's Puritan descent and training, and his Scrope traits, shy of every publicity, inexpressibly horrified at the publicity of crime, made this circumstance peculiarly horrible to him, particularly as his vivid imagination reinforced it with all its possible associations and consequences ; and it was not until after many repetitions and enforcements of the arguments which the reporter used, that he could, even in part, recover from the shock. He however thanked Bird, very justly, for letting him understand exactly how the matter stood.

" Now," he continued, " I want to see this Olds. I want to judge for myself what manner of man he is. By what Mr. Van Braam said, he must look something like a prize hog. I never should pick out such a creature for a detective, I 'm sure ; and it makes me uncomfortable to think of his rooting and snouting about within a hundred miles of Civille."

And, in truth, anybody out of all the thousands who in those days saw this eminent detective laboring along the street while he was in the full career of his usefulness, might very naturally have made the same observation as to his zoölogy.

" Necessary evils, detectives are," said the reporter. " Some very bad fellows among them, and some very decent ones. As for Olds, don't you see that his very waddling and wheezing, and general tallowy, stupid look, may be an excellent disguise ? If he can make a thief think him just that, it helps catch the thief. Well, he has a sort of whim of never being at his rooms except in the evening ; and I can't go with you to-night, for I 've got to arrange down at the office, so that I can be at Mr. Button's celebration. I 'll just give you a card. Olds knows me, and he 'll be civil."

So he wrote " from Bird " on the back of a business card, and gave it to Adrian, noting at the same time the address, which was in a " public building," on Broadway, near the New York Hotel, and the young men parted.

CHAPTER XXIII.

It is not quite true philosophically, though it may be practically, that

" *All* thoughts, *all* passions, *all* delights,
Whatever stirs this mortal frame,
All are but ministers of Love,
And feed his sacred flame."

Not quite. For instance, try anger ; try hunger ; try fright ; try love of property ; try love of power ! Not quite all, dear Coleridge ! But a good many of them. Love, full, complete, perfect human love, is to feel, and express, and receive the counterpart of, all the attractions which make one human being desire another ; admiration, respect, friendship, enjoyment, sympathy (*i. e.* co-enjoyment), affection, passion. All these are unselfish. As for the selfish consciousnesses which the wonderful English minnesinger, by a noble material fallacy included in his assertion, they are comprehended, if at all, only negatively, as crime and misery are included in Christian society, to be reversed and eliminated. But without any one of those unselfish elements, Love, though it may be Love, is imperfect. Still more, or rather most of all, is any one of them alone an imperfect love. The old saw that " Pity is akin to Love," is just as true, and no more, as that beauty is concerned with love. The beautiful object must be lovable too ; the pitied object must be lovable too, before there can be a love in consequence of the beauty or of the pity. When Xerxes bejewelled the beautiful tree, he showed how love for a tree is not love. Whatever love comes of pity may be felt for a dog. Of sympathy in the sense of co-suffering, of pain by reason of the pain of another, the like is true. Whatever love comes of such sympathy, may be felt by man for beast, or by man for man. It is the sympathy of co-enjoyment which is a necessary part of love.

Surrender is the measure of love. This is true equally towards God and man ; the truth is so deep as to be of the substructure of both loves, and it is conclusive accordingly of the criterion of unselfishness for human love. And let no one say that such an analysis is cold or passionless. It is, or at least is susceptible of being, vivid with a sustained, deliberate passion which is to any other what the sun's steady, white heat is to the thin flash of tinder.

No such analysis as this was passing through Adrian's mind, however, as he approached Mr. Button's mansion that evening. He was in a somewhat confused or questioning, and waiting frame of mind, from a number of causes.

He had visited Mr. Olds, the detective, early in the evening. That immense personage had wheezed and gobbled forth an awkwardly worded, but sufficiently clear statement, agreeing in substance with what Adrian already knew. This, indeed, was not what Adrian went for ; he wanted, to use a scriptural phrase, to discern his spirit. In this he was puzzled, as was natural enough. We get our impressions about a man's soul exclusively through physical media. If these media are unfamiliar, we cannot recognize the impressions ; and this exceptional, vast, fat grossness acted as a perfectly impenetrable curtain before the soul of Mr. Olds. The best Adrian could conclude was, that the big man seemed to show a rough and vulgar good humor as well as good sense ; but this was not enough, and Adrian remained accordingly in doubt what might be his influence upon the fortunes of Civille.

Burdened, therefore, with the constant pain of this heavy doubt about herself, and with the perhaps keener pain of a sympathy for her poor old father, Adrian was to do his best to make the evening a pleasant one to both. But he was to do this in the very focus of other interests, all converging upon him like a succession of burning glasses on one and the same object. He was hourly becoming more and more conscious that he was engaged to Ann Button. This engagement had subsisted, almost unfelt, hardly more than an acquaintance, for a year or two ; permitted rather than encouraged, as the couple were so young. Adrian's offer to her, as Civille told Mr. Scrope on the evening when he first met Adrian at her father's, had been really an effect not of love, but of sympathy and pity for unhappiness. Ann was, not to the extent of being persecuted, but to that of being unpopular, a solitary and unloved girl; dry-natured, close, jealous, bitter, resolute, fearless, hard, exacting. The mere kind-heartedness of the young man,—none but the impulsively benevolent can comprehend the statement,—the mere unresisted power of kindly impulse, had sent him to her side, had devoted him to her service, had caused him to offer her his whole life, as one takes up the cause of the deserted and helpless. It was greatly less strange that she should accept him; he was a goodly young man, and it was a real triumph, one which she very deeply enjoyed, that with her homely features and unlovely ways, she should carry him off from so many bright and attractive girls, although she had never seemed exactly to be conscious of the way in which they regarded — or disregarded — her. It was of course, too, that she should be the very last to see what his real motive had been. Whatever she did not attribute to her own attractions, she attributed to her father's wealth; and it did not trouble her that this should avail in her behalf. Indeed, to a nature like hers, it seemed a perfectly satisfactory motive. And it is — within its proper limit. How should she know his real motive? She had not the faculties to recognize such a motive; he did not know what it was himself. Neither of them knew love; whatever sentiment they had for each other, in him compassion, in her selfishness and pride, they ignorantly thought was such.

Now, however, to the stinging of his suffering for the unconscious Civille, and for her sensitive and too conscious father, was added the uneasy questioning of a half-awakened consciousness of his own, which took the shape of a feeling of remorse and shame for becoming recreant to his highest obligations; and the steadily increasing repugnance which he was hourly feeling for Mr. and for Mrs. Button, for their son, and all their works and ways, was growing and growing, also in the form, as he saw it, of wrong feelings which he ought to subdue. And all of them, in a fashion which he could not understand at all, seemed only to be the stronger for his struggling against them; a sorrowful puzzle it was. Then over and above all this were the business offers of Mr. Button, guardedly made, it is true, but yet in such a way that, as Adrian knew perfectly well, he had only to consent, to receive an establishment for life and ample wealth. The very greatness — pecuniarily speaking — of the opportunity oppressed him. It is only a low nature that will grasp with unconditional eagerness at money chances or money certainties. Adrian liked the use of money, no doubt; but it was with a genuine and profound repugnance that he thought of giving up, as he must, if he bowed his neck to the Buttonian yoke, the whole of what he loved,—accomplishments, knowledge, all beautiful and noble growths of mind and soul. Were such hesitations foolish? The road along which Mr. Button pointed was one where angels would fear to tread, and surely a pure and brave young soul was excusable for hesitating.

However, Adrian, among his other good gifts, had one right rare one.

He could put troubles and perplexities aside by a resolute exertion of will, and occupy himself fully with rest or recreation, still more with contributing to the enjoyment of others. So, as he was shown up the tall stairway to the gentlemen's dressing-room, and laid off his overcoat and adjusted his costume, he also laid off his cares, and adjusted his mind. Mr. Scrope and Mr. Bird, who had just arrived, were also, as the reporter remarked, " putting the last touches on their war-paint," and all three went down to the parlors together.

Mr. Button's home was what they call in New York, with an apparent contradiction of terms, a "high stoop" house; having a lofty flight of steps to the front door, so that there was a pretty high basement. in which was the dining-room. The first floor was entirely filled with the long range of three great parlors : lofty and richly furnished rooms, but hopelessly stiff and cold in effect, as if Mrs. Button herself had stood still in the midst thereof and let the rooms emanate from her. Even such attempts as there were at art decoration only made the frost more arctic, and the very north and south poles, one might say, were a couple of fearful full-length portraits, one of Mr. Button, and one of his spouse, that stiffened at each other from opposite places on the walls. There was a pretty numerous and friendly assembly, however ; for the requisite number had easily been made out by inviting plenty of young and old from " the church "; so that, in fact, it might be considered a sort of love-feast jointly celebrated by Dr. Toomston's church and the Scrope Association. In the midst of them, here and there, were a few celebrities, literary and other, such as the hostess had

contrived to gather at short notice. But in New York, as of old, you can always fill the places at the banquet in some way, if not with somebodies, then with common folks. Nobodies all are better than nobody at all.

In gatherings so unforeseen and hasty as this, the progress of affairs is always more or less like that process of hatching eggs which embryologists call segmentation. The company keeps gathering into small groups of such as know each other. These hang together in a comfortless, helpless way, very like the ship-wrecked sailors of the " Polaris " on their little floe, until there intervenes a supper, or music, or a reading, or something of that generalized kind, which at once resolves the whole into separate atoms again. The entertainer, if skilful, is constantly circulating about, breaking up or recombining these groups, as they stir maple sugar in the kettle to keep it in the grained state. Now Mrs. Button and Ann were only moderately skilled in this art, and so their guests were a little too segregate. Adrian, however, and Civille, having good capacities for the work, circulated and chatted, and served as a kind of aides-de-camp, and kept things going with immense vigor and perseverance, and a good deal of success.

First, however, of course, the three young men did obeisance unto Mrs. Button, who was all shiny in a new purple silk, almost as stiff and resplendent as japanned tin ; and then to Miss Button, standing near, whose costume made a surprising exhibition of her anatomy. The tendency towards low-neckedness of dress on the part of ladies other than fat, is undeniable, but easily explained. It is the flesh, and not the bones, that we are shy of showing ; as it is the flesh, and not the bones, whose temptations we are commanded to shun. Therefore, of course, the leaner a lady is, the lower her dress may be cut in the neck without impropriety.

The official greetings over, the three friends were quickly launched upon the tide of social enjoyment by Mrs. Button herself, who presented all three, as a beginning, to a group of substantial persons, which included Mr. Button, Mr. Stanley, old Mr. Adam Welles, who looked rather apprehensive and out of place, a few others of the Scrope connection, and also the famous Mr. Kalokagathos, from Greece, now investigating the social and political situation of the United States; the celebrated German philologist, Herr von Kladderadatsch, and the eminent female reformer, Mrs. Hetty Maginn, so often and impertinently nicknamed "Hit-'em-again" by those jackanapes, the newspaper men, by reason of her energetic and combative ways. But, as she often said herself, the leader in a great cause must have the qualities of a fighter as well as a commander. And, indeed, her coarse, red face was appropriate, and her brawny and athletic figure, and strong, rasping voice, might have made her part good in any melee.

Any crowd magnetizes. The life and light of the large rooms, whose cold and stiff appointments were greatly relieved by the throng that stood or moved within them, instantly acted upon Adrian, who was already resolutely bent upon enjoyment; for himself if possible, for others at any rate. His eyes shone already, the color already rose in his cheeks, and before a word had been said, he felt a sort of light and elevation in his intellect; all his wits and all his

senses — and his nonsenses, too — sprang up, wide awake, and danced with impatience for some activity.

"Good-evening, Adrian," said Mr. Button, with hospitable fervor, and with a heartiness which was, in fact, increased by his greatly increased respect for Adrian since his prompt action and forcible speech at the association. "Glad to see ye. Now fust thing, be sure and look in't the office to-morrow morning at ten exact, will ye?"

"I will," said Adrian, "if I'm alive."

Then they all greeted him as he was presented, and Mrs. Maginn, looking approvingly upon him, observed, —

"You don't look now very much as if you would be dead to-morrow, Mr. Chester!"

"I don't feel so either, madam; but I think very likely some of the people on whom the tower of Siloam fell were as lively as I am at the moment."

"Mercy!" said the lady, "I hope you don't mean that this house is the tower of Siloam, and going to fall on us?"

"O, no, madam," with a smile and a polite bow. "I feel much more as if it were the pool of Bethesda, and I saw the angel just come down to stir up the waters."

"O, thank you! Very pretty indeed," said the stout old angel, highly delighted, as everybody really is at a compliment, no matter if they know it is mere talk.

"I have been at Jerusalem last summer," observed Mr Kalokagathos, in pretty good English.

"Wal," inquired Mr. Button, "is it a fact that they have better artichokes there than anywhere else?"

The Greek gentleman stared and

said, " I beg your pardon !" Adrian, however, interposed, saying rather impertinently, it must be confessed, " They've dug them all up excavating for the Palestine Exploration Society."

" Ah, ja," here remarked the German philologist ; " very interesting mason's marks and remains there, on the wall of the Haram."

" Numbers to direct the builders, are they not ? " asked Adrian.

" I could not array them in a numerical order," said Herr von Kladderadatsch, in his queer English. " But I think to have a similitude with Runic numerals on the Dighton Stone traced, and some more on an Indian relic to New Hampshire out."

"Ah ? " said Adrian. " Then you are studying Indian philology ? Their numerals are very curious, some of them. I remember when I was a boy, learning a Popatomcock numeration table, to a scale of five instead of ten."

" What was that ? " asked the German, eagerly. " Will you it put down for me, please ? Can you remember him ? "

" O yes." And Adrian solemnly recited the following mysterious list, sometimes taught to young persons in New England.

" Een, teen, tuthery, futhery, pip ; sayther, layther, co, jelfrey, dix ; eendix, teendix, tutherdix, futherdix, bump ; eenbump, teenbump, tutherbump, futherbump, giggets."

" Ah, so ? " cried the German, in great excitement, " this is all most wonderful ! And will you note him for me down ? "

" O, certainly." And Adrian wrote the words on a card, while the others looked on with sufficiently puzzled faces, and the linguist plunged into an oration on the parallelisms of een and ein and one, pip and fif or five, dix and decem, and many others which he found amongst these numerals and the German, Latin, Welch, and forty or fifty sets more.

Then he began to inquire for the authorities about the Popatomcocks. The tribe is extinct, Adrian said ; it used to be established near where New Haven is now. Authorities very scanty ; and he referred him to 'that profound work, De Forest's History of the Indians of Connecticut, but added that he had learned their warwhoop when he learned their numerals. This the philosopher was eager to hear, and Adrian, without stopping to think, gave a tremendous Indian yell, slapping his mouth with his hand *secundum artem*, insomuch that his audience almost jumped off the floor with astonishment, and a small chorus of little squeals from all the women, and then a surprised silence, followed.

Mr. Button looked rather confounded, and was just saying, " Wal, young man," when Doctor Veroil's pleasant voice was heard ; he laid hold on Adrian's shoulder, saying, —

" Here, what nonsense are you up to now ? — how are you, Mr. Button ? Good evening, Mrs. Maginn ; come, Chester, the girls want you and Scrope and Bird."

And the jolly physician hauled them away, leaving the astonished seniors to compose their minds.

Civille, Ann, and a little knot of young people, were gathered near the folding-doors.

" What was that awful noise ? " asked one of them.

" This young Sioux here," said the doctor, pointing to Adrian, " was shouting his war-cry, that's all. He'll scalp you if you irritate him, so look out."

" He could raise my hair easily enough," said the saucy girl, — a merry thing with bright black eyes, — " without troubling my scalp "

Miss Button looked very prim at so open an avowal, but the others laughed, though they blushed.

" Switch, hey? " said the doctor. " Well, you deserve another kind of switch for wearing that kind. What horrible nonsense it is ! "

" What nonsense? " inquired Mrs. Maginn, who liked to be where something was going on. and now sailed up.

" Wearing false hair," said the doctor, " and feminine humbugs generally."

" You men are to blame." said Mrs. Maginn ; " we are fools enough to adorn ourselves to please you."

" Nonsense," cried the doctor ; " you dress to please each other, or rather to plague each other. Just see how you women quiz each other's rigs in the street : so you do here. There is n't one of you now, that could n't shut her eyes and make a full inventory of every visible article on every other woman in this set ! "

They laughed, but they did not deny it. Mrs. Maginn candidly avowed that it was a shame to them.

" Yes," said Veroil, sharply, " and a stumbling-block to you women suffragists in particular. If you can't improve such a small matter as women's dresses, you certainly can't improve their social and political situation. Idiots and Indians don't vote, nor babies. What's the reason? It's because they are all alike in being undeveloped in mind — all substantially savages. You women — your dress is savage. It's out of the question

for a man to vote as long as he is so savage as to stick feathers in his top-knot and paint his face and flutter himself out with streamers and things, as only a savage, or a fool, or a child, or a woman, does. The quality and quantity of mind that permits the ornament prohibits the vote. I tell you, until you can make the women quit rigging out those spanker booms behind them," — here the doctor pointed with a grin at a finely developed *panier* or two. whereat the wearers thereof instinctively smoothed down the same as if to quench them, and then looked both annoyed and vexed, — " and those wild jungles of things on their heads in the street, and hair off corpses, and all such savage fooleries, — until you can make them quit all that, there's no danger that you 'll get the suffrage ! "

"There 's too much truth in what you say, doctor," said Mrs. Maginn.

" But, doctor," said Adrian ; " you said the young ladies wanted me. What for ? "

" O, only on general principles. They always want gentlemen."

" Why, you villain ! " cried Mrs. Hetty Maginn, with a great affectation of fury. " We don't want him nor you any more than a toad wants a tail Now you're here, you may as well entertain us, though. You must either sing a song or tell a story — that 's the old rule."

" Very good," said the doctor. " I 'll begin. I can't sing a note. — was put out of the class by the singing-master because I put all the rest out if I stayed in. So I 'll give a song."

And sure enough, he struck up with the most extraordinary tuneless croak that can be imagined, but with so little noise at first, that everybody listened carefully, — those graceful words of Longfellow's : —

"I know a maiden fair to see,
  TAKE CARE !"

he shouted suddenly, without the least notice; and there was such jumping and such squalls ! —

"There," said he coolly, to Adrian, who, the fact is, had really been as much startled as anybody, — "that's to pay you for your yell just now! It's your turn : so now for your song or your story."

"Well," said Adrian, — "but perhaps Herr von Kladderadatsch"— the philologist was just passing by — "can tell us some German ghost story?"

"O, ja!" said he, good-naturedly; "let me to think. So — yes. Not a ghost story, exactly, but of interest, — 'The Story of the German Pastor.'"

And he began in a steady, even, slow, delaying way, as if he were translating it all deliberately inside as he went along, as no doubt he was : —

"As I was walking upon the sea-shore one morning (this is what the German Pastor said), I saw a man standing by the shore of the sea, and holding a pistol to his head. 'My friend,' I said, 'why do you hold a pistol to your head?' — 'Because I will shoot myself,' said he. 'But,' said I, 'why will you do this wicked thing? Do not commit so awful a crime!' — 'Because,' he replied, 'I am plunged in the deepest misfortunes. I have lost my estates, I am exposed to the utmost legal persecutions; my hopes are ruined, my future is only misery. I am at the present moment pursued for a debt by one who will cast me into prison, and therefore I will shoot myself.' —'But,' I said again, 'my friend, this is a terrible violation of all the laws, and will remedy no evil. What is the amount for which you are pursued at present?'—'Fifty crowns,' said he. 'Well, my friend, now come with me to the parsonage and I will lend you fifty crowns; and by no means pursue or repeat this criminal design of shooting yourself.' He accordingly accompanied me, and we set out to go to my home. As we approached, I saw that the door was shut, and going up to it, I knocked. No person came. I then knocked a second time at the door of my house. Still no person came to the door. I accordingly knocked a third time, and my little daughter Fanny came to the door. Having opened it, she started back at seeing me accompanied by a person whom she did not know, and exclaimed, 'My father, who is this strange man whom you have brought home with you?' Said I, 'My daughter, as I was walking upon the sea-shore this morning, I saw this man standing by the shore of the sea, and holding a pistol to his head. "My friend," I said, "why do you hold a pistol —"'

"There, there," interrupted Mrs. Maginn, "you will kill us all. How many times would that long story be repeated?"

"As often as a new circumstance arises in the narration, Madame," blandly explained the Professor.

"And how long would they arise?"

"As long as it might please the ladies," replied the Professor, his eyes twinkling through his spectacles.

"That's two abominable deceits," said Mrs. Maginn. "Come, we'll try who has the nimblest tongue, — no, let's try 'Burying the City' first. I only learned that last week, and I made one to-day that I want to try you with."

All acquiesced politely, and she recited the not quite unknown specimen, —

"In the next room a man was almost at the last gasp, and all night long his constant hic! hic! agonized me"

"Chicago," said somebody, after a few moments. Several others were offered; and at last Adrian recited what he called, —

"LINES FROM 'THE RUSSIAN PROPHECY.'
When Slavon sinewy, or Kalmuck fierce,
Through all embattled Europe west shall pierce."

It took them quite a while to disinter "New York" out of that; and then Mrs. Hetty, who had in spite of her zeal for big reforms, a decided liking for such childish rattletraps as these, insisted on her nimble-tongue exercise, as she called it. This was only the very juvenile amusement of trying to repeat, without error, divers difficult combinations of sounds; such legends as those of Peter Piper, of Crazy Craycroft, and Theophilus Thistle-sifter; that polar poem which tells how

"Midst thickest mists and stiffest frosts,
With strongest wrists and stoutest boasts
He thrusts his fists against the posts,
And still insists he sees the ghosts."

Mr. Adam Welles, who drifted up to them, with Mr. Philetus Stanley, suggested the short rural narrative, — "A skunk jumped off from a stump into a skunk-hole." Mr. Stanley gave, to be repeated four times very rapidly, "She sells sea-shells." One of the young ladies suggested one which will be found still more difficult, also for fourfold repetition, — "Shoes and socks shock Susan." And Mr. Bird, who had been listening very quietly, finally suggested the hardest though the shortest of all, to be repeated in like manner, very fast four times — "Black bug's blood."

After they had all tried and all failed on these last two, and indeed it is surprisingly difficult to say them in this manner, Adrian was called on for his song or story.

"Yes," said Mr. Stanley; "if you had heard him give the argument on the Scrope genealogy yesterday, you would know that he has a great talent for narrative."

"We'll ave both," said Mr. Scrope; "e sings like a nightingale."

"Well," said Adrian, somewhat embarrassed by the compliments, "but one at a time, if you please. I have n't Sergeant Odoherty's talent of articulating and accompanying myself on the trombone. I'll tell you a ghost story, and it's a real one. It happened to me, last summer — "

At this moment, Mr. Bird, who had been standing quietly close by, exclaimed, as if to himself, "I declare, I've left my handkerchief upstairs, now!" and ran out to get it. Adrian, casually looking out into the front hall, through the open door of the back parlor, near which he was, could see part of the stairs; and on this, he saw Bird, who was springing swiftly up, pause and draw to one side, to let a woman pass down,— one of the servants, — and, as Adrian remarked by her dress, the same who had a few moments before brushed past him on some errand or other, and had herself proceeded up-stairs. But he fancied that the pause on the stairs was a little particular, — long enough, in fact, for some words to be interchanged, — and though he heard nothing, something in the carriage and movement of their heads made him imagine that Bird spoke, and the hired girl assented. With a moment's displeasure at such an unsuitable flirtation, — for Bird, as Adrian had already often reflected, was too much of a man and of a gentleman to be indulging in some of the low pursuits that he seemed to enjoy, — Adrian turned again to his audience.

The young ladies showed evident signs of fearful interest ; and Adrian, assuming a grave and impressive manner, related as follows : —

"THE DEAD INDIAN.

" Just without the southern limits of my own city of Hartford, runs from north to south a ridge of trap rock commonly called Hartford Rocky Hill ; and which, as I recollect, is figured and described in an early number of Silliman's Journal of Science, as affording a remarkable instance of the junction of trap with sandstone. Its southern portion was formerly the scene of public executions, and was called by the ill-omened name of Gallows Hill Its precipitous western face has long been quarried for stone ; while from its crest the ground slopes eastward in a broad and evenly inclined plane of fertile farming land. The northern portion of this slanting tract is intersected by various lanes, now, however, disappearing as the growing city stretches southward, throwing forward its feelers of surveys, and empty new streets, unsightly scars upon the bosom of the earth.

" There stands, or stood, a year ago, in Zachary's Lane, as one of these narrow semi-rural ways is called, a huge sycamore tree, one or two of whose lower limbs ran out horizontally to a long distance. Crouched under the protection of this old giant, just at the top of the sloping green bank by the roadside, was a miserable stone hovel, floored even with the ground, and with a cellar to which admission was gained in front by a passage cut into the bank. As far back as any local memory extends, this hut had been occupied, when occupied at all, by one or another disreputable negro family ; but there was an obscure tradition that the spot had been the site of the wigwam of the sachem who ruled the neighborhood almost two hundred and fifty years before, at the first coming of the white man ; and whose name is variously spelled in the ancient records of the colony, but most frequently Sunckquasson or Sequassen. In this dilapidated edifice some of my friends and I used last summer to pass an afternoon ; sometimes in trifling amusements, sometimes in conversation, often very serious and earnest. We had added nothing to the accommodations of the old hovel except a few logs and blocks, which served us as seats, and the fantastic decoration of a human skull, which one of us, an admirer of Edgar A. Poe, had nailed up on the low, horizontal branch which stretched along above the hut, in a sort of imitation of that which plays so important a part in the story of ' The Gold Bug.'

" On one particular afternoon, a warm and pleasant summer day, we had gone out to the hut, and as the preference of the hour was for conversation, we took nothing for diversion or refreshment except a wine quart of claret, iced.

" We sat a long time, first on the green bank outside, and then within the single little room of the old hut, pleasantly discoursing upon a great variety of subjects. All the latter half of the summer afternoon glided rapidly away ; the fleeting July twilight crept swiftly upon us, and deepened rapidly into the shadowing darkness of early, moonless nightfall.

" There was a small projection from

the back of the cottage, within which a door opened upon a stairway to the cellar. I sat upon that side of our little circle farthest from this door, and of course facing it. While we still talked, and the shadows grew deeper and deeper, I happened to be looking directly at the cellar door. As I was doing so, it deliberately opened, and an Indian coming forth from it, stepped forward to one side of the little room, and halting, gazed steadfastly down upon us, as we sat on our blocks on the floor. He was of magnificent proportions; almost colossal in stature, broad-shouldered, deep-chested, straight as a pine-tree, and of singularly stately carriage. As he looked down upon us, gravely and in silence, though we all looked at him, we seemed to have no power to stir; and I clearly recollect how a warning against doing so seemed to take a tangible shape of oddly characterized distinctness before my mind. It was as if I saw a printed line worded and lettered thus: 'There will be a PREJUDICE against UNNECESSARY movement'; and I found the unintelligibleness of this monition accompanied by terrors that were vague but profound, at what might be the consequences of disobeying it. But there was something much more frightful. As the lineaments of the Indian's swarthy face became distinct before me, I saw plainly that though all the rest of the face wore the appearance of perfect health, the eyes were dead, and the flesh about them was dead; and though they seemed to look at us, there was something indescribably horrible in their livid shrunken look, and the fixed unmoving stare from under their purplish half-shut lids.

"After standing a few moments in utter silence, the Indian turned, silently retraced his footsteps, and, bowing his haughty head, disappeared down the stairway. We sat a few moments in the same motionless terrified silence. Then one of my companions, moving as if in a dream and apparently unconscious of the presence of any one else, slowly arose, stepped silently to the door of the cellar, and deliberately went down out of sight. In a few moments more another in like manner arose, and with the same strange appearance of unconsciousness likewise disappeared in the cellar. After another short pause, the third did the same. I sat a moment alone, and found myself slowly rising to follow their example, when the door was flung violently back, and Sam H., who had gone down last, sprang back into the room, shaking and stumbling with terror, his face white and his eyes almost idiotic in his fright. The sight of this natural human action broke the spell which had been holding me. 'For God's sake, Sam,' I cried, recovering my speech for the first time, 'let's get out of this!' And we rushed headlong out of the door. As we passed the outer entrance to the cellar, I summoned courage to approach it and look within; but all was dark, and its more distant portion was shut out of sight by a partition.

"Not daring to explore further, we ran homewards. As we went, my companion informed me that he had descended the cellar stairs and there saw our two friends seated at what seemed to be a table, on which was something that glimmered, while behind it stood the Indian, his head crushed up among the timbers of the floor, and as it were preaching to them, with fluent words and many gestures."

Adrian stopped. He had told the

fantastic story with so much local detail, with such gravity and intensity, that all the women looked properly frightened.

" But is that all?" demanded Mrs. Maginn; " how horrid! you look as scared as any of us."

Adrian shook his head, and with entire sincerity said,—

" It was horrible — horrible— and it is because it was so frightfully true that you can't help feeling it. When I woke up — "

There was a general cry of relief; and the saucy girl who had defied the scalping knife, at once testified that she had known it was a dream all the time.

" But wait," persisted Adrian; —" when I woke up, so perfectly impressed was I with the reality of it, that I *knew* that Indian was standing at the bedside behind me in the dark, looking down at me with those dead livid eyes, and it was minutes before I could summon up courage to pull off the two poultices I had to keep on my eyes at that time, so that I could look."

" Ah," said Dr. Veroil, " very good; very well told too; those poultices were the dead eyes, and all the rest of the dream crystallized round them."

" Yes," said Adria.

But Civille, who had been gazing with her whole soul at the narrator, said softly, as if to herself, " I think the old chief is there! "

Before Dr. Veroil had time for the joking reply which he seemed about to make to this observation, one of Mrs. Button's progresses broke up the little set, and the ladies and gentlemen were sent circulating on rounds of one and another duty. Other similar gatherings, other chats and conversations followed; some

serious, around good old Doctor Toomston and some of the elders; some comical, wherever there might be Dr. Veroil with his satirical sensible good nature, or Mrs. Hetty Maginn with her vehement blunt joviality, or even Mr. William Button, who had a decided taste for whatever of the funny sort he could understand. At the proper time came supper, and in the laughing and chatting procession down to the dining-room, there went just together, as it happened, these couples: first, Mr. Bird and Civille; next, Mr. Scrope and Miss Button; and behind them, Adrian and Mrs. Maginn.

"Do look at those shoulder-blades" said Mrs. Hetty, softly, to Adrian, pointing to the articles in question, very visible over Miss Button's dress, — the good lady knew nothing of any existing kinship or proposed affinity between her theme and her escort, — it must have been with reference to the funny *malapropsities* arising from such ignorances that the poet's wise observation came, about ignorance being bliss, —" do look at those shoulder-blades! You could drop a bullet through there to the floor and she'd never know it! I believe they put dried mutton-bones in a parchment bag nowadays, and call it a girl! "

Adrian, who could not consistently laugh, did the best thing he could, with another compliment,—

" Perhaps if she lives to be as useful a reformer and as delightful a companion as you, Mrs. Maginn, she will become as plump."

" Why, what nice compliments you make," said the good lady; " it would be ravishing if one could believe one single word of it! "

At the foot of the stairs stood one of the servants, waiting to go up.

Adrian, looking carelessly down at her, saw that it was the same with whom he thought Mr. Bird was exchanging confidences in the hall, and at the same moment he also perceived with surprise that it was the same blustering, scolding Irishwoman who had gone off in such a fury from Mr. Van Braam's on the night when he had escorted Civille home. At the same moment he saw Civille recognize her too, and heard her say, smilingly, —

"Why, Katy, is it you? I did not know you were here."

"Yis 'm," said the girl, with that very same venomous, bitter, quick utterance, — and she added, "if ye 've missed anything I could account to yez for it."

"I have not missed anything, thank you, Katy," said Civille, in her sweet, quiet voice, and passed on, completing some half-laughing remark that she had been making to Bird. Ann Button, Adrian thought, started. She certainly looked sharply at the girl. "What do you mean by that?" she demanded.

"And this young gintleman can tell ye that he set out to search me bundle," said Katy, pointing to Adrian, and all in a quiver at the recollection of the outrage. Adrian briefly explained to Ann how oddly the girl had acted on the evening in question; and they went forward into the supper-room, where abundant and luxurious refreshments were awaiting their doom, — and received it.

In due time, they all came back to the parlor; and now there was a renewed demand for music; and various instrumental and vocal pieces were given, some ill and some well. Thus, one was a spirited nautical song, by a gentleman who articulated a little too distinctly as he gave one and another successive note to

the same syllable, producing the following pleasing effect : —

"Aha, my bo-haw-haw-hoys,
    These are the jaw-haw-hoys
Of the no-ho-ho-bul and the bray-hay-have,
    Who love a life-fife-fife
    Of toil and strife-fife-fife,
And a ho-ho home on the bow-wow-wounding wave."

After a time, Adrian was called upon, and complied very readily, like a man of sense who is willing to do his best. For a moment or two, he could not collect his wits; and while the music was going on, and exciting him, as music always did, he had yet suffered his thoughts to fall back from their busy purposeful employment about the people around him, and although he promptly arose and went to the piano, his mind as he sat down was full of trouble; all the pains and doubts that he had thrust one side at entering the parlors, thronged back, more urgent than ever for having been shut out; and in spite of the trifling nature of the circumstances, and the perfect competence of the explanation which he had already given to himself, that momentary pause on the stairway, and the strange impertinence of the Irish woman at the stair-foot, plagued him; for by one of those associations which make themselves for us, the parcel of laces from Jenks & Trainor's, and the something which the girl implied that Civille might have missed, locked themselves together in his mind.

When, therefore, he took his place at the piano, he touched a few chords almost without knowing what he was about. The rich, strong sound of the noble grand piano in some measure awoke him; but yet no words, no air, would take form in his recollection.

"Do I know any songs?" he said, half unconsciously.

"Yes," said Scrope, who was near by. "Give us 'The Child's Three Wishes' again."

"Give us 'Sparkling and Bright,'" said Doctor Toomston.

"That would be an anacreonism," punned Doctor Veroil.

"O, I did n't mean the rum version," said Doctor Toomston, rather indignantly.

But Adrian still tried in vain to remember, until he began to feel ridiculous, and with a sudden effort, he threw off all his preoccupation. At the moment there came into his mind a song that he remembered; and without waiting to choose, he struck at once into a prelude of strong, full, reverberating chords.

"I 'll give you," he said, " the —

BEDOUIN LOVE-SONG.

From the des - ert I come to thee, On a stall - ion shod with fire, And the winds are left be - hind...... In the speed of my de - sire;

leaves.... of the Judg - ment Book un - fold.

The company had excited him. The music, mediocre as some of it was, had excited him still more. The air to which he now sang, monotonous, if not heavy, has yet a recurring, persistent chant character that in some sense throbs along with the passionateness of the words; and the pitch was just right for his mellow and sympathetic barytone voice. Civille was leaning upon the instrument, and without intending it, Adrian looked at her as he sang —

"I love but thee! I love but thee —"

And as he did so, the intense passion of the verses seized him, and he was gone; he sang the rest of the wild, lawless song to her, to her only. She perceptibly trembled when he first looked; then cast down her eyes and stood silent, without looking up at him again. If he had known what he was about, he would assuredly not have sung it. He felt before he had sung the first stanza through, as if every one in the room must see exactly what he was — in spite of himself — doing; making an avowal of uncontrollable, passionate love to one woman, in the home and under the very eyes of another woman, to whom he had promised marriage.

But he sang it through, although with no very distinct consciousness of his manner of execution. He arose without a word, — there was a silence as dead as that of his Indian ghost,

— and without looking up he moved off in a kind of dream, and sat down in the first chair he came to. In a few moments the applause and compliments began. Several of the ladies asked him where he got the music. He answered that he did not remember exactly, — he believed he had it at home somewhere. But Civille, who was passing behind him, moved perhaps by an impulse as unconscious as his own, bent down for a moment and said softly, so that nobody else could hear, —

" I know — *you* made it ! "

It is possible that a few of the more enthusiastic votaries of pleasure — unblamable as the pleasure must have been, since neither cards nor wine nor even dancing were allowed — might have stayed a little too late; but there came an incident to disperse even the chatty familiars of the house who were last to go. These, mostly young friends of Miss Button's, including also Doctor Veroil and one or two others of the more youthful elders, had fallen into a reminiscent vein; also Miss Button, Civille, and one or two more who had, as it appeared in time past, attended the same school with them. One and another of their schoolmates, it quickly appeared, were married; one and another had disappeared. Disappearing is very common in our American city life, where society is an encampment rather than an establishment, and where riches gather like one of those volcanic islands that grow up from under the sea in one night, and disappear in another, yet hot with the fury of their accumulation.

"Where is that lovely fair-complexioned Mary Gray?" asked Civille at last; "don't you remember how she used to make the awfullest recitations, and she was so sweet and loving that even old Miss Piquette, the French teacher, could not find fault with her? She said she always hated books; but O, what perfectly splendid embroidery she used to do! I wonder what became of her?"

"I believe her father failed and died, and her mother, I think, was dead before. I don't know where she went to, I 'm sure," said Miss Button. "Do you, mother?"

"No," said Mrs. Button, "I don't."

"Who's that?" asked Bill Button, coming up to Adrian's side.

It was Doctor Veroil who answered, with a significant tone and manner, looking keenly first at Ann, and then at her brother: —

"She died *Sunday morning*, Miss Button. Mary Gray, Mr. William Button."

Ann turned pale, for the meaning tone in which the physician spoke informed her plainly enough what he meant, and so it did her mother. But neither of them asked any questions. William, however, started violently, and caught hold of Adrian's arm.

"Hold me up, will you?" he said, "I 'm faint." And before Adrian and the doctor, both of whom instantly caught hold of him, could carry him off, he sank quietly down on the carpet, his limbs shaking, his face injected with blood, his eyes turned and set in his head: a frightful spectacle enough.

"Get away, all you visitors!" said Veroil, peremptorily. "This is not dangerous; he will come out of it; but do you all go home."

Nobody tarried to dispute so very proper an order, except Adrian, who waited to see if he could be of use.

"It 's epilepsy," said Veroil, after a moment; "a slight attack; he will come out of it in a few minutes. Give me some ice-water. Has he been so before?"

Neither of his parents nor his sister had ever seen anything of the kind. Adrian told the doctor, aside and in few words, of the attack in the billiard saloon.

"Hm, — must be attended to," was the only reply, and the doctor applied himself to the usual simple palliatives, dismissing Adrian about as brusquely as he had the rest.

So the young man went away, the circumstances abridging all leave-takings. As for Civille, her father, who had not been present at the party, had called to escort her home.

PART IX.

CHAPTER XXIV.

THERE are people who receive a knowledge of men's states of mind and of the complexion of their own circumstances by a method like the chemico-mechanical one called endosmosis, — a quiet, unconscious transpiration of impressions through physical mediums into the mind. *They find they know* what somebody wishes, or how things are going, but very likely they could not tell how they came to know. Such people will sometimes sit for a whole evening in company apparently without any consciousness of what is done or said around them.

Perhaps they even do not answer questions, nor hear what is said directly to them. Afterwards they can tell who was present, what was done, what was said; though at the time they could not tell, and did really not know.

Adrian, who possessed a pretty good share of this faculty of " unconscious cerebration," as Prof Carpenter calls it, had also a pretty good share of the more ordinary faculty of conscious cerebration He reflected a good deal, before the time of his interview with Mr. Button on Wednesday morning, upon the whole situation of his affairs, and he decided that he would accept Mr. Button's offer; proceeding somewhat as follows : —

He felt — and with a pleasurable glow of honest satisfaction — that he was at present considered somebody. He remembered the curiously delightful sense of controlling men, which had moved him while proving his case and convincing the assembly, in his little argument before the Scrope Association ; the intense watchfulness of the faces to which he spoke ; the little thrills of surprise, conviction, delight, which had moved across the audience like the small waves upon a field of grain before a light breeze, as he developed point after point in his closing summary ; the genuine enthusiasm that had responded at the close, — in words and voices, and in the far more affecting and conclusive form of lawful money. He now remembered the consciousness which, he felt, although at the time he had not clearly apprehended it, had surrounded him during the evening of the party at Mr. Button's, with an atmosphere stimulating like nitrous oxide, — the consciousness that he was an object of attention and approving interest. " Yes," he said to himself, — " that was it ! It's agreeable, no doubt, but — now, for instance, if it had n't been for that champagny kind of excitement I should n't have executed an Indian yell in mixed society, even to instruct a German Professor ! I wish I had n't !" And perhaps the annoyance at a breach of etiquette committed from an over-ready willingness to do as he was asked, and a real readiness to give information, neutralized any pleasure that came from having been the hero of the occasion.

More direct and practical than this generalizing self-gratulation, was Adrian's consciousness of having greatly risen in the estimation of the great capitalist, Mr. Button himself.

It was perfectly without intention that he had done so, too. Button, not appreciating any worth except the worth of doing, had been successively surprised, pleased, and convinced, as Adrian could not but know, by one and another proof in practical and practicable suggestions, beginning with a simple theory of penmanship, and culminating in the occurrences of the Association meeting. No wonder. In a young man like Adrian there is a fund of undeveloped power which neither others nor the possessor knows of, nor can know, until a time comes to use it. Then it rises and acts as it were of itself. In cases where this power is great enough in quantity and high enough in quality, its spiritual elevation, its apparently (not really) superhuman promptness, adequateness, inexhaustible force and efficiency, entitle it to the name in such cases conferred. It is Genius. So far as Adrian's action had partaken of this quality,—not very far, though unquestionably to some extent,—the action had produced its legitimate results; success in the object sought, and the admiring acquiescence of others in the means used.

This defining, however, was no part of Adrian's reflections at the moment; he was simply "orienting himself," —getting his bearings and deciding his course. He may be considered as a point acted on by several different impulses; in fact, as the resisting point in a problem in the resolution of forces. The forces acting were four, to wit :—

1. Business; being the proposition which he knew perfectly well Mr. Button was going that morning to make him

2. Study; the lines of acquisition of knowledge and æsthetic culture towards which his own mental nature

impelled him, but which he must definitely resign if he accepted Mr. Button's offers.

3. Betrothal; the fulfilment of his engagement with Ann Button, which would weld him with irrevocable oneness, even more than a mere business contract, into the circle of life where revolved the Button family and Dr. Toomston's church; — for this last, oddly enough, the young man found himself considering as a kind of appendix to the Button interest; and having no great reverence for institutions and forms merely as such, Adrian caught himself asking, like the funny man in the play, whether the tail wagged the dog, or the dog the tail?

4. There was another influence, however, the newest of all, and, if not the strongest of all, yet the decisive one at this time in bringing Adrian's mind to determine upon the consent with which he resolved to meet Mr. Button's offers. And yet it was the least distinct of all; perhaps even it would be most correct to call it an apprehension that there was such an influence. For, whatever it really was, Adrian did not name it even in his silent communion with himself; he had not expressly named it, even in that unresisted and sudden revelation of last evening. He felt that it was not best nor safe to name it nor to admit its presence. He only asked whether it was possible that it was present. He said, Is it here? and added straightway without waiting even to say No, or Yes, —If it is it must be put out; so that if he recognized it even as possibly present, it was only to flee from before it. There was nothing to make him believe that the power in question was really a living force tending to draw him any whither—at least,

nothing distinct. One kiss, one song, one look, one whisper. Yet whenever he remembered either of these, — and since last evening, — as he now recognized with a strange feeling of spiritual happiness which wavered moment by moment into something like fear and pain over wrong-doing, with a swift shimmer like the colors on a changeable silk, — since last evening he knew all of a sudden that for days he had lived in one unbroken dream upon one or all of them, — yet whenever he remembered articulately either one, his heart beat; he felt his cheeks flush; and at once, resolute to keep faith, he would say, No! and would set himself anew to the steady contemplation of what he had promised, and of the yoke to which he proposed to bow himself, as a means of effectual self-constraint to observe that promise. And as in dreams one is forever beginning something that will not end, or avoiding some phantom that incessantly rises again, so in this dream, Adrian, shutting and shutting the door to a paradise, and in resolved self-denying honor steadfastly turning away, forever found himself with the same door opening before his face, the lovely air of an unknown heaven breathing forth upon him through the portal, his heart and his senses acknowledging the divine abode, and his foot unconsciously lifted to the threshold.

For, sweet as the invitation was, yet the strongest impulses of the young man — and noble ones they were, no doubt — called him to refuse; a generosity even unreasonable; an untried instinct of self-denial; an impulse even beyond the line of justice, to surrender not merely his rights, but his wishes, for the sake of seeing others happy in possessing their wishes; a conscientiousness not yet trained to the wise recollection that one's self may no more be wronged than one's fellow — all these ruled him. Happier than the strong god of the old fable, he was ruled by several virtues against one happiness, and that an unknown one. No wonder that that majority carried him

So he hasted down to Mr. Button's office as fast as he could. He did not know why he went so fast; it was to get the business over and done with, and lock that door. On arriving, he found Doctor Toomston seated in consultation with the publisher, in the private office. Mr. Button, as Adrian entered, looked at his watch.

"Ten minutes ahead of time, hay? Wal, that's better 'n ten minutes behind," he observed, not ill-naturedly, adding, in his half-sarcastic way, "'Go not before ye be sent,' is a good rule in business as well as in Scripture: ain't it, Doctor?"

"I can't refer you to that text," said the doctor, with a smile, — "it's not in my Cruden, Mr. Button."

"Wal, it's good sense all the same. But I'm glad to see ye, Adrian; and now seddown and look over this memorandum for a minute, while I finish with the doctor." And giving Adrian a stout filed document, he pointed to a seat, and resumed his consultation with the clergyman. Adrian, unfolding the paper, found it headed, "BUTTON THEOLOGICAL SEMINARY"; and the surprise with which he read this noble title was not diminished when he beheld, as he read, a plan, worked out in considerable detail, for a complete institution. It was provided with a "form of sound words," or profession of faith, of the strictest old-fashioned orthodoxy and compactest verbal architecture, to be signed by all the professors forever; a set of professorships, and a well-digested course of study, were set forth; even the blank "Form of a Bequest" was added at the end, after the pleasing model of the catalogue of Rutgers College in New Jersey, with five different alternatives, adapted to the more general or more special ways in which any moribund might probably prefer to have the institution profit by his decease, and as if to be distributed to all wealthy persons intending death. He had read it carefully through, and sat considering, when the capitalist said, suddenly, —

"Wal, Adrian, — have ye agreed upon a verdict?"

"Why," said the young man, "I see what there is there."

"Seems to me you speak as if you was thinkin of something that is n't there?"

"I was noticing the assortment of Theologies," said Adrian, "and I did think of a couple of chairs that I should have added to the list, even if I had dropped two to make room for them."

"Indeed, young man?" said Doctor Toomston, mounting rapidly into the sacred desk; for the good old divine had, even from his one or two brief interviews with Adrian, become imbued with a deep distrust of his character and influence. If he could have prevented it, Mr. Button would not have called this unregenerate youth into their counsels; and he was wroth in advance with whatever observation Adrian should make; — "Indeed, young man? It will be a fine thing to know your mind respecting an institution which, we hope, will be a school of the prophets long after we three are resting beneath the clods of the valley."

"There, Adrian," put in Mr. Button, "you see the doctor wants to know whether Saul also is among the prophets!"

Adrian, however abundant in sweet and kindly impulses, was by no means deficient in the sterner ones. Indeed, if his tendency to benevolent actions was unregulated and excessive, his tendency to resist every semblance of injustice or imposition was certainly not less so; nor had he the self-control of experience, that waits to consider its own impulse before even revealing what it is, and then waits again to consider how and when best to reveal it. He had also already instinctively felt the hostility of the clergyman's sentiments, and he heard it now rasp anew in the sharp tones of his voice. He answered therefore, with perceptible emphasis: "Doctor Toomston, I believe *I* shall not 'rest beneath the clods of the valley'; I hope for a happier future. I think the habit of assuming that we are in the grave, is a heathen habit of thought and a heathen expression, and not Christian at all. Now, these professorships are: Historical Theology, Exegetical Theology (and Biblical Literature), Ecclesiastical Theology, Systematic Theology, Polemic Theology, Didactic Theology, and Pastoral Theology. All I have to say is, that even if I had to omit two of those, I would have two other professorships: of Practical Theology, and of the Christian Religion."

"Well, sir," said the divine, as he rose and took his hat, "whenever you will endow those chairs, we will try to reap the advantage of your great wisdom and ripe Christian experience."

"Don't go, Doctor," said Mr. Button. — "I'm sorry you and Adrian don't hitch horses no better; but I want ye to hear what I'm a-goin to say to him, for it may have a bearin on the futer of the church, and may bring him under savin influences, too. You hain't no right to miss that opportunity."

But Doctor Toomston was not at present in a disposition to seek the enlistment in his flock of so black a sheep. He would rather have bought the certainty of his exclusion with a great sum. Nor is it strange that the good old gentleman, having lived so long in conditions that made him a kind of pope, — or, should the diminutive of affection be used, a kind of poppet? — was intolerant of what seemed to him such presumption. And having at the same time a good deal of sense under all his habit of domineering in things spiritual, he was, though he did not know it, afraid. Here was a young fellow who said, " You're only a man. Come down out of your sacred desk, and let's see if you are right or wrong." And he was in the right to be afraid. It would have been an injustice to expect him to appear well on an arena from which his whole life had estranged him. And it would have risked a terrible lowering of himself in the eyes of his powerful parishioner. So, with real wisdom, and a sufficient show of dignity, he solemnly withdrew, pleading important duties, and hoping that all Mr. Button's counsels and plans might be guided and overruled if necessary, for the best.

" Overruled, hay?" commented the publisher, when his pastor had departed; " I reckon I know jest what I want, all the same. Now the old man thinks he's sejested the hull o' that are seminary to me, and it does him a heap o' good to think so. All right! I couldn't git the right

influence to bear if he did n't. Them parsons do hang together most remarkable. — Wal, I'll talk to ye another time about the Seminary. But fust of all, my boy, I really wish you could see your way clear to jine the church. I come to this city more'n twenty-five years ago. I had n't more'n looked round, before I made up my mind that that very thing was the best one thing I could do, and I did it. And it's been a great deal o' money in my pocket every year since that time."

The perfect good faith of this recommendation of what may be called an American simony, which contemplated not exactly buying the Holy Ghost, or even church preferment, with money, the same crime turned end for end, viz. buying money with position in the church, — the evident and entire sincerity of this advice startled while it amused Adrian. But he was at the moment in a complying attitude of mind towards Mr. Button, and not in a critical one; and he only answered that he would certainly do as he was requested whenever he should find himself a fit person.

This particular ceremonial was however not what the publisher had chiefly at heart; for he accepted this answer without comment, and proceeded at once to the main business of the occasion.

" Now, about our affairs. You see, there's more in you than I thought. If I'd seen as much of ye 't other day as I have now, I'd a made ye a distink proposition then, instead o' talkin kinder round the question. I liked the way you did up that meetin Monday. You put the case fustrate. I ain't no hand at chin-music, but I know a good style on 't.

" Wal ; the long and the short on 't

is, Adrian, I want a partner. My business here's enough for any ordinary man, and within a year or two my outside concerns have got so that I've been a-workin double tides this two or three years, and I can barely keep up. Then I've got some views for the futer — but they'll keep for the present. But I can't go on this way alone. My son won't be no great stuff to my old age, I expect. Fur's I c'n see he'll be lucky to keep his wits. No use thinkin about that. And I must, too; for if anything should happen to me, 't won't do for William to have control of my property. It's a trustee of my estate that I've got to provide for, as much as a partner in business."

Thus opening at once the main features of his purpose, Mr Button proceeded at some length to set forth his wishes, which were judiciously intermingled from time to time with compliments to Adrian's abilities, and compliments to his own perspicacity in discerning the same. He finally stated to Adrian a distinct proposition, to become his partner, to have the management of his correspondence and general office business at first; and to work into the control of the training department, as it might be called, being that of the choice and management of agents and canvassers, as soon as practicable; to give whatever aid he could in all other undertakings of Mr. Button, so far as desired; and to act, should the occasion arise and the means be provided, as trustee, or as guardian, or both, under such proper instrument as Mr. Button should execute for the purpose. A liberal revenue, by a percentage on the whole business income of the concern, was provided. In conclusion he referred to his unexpected satisfaction at finding such valuable business qualifications in one whose proposed very close connection with his family made their possession peculiarly important, and he suggested how greatly the same connection would promote and strengthen the arrangement he wished; and he ended with a specification of the first enterprise to be carried through under the new reign — the issue of his proposed ' History of the Bible." "If I can git that shoved under folkses noses as handsomely as you put them pints Monday, that book'll make a few-roar, certain — and a good many roar too, it's my opinion. And there hain't no sech chance been offered to a young man in New York city this fifty years, I reckon. — Wal, Adrian?"

What Mr. Button said was doubtless quite true. Adrian had only to say one syllable, and he was rich. Nor was he one of those imperfectly organized persons who are indifferent to riches. Money is like other temptations: not to resist it is wicked; but not to appreciate it is foolish. And Adrian had come with the definite resolve to say this Yes, as being the short straight road to the honorable performance of all his promises, and to a creditable and perhaps sufficiently useful position in life.

But at this last moment he found in himself a profound reluctance; just as many an intending suicide has stopped when the cold steel touched his flesh, or when the cup with the dose poured out was sloped towards his open mouth, or when already bent over the dark cold water. He absolutely could not utter the word which he had as it were lying ready made upon the very tip of his tongue. But this reluctance was from no victory of selfish wishes over unselfish resolutions What Mr. Button had been rehearsing had brought before him with renewed vividness considerations that it was quite right for him to pause upon. It was a profound love of the good and the beautiful and the true, a profound horror of the evil and the ugly, that bore his soul backward from the verge to which his reason and his will had brought him. Even the unusual kindness and softness of Mr Button's manner, while it affected Adrian deeply, yet — and to his astonishment — repelled him strongly. No wonder, however; it is always so with affectionate demonstrations from the unfit.

So he hesitated at the very last moment; he was seeing with the swift vividness of a strong imagination all the distress of future years: the interminable company of bitter-minded women: an imbecile and brutal-mannered ward furious at being deprived of the control of his own property; a hard slavery to business, and loss after loss of all the knowledges that he loved: a shrinkage and hardening of life instead of its expansion; — no wonder that the dollar question did not greatly weigh with him. A valid check to bearer for the whole of Mr. Button's means, waiting only for his fingers to close upon it, — but indeed it was something very like the equivalent of such a paper that he was delaying over, — such a check all ready before him, or even the sum itself in actual money, — in the mood of the moment, — would have affected him as much as the phantoms of values with which the frugal reverence of the Chinese cheats the ghosts of their dead.

But the tenderness of men like Mr. Button is not to be trifled with. It is too unnatural a condition not to be almost a mortification in itself; and especially if it is not responded to, it is likely to react into an excess of violence. This Adrian felt; but indeed all these phases of feeling had been passing through his mind while Mr. Button spoke. So he paused but a very few moments before replying. As the capitalist ceased speaking, Adrian, who had been looking at him, naturally looked down as one who considers. Mr. Button, surprised at even this pause, repeated his last words, with some impatience of tone, —

"Wal, Adrian?"

"I mean to accept," said Adrian at last, frankly, and yet with an effort, and a shade of constraint in his voice, — " but I want to know about one or two matters of detail."

"Mean to accept?" replied Mr. Button, with some asperity, but not yielding entirely to his dissatisfaction, — " why don't ye, then? We can fix up the details afterwards, can't we?"

"Well then, — just one thing that troubles me," said Adrian, almost ashamed of himself, and yet unconsciously, — and perhaps in consequence of that very embarrassment, bringing up the most dangerous subject he could have suggested, — not that it was not the right thing to do, — "just one thing. You don't know what some of your tenants are using your real estate for. Now, could I have a chance to show you the facts, and have some of those infamous places cleaned out?"

Mr. Button was angry. instantly; triply angry; with a sense of kindness abused, a sense of being impertinently meddled with, and last and hottest, and least conscious of all, with an apprehension lest he should be forced to know something that he did not mean to know, and so made to lose rent.

" I have n't a piece of real estate that is n't in the hands of perfectly respectable men," he said — " not one. If there 's any irregularity it 's against my express orders, and they don't like it no better 'n I do ; and they 'll stop it as soon as they can. Sech things will naterally happen in a city like this, without anybody 's bein to blame. But my real estate 's all satisfactory to me, and I can't break up my leases, either, jest to please your squeamishness, Adrian."

All this was excuse, and bad excuse too, and Mr. Button knew it, and the knowledge made him grow angrier as he spoke.

" Wal, I snum !" he exclaimed, in continuation, with the New Englander's attempt to get the relief of an oath without the guilt of it — " I snum ! I might a known, after all, how 't would be ! I 'd a darn sight better a waited and let ye come askin me. Offered sarvice allers stinks, my old father used to say. I 'm sorry I offered it to ye. I 'm sorry, almost, I offered any sarvice to old Van Braam too. Confound sech a high-flyin crowd ! I guess if I should send him in a bill for rent o them premises he occupies, he 'd find out, and so he would about that secretaryship o his'n, if I did n't keep him in it. I don't think no great o him ; I 'd jest as lief anybody 'd know that ; so I would that I 'll stick by those of my blood — if they 'll let me. Wal, I 've a great mind, jest this minute, to cut off all round, and let every man skin his own skunks. General Jackson said he heard of a man once that made an independent fortin a mindin his own business. That 's the way I made mine too. And if you ever

do make one, Adrian, it 'll be the same way, I can tell ye that ! "

" But I did not mean to displease you, my dear sir," said Adrian, who did not know the secret of what a sarcastic wit once called " the virtuous indignation of a guilty conscience," — " I meant to do you a real service, and I thought you would be glad of it."

" O yes, — wal, I hain't no doubt on 't, Adrian — not a bit. You 're like the Baptist minister that had been a-layin down the law to God Almighty in his prayer, and then apologized by sayin, ' Oh Lord, we don't presume to dictate, but only to advise !' You 're altogether too fast, — altogether. You must n't be in sech a hurry, or you 'll find you 've washed more close 'n ye c'n hang out, right off ! "

Adrian was too much displeased with the vulgar anger of Mr. Button, to take any note of the interesting illustration which these observations afforded, of the natural tendency of strong rude intellects to the use of such concentrated wisdom as these proverbial and anecdotic enforcements. Yet they were signs of native powers which might have made the vulgar angry brute a great orator. Intense passion, pictorial representation of it — what more is needed to sway a popular assembly ? Indeed, it was an obscure consciousness of these very powers that made Mr. Button wish to be a member of Congress, or a public man of some kind ; and one of his motives for securing Adrian's confidential services was, a half-defined purpose of making some sort of a finishing preceptor of him — a piece of literary sand-paper, so to speak. But his wrath was inexpressibly repellent to Adrian, and far more so was his reference to the assistance he had conferred upon Mr. Van Braam. " I don't think I can possibly expose myself to any such suggestions as that," was Adrian's feeling, and under this apprehension of personal indignity, his predetermined Yes instantly turned into an approximate No. He rose at once, saying, —

" Well then ; I can't expect you to continue your offer, since I have been so unfortunate as to offend you so much. You are quite right in calling it a liberal one ; I never heard anything more handsome ; and although I look upon it as withdrawn, I am really and very thankful to you for having made it." And he held out his hand to the publisher :

" Wait a minute," said Mr. Button ; and he put his two hands to the back of his thick, strong neck ; — " wait a minute. There 's that pain again. It 's queer. Sometimes I think I 'm altogether done up. Seddown, seddown You 're too fast."

Adrian resumed his seat, but kept his hat in his hand. Mr. Button sat silent, evidently recovering his self-command. After a few minutes he said, —

" There 's no use in concludin now, — I had n't no call to fly off the handle, whether or no. I won't take an answer from ye to-day. It 's too important a matter to hurry. But you 've got my proposition, any way. Now go and mull it over at your leisure. Take time for it ; and make up your mind deliberately."

Certainly this was fair reasoning ; and Adrian, feeling that he could not refuse, assented, and so went away.

CHAPTER XXV.

As Adrian purposed to set out for Hartford the same afternoon, he went from Mr. Button's office to his boarding-place, with intent to prepare for departure. He went leisurely, and stopped, as was his custom on occasion, to see divers sights, and more particularly to examine the stock in trade of one or two print-shops, in order to find, if he could, a suitable substitute for the unhappy print which he had destroyed from over Mr. Van Braam's mantel-piece.

In choosing this picture he experienced a good deal of difficulty. His modest finances would not admit of a good oil-painting, or water-color drawing ; what people call a " chromo," he despised almost to a Ruskinic extreme ; the various sun-pictures he truly estimated as studies rather than pictures, so that he was left to do the best he could with engravings. So he examined lithographs and steel engravings, etchings and mezzotints ; landscapes, sacred subjects, comic pictures, domestic and sentimental groups, war-pictures, portraits, historical scenes, in endless variety, trying to choose something with thought enough to bear acquaintance, with happiness enough of some kind, whether human, animal, or the representative happiness of joyous landscape, to be a comfort, and with artistic merit enough to bear fair criticism. A good copy of Henriquel-Dupont's immense plate of Delaroche's Hemicycle tempted him, but were too big and too costly. A Marie Antoinette before the Revolutionary Tribunal after the same powerful master, the noble Ecce Homo after Guercino, a dark, cold, strong picture of Odin speeding over the northern snows on some errand of death, with his raven at his side, Kaulbach's weird battle of the phantoms, fighting again in the air over the heads of the furious fleshly warriors on the earth, he examined and rejected. A sad or gloomy thought, whether great or small, complex or simple, weak or strong, is no good possession, if to be used alone. Next he found a large photograph of the pyramids and the Sphinx, whose exceptional portrait value redeemed it out of the class of mere studies; and he was specially attracted by the funny expression of undismayed joviality upon the gigantic battered phiz of the Sphinx, who seemed to "come up smiling" from her terrific punishment by the ages, although their pounding had beaten a vast hollow where her venerable nose had originally been. Yet upon reflection this picture, while a capital one to be included in a portfolio, seemed too peculiar to be placed alone in a sitting-room. In such a place, geniality and breadth of association, not grimness and separated quaintness, are wanted. Then came Hamon's delightful little fancy, "Ma Sœur n'y est pas"; then Holman Hunt's burglar-like "Light of the World." At last, just as he was on the point of giving over the pursuit for that time, he found what he wanted, — a steel engraving it was, broad in execution, yet so soft in parts that at first sight you took it for a lithograph. It had no name, nor any designation of either painter or engraver; but its level, strong meadow plane, its long, long vista straight and far into the distance, its perfect atmospheric perspective, the enjoying, powerful, thoughtful skill of the whole management, proved it to be after Rousseau. It was a partly wooded foreground, from which you looked out beyond and through one open glade after another, until you seemed to glide miles upon miles away to the distant horizon, carried evenly and resolutely by the strong will of the artist, over the vast and fertile plain. In the shade of this foreground sat a young couple, the lady with some work, the gentleman reading to her. That was all — but it was enough. Paying what was asked, without bargaining, Adrian took it under his arm and passed on, well pleased.

At entering the door of his temporary abode, the servant handed him a letter, which, she said, had been left there for him some time before. The superscription was in the handwriting of Miss Ann Button, and something was enclosed. With a curious mixture of presentiments, Adrian hastened up to his hall-bedroom, and opened the letter. The enclosure was the ring which he had last seen on Miss Button's finger, — the engagement ring which he had given her, — and the letter was a peremptory dismissal, dated about an hour back. Thus it ran: —

DEAR ADRIAN: — It is with much pain that I send you back your ring. I have for some time been convinced that it would be a greater mistake to keep on with my engagement to you, than to discontinue it. Recent occurrences have made me more certain of this than ever; and the prayers and counsels of one whom I revere almost as a parent, have this very day, and not for the first time, warned me, not to be unequally yoked with an unbeliever. I have been greatly wounded by recent expressions of yours upon religious subjects, and so has my mother. It is with her advice as well as that of my beloved pastor that I now act. We had better not see each other for the present. Let us, however, still be friends. I wish you every happiness in this life and a better preparation for that which is to come. Some things which I have observed have made me think that you have already discovered a more congenial companion than I could have been. I need not forgive her, for she has not done anything wrong, in this matter at least. Yet I cannot conscientiously ask the blessing of Heaven on any human relations unhallowed by the consolations of religion. May you be brought to know your sinful condition before it shall be forever too late.

Your Friend,

ANN J. BUTTON.

Adrian read this stiff and cold letter —a very corpse of a letter— twice through, with feelings that seemed to him thoroughly improper in a rejected lover. He wanted to laugh, and to hurra, in fact. " I ought to be mortified, seems to me," he said to himself, " and here I am, feeling like a prisoner unexpectedly let out of jail!" And catching a glimpse of his own delighted countenance in the glass, he did laugh aloud, in spite of propriety.

Then he set himself to consider what might be the facts of the case. Had he been to blame by neglecting Ann, or in being too attentive to others? Certainly not, unless — and here his conscience did give him a sort of dig — certainly not, unless in the case of Civille. With her name a profound wave of happiness and hope swept through the young man's soul. And he no longer resisted it ; he floated away into the dream-world of love. He had never known of it before ; the thrill and glow of his own emotion — when he came to a consciousness of his thoughts — almost scared him. Then, with an effort, he resumed his process of reminiscence. He had been as attentive to Ann as she would permit. But her cold close nature had mostly forbidden even the discreet intimacy which is thought proper in such cases. How cold and secretive she was, appeared plainly enough in her utter silence about these recent griefs of hers, until the last moment, in the severe air of reproving sanctity with which she conferred damnation on her lover, and in the prompt and almost brisk decision with which she cast him out of her — hands. But again ; had he done wrong in the matter of Civille? He thought and thought ; he could not see that he

had. At the most, he had without consciousness or intention suddenly found himself dangerously delighting in her ; and as soon as he saw this, he had in good faith tried a short road out of the peril, without even waiting to see whether his wish coincided with his duty. And on this short road, he had received already two stout and unexpected rebuffs, from the very persons in whose interests he had been acting, and acting in perfect disregard of any preferences of his own. Mr. Button had shown him very plainly that he meant to permit no ethical views to be confounded with his financiering. And now Ann, for whom solely — except so far as the keeping of his own faith with her might be a separate motive— for whom solely except for this, he was escaping away from heaven as fast as he could, stood up and thrust him irresistibly back. " It is good that I did not stop to think about it all," reflected Adrian, " or I believe I should have spoken first !" And he yielded to the stroke thus aimed at him, without wish or thought of warding or returning it ; back he hastened into paradise as fast as he could.

First he sat down and wrote, briefly, but kindly, for he felt so happy that he wished well to everybody in the world, to Mr. Button, enclosing Ann's note, and saying that this step of hers totally changed all the relations of the parties to each other ; and that accordingly it was necessary to postpone all their proposed business plans for the present. And he explained that he believed Ann had really done what was best for all concerned, and expressed what he really felt : sincere regard for her, and respect for the perspicacity which had discerned the state of her own feelings, and for the decision which had so promptly acted upon them.

Then he completed his small task of packing up. Then he took his picture under his arm and hastened to Mr. Van Braam's. He found Civille in the parlor, but not alone. She had lying on her lap a little baby, rather dark-complexioned, and with black eyes, that kicked and crowed while she played with it and laughed with it. The mother stood by, — a rather good-looking mulatto woman, with that glossy, wavy hair which indicates some mixture of Indian blood, and with that combination of intense passionate and lowering looks in her features, which is so often seen in the negro-Indian half-breed.

"I can't bear to have you carry the dear little thing away," Civille was just saying, as Adrian was shown in. "I'm ever so much obliged to you, Mrs. Barnes," she continued, as she exchanged greetings with her visitor, "for letting me have her so long. You'll bring her again, won't you?"

Mrs. Barnes promised; but the baby, having the babyish faculty of knowing who loved it, felt the strong sweet yearning that surrounded her, and at being held out to its own mother, set up a terrible howl. Mrs. Barnes' bright black eyes flashed with unreasoning anger.

"Not if you make my child love you better than me!" But she added in a moment, "Beg pardon, miss, but it hurt me to see her cry at having to come back to me. I've got a terrible temper. And God knows it's but a bad home the little thing will get with me, and a right poor prospect. Thank you kindly; and I'll be sure and bring her. Perhaps it would be the best thing could

happen to her, after all, to forget her own mother entirely."

"Good-bye, dear," said Civille, kissing the poor little thing, "we'll both love you, baby. And Mrs. Barnes, I'll do anything I can for you too; for baby's sake and for your own."

"You're very good, I'm sure, miss," said Mrs. Barnes, as she withdrew.

"That's the poor little baby they turned out of the Shadowing Wings last week," said Civille to Adrian, her beautiful eyes full of tears as she spoke; — "Dear little funny thing! I'll tell you a secret, cousin Adrian," she continued, — "I mean to adopt that little girl, if her mother will give her to me."

"Do you?" said Adrian, who was not in any mood of mind to disapprove or oppose any wish of Civille's — at least directly — "that is very lovely in you."

"I did not tell Mrs. Barnes so; but I wanted to."

Now, lovely as Adrian found the disposition which was impelling Civille, this particular baby, if any existing baby, was not the precise one to which he would on the whole have first directed her maternal instincts. But he had too much tact — and his sentiments towards Civille at present reinforced that tact — to say just that. So he executed a flank movement.

"You must consider one immediate question, and one future one, before you fully decide," he said, "for a real adoption, you know, is for life."

"Yes, — I know it."

"Well; I think you were telling me one day about your pets that died?"

"Yes," said Civille, as a sad look

came over her face, — " my poor little canary, my little dog — all of them — "

" ' All my little ones, — all ! ' " quoted Adrian. " But, my dear cousin, will you please also to consider what your father or yourself also told me about your own health having somewhat failed since you came to this house to live? And I know, myself, that you are not as strong as you ought to be. Anybody can see it that knows how to look at faces. Please to confess that you are more nervous, and more easily tired, than you ought to be."

" Yes, — I am," said Civille ; " but what do you mean, Adrian ? "

" And see how magnificently your plants grow," continued he, pointing to the luxuriant leafage and rich blooms in the little flower room. Civille looked, but was more puzzled than ever.

" You live here, and don't perceive what I do, who come from the country. The moment I was well within New York city, I felt the air to be dead, and dirty. It feels so and smells so to me all the time. I don't believe I could bear to be locked into such an infected place for life. Now that same difficulty is worse here in this old house, for it does not ventilate well ; you know your father keeps it as much shut up as he can, and the drainage certainly is not right. I know it is n't, for I never come in here without being reminded of it. And remember that plants will flourish in air that is abominable for animals. It is this close old house that killed your poor little pets, Civille ; it is keeping your own health down ; and if you do adopt this nice little baby, don't you do it while you live here."

The force of the facts, and the

earnestness of the manner in which they were put, made Civille look very thoughtful ; she considered a moment, and then agreed that she would at least wait a little.

" Ask Doctor Veroil," said Adrian ; " he 's a man of capital good sense as well as a kind heart ; he likes you, and he 'll give you the right advice. In fact, I 'll abide by what he says — I 'm not afraid to promise that in advance. I wish you would too ! "

Adrian felt quite safe in this offer ; for the truth is that he promised himself to see the doctor and get him well primed before Civille should have a chance at him. But he resumed : —

" That is the immediate consideration that I meant. The distant one is not so pressing, but it is worth considering. You ought to remember the chances that this little girl will grow up bad, in spite of you. She is not of a hopeful strain. Have you looked at Mrs. Barnes' eyes? There are some very wicked looks in that woman's face. I have n't the honor of Mr. Barnes' acquaintance "

" Oh, don't," said Civille, tearfully. " Adrian, why do you fight my poor little baby so ? "

" Dear Civille," said Adrian, " answer me one question. Had you thought of either of those things yourself ? "

" Why — no."

" Then was n't it best that you should be brought to consider both sides of the question ? " .

" — Yes — I suppose so," said the young lady, who very naturally hated to admit it.

" And if I was really fighting the little thing," said Adrian, " how evident it is that my policy would be to get it here as soon as possible, since I believe this house unhealthy for it ? "

So Civille was silenced, if not convinced. But she agreed to ask Dr. Veroil about it; and then she asked what was in the parcel. The picture was produced, and was liked; and was found to fit sufficiently well in the frame which had so long displayed the agonies of the Dying Camel. Then Civille returned to the sofa where they had been sitting, and Adrian too came and sat by her where he had sat before. He said,

"Cousin Civille, I would like to hold your two hands once more just for a moment, before I go back to Hartford this afternoon."

"Yes," she said, promptly and simply, and held them out to him. He took them, crossing his own, as he had done at the room of Mrs. Babbles in Depau Row, and looked once more into the deep limpid gray eyes.

"Ah," she said, "you must n't! You must n't put me asleep again, cousin Adrian!"

"I won't," he replied. And the emotion that arose within him gave her a troubled feeling; and an expression of perplexity, with a shade of apprehension, came over her face. "What is it?" she asked, with a shy smile and a faint blush

"Dear Civille," he said, "something has happened to me to-day that I should have said I ought to feel sorry for, and I am as glad as I can be. And it has explained something else, that I was afraid about before; but now I am glad of it. And still something else has happened which most people would think me very foolish for doing; but I believe you will think I am right."

"What a string of riddles!" said Civille, looking more perplexed than before, but yet somewhat comforted by the earnest gladness of Adrian's tone and manner. "What a string of riddles! And is any reward offered for the best answers to your three conundrums?" she said, almost gayly.

"A reward? No, I am not offering one; I am seeking one; before I have earned it, too. Civille, what is the reason that instead of wanting to keep things secret from you, as I usually do with other people, I always enjoy the idea of telling you?"

"Why, you have never told me much," she said.

"Have n't I?" he replied, impulsively. She blushed again and looked down, and he felt her draw a little away from him. But he held fast, and hastened. "Wait just a moment," he said, "I am going away.—Civille, Mr Button has offered me a partnership, and I have refused."

She looked up with surprise, yet not with displeasure.

"I had decided to accept, this morning, though."

"What changed your mind so suddenly?" asked the young lady.

"Chiefly," he said, "Ann's note, which I received afterward, dismissing me."

Civille started, and looked up at him with a mixture in her expression of sorrow with something that Adrian could not quite make out. But his carefulness and deliberation did not last him any longer. "Yes," he said, "she wrote to me that she would not be unequally yoked with an unbeliever. That was Doctor Toomston's text Sunday. Perhaps he meant me. She says he advised her, at any rate. So did her mother, she says. But, Civille, she was right. She did not love me, nor I her. It is you that I love. Civille, love me?"

"I love you, Adrian," she said,

softly, but with a feeling too deep for passion, and blushing a little, she looked for a moment, as she spoke, directly into his eyes; and she received, and returned, the kiss that he gave her.

"Yes, Adrian, I love you. But I ought not to have said it. I ought not to have kissed you. Let go, please! Don't, dear!"

For he was, naturally enough, seeking to draw her still nearer. But the beseeching tone of the last words was too urgent to be resisted, and he could not but withdraw a little, as her two slender hands, with soft impulse, even pushed him a little away.

"I can't," she said. "Dear Adrian, I know what you said, last evening, and I have been wickedly happy ever since. I should have kept on so, too. But I did not know this would happen. Poor Ann! She will not let anybody love her!"

Adrian did not know what to make of this mingling of confession of love, of reprobation and refusal of it, and of discursive benevolence.

"Nor you either, it would seem," he replied, almost discontentedly. "I don't understand it at all, Civille. I felt so sure! Well, I had no right to. But you don't mean it, Civille?"

"Yes I do, dear. And you will say I am right when I tell you the reasons. Now, you mustn't look displeased. Dear Adrian, if I hadn't thought about you more than I had any business to, could I have had an answer all reasoned out, ready for you now?"

It was true; the fact that she had indulged in dreaming of him even as a refused lover, was in some way an alleviation of the painful sense of lonesomeness that began to arise in him, as he felt that Civille's real meaning was a refusal. But still, it was a man's reply that he made, —

"I wish you had not given me one single kiss, then!"

"I don't," was the woman's answer. "It would be sweet to me always, even if I should never see you again."

"You are right, Civille. But now — tell me?"

As he asked, the front door was heard to open. "It's father," she said, — "to lunch. Don't let him know. I'll write to you. You have a right to be told; perhaps I can write more easily."

"I am not sure but that I would prefer a broad, plain, gilt frame, after all," said poor Adrian, in a tone rather louder than usual, jumping up so as to be standing on the hearthrug as Mr. Van Braam came in. "Gold always lights up a picture."

PART X.

CHAPTER XXVI.

"GOLD lights up the picture," Adrian repeated to himself as he walked slowly away from the old house, in a most discomforted and unsatisfactory frame of mind. He could hardly have told how he got out, and he wondered what Mr. Van Braam must have thought of his confused appearance, his hurry to escape, and his incoherent attempts at conversation.

But habitual good manners cover a multitude of sins. Only a very keen penetration could have discerned the disorder which to Adrian himself, struggling to repress it, seemed almost an uproar. The very effort however was of itself quiet; and the perfect unsuspicion of the old gentleman was an abundant supplementary protection. The phrase upon which Adrian had fallen in effecting the sudden diversion which had been necessary, meanwhile ran in his mind, or rather floated atop of it, as mere phrases will sometimes do most perti-

naciously when the real thoughts are profoundly absorbed. "Gold lights up the picture," he kept saying, until when he had repeated it a few times, a larger meaning flashed upon him all at once, and he laughed a short uncomfortable laugh, at the thought of the gold he had refused that morning, and of the picture which that gold was to have lighted up.

The fact was, the young man had not his wits clearly about him. He was stunned, or dazed, in a manner. He had been so certain — he had so *known* — that Civille would respond to his request instantly, gladly, utterly, — that her refusal perfectly confounded him. Even now, he could not realize that she had refused him. As he walked on, and the disorder of his feelings and thoughts cleared up a little, he could not feel the bitterness and shame of one who has been refused. He only felt a sense of immense perplexity, colored with trouble. The question as it lay before him, though not consciously so recognized by him, was not, Why am I rejected? but, Why am I delayed?

Nor was this refusal of his to acquiesce in the disappointment a piece of conceit. It was the persistence of a profound conviction of the suitableness of two souls for each other. Thus he continued in the same mind, not from a mere effort of will impelled by motive, but from an impulse like that of gravitation; constant, unvarying, acting not as a motive superadded, but as a quality innate, and thus carrying him by a grasp upon the deepest substructure of his whole being, so that his will, or will not, had nothing to do with it, but was carried along irrespective of any determination. So we sweep along on the round world and whirl round and round as we go; and let us be as obstinate for motionlessness as we choose, let our indignation be as white-hot as it likes at the idea of motion, let us do our best to contradict the universe by hurrying in a contrary direction, it is all in vain; round and round we go, indignation and all, a thousand miles an hour, — less perhaps thirty miles an hour that we can do by rail due westward towards nullifying the earth's rotation, — and forward we sweep nineteen miles a second, without being able to pull back an ounce or an inch — not to mention the general·motion of the whole solar system towards a point in the constellation Hercules at the swiftest rate of all, forty-nine miles in a second! Truly, when astronomically considered, a man is a miserable helpless mite!

However, Adrian neither analyzed his own mental structure, nor sought out analogies in solar and stellar astronomy. He simply hurried. It is an instinct of strong healthy positive natures, to act. In no matter whatever has man more the advantage over woman, than in being so much better situated for escaping trouble by activity. Ruin, shame, pain, loss, disappointment, bereavement, any thing can be lived through by a man, who has the resolution (and vitality) left to plunge over head into some occupation. It is a wise suicide of suffering. He drowns himself as to his misery, by leaping into the deepest abyss of occupation he can find. Not that this is a sure cure for all. But it is a great relief for almost all.

Nor was Adrian's state an awful immeasurable grief. As just shown, it was not a destruction, but a storm. It was however an indescribably painful condition, for it was his first real disappointment, — and the first real disappointment, though it be recovered from, has a murdering fatal force like the first blow of the executioner's iron bar upon the malefactor bound to the wheel. The sufferer may even laugh at the second.

Accordingly, confused and unhappy as he was, he simply hurried. He walked swiftly to his lodgings, completed his few arrangements, found that he had yet time to walk to Peck Slip, — for he took the steamboat to New Haven rather than the all-rail route, — and taking valise in hand, he set out at once, getting over the ground at a tremendous rate. He thought of stopping at Dr. Veroil's, but concluded to write instead; and without meeting any experience of importance, he proceeded swiftly through Broadway, the City Hall Park, and Beekman Street, turning northward a little way after he had reached the docks; for he did not know the city well enough to take the shorter way down the Bowery and the New Bowery to Peck Slip itself, or the cut across the Park, and down Spruce and Ferry Streets through "the Swamp." However, he was just in season, and stepping aboard, intrusted his valise to the Afrite who brooded darkling over the hidden treasures of the baggage-room, and who, unlike his brethren of the Arabian Nights, himself furnished the magic token which on being rubbed (i.e., shoved back to him) should rescue its proper treasure from his necromantic power.

This done, and his ticket purchased, he resorted at once to the engineer's room, — his constant habit on steamboats, — to look at the engine. This pleasure is not for a grown person what it is for a child — mere gratification of unintelligent curiosity — it is a real and high grade of enjoyment, whose strange and remote nature it is not easy to express. It is like the pleasure of watching a great fire, a volcanic eruption, from close at hand; of going out into the heart of a furious storm; of creeping up close to the main waterfall at Niagara and looking up the vast sheet. Is it imaginative, or spiritual, or rather mingled of both? Is there a magnetic element in it? It is a state of excitement, — emotion, rather, — which will be found to arise from being close to any vast force in action. It was not foolish curiosity merely, but in part at least the unconscious perception of this influence, which made the children of Israel press near to Sinai. So Adrian leaned against the door-post and waited; and shortly *bang!* went a brass gong over the head of the bearded engineer, who quietly hooked on the eccentrics, set his lever, and whirling one valve one way and another another, started the monstrous machine. With long, dreary, quivering groans, as if the hot steam agonized its very vitals, the vast

structure slowly, very slowly, stirred and moved; then as the valves were opened wider and wider, the steam itself took the work off the hands of the engineer, who replaced the long bright lever upright in its socket; and as the boat glided cautiously out of the slip and headed northward at half-speed, Adrian watched with quiet delight the steady play of the rock-shaft with its well-oiled "toes," and followed in imagination the alternating rush of the groaning steam through the valve-cylinders and ports into the great main cylinder first above and then below the piston. A rough-looking man who stood by him, also watching the work of the engine, was evidently a guild-brother; for after a few moments he stepped into the engine-room with an air of familiarity, shook hands with the engineer, and sat down by him. Then, looking up with disapproval towards the snapping rattling Sickels cut-off which was perched aloft upon the valve-cylinder, he said,

"Hmh! Don't like so much old iron hitched up round. That snippety-snap Sickels cut-off makes an engine-room look like the inside of a Jurgensen watch!"

The engineer made some remark in defence of his immense hot pet, which Adrian did not hear distinctly; and having for the time gazed his fill, he strolled up into the saloon, and having for the moment exhausted his external stimuli, he began to pace moodily along the length of the boat, and to reflect upon his sorrow — to eat his heart, as the barbaric phrase is. But before he had half completed half one length, he was called by name, and looking up with a start, he saw Mr. Adam Welles and Mr. Philetus Stanley, who greeted him with much cordiality. Adrian, notwithstanding a moment of melodramatic longing after solitude, made the best of it, put on a pleasant face, and returning their salutation, took the seat which they gave him and fell into talk with them.

"I was just observing to Mr. Welles," said Stanley, in his precise dry way, and with his usual cold smile, "that in order to accommodate him, I would take his share in the Scrope Estate speculation off his hands at cost, at any time."

"I saw you did not believe in the business," answered Adrian, replying to the thoughts and not to the words of the other, "at the meeting. I think if it hadn't been for me, Mr. Stanley, you would have smashed the machine, as the politicians say."

"Not believe in the business!" exclaimed honest old Adam Welles, — "Why, Mr. Chester, what can you mean? Mr. Stanley believed in it fifty dollars' worth, I'm sure, for I saw him pay it with my own eyes."

"Never mind, Mr. Welles," said Stanley — "I'll abide by my offer, remember."

"Well," said the old man, with a smile at his own shrewdness, "I accept provided I find I'm going to lose, but not if I'm going to win. I'll shake hands with you on *that!*"

So he and Stanley went through the form of shaking hands, and Adrian moreover was invoked as a witness, whereupon, with much solemnity, and to the amusement of Mr. Welles, he took out his memorandum-book, and noted down the agreement, with a date.

"But now," said Mr. Welles, "Mr. Chester, I beg you to allow me to congratulate you upon the able manner in which you convinced the assembly Monday. I don't remember any thing better since that short and sensible address of the Town Clerk of Ephesus."

Adrian thanked the old gentleman, very cordially. There is always something peculiarly affecting in the hearty loving pride with which an old person regards the success of a young relative or friend. The emotion must be by the nature of the case so perfectly disinterested and genuine, that it has its full legitimate weight.

Mr. Welles talked on for quite a while, laughing as he recounted his recollections of the turns in the debate, and dwelling on his own satisfaction at being a relative of so many persons of present or future eminence, — for, he said, if he lived a few years more he expected to see Adrian with a national reputation. Then he came back once more to Adrian's unaccountable idea, as it appeared to him, of Mr. Stanley's being sceptical of any gains to accrue to the members of the Scrope Association, from their English inheritance.

"Do you know," said Mr. Stanley, suddenly, "the value of all these estates in England, and the value of all the real estate in England, Mr. Welles?"

"No," said the old man, puzzled.

"Well, I had the curiosity to get together the figures," rejoined Mr. Stanley. "I found that all together, Chase Estate, Townley Estate, Jennings Estate, Brown, Smith, Burnham, and so on, — all together, those that I know of, amount to so much, that if you sell every foot of ground in England to-day, and get the appraised value for it, — and that would be the best forced sale ever made yet, — even then you will be between six and seven million pounds sterling short of the amount claimed by

American heirs alone, not to mention such as may turn up in Australia ! ”

Poor old Mr. Welles gazed at the speaker with a most rueful expression. Stanley went on :

“ Then, what do we know about this Scrope ? He brought decent enough letters, no doubt. He has a right to his name : he is our kinsman. But is he competent to manage so weighty an undertaking ? We can't control him, nor help him, at three thousand miles off. And if he lays hold on several million dollars, who knows whether he will render a just account ? You must remember, he comes from the royalist branch, not the Puritan ! — I don't mean that the cavaliers were dishonest. But they were thriftless, improvident, and unsuccessful, certainly.”

“ But why didn't you argue this way at the meeting, Mr. Stanley ? ” asked poor old Mr. Welles.

“ Could I do more than I did, Mr. Welles ? ”

“ — No, I don't see that you could ; but in that event, why did you subscribe ? ”

“ Yes,” added Adrian : “ I should like to know that, too.”

“ Well,” said Stanley, with an icier smile than ever, — “ I'll tell you. I didn't mind letting our good friend Mr. Button carry on the enterprise, if he wanted to — as you see he did. I thought if I put down a little, it would encourage him — and it did. Now, gentlemen, honor bright ! Don't you repeat it : I have told you in strict confidence. — And now, Mr. Welles, why did *you* subscribe ? ”

“ Why,” said the old man, with an uneasy half-laugh, — “ to make some money. And to set up the family connection. And I thought very

likely that in the course of the investigations those lost books might turn up somewhere.”

“ Yes,” said Adrian : “ I remember Scrope said one day while we were talking that he felt very sure those books had either never come from England at all, in spite of the Scrope will, or had been shipped back there. He said he had an old chest himself that he was sure was the Scrope Chest ” —

“ Pshaw ! ” interrupted Stanley, — “ we know that the Scrope Chest was in Thomas Hooker's old house at the foot of Prospect Street in Hartford as late as the year 1790 — might be there this very moment, if the house hadn't been a tenement-house this thirty years. And ” —

He interrupted himself ; for he had already gone much farther than was usual with him in the way of communicating information. Then he added, — “ And you, Mr. Chester, — what made you subscribe ? ”

“ Pretty nearly Mr. Welles's motives ; — though I took it for granted that you and he together had found out all about the Scrope Chest and its contents long ago. Indeed, it wouldn't surprise me, Mr. Stanley, to learn that you had picked up full half of the Lost Library, book by book, and had them on your shelves at this moment, every one with “ Adrian Scroope ” written on the fly-leaf. Have you ? ”

Stanley shook his head, and looked rather annoyed. “ I believe you have the only known autograph of Adrian Scroope of Hartford ” he replied, “ except that in the archives at the State House.”

“ For my part,” said Mr. Welles, “ I don't believe that even the glory of adding to such a collection as Mr. Stanley's would tempt me to part with such a book if I ever found it. Ah, how many, many thousands of volumes and hundreds of tons of trash I have handled and scrutinized and sifted in hope of coming on some of those books!"

" You must have found a great many curious things," said Adrian, who had seen Mr. Welles's own collection, a wondrous mass of items, bearing somewhat such a relation to a library, as a pile of "scrap tin" in a ditch does to coined gold.

"Ah, indeed I have," said the old man, — "you have seen my books yourself; but the best of them " —

A glance from Mr. Stanley stopped him. That astute gentleman had no wish that the old foreman should specify the rarities which he had furnished to the well known Stanley Collection during the last twenty years, at prices which the old man himself thought handsome, but which would have made Andrew Purvis perfectly crazy.

" Well," Mr. Welles began again — " I only wish I could fill some of my broken sets. Now I've got some curious French odd volumes. I can't read them, but I can pick out the meaning of some of the words. There's tom one of Mister Poitcevin Peetavy on the jewks florawks dee Towlowz." —

As he innocently recited this fine specimen of Connecticut French, looking down in the careful solicitude of his recollection, Mr. Stanley, catching Adrian's eye, winked, but with a perfectly grave and steady countenance. Adrian almost laughed, but the consciousness of the cruel unkindness that a laugh would be to the good old fellow overpowered even the extreme funniness of the recital, and with one spasmodic repression, he remained as impassive, in appearance, as the sardonic Stanley. The old man went on with quite a list of his treasures.

Some of the titles he recited were almost as valuable, philologically, as that about the floral games, and as he mentioned them, the wicked Mr. Stanley more than once darted at Adrian another composed, but discomposing look of cold keen fun. Truly, there is something very ludicrous in the grotesque results produced on either English or foreign words, by thoughtful accurate reading people who have never heard them pronounced, and who honestly do the best they can on general principles. But Adrian, keen as was his sense of the funny, was still more sensitive as to kindness or unkindness. It dawned upon him that Stanley must have in some sort helped on the old man in this line of vocalizing — as was indeed the fact — for his own amusement; and it affected him painfully, as being a piece of cold sarcastic selfishness. And he had hardly any further impulse to laugh, even when Mr. Stanley was so good as to lead up himself to a particularly good point, when Mr. Welles was speaking of a suggestion of his about certain old papers : —

" That's one of your bright thoughts, Mr. Welles," said he; "one of your March notions, isn't it ? You see, Chester, Mr. Welles is a Shakspearian student too."

Adrian was puzzled, but said, what is very true, — that he had no doubt a sensible Yankee might know of his own knowledge a good many things about old English, that neither cockney nor provincial in England could very well understand.

" Yes," said the old man ; " you see, Mr. Chester, it occurred to me that there's a plain meaning to a passage in Julius Cæsar, ' Beware the ides of March,' it says. Now, why didn't that old prophet fellow mean simply that folkses minds are more active in the Spring, just as all the rest of the world is, and that Cæsar had better look out, in consequence? I don't see why a common sense notion of that sort ain't as good as any other?"

"Yes," corroborated Mr. Stanley. "Now I think that very suggestion is one of the ideas of March. Don't you, Chester?"

"Well," said Adrian, who had to say something, "I'll tell you what 'tis, Mr. Welles: I can't offer to take financial obligations off your hands, as Mr. Stanley has done; but if you ever publish an edition of Shakspeare, I'll subscribe for a copy."

They talked a good while longer — indeed, most of the way to New Haven, in a rambling discursive way, on topics of antiquarian and modern literature, family genealogy, and so forth. Stanley and Welles had nothing better to do, and Adrian was sensible enough to prefer any occupation to meditating on discomforts of his own for which there was no present help. But the effort of repression, and the effort of taking an interest in the conversation, grew very burdensome; and at New Haven, instead of taking the cars with his companions, he made an excuse and stopped over night at a hotel.

CHAPTER XXVII.

On the north side of State Street, and of the State House Square, which square is a three-cornered area in the middle of the ancient city of Hartford, there stood, on the forenoon after Adrian Chester's conversation with Mr. Stanley and Mr. Welles, a house. It was of wood, roomy, old, white, low "between joints," with a hipped roof, and a large front door painted dark green with old hard paint that had shrunk into little square sections. This

door was built in ha. res, an upper and a lower, bolting together when required on the inside. It had moreover a great bright brass knocker in the middle of the upper half, and the door itself was in the middle of the front of the house — half way between eaves and underpinning, as well as between end and end. And by way of access, a long steep flight of narrow freestone steps was laid up against the side of the house, like a vast nose that had been quite smashed down to one side upon a face. One iron rail at the outside prevented this tremendous ascent from being almost as terrible as the mysterious steps up which the neophyte scrambled in the dark in Moore's imaginative little story of "The Epicurean," every step, as he lifted his foot from it, falling down slop! into unseen water far below. The substance of the front steps of this goodly old mansion dated back to the Old Red Sandstone period, — any number of years you like, as a few millions are of small account in such matters. Its woodwork dated back some three or four centuries only; as within that period probably sprouted the acorns whence grew the straight white oaks that furnished its square and massive timbers. The odd arrangement of its front was of not more than fifty years' age or so; it was at that time, or not far from it, that a high bank of earth, previously bordering the street, was cut away from under the houses. These were shored up and built under, instead of being let down, and thus for once it happened that some houses had their chimneys and upper floors built and finished before the lower floors and foundations. The lower floor of this particular house was put to the lower uses of trade, and thus served very nicely to maintain by the vulgar but increasing revenue of business, the old fashioned aristocracy that staid up-stairs and grew poor. And lastly; to a period somewhat more distant than the era of the rebuilding, yet a good ways this side of the era of the acorns, there dated back the lady of this house.

An Aunt is not to be found on every bush. The ignorant may perhaps suppose that the quality of Auntness inheres in every sister of a parent. In form, possibly; but in substance, not necessarily by any means. An Aunt is a being who can only exist for children. Grown persons cannot (unless they are childlike) have *real* Aunts. For those who can, the Aunt is a delightful personage who has all the merits of a mother, but in a more exalted degree, and none of those defects of harshness, discipline, infliction, peremptoriness, and the like, that so often and sadly mar the natural sweetness of the filio-parental relation. The Aunt, you see, can permit, but cannot forbid. She is a beatified mother. And any person claiming to be an Aunt, and falling short of these attainments, is an impostor.

It was Adrian's not only Aunt, but his Great-Aunt — his grandfather's sister, — who was upon the morning in question trotting nimbly to and fro in this old house. She was a thin, straight, active little old lady, with eyes that notwithstanding her age were black, quick, bright and snapping. Adrian's father and mother, both well and strong. were seized with a fever when he was a little baby, and instead of living to be old as their kin usually did — for they were both of long-lived families — they took divers quantities of calomel, and lost divers quantities of blood — "which is the life," God Almighty says — under the heroic treatment of an old fashioned doctor of the day, and so they died. The Aunt aforesaid, — Mr. Chester's aunt, who had a tiny income of her own; about a hundred and fifty dollars a year, secured on this very house and land, was living in her nephew's house, in her professional capacity of Aunt, when he was taken ill. She watched over him along with his young wife: after he died, and the widow was taken ill, she took care of her too. She promised the poor young mother to take care of the baby, and she did it. She cared nothing about men, she always said; at any rate she never married, and seemed always perfectly satisfied with her stated work as a Tract Visitor, her weekly Sunday school class, her housekeeping, her small circle of friends and her reading. With occasional misadventures and losses, she had fought one unbroken campaign against speculators, selectmen, city government, and mankind in general from that day forward, to maintain her garrison in that old ancestral-house. Sometimes people wanted to buy it to pull down and rebuild; sometimes there was a plan to cut a new street through; sometimes wise friends exhorted her to lease it and go and board somewhere. No. It was Adrian's home and hers, and she would stay in it as long as she lived. Taxes and expenses grew heavier and heavier; her little income remained a hundred and fifty dollars; but the valiant old lady managed and fought it through, getting an important contribution of course from the rent of the two stores on the ground floor. She had brought up her grandnephew on the best old fashioned Connecticut principles; had secured him a good education, got him fitted for college, and would have sent him thither, but he preferred trying a clerkship, which he afterwards left for the post of assistant librarian at the Young Men's Institute, for the sufficient reason that he found he liked giving out books better than keeping them.

Miss Chester had, no doubt, some peculiarities: it is hardly possible for a person of energetic character, who lives a life at once active and solitary, to avoid becoming peculiar; but thus far, they only rendered her more piquant and agreeable; for she had too much strong sense and good judgment to become actually "queer." She was, as usual while employed about her household duties, singing — or rather vocalizing, after her invariable habit, with a rather tremulous and thin but still sweet voice, to the tune of "Long, long ago," and using instead of the monosyllable "ah," the monosyllable "pee," — thus:

Pee, pee pee *pee,* pee pee *pee,* pee pee *pee,*   *Pee* pee pee *pee,*   *pee* pee pee *pee.*

She had got through all the dishes and done almost all the dusting, and was now setting in order the non-literary items of Adrian's own room — for she had attained to that rare and almost incredible state of grace and wisdom which enabled her to let the young man's books and papers entirely alone — when the bell rang, and the small servant-girl who comprised in her brief person the whole menial train of the establishment, having answered the bell, announced a gentleman in the parlor to see Miss Chester. So, laying aside her dust-cloth, the old lady trotted down stairs, doubting in her own mind who this might be; but as most of the "gentlemen" who called to see her for the last twenty years had done so to demand money or to try to get away her home from her, she reasoned that here was probably another attack, and entered the old-fashioned parlor all ready for the combat. But she did not expect the fearful experience that awaited her.

A small man stood in the farther corner of the room, his back towards her, intently studying the antique closet or "bo-fat," as Miss Chester called it, which was built across one corner of the room, and through whose glass door might be dimly seen a tea-set, and certain other articles, all of real old china, the pride of their owner's heart. As she entered, the gentleman turned round and made her a polite bow:

"Miss Chester, I believe?"

"Yes, sir."

"I couldn't help admiring this curious old cupboard, madam. Such a fine old house, too," he went on, looking at the heavy beam that crossed the room under the middle of the low ceiling. "Just like my grandfather's old home where I was brought up."

"Indeed?" said the old lady, unexpectedly pleased. . . .

[Intermission of one hour.]

Adrian Chester had come from New Haven by an early morning train, and had occupied himself on the road by examining a document which he had been carrying in his pocket for a few days, being no other than the code of instructions to canvassers, of which Mr. Button had a few days before given him a copy, at giving one to Mr. Jacox. It was a very curious document, filling both sides of a large sheet of paper in a close type, and containing nearly six thousand words, equal to twelve or fifteen duodecimo pages. It consisted of a caption in a bold clear letter, and just forty different propositions. The caption consisted of pithy maxims like the following :

Commit this to memory word for word. Hold the Book you are selling in your own Hands. Don't let the customer take it unless necessary. Don't merely say you have got it and talk about it, but show it. Don't ask the customer to buy it, except as the very last resort; but show it and describe it until he says, " I will take one." Don't tell what it costs until he wants the book. When he is ready, hand him the Order Book and pencil, and he will see the price extended opposite the names already in. Remember, you must make the customer want the book, before you try to sell it. He would not buy coined gold if he did not want it. Begin talking as follows:

Here followed the items of this Catechism, laid off with shrewd sense in short paragraphs, numbered in order, being an elaborate exposition of the merits of the book. For instance :

I. I have here, Mr. ——, the best book ever printed except the Holy Bible, and one that every one is pleased with. This may seem extravagant; but seeing, you know, is believing, and here is the book. [*Read the title on the back, carefully and distinctly*] "A NEW AND COMPLETE HISTORY OF THE BIBLE, by the Reverend Hocum Hotchkin, D.D." Or, as the gilt stamp on the side of the cover says [*read the side lettering carefully*], "THE HOLY BIBLE, ITS HISTORY, WORK, AND INFLUENCE." [*Now open to the title-page and read it ; then open to the Introduction, and remark, looking your customer squarely in the face,*]

II. The Bible itself authorizes us to believe that many persons even of intelligence cannot fully understand what they read in it, unless some man should guide them. See Acts viii. 30, 31. This is what the Reverend Hocum Hotchkin, D.D., says in beginning his Introduction to this great work. The very Table of Contents [*turn to it*] will convince you how necessary this History is, in order to understand the Word of God. [*Read fifteen or twenty of the first items in the Table of Contents.*]

And so on ; a shrewd, practical discourse, adapted with comical skill to the character of a serious, Bible-reading and meeting-going public. And Adrian, in order to experiment upon his own abilities in the practical details of the business to which he had come so near devoting his life, set to work with a hearty good will to master this composition; and having what actors call "a quick study," by the time he reached Hartford he felt so well prepared that he thought he could even sell his own dear great-aunt a copy of the History of the Bible, if he had it, notwithstanding the furious and implacable hatred which as he well knew she bore to the whole race of canvassers, — a hatred far beyond her sufficiently energetic hostility to mere tax-gatherers and house-hunters, who, vile and noxious as they are, can be considered human beings.

Walking up Asylum Street from the station, valise in hand, Adrian calmly and unsuspectingly ascended the steep old freestone steps, entered the house, laid off his overcoat and hat, and hearing a voice in the parlor, he went in. What a spectacle ! Can any thing be more frightful than to find one of our most beloved ones, without warning or expectation, smitten by a cruel calamity ? Especially if we come suddenly upon the height and paroxysm of the agony.

As he softly entered the room, his poor old aunt, almost exhausted, was pushing from her with a feeble hand an open book and pencil, which were held out to her by a little man who sat opposite her by the table.

"Oh dear, dear," she said, or rather sighed, in a faint and weary voice, —

" I don't want a History of the Bible any more than a hoptoad wants a fine-tooth comb. I can say more than half of it by heart already."

" You are aware," said the little man in a glib peremptory tone, " that it is one thing to read a book, and quite another so to read it as to understand its contents and thoughts and make them our own " —

Here Adrian, who recognized in these words No. xxxv. of Mr. Button's code, interrupted, while his aunt gave a jump and a cry at the sound of his voice. He took the very words out of the little man's mouth, and proceeded with a majestic and stately delivery; —

" Yes ; and this is pre-eminently true with reference to the Book of Books. The Bible may be read daily and even thoroughly, so far as the letter, the verses, the chapters, and the books, are concerned, and yet comparatively little may be acquired or apprehended of the great truths which it teaches, or of the grand and various topics which are unfolded in its sacred pages. Number three exes, vee, i. Not a few individuals have read the Bible through and through repeatedly, and yet have wondered that they could retain so little of its teachings, and had such an indistinct impression or knowledge of its varied topics or discourse, Mr. Jacox ! "

Miss Chester looked perfectly stunned. As for Jacox, for it was he, he looked a hundred times more astounded — if such a thing be possible — than she at seeing this interloper thus proceed to steal and fire off his own thunder, and with the obvious effect of re-assuring the almost surrendered victim. For the old lady had fought a good fight, but she was too much of a lady to be absolutely rude to her assailant, and unfortu-

nately for herself, she was too much of a woman not to talk with him. Under such circumstances, the business could have but one termination. A book agent spares neither age nor sex. He would assuredly have had her name in his little book in two minutes more, if Adrian had not appeared.

" Oh Adrian," said the dear old lady, " I'm *so* glad you came! But for goodness sake what's the meaning of all that lingo ? "

" Mr. Jacox would have said it to you if I hadn't — hay, Mr. Jacox ? "

The canvasser looked pretty angry.

" Come," said Adrian, " how do you know but I can be of some use to you after all ? Mr. Button gave me a copy of those directions, when he gave you yours. Don't you remember ? I committed every word of them to memory this very morning. And how do you know but I wanted to sell a copy of the History of the Bible to my aunt here ? Won't you let me supply my own family ? "

Jacox made a great effort, and with the aid of his recollection of Adrian's presence in Mr. Button's office, managed to look at the situation somewhat like the joke which it was. Adrian, who was well pleased at the success of his little extempore scene, put him into perfectly good humor by volunteering himself to take the copy of the History of the Bible which was to have been the property of Miss Chester, and wrote his name in place of hers in Mr. Jacox's little book.

" You mustn't think too hard of me," said the little agent, as he prepared to go; " I thought I'd lost my hour's hard work. Much obliged to you, sir. I like a joke as well as anybody, if it don't cost me too much. But I must say the Button connection is pretty near too much for me. There's two cousins of his came pretty near spoiling a good suit of clothes for me this morning."

"Cousins of Mr. Button's?" said Adrian.

"Little hip-roofed brick house out on the Newington road," said the agent.

"Why, it's Deemy and Dosy Tidball!" said Miss Chester. "What on earth made you try to sell them a book?"

"Well, you can't never say where you mayn't find a customer," said Mr. Jacox. "And they sell books, if they don't buy 'em."

"How do you mean?" said Adrian.

"Why, I came by there this morning, and saw 'em just taking their pay of a rag peddler for two or three barrels of old papers and books and things. I went to work to get hold of the cash myself, and spent pretty nigh an hour at it, but when they found out 'twas a book of Mr. Button's I had, one of 'em said they were cousins of his and he would give 'em one, and the other, she said he was too proud to recognize 'em and too stingy to give 'em any thing, and then the first one said if I didn't leave she'd heave the swill at me ; and that would have spoiled my clothes ; and then I was just leaving, when Stanley of East Hartford drove up — I knew about him when I was to work for Noyes & Skittery round here. I like to know what's going on when I can just as well, so I went kinder slow, and I had some satisfaction out of those old Miss Tidballs, anyhow!"

"How was that?" asked Adrian.

"Well, Stanley he was in a great hurry, he said, for he'd got to drive out to Newington Centre and look at some papers and things of the Reverend Mr. Brace, I believe, that used to be settled there : but he just stopped to ask if they hadn't some old papers in the house. Said he'd just

heard old Mrs. Goodin say 'twas very likely, and he'd give 'em a good price for 'em. Then one of the old ladies — the tall thin one, she said they'd had a lot of trash that belonged to old Clerk Tidball ever so many years ago, but they'd sold it to a rag man that very morning for two dollars and a half. Then Stanley he looked as if he'd have a fit — he was the maddest man! But he held in, and he took out some money, and jest said, sorter quiet like, says he, 'Well, Miss Tidball, do you see those ten ten dollar bills? I'd have been glad to give you those for that trash, as you call it. One hundred dollars, ma'am. That's all, ma'am!' And he hopped into his sleigh and went off to Newington; and if them two old ladies didn't give it to each other! 'There, Deemy Tidball,' says the fat stumpy one — 'I always thought you was a fool, and now I know it.' — 'Well,' says the tall one, 'you Dosy Tidball, don't you tell me! You've been at me to sell those old things this two years, and now I've done as you said you call me a fool? Well, I was, for doin' as you said, and always would be as often as I did.' They really screeched and hollered at each other so that I was kinder ashamed, and I came along into the city."

"Poor girls!" said Miss Chester. "I don't wonder they felt bad! And I remember them such bright pretty young things! I must go out and see them."

"But I should like to know," said Adrian eagerly, "what became of that rag peddler!"

"He came to the city," said Jacox, "and he was loaded cram full ; so he's gone and sold out somewhere."

"What do you want of him?" said Miss Chester.

"Why, aunty, don't you know old

Clerk Tidball was supposed to have a lot of very valuable old documents in his hands? We've always expected we might find some Scrope facts if we could get at them. It's only a little while ago that these two old ladies got the Tidball things, — they'd been out in Pennsylvania somewhere, nobody could find out where. And the Tidballs were so touchy and spiteful and suspicious, nobody could do anything with them. I wonder they didn't throw the swill on Mr. Jacox without notice instead of threatening it."

"I'll tell you what," said Jacox, who seemed inclined to do Adrian a good turn in exchange for his subscription, "I know what I'd do if I were you. I'd go straight over to the old Barnard Paper Mill in Manchester. All the rag peddlers know that their best chance for old books and such kind of stock is to take 'em right there. . Old foreman Welles'll pay double prices, very often, for such things, and then they save the profit of the dealers here in the city too. And I'd go right away. Stanley'll be out there this afternoon as sure as death. I know him."

"So he will," said Adrian. "I must try the dealers, though, and then I'll go over. There's only two of them, and they'll tell me. I'm much obliged to you, Mr. Jacox. When the book's ready, we'll take it with pleasure."

And hastily resuming his outer garments, he left the house with Mr. Jacox, his aunt in vain recommending him to wait till after dinner. He flew to the cellars occupied by the two paper-stock dealers, but found that no goods had been sold to them that morning. And moreover, one of them, whose establishment was near the Great Bridge, informed him that he had seen David Hertelchick

the rag peddler, drive over the bridge eastward with a heavy load.

This was enough, and Adrian darted round to a livery stable, which he occasionally patronized. It was a warm bright day, the snow was melting, and everybody was making the most of the sleighing; there was not a runner left in the establishment.

"Confound it!" said Adrian, "I must get to Manchester!"

"Take Smarty," suggested one of the men; "you can ride, Mr. Chester, and we had her sharpened this very morning."

The liveryman, after some little hesitation — no livery stable keeper likes to hire out his favorite horse — consented. "Saddle Smarty, John," he said, "and be lively about it. But Mr. Chester, remember, the mare's frisky, and she hasn't been out of the stable except to get shod, this three days. And she's awful tender-mouthed, too. You'll be very careful, won't you?"

Adrian promised, and the bay mare, a beautiful animal, was quickly brought out saddled and bridled, dancing and sidling along as if it was difficult to keep her feet down to the ground, whisking her long tail, and arching her neck, while her thin delicate translucent ears quivered and turned to and fro, and she snorted and snuffed in the fresh air.

After some little trouble, for the mare was as full of frolic as a kitten, Adrian got into the saddle, and after she had paraded about a little on her hind legs, she came down to business. At an easy canter, Adrian went off down State Street, intending to turn northward at Front Street and to cross by the bridge; but as he approached the foot of the street, the broad level surface of the river tempted him, and he took the mare straight over in the wagon track on the ice. The pure cool air, so different from the lifeless dead stuff that they defraud themselves with for an atmosphere in New York City, stimulated him, and so it did the spirited animal under him ; as he crossed the broad motionless river, the easy canter stretched into a long stride, and before he had reached East Hartford Street, the fleet mare was racing along at that glorious greyhound-like undulating full speed that takes away the idea of effort, and is the most beautiful motion on earth, except perhaps that of the greyhound himself, or that of a swift boat before a strong breeze. Up hill and down, and across the levels of that sandy region, sped the strong swift creature, as if she enjoyed the expedition as much as her rider ; sometimes, it is true, slackening her pace to an impatient walk, along some piece of road where the snow was soft ; but it was not much over an hour from the time of starting, when Adrian rode up to the door of the counting-room of the Barnard Paper Mill some twelve miles away. Old Adam Welles, who was at that moment in the counting-room, came to the door.

" Ah ha, Mr. Chester, glad to see you ! Young man Chester, welcome to old Manchester." And he laughed heartily at his own wit, and then looking at the mare's smoking flanks, he exhorted Adrian to dismount and let her be taken care of. Adrian readily complied, and without waste of time, told the old gentleman just what had brought him out there.

" Old town-clerk Tidball ! " said Adam Welles, with great interest, — " you don't say so ! Well, I dare say the stock's in the sorting room this minute. I know there were three or four loads brought this very morning,

and we were rather short of stock, so they've gone right in to be sorted. Come on, Mr. Chester." And sending the mare to a stable to be rubbed down and taken good care of, the old man led the way to the sorting room.

This was a large loft, where a number of women were handling away at great piles of all manner of waste paper and rags, and swiftly laying out the different classes of "stock," for the devouring maw of the mill. They stopped at the door for a moment to look at the busy scene, and Adrian observed,

" What a quantity of curious things must turn up here in the course of a year ! "

" Yes indeed. One of our women found an envelope full of banknotes a little while ago."

" Didn't the company want them ? "

" She was shrewd enough to slip the envelope into her bosom the moment she saw what it was without saying one word, and she went straight on with her work until the end of the afternoon. But she didn't come back any more, and she and her husband had left town before we found out. I heard they'd bought a farm out West somewhere."

" Oh, a husband ! No chance for you, then, Mr. Welles."

" No, thank goodness ! " said the old gentleman, who professed to hate and despise women in a far more cynical manner, at least in assumption, than Miss Chester's towards men, — " no indeed ! Pretty muss a woman would make in my old den ! I'd sooner set it on fire. Mr. Chester, women are Apollyons ! "

He delivered this frightful sentiment with a concentrated earnestness which was quite funny.

" Why, Mr. Welles," said Adrian, " what an awful heretic you are !

Now my aunt talks about men a good deal the same way, but she does think marrying is good for half of us. 'Every man is a fool that don't marry,' she says, 'and every woman is a fool that does.'"

"Well," said the old man, "I agree to the last half. And there'll always be enough silly people to continue the species, so I can have my own way and my own wisdom without doing any harm. — Well, let's see if they've found any thing."

So he advanced into the room, followed by Adrian, and asked the forewoman of the sorters if any thing was laid out for him.

"Oh yes, Mr. Welles. There's near a bushel of stuff," — and she pointed to a pile on a sort of counter at one side of the room, which the old gentleman and Adrian eagerly hastened to examine.

It was a heap of utter rubbish ; — such as privately printed poems; a stack of account books; some files of old receipts; an edition of an occasional sermon, — "There's the whole edition," said Mr. Welles, — "seven bundles of two hundred and fifty each; and that poor old fellow thought he was going to make a little fortune out of it!"

They inspected every item, and had shifted the whole pile, without finding the least scrap of any value. Adrian picked up one of the last three papers that were left, saw that it was a blank certificate with the name of Joash Tidball signed to it.

"Here's one Tidball paper," he said. "There ought to be more."

"Another armful," said one of the women, at this moment bringing up a further instalment, which she threw down upon the counter. This lot looked a good deal like the other. Adrian and Mr. Welles each lifted

out of it, to begin with, an old account-book. Mr. Welles's was bound in old fuzzy calf, Adrian's in crackly yellow old parchment. Having opened them and inspected them for a few moments in silence, they looked up at each other at the same moment, both flushed and smiling.

"Here's Mr. Button's father's own account book," said Adrian, "with a genealogical record in the back end."

"Here's the lost second volume of the Hartford Town Records," said old Adam Welles. "It's been missing over a hundred years!"

"I declare!" exclaimed Adrian. "See if the other half of the Scroope will isn't there!"

Eagerly and slowly the two men turned over leaf after leaf, from one end of the book to the other. They did not find the torn leaf; all they could discover that might have related to it was, a very narrow strip between two leaves, as if the leaf had been carefully torn out as far back as possible. All the rest consisted of entries of the miscellaneous sort that used to go into the early town records; an invaluable mass of materials for the early history of the town, but showing no signs of any Scrope information.

Then they inspected the other book, in the same careful way. The account-book part was an ordinary series of business entries, carefully and clearly made out, but sadly misspelled. The genealogy which the old gentleman had noted on the blank leaves at the end, was of more importance. Having read it through very deliberately, the two men once more looked at each other, but this time with a surprise by no means agreeable.

"Can that be so?" said Adrian. "That makes Mr. Button a descendant of the Lebanon Throops and not of the Bozrah Throops! No relative of ours at all!"

But so it was. Old Adam Welles, a shrewd and clear-headed judge in such matters, was convinced that this was proved by old Phineas Button's entries.

"And here you see how they came to think they might use the Scrope arms, too," said he, pointing to a separate entry on a fly leaf. Adrian read it:

"Arms of one of the Scroope families, used by some of the Throops. Found in a book of heraldry. Azure a bend or."

"Well," commented Mr. Welles with a smile, "he thought he had as good a right to one Scroope coat as another, and so he might as they say 'pick his choose.' And so he had!"

This discovery instantly filled Adrian's mind with many thoughts. First came the reflection that here was a mode of accounting for the different character of the Button family from that of the rest of the connection. This occurred to Mr. Welles too, at the same time; for he said,

"Well: he didn't seem just like the rest of us, that's a fact!"

"By George!" said Adrian, "he'll want that five hundred dollars back from Scrope now, if he finds this out! I wish he may get it!" And the young man stopped short, as he remembered that this discovery would also, very likely, as soon as Mr. Button should know it, impel him, rough and selfish as he was, to deprive old Mr. Van Braam and Civille at once of home and living.

"What shall we do with these books?" he said, perplexed and uneasy.

"I think if Mr. Stanley were here," said Mr. Welles, with a laugh, "and we did not let him have them, he would kill us."

After some discussion, it was decided that Adrian should take the record volume to Hartford and deposit it in the town-clerk's office; for though neither of the two men said so, they both knew perfectly well that if intrusted to Stanley, it would disappear as effectually as it had with the deceased Tidball. As for the account book, Adrian left that for Mr. Welles, who, as he knew, would give it to Stanley. He could not bring himself to undertake to forward it, or its disagreeable information, to Mr. Button. He was conscious that the publisher ought to be told. He knew that Stanley was a grave, and not a trumpet, of information. But yet, he felt that he must for the present at least hold his tongue. "The truth is not to be told at all times," says the proverb. This does not mean that you may tell a lie, but that it may be right to hold your tongue.

So he tied up his record-book, and with a friendly farewell to Mr. Welles, he rode back to Hartford, depressed and thoughtful.

PART XI

CHAPTER XXVIII.

WITH women, love is a business; with men, business is a love. This does not mean that women are mercenary in love or that men deal in the spirit of love in their ordinary business. It means that love is to women, yet more than to men, an occupation, absorbing, that fills and uses much of life; that to men, business fills and uses much of their life in much the same way. As human life is at present ordered, this apportionment of activities is unavoidable and appropriate.

Thus it happened that Adrian, rejected both by the lady to whom he had been betrothed and whom he loved in what may be called a conventional sense, and by the lady whom he loved really, to whom he had offered himself as it were unconsciously, from the impulse of a genuine, intuitive and profound love, was yet not disabled in any sense by his grief. It is true that his own fortunate instinctive good sense and native self-command enabled him to do what many a man has died for not doing; to drive out his sorrow by filling the place of it with incessant activity. It hardly occurred to him to mope, and if it did, he set himself resolutely to get out of moping; and as to suicide, there was in his healthy active mental constitution no idiotic — or lunatic — vacancy to receive the idea.

None the less however did his longing return upon him when an hour of leisure came. He rode back home from the old paper-mill without adventure; returned the lively mare to the charge of the livery-stable man, who complimented him upon the good judgment with which she had been used; went home to the old house, and told his aunt, during tea-time, all about his trip and his discoveries, and above all, he showed her the Scrope Genealogy, at which she was properly amazed and delighted.

After tea he still sat talking a while with the old lady, whose questions were many about his experiences in New York. To some of these inquiries Adrian replied with freedom and fulness; but the answers which bore upon his own personal relations to people in New York he found himself measuring and considering, so as to avoid telling any thing about Civille or Ann. Their interests, however, were so combined with those of other people, and therefore kept him watching and shaping his replies to such an extent that the shrewd old lady suddenly exclaimed,

"What's the matter with you, Adrian? You hitch and boggle as if you were afraid I should find out that you've been committing murder!"

"Why," said he, not liking to confess the facts, "I don't know of any murder; but I'm pretty tired. I think very likely I can tell a straighter story to-morrow."

This excuse was readily accepted; and Adrian went rather earlier than usual to his own room, with full intention of going straight to bed. Having however shut his door, and sitting down before the fire for a few moments of quiet solitary thought, his mind reverted with magnetic promptness to Civille, and he unresistingly permitted himself to float away into a long deep love-revery.

Perhaps such a state is a real communication. Not every one is capable of it. As man is made in the image of God, so the love of man should be in the image of the love of God. Perhaps not many in this life can enter into the fulness of either. Perhaps not many can love with absolute wholeness of being — "with all thy heart (body) and with all thy mind (soul) and with all thy strength (giving one's self totally and all together)." Nothing else is full love. But it absorbs the whole being. When we become seraphim, we can do nothing else, perhaps: but while we are human, we must do many things else, and as human, must cast ourselves whole into them one after another, but must from time to time come wholly (so far as consciousness is concerned) out of each.

For the time, however, Adrian neither knew nor felt any thing but a longing passionate love for Civille. He had repeatedly been vividly conscious of her personal charms. He had had less consciousness of the far higher and rarer charm that dwelt around her and radiated from her — the charm of her sweet controlling spirituality. Yet it was exactly this that had most attracted him. Neither at any other time, nor now, however, did he analyze or reason about her. He surrendered himself to an emotion, an impulse, powerful, profound, lovely, beyond any thing he had ever known. His heart beat, his cheeks flushed, he felt tears almost coming into his eyes; he sighed, he said half aloud, "Oh, Civille!" and held out his arms as if

his prayer could have reached her and drawn her close upon his heart. — But the spoken word and the movement awaked him: and man-like, he blushed to be capable of such sweet and deep emotion. Yet the longing wish to commune with the inaccessible one still thrilled throughout him; and turning to his desk, he wrote:

DEAR CIVILLE: This is not to beg nor to annoy. — As long as I don't hunt you and try to make you do or say what you don't wish, you will let me tell you my thoughts, won't you? You are kind. I am sure you will.

— Now, dear, I don't get you out of my mind at all. And (please not to be displeased) I don't feel as if you had refused me. What I mean is — I think — that I know it was not out of dislike. And I know we need not be shy of each other on account of it. You would ask me to serve you if there was a chance, just as soon as before — wouldn't you? You ought to, sooner. — I don't feel as if I were setting down words to you. Nor did I ever feel as if I were talking to you, exactly. — I want to say what some people would think very irreverent and wicked, but I can't show you what I mean any other way. — The feeling I always had with you was *a sense of oneness with a higher existence.* And yet this has never been a consciousness while it was happening — it was always a remembrance after I had left you. How can I express the depth, the force, of such recollections? Will details do it? They add lifelikeness to a picture. Let me try:

About four minutes ago, that is, ten minutes before eleven, which means, you know, fifteen minutes and seven seconds before eleven, where you are, and just before I began this letter, I was sitting still before the fire in my own room. I have had a long and fatiguing day, but I know now that a consciousness of you had been underlying all my riding and hurrying, like a level vein of gold under rough hills. When I came and sat down here alone all the upper strata vanished and the gold-bearing one appeared. So it was as if you were by me, I think; and I held out my arms and called you, and my voice, instead of calling you to me, recalled me to myself, and I awoke, and wished you were here.

So you have not made me dislike you. — I had some entertaining talk with Mr. Stanley and Mr. Welles on the boat coming home. This morning I thought I had a chance to find some of *the* books at the paper mill where Mr. Welles works — went and hunted — did not find them, but did find something else — two somethings. One was a volume of Hartford town records that has been lost for a hundred years. Another was an old account book of Phineas Button, *our* Mr. Button's father. There is a record of births and deaths in it which shows something that I will tell you, in confidence — *Mr. Button is no relative of ours* — he is of the Lebanon family, not the Bozrah family. Now, you will see on considering that if he should find this out it might cause you and your father some inconvenience; and if that should happen, and my aunt or I could be of use — or if we could for any other matter, and you will give us the refusal of serving you, then I will forgive you everything! If you should ever prefer anybody else to us in such a case, I don't think I will ever forgive you! N.B. my dear cousin, you must figure to yourself that you saw my face while I was saying these last things; or else you will take the threats for true as well as the good will. Tones can't be written any more than printed.

But I shall not tell Mr. Button, and very likely there's no harm after all. You may tell your father if you think best; for you are a discreet person; I have great faith in you. My writing to you in this way proves the faith, doesn't it? Perhaps you will answer that your treating me in *that* way proved the discretion?

Dear Civille; you wouldn't guess it, but (in a proper, cousinly, harmless, inoffensive way,) I love you.   ADRIAN.

"Aunty," said Adrian, next morning at breakfast, looking up suddenly from his paper, "they are going to pull down the old parsonage at the foot of Prospect Street."

"Are they?" said the old lady. "Well — it used to be a mighty fine house — I can remember when old Madam Woodbridge used to live there. She was old Parson Woodbridge's grand-daughter, and nobody but ministers or their folks had ever occupied it. It was built for the Reverend Thomas Hooker, you know."

"The beginning of it was," said Adrian, who was a more accurate local antiquarian than his aunt; "but only the first floor of half the ground plan. You know it was determined long ago that the great chimney had been partly rebuilt. It was at one side of the house first, and had to be enlarged when they built round it, so as to make room for fireplaces and ovens on the other side."

"Well," said Miss Chester, "the odor of sanctity was drowned out by the smell of rum and tobacco a good while ago, and I'd just as lief the old house should come down."

"But I thought," suggested Adrian slyly, "that the smells of rum and tobacco were of the most sanctified sort amongst the old fashioned Connecticut clergy?"

"Oh, very well, — there's been plenty of Germans there too; say lager and sour krout, if you like."

"Yes," said the young man, "it has been a tenement house this long time. But I must go and stand guard while they pull it down. Stanley got his Higley copper in the underpinning of the old Webster place, and they found a perfect pine-tree shilling on one of the sills."

"How do you know it is to be pulled down to-day?" said the old lady.

"I'll tell you," said Adrian; and he read out a local item from the Daily Courant:

"ANOTHER OLD LANDMARK GONE. The devastating hand of improvement will to-day erase from our midst one of the very few remaining monuments of the days of the Pilgrims. The former parsonage of the First Church in Hartford, long hallowed as the abode of Thomas Hooker and his successors in the ministry, after having been desecrated for half a century as a boarding-house and tenement-house, is to be pulled down, this very day, to make room for the new brick block to be erected by the enterprising firm of Bobson and Bull. The designs were drawn by that accomplished architect English Bond Esq.; and the contract for the whole building has been taken by the energetic firm of Wood and Stone. We trust that the spectacle of prosperity which the new edifice will offer, may propitiate the venerable ghosts of the departed. The building is to be embellished, we understand, with a handsome white marble memorial slab in the centre of the front, upon which will be carved the appropriate and honored name of 'Hooker Block.' *Tempora mutantur.*"

"Well," mused Miss Chester, "I never thought I should outlive that old house. I s'pose this one of ours will go next. The common council's tried to get rid of it often enough. They seem to be as set against an old house as they are against an old tree. They've cut down all the old elms and poplars on Main Street. Here goes the oldest house in town. Ours'll come next, I guess. They'll have an ordinance shortly, I expect, to kill all the old folks. Now I wonder what can be the reason that an alderman naturally hates a tree?"

"Because," answered Adrian, "an alderman is afraid of a tree. He's a wooden headed rascal himself, and wants to get the raw material out of the way, for fear the carpenter should hew a better one out of a tree-trunk."

"Well: they might perhaps have cause to be afraid of a poplar candidate," said the old lady slyly; "but elm-wood is for coffins; they'd better keep that growing."

"I wish an alderman had been hung in State House Square for every elm cut down!" said Adrian, hotly. "Then it would be some small consolation to bury each of the beasts in the very tree he had murdered."

"Look into the garret, Adrian; don't forget that," said Miss Chester.

"Well, I will," was the reply;—"but what can there be there now?"

"Never mind," said the old lady; "the way to find things is to look in the unlikeliest places first. I don't

expect the Scrope books are there, but look, at any rate. You know old Miss Woodbridge used to say she believed the Scrope Chest was there when she was a girl."

"I've heard you say so," answered Adrian; "but I guess it was only her fancy. The chest and books seem to have disappeared together from the time of the will,—in 1727, though Stanley says the chest was there seventy years later." Miss Woodbridge couldn't remember so far back as that.

"She remembered her grandfather, though—unless she imagined him from that stiff wooden looking old portrait in her keeping-room, She used to tell me of things he said, and things he did; but all that may have been told her too. But there's that other old story of one of the three regicide judges being kept hid in that very house—they seem to have been into every town in New England!—still if it was so it would be very natural for Adrian Scroope and his goods to be there too."

"Well," repeated Adrian, "I'll watch every splinter and scrap of the old place; but I must run,—they may have it half down already for what I know."

And springing up, he seized hat and coat and hastened out.

<h2>CHAPTER XXIX.</h2>

ADRIAN crossed over at the east end of the State House Square, and walked swiftly southward down Prospect Street. The distance was not great; it was but a few minutes before he was descending that rather positive incline at whose foot Prospect Street turns into Arch Street. The ancient mansion in question stood just at the confluence of these streets, upon the farther or south side of Arch

Street, on the narrow space between that street and the steep high rocky bank of Little River, that tributary to the mighty Connecticut which meanders so charmingly through the very middle of the wealthy old city. There is a horrid tradition that this stream is properly — improperly would be the right term — called Hog River; but the vile story is only alluded to here that it may be abhorred — as they nail up a crow on the barn door.

As he came out upon the upper part of the slope towards the river, Adrian was startled to see the destroyers already at their fiendish work. Several men, with axes and crowbars, were pounding and ripping away at the roof with that species of inhuman delight that attends all destructions; while clouds of dry dust arose in the clear cold air, and shingles, timber and bricks rattled and crashed down into the street below. And just crossing the street to enter the old house, was Mr. Philetus Stanley of East Hartford. Assuredly! Not cart-ropes could have kept that keen and tireless hunter from such a quarry. Can any New England mansion of the better class, and two hundred years or more of age, be pulled down without the bringing to light of some treasure? It may be manuscripts or pamphlets or books or coins or furniture or utensils or what not — but something ancient and curious there is sure to be. And Hartford is within sixteen years as old as any town in New England, and was from the first one of those substantial and intelligent communities who have things worth keeping, and therefore worth losing and worth finding again two centuries afterwards. And many a prize had Mr. Stanley gathered from the ruins of such old houses, to be borne into that mysterious treasure-chamber in his own old house — a room whose fame was known to every antiquarian in New England, but whose interior had never been beheld by one mortal of them all except its owner.

However, here he was, all the keener for what he had already amassed, as is the wont of misers. Adrian gave one groan at seeing his rival, but truly it is to be feared the young man was not quite envious and miserly enough for an ideal collector. So he appended a laugh to the groan, and only sped onward faster than before, dislocating and misapplying a very respectable quotation as he did so, as if to justify himself: "On, Stanley, on!" said Mr. Adrian; "Chester is charging after you!" Moreover, he charged to such purpose that he was close at Stanley's heels before that gentleman had ascended the steep huddled flight of stairs that turned three square corners within the little entry before reaching the second floor.

"Good morning, Mr. Stanley!" he cried out cheerfully — "I follow in the footsteps of my illustrious predecessor!"

"Good morning," said Stanley, very grimly, for he was enraged; but there was no help for it, and they went on together. The house had been emptied, stripped to nakedness. Even the last old shoes and bonnet-frames and skirt-skeletons were lying out in the street waiting for the more solid rubbish. The bald nakedness of the rooms was inexpressibly dreary. The two men had not looked into the lower ones, and only hurried through the upper ones to get into the garret, which they both knew perfectly well was the first place to search. But even in two seconds Adrian's quick eye took in a squalid gloomy vision of battered plaster, soiled cheap wall paper, grease-spots at head-rest height around the wall, and smoke-marks upon the ceiling. In another moment they were in the garret, in a dust of old lime and dirt so thick that they could hardly see, with a rain of shingles, and bits of wood, seasoned with brick-bats, falling around them, and the prodigious banging of the workmen resounding on the hollow roof and thundering in their very ears.

The garret had been partitioned off into small rooms. As they made their way alone through these, the chief workman met them, all powdered white with lime-dust. In reply to an inquiry, he bawled out through the racket that there wasn't a relic in the whole house, from ridge-pole to cellar bottom, but he made them welcome to hunt as much as they liked; only recommending them to wear buckets on their heads against brickbats.

"Now, what is there in here, for instance?" shouted Adrian, rapping on an old partition of perpendicular oak planks that extended from one corner of the great square shaft of the chimney, across to the eaves.

"Oh, nothing; only another room," said the chief Apollyon. Adrian walked back round the chimney to see. The others followed.

"There's a room," said Adrian, "no doubt; but that's a double partition, and there's more than two feet between them," he added, pointing out the facts to the carpenter.

"Yes," admitted the workman; "it's a closet; there's the door, close to the chimney; that single board hung on leather."

Adrian opened it and put in his head.

"Pitch dark, and smells very rank of old shoes," he observed. "Hold on a moment." He struck a light with a match, and then added, "This closet don't go clear out to the eaves. There's a cross partition. May I get an axe?" he asked eagerly. Good-natured — and inquisitive — Mr. Carpenter ran off himself after one.

"Halves, now," said Adrian, "if we find any thing, — honor bright?"

Mr. Stanley, a little reluctantly, agreed. The axe was quickly brought, and a crowbar too; and the vigorous and skilful enginery of the athletic workman quickly started a plank or two from the neighborhood of the cross partition which Adrian had noticed. The carpenter thrust in his head. "Nothing in there, I reckon," he said.

"Let me see," said Adrian. — "Yes there is — come, let's have the rest of these planks down. There's an old box."

Bang, rip, crash, down came half a dozen more of the ancient oak boards; and the small triangular recess close under the eaves was laid open. An old fashioned chest, of dark colored wood, panelled and carved, stood within. Adrian and Stanley looked at each other. The workman, creeping in under the sloping roof, seized hold of the chest and heaved at it.

"Pretty solid, that!" he exclaimed, finding it much more heavy than he had expected. Adrian crawled in also, and the two men hoisted the box out into plain sight.

"The Scrope Chest!" said Stanley, and he pointed to the escutcheon carved in the oaken front, with the well known bearings, Azure a bend or, properly indicated by dots and lines, and the word "Scroope," in old English letters, beneath it.

Just as one gazes at the outside of a letter, wondering whether it brings good news or bad, or who the writer may be, so the two zealots stood gazing for a moment at the outside of this old chest. Each was saying, That is the Lost Library ! Each was preferring the room of the other to his company, with a silent fervency that if translated into act might, it is to be feared, have extinguished a valuable life. Here, in the middle and very heart of the region, even in the very house, no doubt, where Adrian Scroope had sojourned, this treasure had lain in silence and darkness all these years, as if mocking their eager search ! And now, both the gentlemen and scholars were cursing each other most heartily in their silence, and longing for some means of appropriating the whole of the discovery. Still, there is no commandment against coveting what doesn't yet belong to your neighbor ; and the two men coveted with all their hearts.

"Confound you," at last exclaimed Adrian, though with a laugh at his own fury. "Confound you, Mr. Stanley, I wish you were in heaven, where you belong ! "

"Oh, well, go there yourself ! " said the other, in the same tone.

All these eager immoralities, however, had drifted across their minds in a moment or two ; and Mr. Carpenter, a direct and practical person, having looked from one to the other of them a couple of times with some wonder, said,

"Wal, you look as if you thought there was a corpse into it. Here goes ! " With a queer impulse of hesitating reluctance, — a sweet reluctant amorous delay, — each of them cried "Hold on ! " but even as they spoke, the workman gave a pull, an old lock cracked and yielded, the two spectators turned white with intense expectancy and doubt, and up came the lid. The box was crammed full to the very brim with unbound printed sheets. Stanley, Adrian and the carpenter each seized a handful.

"Pshaw ! " exclaimed Stanley, — "a lot of copies of Stiles' History of the Judges."

"Let's see if that's all," said Adrian, and they quickly emptied the old chest ; but it was all. They repacked the whole ; handed the workman a proper fee ; and one of the contractors who had bought the building having by this time come to supervise his men, Mr. Stanley, acting for himself and Adrian, easily purchased the chest and contents, at a cheap rate.

"See here," said Adrian, when the bargain was concluded, "I want the chest, Mr. Stanley."

"So do I," curtly answered the other.

"Well ; you want that edition of Stiles too, don't you ? Scarce book, — brings from $2.00 to $5.00 at auction — here's some two hundred uncut perfect copies : — splendid chance for exchanges, if you carry 'em home and keep the facts to yourself."

Stanley grinned. "Well," pursued Adrian, "now, see here : — You just buy of Mr. Wood the refusal of every thing else on the premises that's in your line : take the sheets, give me the chest, and I'll retire ; who knows but you'll find all the treasures of the Egyptians ? "

Stanley, after brief consideration, agreed to this proposal, and even added the liberal gift of one of the copies of the book. Adrian hurried away for packing paper and twine ; tied up the books, handed them over to Stanley's charge, and getting a dray, drove home in triumph with the Scrope Chest. Nor did he regret his bargain, notwithstanding the well known result. As all New England antiquaries are aware, the demolition of the old home yielded to the eager hands of the happy Stanley, not only divers coins and other small matters of interest, but a very considerable mass of the sermons and private papers of the Reverend Thomas Hooker himself, the same being found in the walls of the house, stuffed in between the outer weatherboards and the inner lining. How or when or why they should have been thus secreted, nobody has ever explained: there is no tradition of Mr. Hooker's having hidden or destroyed these or any other papers, as some men have done in their last days; nor is any thing known of any risks or dangers of any kind which could have occasioned the concealment. There at any rate they were, yellow and stained, a few of them wasted away by dampness and nibbled by vermin, but enough of them left legible to form a valuable addition to Mr. Stanley's hid treasures. It will not do to say to the historical treasures of New England, until the death of Mr. Stanley shall release them.

As for the copies of President Stiles' well-known and well reputed but not particularly valuable work, it is too late now to seek to trace their transfer from the printing office of Elisha Babcock in 1794 to the Scrope Chest in that old garret. There certainly was some mismanagement or other in the publishing of the book, perhaps in consequence of the death of the author, not many months after it appeared. The high reputation of the writer and the local interest of the subject would naturally have caused the printer to strike off a good number of copies, whereas the work has always been rather uncommon, and is now quite scarce.

But whatever the facts might be about these ancient matters, the Woodbridge reminiscence was substantiated. The Chest, doubtless with its cargo of printed sheets, must have been stored in the old house about 1794; and the partition which had protected it so effectually being put in not long afterwards, books, chest and all had quietly faded out of remembrance, as deaths, removals, changes of ownership and occupancy, and the other vicissitudes of so many years had arisen one after another, as additional veils between present and past.

The discovery of the chest and books was not kept so quiet as was intended. Such things never are. Good Messrs. Carpenter and Contractor, although they readily agreed not to mention the little circumstance, must have communicated it, of course under the same condition, until everybody in Hartford knew all about it, on condition of not mentioning it to anybody. Then the newspapers — which are what Goethe called Nature, "the Open Secret" — had a paragraph or two, and then quite a number more, on the chest, on the Scrope Will, and in particular on the Scrope Library.

The general conclusion about the latter was the same to which Adrian himself, and his aunt, had come at once; that as their depository was here, they themselves must be in the neighborhood. The notion that they were probably to be sought for in the old town of Bozrah, or in Windsor, where lived Adrian's ancestor John Chester, was definitely surrendered, and the only question suggested as remaining for discussion was, Where in Hartford can the old books be?

CHAPTER XXX.

CIVILLE answered Adrian by return mail, kindly enough, but in a note so brief as to be little more than a mere acknowledgment of receipt. Indeed, she apologized for this brevity, but with such generalized specifications about health, employments &c., that Adrian, reading the neat little document over and over, and pondering upon it, could not help concluding, Either she don't care at all, or she cares so much that she is afraid. He now, moreover, resumed his post as assistant librarian at the Young Men's Institute, and betook himself to his regular avocation of covering, stamping, marking and shelving books, of running to get novels for little boys, of first informing young ladies what books they wanted and then handing them out, of comparing his own critical estimates of great writers with those of middle-aged single ladies, and of doing all other those acts and things which are proper to the office of assistant librarian. He had overstaid his vacation by a number of days, but a proper acknowledgment to the cantankerous members of the Board of Directors served to adjust that; the accommodating members remembered all the extra hours and days and labor that the young man had so often bestowed upon the institution, without talking about it. And he flung himself into his work harder than ever, in part purposely, to make up for lost time, in part without any conscious purpose, but as the result of a necessity to escape from useless wishes and mere lamenting reveries. In whatever time he had to spare from work and sleep, he did however devote himself to a thorough re-examination of the question of the Scroope books; inquiring of all the living authorities (except Mr. Philetus Stanley of East Hartford) that he could reach, and searching records in every direction. It was however all in vain; he could

not find the least hint of the books subsequent to their disposition in the Will, nor any of the chest itself, whose presence in his own room was proof enough of its own existence now; but he used sometimes to think of the old witchcraft notions, and to wish he could extort a revelation from the hard and blackened oak timber, like Canidia, who used to make the moon dance and bow, or as Khawla in the Domdaniel extorted speech from the dead Teraph.

But one day about a month afterward, at noon, a telegram reached him at the library to the following effect :

"Come at once. Van Braams are in trouble.   C. Veroil."

"I must go to New York by next train," said Adrian promptly to his principal. "Some near relations are in trouble there."

"Very well," said that gentleman, quite courteously, "I can't say a word against that; but will you please notify the Board?"

"Certainly," said Adrian, — "instantly; but I can't wait." So he wrote a brief note to the President; as he began he remembered the cantankerous minority; and with a decision that was to him easy because it was natural, but which is more admired than practised by prudent people, he shaped the note into a short statement of his departure and its reasons, with a resignation of his post, should the Board under the circumstances think it best to accept the same.

To show a board of young men, — or old men either, — that their subordinate feels independent of them, is a tolerably sure and short road to a dismissal. The opposition seized on the chance; Adrian's lukewarm friends permitted themselves to be displeased or indifferent; his strong friends felt themselves at a disadvantage; and after some debate over the imputed brusqueness of the present action and the alleged carelessness of the interests of the library in his recent vacation, the resignation was accepted by a decisive vote.

Having sent his message at once to the President of the Board, and having answered Dr. Veroil that he would reach New York that night, he went straight home, notified his aunt, and made ready. The stout-hearted old lady instantly offered to go with him, but this he declined, promising however to send for her if necessary.

The journey was without adventures. Reaching that city, Adrian went at once to Dr. Veroil's. That hospitable and genial gentleman was at dinner, and he made Adrian sit down and eat, although the young man felt no great appetite. But the doctor, in his own jolly forceful way, simply constrained him.

"You must," he said, "for probably you'll have to be up all night; and a hearty meal is indispensable in preparing to sit up all night. So come in!"

And he haled him forth of the office into the comfortable dining room, and presented him to Mrs. Veroil, a comfortable smiling dame, and to his two plump children; and while he prescribed and administered abundant and succulent viands he told him whatever was to be told.

This was, in short, that Mr. Button had all of a sudden and without visible cause, warned Mr. Van Braam to quit the house where he was living, in consequence of alleged intended improvements; and at the same time the insurance secretaryship from which the old gentleman had drawn his support, had also been taken away from him, undoubtedly by Mr. Button's means. These misfortunes, amounting to instantaneous ruin for a man so old, so poor and so nearly friendless, had come upon him when if not ill, he was somewhat indisposed, and had aggravated his complaint into something so much like a typhoid fever that it might be a question whether his ailment was not really such a fever, produced by the unhealthy air of his house. If he had a place to go to, the doctor concluded, it would be the best thing that could happen to him to be driven neck and crop out of that old shanty.

As Dr. Veroil thus recounted, it flashed across Adrian's mind that Mr. Stanley must after all have sent Mr. Button the information in the old account-book. Stanley's rather mischievous disposition, and his bitter contemptuous dislike of Mr. Button had, if this was the case, prevailed over his love of keeping a secret; there was no reason to suppose that he had thought that any evil would enure to any third parties.

As Dr. Veroil made no allusion to that other matter which had been expressly left in charge of himself and Mr. Bird the police reporter, Adrian also refrained in like manner. He did indeed, as the doctor's narrative closed, give one inquiring look, which however the physician answered by an almost imperceptible shake of the head and contraction of the eyebrows. Adrian therefore inquired only about Mr. Button's prosperity in general. His business, the doctor answered, went on as usual; his political prospects were understood to be beginning to brighten, as he was to have a nomination for member of Congress at an election about to take place to fill a vacancy in his district.

When dinner was over. the doctor summoned Adrian into his office and gave him final directions about Mr. Van Braam, their substance being that as the old man was in a very weak state, it was for the immediate present critically important that his tonics should be frequently and punctually administered. He (the doctor) was to look in, if possible, before bedtime, and at any rate in good season in the morning, and hoped to find every thing going on well. He wanted Civille to rest well for a few nights, he added, or else she would be down sick too. And then he said that as to the other matter, Mr. Bird had told him that the thefts at several of the largest retail dry-goods houses had begun again a week or two ago, and that measures were concerted to detect the criminals, though so far nobody had been caught except a few of the ordinary shop-lifters. And he added, that of course considerations connected with these affairs had had their influence upon Mr. Van Braam; affairs about which, of course, nothing whatever was to be said unless in case of absolute necessity.

Well fortified, therefore, as to his physical man, but not so comfortable in his mind, Adrian left the abode of the genial doctor. For, no matter how ready one may be to assist those who need, it is depressing to feel all at once that it is upon us that the helpless person is to be laden.

It was that same bitter-tempered Katy, who opened Mr. Van Braam's door.

" What, you here again? " exclaimed Adrian, not at all pleased.

" Yis, what I'm here agin, sur ! " said the woman, in the same sharp ill-natured manner; but she seemed to relent a little as she added,

" But it's glad of ye Miss Civille will be, faith ! Walk in sur, till I tell her."

He entered the parlor, where there was a fire and a light; and in a moment Civille came in. He rose to meet her, and had hardly time to see how thin, and white and weary her face looked. Involuntarily the tears came into his eyes, and involuntarily he held out his arms. The poor girl, as if upheld so long only by the iron necessity of her lonely situation, gave way at once. She burst into tears and almost fell. He caught her and supported her to the sofa, and soothed and comforted her, stroking her soft hair as one comforts a baby, and letting her cry, as one comforts a woman.

" I knew you would come," she said at last.

" I would have come before," said he; " you ought to have sent."

" Until yesterday I hoped we could fight it through alone," said she; " but father is worse, and I got so frightened ! "

Poor child ! She had never had wealth, but her father's solicitous care had hitherto kept her in comfort. Her wealthy friends had always treated her with that kind of civility which we confer upon agreeable inferiors who don't ask us for any thing; and this, her sweet nature took it for granted, was affection. She felt a real affection for them; and the most genuine affection is the first to believe in the genuineness of a response. Now, all at once a great distress came, as if an earthquake were shaking the very ground away from under her feet, and it was as if everybody ran away on purpose to leave her to fall into the pit.

" I did not think Ann would have treated me so," said she, crying quietly. " I loved her; and I love her now. It was not just because they were all cousins. I don't see how they could do so. But Ann actually refused to recognize me in the street, and so did her mother. Oh, if I had become suddenly infamous, and good people had cast me out, I know how it would have felt!"

"Well, dear," said Adrian, "Doctor Veroil will stand by us. He's a man! And as long as my aunt and I own that little old house in Hartford, we shall all have a roof over our heads at at any rate. And Civille, — I don't think it would even make my hand tremble in smoothing your hair — how silky and fine it is — if you should become suddenly infamous, as you call it. You can't be any thing to me except what I know you to be, Civille. I defy you to change."

"I don't want to, Adrian," she said, simply; "and I feel better to have you pet me a little," she added, contentedly, and almost nestling to his side; "I am not to be afraid of you, you know, and you are to help me now that I need it."

"Yes," he said — he could not well have said less — or more. — "And now, dear, you must show me about the nocturnal affairs, and then you must go to bed and sleep all night."

"I begin to feel sleepy already, Adrian; you can put me asleep, you know.— But that is not very complimentary."

"I think it is, very," said he, — and indeed the perfect trust that was implied by the fact, and that thrilled through the soft heartfelt voice, all the more touchingly because it was veiled and languid with weariness and sorrow, filled him with a happiness such as he had never known before — the happiness of satisfying one beloved.

They went up stairs to the sick room. Mr. Van Braam lay quietly in bed, asleep; his bloodless complexion and thin high features, sharpened by illness, giving him a deathly appearance that was only removed on watching the faint slow respiration. The rubric for the night was brief; Give the draughts punctually every half hour. Katy, who sat silently by the fire, was dismissed; Civille went away, receiving quietly a kiss on the forehead from Adrian, "for good-night;" and Adrian stood on the hearth-rug a few moments, observing the economical appointments of the room ; then turned to the shelf, where he found a few books, from which he selected a volume of Sainte-Beuve's *Causeries;* and he sat himself down to read, to think, and to make notes.

The half hour soon came round, and he waked the patient and gave him his dose. Although the old gentleman recognized Adrian, he was too weak, apparently, to ask or even to consider, how he came to be there; he opened his eyes, smiled faintly, swallowed the draught, made a feeble grimace of discomfort, lay down again and relapsed into his immovable condition. Adrian wrote down passages quoted or written by the accomplished French critic, somewhat in the following style.

JOUBERT. "Looked like a soul that had met a body somewhere by mere accident, and had taken up with it and was doing the best he could with it."

IMPERFECTION. Le Sage says, "The best people are those that have the fewest vices." Chester compares the military observation that the question between two opposing generals is, not which shall make no mistakes, but only which shall make the fewest."

And so on: translating, paraphrasing or commenting, as the case may be : then laying down his book and looking at the fire ; then listening (so to speak) to the utter stillness in the house. He had never tried his hand at nursing before, and he smiled as he said to himself, after about an hour, " I guess I was made for a nurse." The smile was first at the idea, and then at the insufficiency of the experience from which he was deducing it.

At the second dosing of the patient, he murmured something about its being " nasty," and a wish that they'd "let him alone." Who has not entertained similar views about medicines of the more plentiful and frequent sort ?

——— ⁄

Ah ? What is this light ?

Adrian sprang up, terrified at once into springing up and into a faintness that almost let him fall down again. Gleams, a glow almost, of white light were in the room. Amazed, he looked hither and thither, and choked down, as it were, a shout of " FIRE !" But he sniffed after a smell of smoke. There was none. He went to the window and looked out. The gray pale light of sunrise was rising over the city.

He looked at his watch — he looked more than once — he compared it with Civille's, that was hung up over the shelf; and as his senses clarified themselves and settled into daylight order after about two minutes of terror and confusion, his reflection upon his eminent capabilities for the nursing business came into his mind with a queer mixture of shame and fright, along with the recognition of its ironic if not direct justness.

But the patient ?

With feelings not entirely unlike those which may be supposed to have occupied the late William Tell on finding that abilities of his own have brought upon him the risk of killing his son, Adrian looked across the room at Mr. Van Braam. He could not see him distinctly from where he stood ; and it required a strong effort before he could bring himself to walk across to the bed. The old man had turned over and lay flat on his face. " The last struggle " thought Adrian — " and I to confess to Civille ! " — But the necessity of the case was supreme, and with a thrill of horror he laid his hand on the — No, not the corpse !

At the touch, the old man moved in the bed. Still less is it possible to express the relief, than the horror, of this so gifted guardian of the sick. Turning his haggard and bony old countenance out sideways, Mr. Van Braam asked,

" What, again ? "

Adrian cried and laughed.

" I'm better," said the old gentleman. " I must have slept."

He was really so much refreshed that Adrian ventured to confess his unfaithfulness. Mr. Van Braam would have laughed outright, had he been strong enough. As it was, he could only smile ; but his next words showed that his wits were not enfeebled, though his body might be. He still spoke very low and but few words at a time.

" Don't tell a soul. — Veroil would kill you. — Good nurse, Adrian ! — Just what I wanted. — Pour the stuff behind the fire. — Don't scare Civille — Poor child ! "

So Adrian carefully poured a proper quantity of the tonic mixture amongst the ashes, freshened up the decaying fire ; put out the expiring lamp ; replaced the volume of M. Sainte-Beuve upon the mantle-piece ; made a hasty toilet ; and assisted his patient to do the same.

With his face washed and his hair nicely brushed, Mr. Van Braam looked quite comfortable, and asked how Adrian came to be there; and Adrian had just answered that Dr. Veroil had summoned him, when there was a soft knock at the door, and Adrian admitted Civille. As things were, he felt at liberty to admire her morning dress, a loose gown of soft shimmering dark gray stuff, with a narrow white lace about the neck, and confined at the waist by a pretty belt. She looked at her father:

" Why ! " — and she bent over the dear old man with a graceful gesture, and caressing his white head with both hands, she kissed his forehead again and again, and then looked at Adrian with such a solemn loving brightness in the deep lucid gray eyes !

Then she sat down and cried a little.

PART XII

CHAPTER XXXI.

"Come," said Civille, brightening up in a minute or two — "what am I crying for? — Adrian, you must go and have a good sleep, you dear good cousin, and then you shall have some breakfast. — What are you laughing at? You too, father?"

"Why," — said Adrian, "at the idea of my ever having to sleep. I am the he-Melusina; I never sleep."

Civille looked puzzled. "Tell her, Adrian," said the old man, feebly. With some hesitation, Adrian did so, to her immense surprise and contentment. But they agreed with one consent not to inform their respected physician.

So the two young folks had breakfast together, Katy remaining with the sick man the while. Civille did the honors of the table, and while Adrian ate and drank, he enjoyed still more than the delicately served viands, her neat-handed, graceful ways, her innocent happy chat, her gracious sunshiny presence. And they had abundance of topics to discuss.

For instance:

ADRIAN. Very jolly coffee, Civille. I say coffee. If it were dandelion or rye or chicory I should be brutal enough to say so, I am afraid. A cheat in coffee is next door but one to murdering a baby.

CIVILLE. Oh, don't! Poor little thing! Well, it ought to be good; I made it myself.

A. Tell me how your father came to be ill.

C. He has been a little ailing for some time. I have sometimes thought he was excited about this Scrope estate business; for he has never seemed quite .well since the very evening when you and Mr. Scrope met here and talked about it.

A. (*Remembering that that was the evening when the detective Olds had called on Mr. Van Braam, but not telling Civille so.*) Hasn't he? Well; I'd rather attribute his illness to an expectation than to my own call, certainly. And these questions of genealogy and inheritance have an immense interest for some people.

C. But father attended to his business, although I know he didn't feel well, until two or three days after you wrote me about that old account book. Then he came home one evening, all broken down, and went to bed; and he hasn't got up since. (*Here Civille began to cry quietly, — the tears slowly dropping one after another; but her voice only trembled a little, as she went on:*) I thought my dear father was going to die.

A. Oh, Civille, don't cry, please. It hurts me.

C. (*Wiping her eyes.*) Well, I won't. But it does me good sometimes to cry a little. You see, that very day when he came home, he had received notice that he must lose his secretaryship and move out of this house. I don't know why he should have felt it so intensely, I'm sure. He and I have been poor enough, and long enough, not to be frightened at that. But he kept talking that evening, and afterwards too, about its being so hard for me. I couldn't understand it. ["Poor thing! I do," said Adrian to himself.] I think it was the Scrope estate business and these other things coming so, all together, that made him ill. I told him then what you had written, of course. He said it was no wonder Mr. Button kicked him out,—he had no doubt Mr. Button felt as if he had been deliberately cheated on system. So we must go, as soon as he can move.

A. Well; I'll help you.

C. I know you will.—It was very sweet of you to come.—I felt as if every thing would be right, the minute I saw you; and when I had left you with father I went right to sleep as quietly as any baby.

A. Even Mr. Button won't trouble you until your father can be moved. Then we will find a place to stay, and look round a little. The world is wide, particularly New York.

C. Adrian:—I heard you call me that evening! You look surprised? Well, if it was not you that I heard, it was a curious coincidence that I should have fancied it exactly at the time. You know you wrote me the almanac difference of time for Hartford and New York. Was that so as to find out whether I heard you?

A. No. I only wrote just what came into my head. But I know this: when I spoke your name that night I felt as if I spoke to you.

C. I was sitting here by the fire, and father was asleep in his chair. I had been singing a little, and I guess I had been thinking I would like to have you here instead of Mr. Bird and Mr. Scrope—

A. Why,—beg pardon—hasn't Scrope gone back to England?

C. Yes; he sailed a day or two afterwards. Well; they had both come and gone, first Mr. Scrope and then Mr. Bird, and so I was left alone. I had dropped my work and was sitting thinking, and all at once it was as if a distant voice called me. —Civille!—It was like your voice, I thought, but sorrowful, as if you sighed. It startled me; but there was nobody. And I couldn't hear wherefrom it came. It was as if it was from deep in my own brain. I went and asked Katy; she had not spoken. So I concluded I had dozed and dreamed it, until your letter came. I remembered the time, because father woke up as I went out, and asked, and I told him.

A. I hope it was my voice you heard, and I mean to believe it was. There are plenty of questions where preference of belief is good ground of belief. Well; has Mr. Bird offered himself yet, Civille?

Civille blushed, and opened her mouth to answer. Katy however at that moment came in to say that Mr. Van Braam would have a slice of toast and some tea. So Civille told her to clear away the things and have her own breakfast, and herself prepared her father's breakfast, giving Adrian the newspaper, which he said he would read, and then, if she or her father had any errands to be done, he was at their service.

He had just perused an account of the nomination, the evening before, of Tarbox Button Esq., for the vacant place of representative in Congress from the ———— District of New York, when a chopping and banging in the yard interrupted him. Looking out, he saw four workmen, two of whom were beginning to cut down two trees, and the two others, with axe and crow-bar, were tearing down the old paling at the side of the house, between the yard and the vacant grass-ground outside. Running out, Adrian found that they were sent by a person with whom Mr. Button had contracted to tear down the house this day.

"But there's a sick man in there that wasn't expected to live, and who can't be moved," exclaimed Adrian, in a rage. "Did Mr. Button tell you, if you found an old man very sick in the house, to murder him?"

"Don't know nothin' bout it, boss," said the chief of the band, roughly but good-naturedly enough. "No xpress orders to murder anybody, furzino, but mighty strick to git this old place cleaned off right away."

After some further parleying, Adrian succeeded in negotiating a delay, on condition however that he should pay for the four days' works, which, the men said, they would otherwise lose, until he could see Mr. Button and secure a delay. It is true that they would doubtless not have absolutely torn the roof down over the helpless family, like a British landowner evicting a tenant, but the trees, fences and outbuildings would have supplied materials for some hours of destruction noisy enough to greatly injure Mr. Van Braam in his weak state.

So the men shouldered arms and marched, and Adrian, in a good deal of indignation returned to the parlor, where he found Civille waiting. He explained the occurrence, with terse remarks upon its ethical aspect.

But Civille, with her own sweetness of heart, sought for excuses. Mr. Button did not know of her father's illness; or his directions to wait had been forgotten or neglected.

"Oh yes," said Adrian, "any thing except to admit that anybody does wrong. You enrage me, Civille. Don't for goodness' sake be too bright or good for human nature's daily food. If you will be so very heavenly, you'll be crucified, sure." And he laughed at his own wrath, and continued:

"But now I must hurry down and see about it. — But Civille, you didn't answer my question. Did Bird offer himself?"

She blushed a little, but answered, with her own natural — yet odd — directness,

"Yes; Mr. Scrope did too. I know you won't tell, Adrian."

"Well," said he, "I don't wonder. Yes, — I do. I don't at their wanting you, but I do at their fancying themselves good enough for you."

Then he blushed, as he perceived the elegant compliment he was paying to himself. — "I mean, dear, nobody is good enough for you. As to Scrope, I guess he is conceited enough to think he's good enough for anybody. But Bird's a fellow of great sense, though he's not very cultivated. I don't understand it. Well, I must go — any errands?"

"No; I must run out myself a little while; I want Doctor Veroil to come early, and I must go and tell him."

So Adrian went off, appointing to return as soon as he should effect the proposed arrangement with Mr. Button; and all the way down to the office, he meditated with the queerest mixture of feelings, on Civille's three offers, which, he remembered he had prophesied out of

Mother Goose on the evening when he had accompanied his rivals from the house. "'We're three brethren out of Spain,' he recited. — Well, she has made us all walk Spanish, at any rate ; and we can all go back to our Spanish castles. A proper fate for men with no better estates!'" But her lovely figure and exceeding grace in the simple morning dress, a certain dainty delicacy in the little ministrations of the breakfast table, an especial tenderness of manner which had perhaps arisen upon her from her sorrow over her father, insomuch that even if she was gay, it seemed as if tears were thrilling through under all her heartfelt tones, and most of all, the unconscious trustfulness with which she reposed in his help, all these influences filled the strong young fellow with an emotion that returned and returned upon him without end, as the ceaseless sea-waves follow and follow up the beach. He did not understand it, nor try to ; but he found a measureless pleasure in the full silent consciousness that if any efforts of his could save Civille from all trouble, or any trouble, the effort should be made ; and the strength of his sense of devotedness translated itself into a feeling that it would succeed.

———

"Wal!"

There was a whole chapter, — a whole volume, — of unwelcoming contemptuous angry surprise in the frown, the twist of the mouth, the falling inflection, the sharp harsh bark, of Mr. Button, when looking up, he saw Adrian enter his back office. Nor did he offer him a seat, nor hold out his hand. Adrian was angry enough before. The discourtesy enraged him so much that perhaps it even steadied him; to his own surprise, he felt quite calm and rather inclined to smile. He made a polite bow, said "How d'ye do, Mr. Button?" and took a chair himself, saying,

"Sha'n't detain you more than a moment."

"That's so. Got to go anyway."

"Mr. Van Braam is very ill indeed, Mr. Button — they were afraid he wouldn't live — it's impossible to move him. Now I want you to call off your dogs, and let the old house alone for a few days ; if you please."

"Hmh! Live? He'll live fast enough's long's he's got somebody to live on. Live on you, 'f ye had any thing. Had to let go o' me, I guess, is what made him sick. You goin to take him up?"

"I've resigned my place at Hartford — at least if the Board chooses — and you know I can't support many people on my investments."

"Reckon not. Wal — the house. I don't know nothin 'bout it — Oh, yes I do, — contracted with what's-his-name to pull it down. Yes — 'twas to-day, sure enough. Forgot all about it — I'll see what can be done. You may come and see me this evening about it. But I don't owe no favors to any on ye, young man."

"Any of me?" asked Adrian with a smile, — "there's only one of me."

Mr. Button gave a snort of irritation. "Hmh! You knew what I meant. Fact is, I wouldn't git back agin into your family connection if I could. I've got other fish to fry. Your swindling, cunning Scrope's welcome to my five hundred dollars, — 's long's I can't git none on't back, — guess all you git of the Scrope estate amongst ye you c'n put in your ear. I won't trust another one o' that crowd, though, any further than I c'n swing an elephant by the tail — I c'n tell ye that!"

There was something antipathetic in the natures of the two men that made them intensely irritating to each other. Adrian had never been in the company of Mr. Button without feeling this more or less distinctly, and Mr. Button himself had shown it before by the rasping anger of his reply to Adrian's suggestion about the use to which some of the publisher's real estate was put. Adrian's natural and acquired good manners however prevented him from very openly showing this; while Button, who restrained himself only from motives of interest, was much more liable to lose his self-command. At present, enraged as he was by the knowledge which it was sufficiently evident he had obtained, through the friendly offices of Mr. Stanley, from the old account-book, this new vexation was added to his older ones, and he "freed his mind" with an alacrity and fulness of wrath and objurgation that boiled out of him so thick and hot as to make Adrian think of a mud volcano. In a moment he broke out again with another mud-flow of vulgar angry bragging:

"I'll let some on ye know what's what, and what aint! I've got over that are trouble about my health, — I haint felt as smart and wide awake as I do this very day, I reckon for ten year! Praps you didn't see in the papers this morning, that I was nominated for Congress last night, in my district? Goin', too! I got that all fixed before I took the nomination, I can tell ye! I don't put my hand to the plough and then look back! Some time before you git into Congress, I guess! Or that old Van Braam, either! I reckon the old fellow 'll find out what tis to have a

man a boostin on him! I've kept the breath o' life in his old carkis, this good while."

"Let not thy left hand know what thy right hand doeth," quoted Adrian quietly.

"Hmh!" again, snorted the wrathful capitalist, with a toss of his head like an angry beast that is hit sharply over the snout — "Hmh! Yes: and I've got my own business in good shape too, no thanks to you, young man! And so you've resigned your place? Fourth of July at your house every day, now, hay? Wal, — have your own way. But I must go. I'm a goin to ketch that are thief that Jenks & Trainor and the detectives cant git hold of; nor Bird neither."

"Why, pray what put that into your head?" asked Adrian, surprised.

"Wal, I got talkin' with Jenks and Bird about it tother day, and they sorter confessed they was beat, and I bantered 'em to let me try, and they took me up. I'm to have two chances; first experiment this morning."

Here he looked at his watch, and jumping up, bade Adrian good day with somewhat less gruffness, now that he had relieved his mind, saying "I don't wish you no harm, Adrian, but you haint showed much judgment, 'cordin to me, in a business point of view — good morning, — I'm behind my time now." And he hurried out, entered a hack which was waiting for him, and drove off.

Adrian followed, more leisurely, inquiring in his own mind how it could be that he seemed to have mounted through his very wrath itself to a region above it, as travellers ascend above the region of clouds. Still, he felt that Button was not a person to be angry with, except as one might be angry with a polar bear or a man-eating shark. As he went musing along, some one seized his hand and sung out, in a jolly tone,

"Why, how are you? Last man I expected to see, but just the one I am glad to see."

It was the good natured book dealer, Mr. Andrew Purvis, whose shop was near by. Adrian, after his first surprise, returned his greeting with cordiality, and asked whether he could do any thing for Mr. Purvis. No, the dealer said, but added a special request to Adrian to look in at his place that day or the next, as, he added, there was a little matter of business about which he wanted to see Adrian; unless he could come now?

But an idea which popped into Adrian's mind just as Purvis met him, caused him to appoint the next day instead of the present moment, and shaking hands, they parted. This idea was, to hurry after Mr. Button at once and to hire the old house of him for a week, purely as a matter of business. In his peculiarly ugly state of mind, Adrian reflected, he might even insist upon going forward with his demolition; and although the sick man might survive an immediate removal, what an outrage and inconvenience together! Whereas, also, it is the nature of a thorough business man never to refuse to consider a business proposition, never to refuse to conclude it if profitable, never to let his evil passions or his good ones either, interfere or mix with his business. A thorough business man will not sell to a church or a charity for one cent less than to a gambler or any other speculator : he may afterwards make the church or the charity a gift of some of the money. And Mr. Button prided himself upon being a thorough business man.

But where to find him? At Jenks and Trainor's, probably. The affair should be closed as soon as possible. However, concluded the young man, I'll go back first and see how Mr. Van Braam gets along, how Civille is, and what the doctor says. How pleased he will be at the effects of his old drugs!

CHAPTER XXXII.

So he speeded back to the old house — if the crawling of a horse-car can be called speed — as fast as he could. Doctor Veroil's coupé was before the door, and Adrian entered, and went up to Mr. Van Braam's room.

"A capital recovery!" said the physician, after salutations, — "we'll have him as lively as a kitten in five days. But what a constitution!"

"But what a doctor!" said Adrian, with an air of grave admiration.

"Oh, thanks!" said Dr. Veroil, with a proper modesty. "No doubt I know what I'm about; but it's a fine thing to have nature help us, all the same. Mr. Van Braam is not so very strong, muscularly, but it is rare to see the recuperative power so elastic and so prompt in a man of his age. It's a pity to have to give him medicine!"

"It is," commented Adrian again, as gravely as ever.

"Where's Civille?" said the old man.

"She went out after breakfast," said Kate, who was in the room. Adrian was surprised that Dr. Veroil did not mention her call at his office, and after waiting a moment, he said;

"She told me she was going to call

at your office, doctor, and then come right back."

Doctor Veroil looked at Adrian, surprised in his turn. Then he glanced at the old gentleman, who looked anxious, then he cast a significant glance at Adrian, and said,

"Oh, yes : she just looked in, and she was so tired out and pale that I gave her a peremptory order to ride up to the Central Park and sit or walk a little in the fresh air there, as it's so pleasant to-day, and try to get a winter rose or two into her cheeks for dinner time."

"Very good advice, doctor," said the old man.

Veroil now gave some directions, and after repeating his encouraging predictions to the old man, went out, but as he went, he made a sign to Adrian to follow him, and went down into the parlor. Turning short round as soon as he was within the door, he showed to Adrian a startled face.

"But I haven't seen Civille !" he said.

A comparison of the hours showed that she should have been at the doctor's office at least three quarters of an hour before he left it for his usual morning round.

"Can she have gone to Mr. Button's for anything ?" said Adrian.

"Hardly," said the doctor; "those women cut her the other day in the street. She's that kind that she will be hunting excuses for them, but I don't think she'll go right into their — pen," he concluded, in one of his sudden rages.

"But what can it mean, then ?" said Adrian, who began to be troubled, in proportion as he saw the annoyance of the doctor.

"Well," said Veroil, "there's no use in hiding anything between you and me. I told the first straight story that came into my head to make the old man comfortable. His misery about her has done more to make him sick than anything else. He is doing splendidly, now, but he hasn't the strength of a child; and if anything should go wrong with her, and he should know it, he wouldn't last two days. I never saw one life so bound up in another — never. And he must be lied comfortable as long as is necessary — or as long as possible."

"Amen," said Adrian ; "but what is your guess ? "

"We must try the police, anyhow," said the doctor. "I *must* make my calls ; you must find her at once. I'll give you a general letter of introduction, to keep in your hands. I know so many people, and so many know me, that a note from me is almost a government commission, taking the direct and indirect influence together. Go first to Olds ; if he knows anything, so far so good. If not, go to Mulberry Street, and have a general inquiry made for accident or arrest of a person answering her description. As soon as you have either good success or bad success, hurry and tell me."

The doctor went to a side table where there were writing materials, wrote the note of introduction and gave it to Adrian, and they went softly out together. As they did so, Adrian, in a low voice, suggested to Dr. Veroil what Mr. Button had told him of his proposed thief-catching expedition. "It's a coincidence, doctor," he said, with a strong sense of pain at his heart.

"Yes, but only a very distant one ; we won't discount any troubles, my boy ; I don't propose to recognize any speculative horrors. — How was my friend Button this morning ?"

"In uncommonly high feather.

Said he hadn't felt so well this ten years, as he did this very day."

Veroil stopped short: "He did!" exclaimed he — "And a day or two ago, he was so used up! Well — it may be all right. But " —

He did not complete his sentence, and going out, he dashed off on his rounds. It did not take very long for Adrian to get across to the corner of Broadway and Washington Place, where the detective's rooms were. The day was apparently a day of opportune meetings; for as he passed the door of that great quiet substantial brick mansion where Commodore Vanderbilt has lived so many years, he beheld the trim and active figure of Mr. Bird the reporter, just coming round from Broadway into Washington Place.

"Let me only meet Civille next," said the young man to himself.

Bird looked quite surprised to meet Adrian, but was as pleased, after his quiet manner, as any other of his friends had been. Adrian did not hesitate to tell him the business in hand; and Mr. Bird listened, with very evident interest. When Adrian was through he said,

"You needn't go up to Olds' room now; I've just been up there myself, and he isn't in. Try head-quarters, first, and then come back; he may be in any minute."

"Well," said Adrian, "I will." As they parted, "Stay," called out Bird; "I've thought of another move. I'll give you a card to Jenks; I've had to see him plenty of times about shoplifters, and other matters, and he knows me perfectly well. If any trouble has been made by Olds, Jenks will know about it; he is the fiercest of them all about these thefts, and I think you may save time by going to him now. If he has noth-ing to tell you, then try the Mulberry Street folks, and then call at Olds' again, and then try back home; you see, she may be back there now, for what we know."

This was good advice, and Adrian followed it, turning back and taking a Broadway car at the corner of Washington Place and Greene Street. This car took him past the entrance of Jenks & Trainor's vast establishment on Broadway, some little distance above Union Park. Everybody knows the monstrous elaborate front, painted white to look as if its pillars and panels and entablatures,. instead of dense tough iron, were. carved of brittle white stone. How much longer will New York architects keep on telling lies with their materials? As if the substance of iron could look right within the forms of stone! What is the natural relation of form to matter is the one discovery for which a genuine nineteenth-century architecture is waiting.

Both ways at once, through the lofty arched doors of this vast mart of woven things, there glided two rivers of well-dressed women. As Adrian stepped from the car to plunge into that one of these interminable processions which entered the sacred place, he was startled to see, in the other, Miss Ann Button coming out. She did not see him; and she turned and walked up Broadway towards home. Upon her features Adrian could distinguish no expression in particular. He did not address her, but passed on into the building, gliding along in the midst of the throng of matrons and maidens, not with a sense of impiety exactly, such as Clodius may have felt while intruding among the feminine votaries of the Bona Dea, but with a feeling of having no business there, which reminded him of the wickeder enterprise of the eminent Roman rowdy.

At one side of the vast store, a little way within the entrance, there was a dense crowd of clerks and customers, such as gathers in the street for the purpose of keeping the fresh air away from any one who is faint. "What is the matter?" he asked of a clerk who was one of those on the outskirts of this throng. "Don't know exactly," said the young man; "somebody fainted, they said." —

"I have an errand to Mr. Jenks," said Adrian; "how shall I find him?"

"Step this way," said the other, obligingly; "I'll get the floor-walker to show you."

This personage was a thin tall man, with iron-gray hair, severely dressed, who looked about him with keen peremptory eyes and walked up and down the floor. and who somehow looked to Adrian like a broken-down business man — perhaps because he was; such posts are well-known harbors of refuge for wrecks from financial storms. Adrian repeated his request.

"Show the gentleman up to Mr. Spink," said the floor-walker to the clerk. Mr. Spink had a small den up one flight of stairs; he was a dry little man with thin red hair and a look of conscious authority.

"I want to see Mr. Jenks," said Adrian.

"About what?" said Mr. Spink, sharply.

"A confidential matter" said Adrian.

"I'm his confidential clerk," said Mr. Spink; "you may mention it to me."

Adrian hesitated. "Can't see him any other way," said Spink, more peremptorily than ever, — "it's that or nothing."

Adrian was greatly inclined to give the peremptory man a beating; he knew nothing of the frantic pressure of all sorts of applicants against which a wealthy New Yorker has to devise a whole system of fortifications. But his errand was a guaranty against unseasonable wrath, and he laid before this Cerberus with one red head the note of Dr. Veroil and the card of Mr. Bird.

"Ah," said Mr. Spink, who now gave a quick inquiring look at Adrian — "yes. That business — Well, you had better see Mr. Jenks, sir. This way, please." And he guided Adrian along narrow alleys among interminable piles of dry goods of all kinds, to a remote corner of the building, where he rapped at an unobtrusive door. This opened from within, and they entered.

"Mr. Chester," said Spink, with skilful terseness, "with introductions." And he disappeared.

Mr. Jenks, a slender middle-aged man, nearly bald, and with a worn and over-worked look, sat at a desk writing. He looked up an instant, pointed to a chair close at the side of his desk, bowed very slightly and hurriedly, said "Take seat, please. One moment," and went on with his writing. Having finished, sealed and addressed a letter, he sat up straight, made a half-face in his pivot-chair, and thus brought face to face with Adrian, said,

"What can I do for you, sir?"

Adrian, always quick to receive impressions, felt the intensity of New York business which was weighing upon the merchant, and made his communications as brief as possible.

"Note from Dr. Veroil," he said; "card from Mr. Bird."

"Mr. Spink saw them," said Jenks, with a nod, as much as to say, "Spink gets my business ready for me; if the introductions had not been right you would not be here."

"Is Mr. Tarbox Button here?" said Adrian.

"I believe so," said Jenks; and taking up the mouth-piece of a gutta-percha speaking-tube that rested on his desk, he blew into it, then held it to his ear, listening to indistinct murmurs as from a shell of ocean, then mumbled something into it, then held it to his ear again, and then said,

"He was here. He has gone home ill."

"Where is Miss Van Braam?" asked Adrian.

"Why," said Jenks, hesitatingly, — "excuse me; in whose behalf do you inquire?"

"Her father has been at the point of death; he is very ill, and a little more trouble will kill him," said Adrian, not able to keep his voice quite steady; "she has not been seen since she went out on an errand after breakfast, this morning, meaning to return in half an hour; the poor old man is inquiring after her. They have no friends here, except Dr. Veroil and myself—I am her cousin. We know the suspicions about her; and Mr. Bird told me you might be able to give me some information. Whatever happens, she mustn't be left entirely alone."

"Mr. —— Mr. ——"

"Chester," said Adrian.

"Mr. Chester," said the merchant, "nothing could be more painful than to feel forced to take such action. But we must protect ourselves. Perhaps you don't know that we often lose five hundred dollars' worth of goods in a day by actual theft over our counters?"

No, Adrian did not.

"We have at this moment two regular customers — married ladies, wives of wealthy men, — who steal, as well as buy, every time they come into the store. We have them watched, and we send their husbands the bills. They pay, and nothing is said about it. We have other cases all the time; some professional female shop-lifters, some respectable women, —so-called, — who steal; and some, what the doctors call kleptomaniacs beside. We can't go into that. We must protect ourselves from theft as far as we can, whatever the cause of the theft."

Mr. Jenks paused, like one who looks to see the effect of his argument. As Adrian said nothing, he resumed.

"I tell you this, Mr. Chester, confidentially; it is proper, under the circumstances, that you should know something of our situation in the matter. I do not wish you to suppose that we have been harsh or hasty in what we have done. With regard to the present case — you know, I suppose, that these kleptomaniacs have very often all the cunning of a smart thief and all that of a lunatic together? — This makes it, often, next to impossible to detect them — next to impossible. In the present case, we have watched for months before taking any action. And I may tell you this: your friend was in the habit of coming with another young lady. We have — very cautiously, I assure you, and without compromising any one, — obtained such information from that young lady as to make the case next to absolutely certain — we can prove that some of our goods were found in your friend's possession. Now, — we know how distressing such cases are, — even now, provided we could be satisfied, — guaranteed, I mean, — that the depredations should cease, we would discontinue all proceedings. As it is, Mr. Chester, your friend is detained with a view to further investigations. But in such a manner as not to expose her publicly, nor to annoy her more than is necessary. We never go any further in such cases than we are absolutely forced to do."

Although in truth all this was little more than Adrian had for a good while been trying to be ready to hear, he was not ready. The statement was only too clear and well reasoned. It accordingly did not affect him with anger. The merchant was evidently convinced that he had caught one more of the ordinary run of respectable female thieves; but this suspicion, or rather belief, did not convince Adrian. It is true that it did perhaps make him a little more conscious of the possibility — only the possibility — that Civille had experienced some sort of alienation of mind. But this, even if he admitted its existence, he felt, — he *knew*, — was a disease, as much as scarlet fever; and temporary in the same sense.

Thus he reasoned in his own mind. While he did so, the merchant turned to his desk, and was instantly absorbed in his letters again. Once or twice a whistle sounded from one of the pipes close to his hand, and he listened and returned prompt and brief decisions. Adrian, in the mean time, like one who has been stunned and recovers, gathered up his scattered wits.

" Well," he began, —

The merchant at once dropped his pen and listened. He was not a hard man; he was in this matter only conducting one of the unavoidable accessories of such a business as his. And he had been giving Adrian, very likely, five hundred dollars' worth of time, because the case was a hard case, and he wished to be considerate.

"Well, Mr. Jenks, I can't find any fault with your action. But you will put me in the way of seeing my cousin, surely ? "

" Yes, — of course." He wrote a few words, signed, and gave Adrian the paper. " Hand that to Mr. Olds the detective, and he will go with you to Police Captain MacMurdo at Jefferson Market Station, and one of them will take you to her. We have to be very particular about such matters. Very sorry, Mr. —— Mr. —— Good morning." And before Adrian had reached the door, Mr. Jenks was absorbed in his work again.

Adrian, hastening down stairs, got into a Broadway stage at the door, and sat quietly while the big clumsy machine bumped and hitched and rumbled in its senseless unfeeling way, down the crowded street. In his state of highly exalted excitement, — for by this time he had gradually become excessively impatient, — he found himself imagining that the driver of the omnibus, the limping beasts that drew it, even the bulky and ponderous vehicle itself, were delaying from an innate malignity, from joy in prolonging his state of suffering and suspense. He wanted to get out and run. He wanted to punish the omnibus for not hurrying. He wanted to defy and vanquish each successive person who halted the stage and got in. He sat eagerly looking forward as if to project his will, like an auxiliary motive power, into the venerable-looking and raw-boned steeds. And the more eager he was, the more deliberate and lumbering was the progress of the stage. It did however gradually work along down to Fourteenth Street; into Broadway; past

Stewart's. At Eighth Street, however, it turned suddenly short out of Broadway to the right. Some one, on this, pulled the strap, and when the stage stopped, got out. Adrian followed, and on reaching the sidewalk, found that the police were turning all the vehicles bound down, off by Eighth Street and Mercer or Greene, while those bound up were coming out of East Eighth Street again into Broadway; and Broadway from Eighth Street downward, was crowded with people. On inquiring of one or two persons, he was told that the New York Hotel was on fire. A little way down the street, the chimneys of several steam fire-engines were visible, pouring out their characteristic dense swift puffs of heavy black pine-wood smoke, and the gigantic iron chatter of their hurried pumping seemed to smash the very air into pieces. Adrian worked his way through and amongst the throngs, finding the crowd more and more compact at every step. Had his errand not been urgent, he would have paused by each of the whizzing throbbing chattering steam giants as he came to it, to watch the swift services of the engineers, to stand close to the monstrous jumping shivering fiery heart and feel its ineffable intense thrill and furious headlong whirling strength. But he did not; although it did seem to him that their eager zeal excited him even more than he was excited already.

As it was in the daytime, no red glow of firelight nor quick licking sheets of flame shone before him; there was only a thickening murky cloud of black smoke, and he could not tell whether that came from a building or from the steamers. He gradually worked along down to the sidewalk on the east side of Broadway opposite the New York Hotel; but with all his gazing he could see no signs of fire in any part of its vast gloomy brick front. The quiet Broadway entrance was open, and he could see people moving about the lighted hall within, who did not seem very much hurried, though two of the engines were jabbering and shivering close before the door. It was not until, nearly opposite the south-eastern corner of the hotel, he came suddenly upon a rope barrier which a strong cordon of policemen within it were strenuously maintaining against the incessant pressure of the crowd, that he saw where the fire actually was. It was not in the hotel at all — it was in the tall building on the opposite corner of Washington Place and Broadway — the building in which were the rooms of Olds the detective.

The rope barrier defined a nearly empty area in Broadway and Washington Place, within which the pavement, all wet and muddy, was crossed in many directions by the hose of the fire department. Here and there sharp fine spurts of water flew out through small faults in the hose, and gathered into puddles. Policemen in their dark blue coats and firemen with their broad-brimmed glazed fire-hats, consulted, stood guard, or moved about. Several men had been passed in at the Broadway door, and led up the stairs out of sight. Others were carried up on ladders planted on the Washington Place sidewalk, and firemen at one or another window directed streams into the inside of the building. From the windows of the upper floors, smoke rolled and poured out in vast volumes, and canopied all the neighborhood; and the fizzing of the waste spurts from the hose, the hiss and rush of the streams directed into the house, the orders and shouts of the officials, the voices of the crowd, and the gigantic humming, chattering and coughing of a dozen steamers crammed the air with heterogeneous noises. Beneath the vast volumes of dense smoke, the crowd surged and squeezed and swore, while the officers, with impassive morose official faces, ordered and pushed them back, totally neglecting the bantering or abusive remonstrances that spattered out at them from those next the rope.

Adrian, by quiet persistent insinuating pressure, worked his way into the very front rank, and had hardly given a single glance at the vivid gloomy picture, when he found himself at the same moment pushed forward against the swaying rope barrier by the crowd behind him, and shoved backward by a tall strong policeman, who quietly laid his "locust" horizontally across Adrian's chest, and pushed powerfully against him, with both hands, bawling out in a rough strong voice,

"Stand back! You must stand back, gentlemen! Make more room here!"

"It's a free country, isn't it, mister?" said an indignant citizen. "How cocky them cops is!" remarked a ragged boy of ten. Adrian, however, shoved back against those behind him in compliance with the order, and looking directly into the policeman's eyes, said with a smile,

"Rather tight times, Mr. Officer!"

"Hmh!" grunted the man, "easy enough if them would stay to hum that ain't wanted here!"

"But I have a message to Detective Olds," persisted Adrian. "He rooms in that building, you know. Have you seen him?"

The truth is, that in spite of the reprobation which has become conventional against certain classes of subordinates — such as police-officers, express-men, hotel-clerks, railroad-men, — the truth is, that if one has any real business with one of them, and states it promptly and civilly, it is very uncommon to receive any other than a prompt and civil answer. The officer, notwithstanding his rough manner, and although all the time he shoved away with all his might against Adrian with his club, became attentive as soon as he saw that Adrian's errand was a real one, and replied, "He may be somewhere about. Better come under the rope and speak to Captain Dorr. I can't stir from here, you see." And he gave a kind of jerk with his head, towards a group of three or four officers and firemen who stood within the cleared space, at the Washington Place corner of the sidewalk before the building. Adrian, with a good deal of difficulty, managed to stoop so as to get under the rope, and while the officer renewed his shouting and shoving, and the crowd their jeers and remonstrances, he went across to the sidewalk, and selecting the police captain by the gold badge on his breast, he said,

"Captain, I have a pressing message for Detective Olds. Have you seen him?"

"Just sent to inquire after him," said the officer; —

"Don't know any thing about him," reported a patrolman, coming up at this instant; "hain't seen him to-day."

"That's from the janitress," said Captain Dorr.

A fireman rushed up: "One of the boys says a man went up by the side door not fifteen minutes ago," he said, excitedly; but the room's all afire, and there's a stream agoin into it now" — and the man pointed up to the fourth floor, the highest but one, where smoke was gushing out at the windows furthest back, next the St. Julien House, and a hoseman, perched on a ladder, was sending a full stream thrashing and spurting to and fro into the inside of the building.

" A man ! " said the captain — "I guess if it was that big porpus he'd 'a known it ! "

— Adrian darted across the sidewalk into the front door of the building, and disappeared up the stairs, too quickly for interference. The policemen and firemen shouted after him, but in vain. The captain swore a deep oath at him for a fool, and the chief engineer, also with oaths, ordered a fireman to follow him and bring him back.

The impulse which sent the young man into the burning house was not a very reasonable one ; it was too instantaneous, too purely an impulse, to be reasoned. It was, indeed, one of those efforts which one's reason would never permit, which if made at all are made precisely as unconscious impulses — which if they succeed are called inspirations, and if not, are at present nameless in English. Such inspirations have made men defy death under locomotive-wheels, have made women spring into the sea, to try to save the life of an infant. There flashed across Adrian's mind two pictures ; the sick old man all alone, calling feebly for his daughter — the delicate and spiritual girl, if possible even more helplessly beset, locked in the noisome cell of a police station. He had counted on the detective to put an end to both these miseries in an hour. Without him, how long might they not last, how fatal might they not be ? He did not wait to enter up the *per contra* — the uncertainty whether anybody at all had really gone in at the side door, the moral certainty that no clumsy creature like Olds would try to clamber up three flights of stairs into that death-trap, the probabilities about his having been in some way caught and detained in his room, and perhaps already suffocated there. Adrian did not even wait to consider that his own remarkable swiftness and agile strength made it less dangerous than for most men to venture into the building. He thought not at all : he only saw the sick man and the young girl, and with the athlete's habit he drew in one full inhalation, and sprang away.

The very utmost force or swiftness of horse or man can only be exerted while one full breath is held. With this one breath, Adrian leaped up the stairs, two steps at a time. He remembered well enough the disposition of the interior — single halls one above the other along the south or inner side of the house, with rooms at each end and others along the north or Washington Place side. He sprang up two flights ; ran to the back end of the hall, turned and ascended another flight, and was on the floor of the room he sought. The fire, which had begun in the fifth or uppermost story, had taken entire possession of that, and was working through the floors downward. Thick hot smoke eddied and rolled along the hall ; the fire crackled and roared through all the house above him, and the streams from the engines splashed and whizzed with steady energy against wall and rafter, ran along the floor and down the stairs. Pausing a moment Adrian stooped close to the floor for two or three breaths of comparatively pure air ; then sprang to the door of the detective's room, which was that across the back end of the building, shouted his name, and without waiting for a reply, drove in the door with his shoulder, and entered. The savage fury of the interior was indescribable. It was filled nearly down to the floor with swirls of dense hot smoke that scorched Adrian's eyes and drove them tight shut in an agony of smarting pain, and was incapable of being breathed; already the fire was snapping and crackling through the ceiling, from which portions of the plaster had fallen; and through the breaches, a roaring hell of red flames could be seen by momentary flashes, filling the space above. And two white strong jets of water dashed steadily in through the windows and with a powerful splashing strength that would have knocked a man down like an axe, flew waveringly against and through wall or ceiling.

Stooping close to the floor, so as to avoid the furious stroke of the waterspouts, Adrian crawled straight to the further corner, where he remembered that there was a bed, and unable to open his eyes in the acrid burning smoke, he felt upon it with his hands. There was something — it seemed like the relics of a wasted man, but all wet with blood — unless it was with the pouring torrents of water. Whatever it was, Adrian dragged it down upon the floor, and with a desperate effort opened his stinging blinded eyes upon it for an instant. It came to pieces under his grasp. Something like a head there was; clothes; a thin unsubstantial caricature of humanity in them; it was as if he was mocked by a goblin like the German Nixy, which is the shell of the front half of a human being, but all open and vacant behind; or as if he were surprised by some new fantastic form of dissolution. He recognized nevertheless, or thought he did, the broad oleaginous features of Olds, as to his inexpressible horror the dripping soft object which was like the ghost of a head came apart under his hands, from the rest of the thing.

It was impossible to endure the situation longer; his lungs were bursting, his eyesight gone; he felt that in ten seconds more he would be lost; and turning, he pointed as well as he could for the entrance, stooped again, and went crawling as fast as he could over the hot sloppy floor. At one and the same moment his head struck hard against something solid, and as he fell, he fell upon something soft.

SCROPE; OR, THE LOST LIBRARY.

BY FREDERIC B. PERKINS.

PART XIII.

CHAPTER XXXIII.

ONE touch showed Adrian that what he had fallen against was the wall, and that what he had fallen upon was a human being. With a final effort of recollection and of strength, he made out that he had in returning across the room, aimed too far to the left; and seizing the prostrate person, he made once more for the door, and this time reached it. Whether he could have got down stairs safely by himself with his load is doubtful, perfectly blind as he was for the time being. Somehow, he struggled onward; just as he reached the head of the stairs he tripped in a ragged piece of floor-cloth, and pitched forward. Down he would have plunged upon the iron-plated steps of the steep stairway, had not a strong arm caught him. It was the fireman who had been sent up after him, and who had been searching in some of the other rooms.

"Just in time, young feller!" exclaimed Mr. Fireman; and they made the best of their way to the street, holding the insensible figure between them, Adrian guiding himself by the movements of his assistant. As they came out upon the sidewalk, defiled and disfigured from head to foot by cinders, smoke, heat and dirty water, a monstrous roaring Hooray! went up from the crowd; for all had instantly divined that the limp and helpless figure between the two men was that of one saved from the fire. "Well done!" exclaimed Captain Dorr, as he relieved Adrian

from his share of the burden, and set the rescued person down on the sidewalk, leaning against a post. — "Who is it?" continued the police officer, as he examined the features of the insensible individual — "Jack Bird, as sure as I'm alive!"

"The police reporter?" asked Adrian eagerly — he could not keep his eyes open long enough to see anything.

"Yes, — Tom," continued Captain Dorr to the fireman, "we must get him to the hospital; here's a bad hole in his head."

"Take me too, will you, Captain," said Adrian, "I believe my eyes are burned out of my face; I can't see at all: I can't stand it much longer."

"Come on, then," was the officer's answer; "we'll go round to the station first." A little escort of policemen was quickly organized; one led Adrian, two carried Bird, and by way of Washington Place, they were in a few moments at the station-house of the Eighth Precinct, in Mercer St., only a few blocks away. Here a physician was quickly in attendance, who reported after a brief examination that Bird appeared to have suffered a concussion of the brain but that there did not seem to be any fracture of the skull; that whichever was the case, it was uncertain when he would regain his senses if at all; and that he should as soon as possible be taken to a hospital where he could be more thoroughly examined and properly treated. As for Adrian, the doctor said his eyes would be all right in a day or two; he might wash them in warm water from time to time, and occasionally use the common lotion of rose-water and sugar-of-lead, which lotion he sent for on the spot, by a policeman. Meanwhile a hack was brought round, and the luckless reporter, still senseless, was carried away, in charge of another policeman and the physician.

By permission of the police sergeant in charge of the station, Adrian sat quietly in a corner, for a while, cautiously sopping his eyes in the cooling rose-water, thinking over the situation of affairs, listening to the noises of the street, to the occasional items of police business that came in, and to the rough desultory talk of the two or three policemen in the room. At last, as the darkness began to come down, he found himself able to see a little, and at once set out for Jefferson Market. Crossing the Washington Parade Ground, and following Waverley Place out to the Sixth Avenue, he reached in a few minutes this important centre of municipal interests — for the three-cornered block commonly referred to as Jefferson Market includes, besides divers minor portions, not only a market, but an engine-house, a fire-bell, a police court-room and a police-station, with their respective appendages all complete. Adrian easily found his way to the station, and went up to the desk. A large red-faced and red-haired officer was upon the throne of the place, behind the desk, and upon a small platform running across the head of the room, which platform was also shut off by a stout wooden rail.

"Captain MacMurdo?" said Adrian.

"Gone out," was the gruff response.

"Can I apply to you instead, sir?"

"Can if you like."

As Adrian was taking out of his pocket a few papers and selecting Bird's card to Mr. Jenks, Dr. Veroil's letter and Mr. Jenks's own note to Bird, by way of credentials, the officer — he was a lieutenant — exchanged winks and grins with one or two of his companions who were lounging hard by.

"I want to get admission to the cells," said Adrian —

"Guess you can run your face for that," interrupted the lieutenant; and he and his fellows chorused with a big Haw! haw!

Adrian, for an instant furious, was lucky enough to bethink himself, as their grinning faces centred upon him, that his features and his costume might really justify their jeers; and not being afflicted with vanity, his wrath became amusement, as he perceived why they had been so ungracious, and he answered in a jolly manner,

"Do I really look so hard?"

Policemen are rough fellows, but they are very often good fellows. Adrian's good nature and good manners set them right in an instant.

"Hard?" said the lieutenant, this time amiably enough, — "hard ain't no name for it. Any man on the force would take ye in on sight."

"Well, that's just what I want this time," said Adrian, — "you have a person — a lady — locked up here, that I want to see. I had a note to Detective Olds, but I found his place all on fire, and I hardly got out of it alive myself."

"Yes," assented the officer; "they've got half our reserve squad over there now." Adrian now laid his documents before the lieutenant, who examined them with care, and reflected a moment:

" I see Mr. Jenks speaks of letting her go," he observed; " 'fraid we shouldn't be justified in that unless Olds himself should say so. But you can see her, sir. Bill, show the gentleman in to number eight."

The New York city police-stations have, — or should have, — besides the office and the quarters for the force, two *obligati* departments; one for confining persons arrested, and one for temporarily sheltering the homeless. The latter is a bare and desolate room, containing a stove for winter, and some strong wooden benches. Comfort is diligently and successfully eschewed, for it would speedily attract a mass of insufferable patronage. The prison part is one or more corridors with stone cells at the side, closed by strong doors. The patrolman addressed as Bill, upon receiving the order, took a lantern and lit the wick of its dim oil lamp; then turning to Adrian with a "This way," he preceded him to the back corner of the room, at the right hand of the captain's desk; opened a door, and led the way through a short entry, then through another door down five or six stone steps into a narrow passage, floored, sided and ceiled with stone. Despite the stove at the far end, the gaslight midway, and the abundant whitewash smeared thickly everywhere, the place was damp, cellar-like and horrible with the odor or flavor that always haunts places of forcible detention. It might almost be believed that souls rot in prison as well as bodies, and infect the place.

" Number eight," said the policeman, opening the door. " You can take the lantern." Adrian entered, holding up the light before him; the officer went away; there were two persons within, both women. One was Civille. " Oh, Adrian ! " she cried out,

as she sprang up, and held out both hands. As she did so, the outer door clashed behind the retiring policeman, and a sneering drunken female voice from the next cell mimicked Civille, calling out again, " Oh, Adrian ! " and adding, " Dear Adrian has come ;" — and then she broke out with the cracked husky tones of an exhausted debauchee, into a song of the war —

"When Johnny comes marching home
  again, hooray! hooray! "

The silence which Adrian had noticed on entrance was indeed only the pause of the inmates of the place while they ascertained what was the new arrival ; and a hoarse and hideous chorus helped the drunken woman through her stave.

Adrian's surprise and horror were great enough ; but Civille's were greater ; even insomuch that Adrian could not understand for a moment the look of intense doubt and agony which she cast at himself, nor why she covered her face in her hands and fell back on the narrow bunk where she had been sitting by the side of her companion. But he remembered in a moment, and said, with a tone of resolute cheerfulness, which he assumed of purpose and almost with a laugh, as he remembered the police sergeant's criticisms upon his personal appearance :

" Don't be frightened, Civille, — I got caught over on Broadway in a room full of smoke and water; I'm only dirty and scorched. Your father is doing nicely ; we shall have every thing right in a little while ; I've seen the people."

He was quite right, as he was quite natural, in never even thinking that it was shame that made Civille hide her face. Modesty belongs to such as she ; but shame never. She looked up at him again, with inexpressible relief.

"I don't know what I thought," she said. "But it's such a horrible dream, that I wasn't quite sure but you were part of the dream."

"I see," said Adrian: "it's as the police sergeant said; he said any officer would take me up, for my looks."

At this moment the singers stopped. As Adrian was about to speak again, the other woman held up a warning hand, and said, in a whisper,

"Hush!—They are listening to make fun again. Sit down here, Mr. Chester, and speak low."

"It's Mrs. Barnes, Adrian," whispered Civille, in explanation; and indeed it surprised him to be so called by name. He remembered at once the fierce-looking rather handsome mulatto woman whose baby he had found Civille holding one day,—the baby that had been expelled from The Shadowing Wings, in consequence of the ethnological Christianity of Mrs. Tarbox Button.

"How do you do, Mrs. Barnes?" said Adrian, politely, and adopting the subdued tone of the company,—*regis ad exemplar*,—"and how is the little one?"

Very well, the mother said; and upon further inquiry it appeared that by good fortune the child was safe with a neighbor of its mother's; and also that the meeting of Civille and Mrs. Barnes in the cell was merely a coincidence such as is constantly happening in real life, and of which people so often say "Such things happen in fact, but it would not do to put them in a story." Mrs. Barnes had been concerned in a furious drunken row, and was in consequence locked up to answer.

There now followed a brisk exchange of questions and replies. It appeared that Civille had been arrested a few minutes after leaving the house that morning, on a charge of shoplifting at Jenks & Trainor's, and had been hurried off to the police station, without being allowed to go back to the house or communicate with her friends. The officers had however explained that the detective who had employed them, would see her in a very little while, and that every facility would be given her for consulting with whomsoever she might wish, as soon as she should be once locked up. These promises, however, had not been kept, and to her inquiries why, the officers had replied that the reason was, the failure of the detective, Olds, to appear as he had promised. She had written to Mr. Button and to Dr. Veroil, not daring to send direct to her father: but until Adrian's coming, Civille said, she felt sure the letters could not have been delivered.

Nor had they been, Adrian replied, at least his visit was no evidence of it; and in turn he briefly told the history of his day, and ended by explaining that he should now return at once to Dr. Veroil and to Mr. Button, and that at the very worst, Civille should be released in the morning. And, he said, she was to keep up her spirits.

"Oh," she said, with a quiet smile, "it was pretty disagreeable at first, and I have been worried about father. But Mrs. Barnes and I have been very friendly and comfortable together,—haven't we, Mrs. Barnes?"

"You're jest as good as you can be, ma'am," said the mulatto woman, impetuously; "if everybody was like you 'twould be a better world than 'tis."

"Oh," said Civille, with a smile,

"there's plenty of good people. There's my cousin Miss Button, who gave you this nice shawl, and you yourself, who made me take it because I was cold."

"Gave me a fiddlestick!" exclaimed the woman; "she's given no end of nice things to poor folks that I know and their children, and there don't nobody like her. But them that knows you, they'd do any thing in the world for you, Miss Civille, and that's the truth."

"Would *you*, Mrs. Barnes? — *will* you?" said Civille, earnestly.

The woman's countenance fell. "I know what you mean," she said, uneasily — "I can't make myself over again; I would if I could. I'll go up for ten days sure in the morning, and then I shall be decent for six weeks or so, and then I shall have a row again of some kind, I spose. It's as if I had fever'n agur regular every few weeks, and you sh'd ask me not to."

"Well," said Civille, "will you come and see me when you come back? You can do that? — And be sure and bring the baby!"

Mrs. Barnes promised. "Perhaps we can contrive up something, between us," continued Civille with a smile, "we two prisoners ought to be smart enough. They say they are always planning something together. I sha'n't be sorry I was put here, Mrs. Barnes, if it turns out to be of any use."

This conversation was delightful to Adrian. His own nature responded readily and earnestly to every call for help, and it was a wonderful pleasure to see the earnest kindness of Civille, whom he loved, — a kindness so sympathetic with his own instincts; and there was repeated in him as he listened, that vague deep strange sweet

feeling, which, he had experienced before — She is myself!

And further, he received another hardly less exquisite pleasure from what the Evidences-of-Christianity people call unconscious coincidence. He found himself reasoning in the midst of his emotions, that it was an absolute impossibility to imagine, still more to believe, that there could be either evil or delusion in a soul so very sweet and kindly. No matter, he continued to himself, if I saw them find stolen goods on her person and in her pockets, — I should *know* that she was perfectly ignorant and innocent of their being there.

And still again, his reason repeated its conclusion, but from a totally different beginning: It is another impossibility for one who has done wrong, to be so unconscious of the prison and of the danger! She is the same pure and lovely and serene lady in this den of abominations, as in her own little parlor at home. Ah! the enthusiastic young man thought, she is best worth loving of all, even if she will not love me back!

So, when half an hour was gone and the officer returned, all that could be said had been said, and Adrian, conscious that he was to go, only remembered at the very last moment that he was leaving the lady of his choice locked up in a petty prison, charged with a vulgar little crime, amongst the very draff of the worst city of one half the earth. And yet, to his own surprise, he even felt more inclined to smile than to cry. The situation was not a disgrace, it was an absurdity. With good courage, which he had received from Civille as much as he had given it to her, he shook hands with Mrs. Barnes, kissed his cousin, promised once more to return in the morning, and departed. As he followed the policeman back to the outer room, he recited to himself with that full sense of meaning which fitting facts inspire into a quotation, Lovelace's well known lines, in his stanzas "To Althea:"

> Stone walls do not a prison make,
>   Nor iron bars a cage ;
> Minds innocent and quiet take
>   That for an hermitage.
> If I have freedom in my love,
>   And in my soul am free,
> Angels alone, that soar above,
>   Enjoy such liberty.

"The real prison, after all," he said, in comment on the plucky cavalier's graceful rhyme, "is in the prisoner."

"Dunno 'bout that," observed his guide, for Adrian had unconsciously spoken aloud — "guess ye wa'n't never shet up, was ye?"

"No," said Adrian; "but I'd rather take the chance of breaking jail than the chance of forgetting if I had murdered somebody."

"Wal, you're right," said the policeman. Really great truths about life are very easy to understand. There are very few people who will deny to begin with that there is a difference between right and wrong. Honest Mr. Policeman was, ethically, in excellent health.

CHAPTER XXXIV.

ADRIAN at once arranged with the officer in charge to prevent Civille's name from reaching next morning's newspapers. This he did by quietly erasing the real name which had been entered in the record of the place, and substituting that of Betsy Jones, obviously quite as good to fill records or constitute items, and which saved the disagreeable fame of having been arrested and imprisoned on a charge of theft, a fame not very welcome, even when undeserved, to any lady.

Adrian now expressed his thanks to the officers, and added a confession that he had not expected to be so obligingly treated.

"Oh, bless your soul," said the lieutenant with a grin, "you're a gentleman. Its folks that comes in to blaggard us that we jest cut up to. Most anybody's glad to accommodate, but it don't stand to reason that abuse makes a feller obligin. You can't ketch flies with vinegar."

"That's very true," assented Adrian, who, finding so much favor in the eyes of the officer, went on to ask for suggestions as to proceedings next morning. The reply was, that in order to set the lady at liberty, he ought to bring either the complainant, (viz., Olds,) or counsel for him, in order to withdraw the complaint. If the detective should not turn up, bail should be obtained. Whoever should come, ought to be on hand at the opening of court next morning, punctually at seven o'clock. With these instructions, Adrian took his leave.

He stopped at the first eating-house he came to, took a draught of water, and bought a couple of sandwiches; for he had actually not once thought of eating or drinking all the day, so intense had been his sense of the urgency of his errands, and so quickly had they followed one after another. Then, entering a hack which he found on Broadway, he gave the driver Dr. Veroil's address, promised half-a-dollar extra for speed, and ate his sandwiches as he rode. The splendid vitality of his youth quickly regained from the meagre refection and the rest, — if the jolting of a hack can be called rest, — of his ride, the strength and activity which he had felt himself losing. Not that twelve hours is so long a time to go without food. It is, though, for one thoroughly used to the ordinary daily three good meals.

Dr. Veroil was out; an unusual thing at this hour — nearly ten o'clock. Adrian decided, late as it was, as the circumstances would be an ample excuse, to see Mr. Button and get a definite answer about the old house, as the publisher directed in the morning, and then to come back to the doctor's. It was but a few minutes' further drive to Mr. Button's. Dismissing his driver, Adrian rang, and was admitted. He was shown into the back parlor, where to his surprise he found Dr. Veroil, agreeably occupied in partaking of cold roast lamb and brown stout. The physician welcomed him with eager interest, demanded his news, and at the same time exhorted him to partake of the viands. Like the policeman and Civille, he moreover took notice of the disorder of the young man's costume and the somewhat deteriorated appearance of his visage.

"You'll understand it all in two minutes, doctor," said Adrian, as he addressed himself with good courage to the eatables. His sandwiches had been little more than a drop in the bucket. He began with the main items, as one puts a list of contents at the head of a chapter:

"Civille is locked up at the Jefferson Market station on a charge of shoplifting at Jenks & Trainor's," he said: "Bird is hurt in the head and is at the New York Hospital; Olds, — I think, — is dead. I want, first of all, bail to get Civille out at seven o'clock to-morrow morning — but doctor, Mr. Van Braam?" —

"All safe," said the doctor; "fortunately opium does not injure him as it does some people, and he is comfortable for the present; it will injure him less than to know about Civille, anyhow. Well?" —

So Adrian began from the moment of his leaving the doctor in the morning and gave a succinct account of his whole day, and ended by saying,

"I went straight to you, Doctor, to be bail, in case nothing is heard of Olds; and not finding you, I came here. Angry or not angry, Mr. Button would hardly refuse to bail Civille out, under the circumstances?"

"I'll do it," said the doctor, — "I'll do it, of course, with as much pleasure as such a service admits. As for Button," he continued, with sudden seriousness, "he won't bail anybody out at present — never, very likely."

"What?" exclaimed Adrian, greatly startled by the doctor's manner, — "what do you mean?"

"I've been here most of the time since noon. — He had a stroke of paralysis this morning at Jenks & Trainor's store — a very dangerous one."

"Ah!" said Adrian, "it must have been he that was in a faint, they said it was, in the middle of a crowd of clerks and customers, at the moment I went into the store. I never thought of that — how could I? And Ann came out at the very moment when I was going in, too, — how could she not have seen? She looked exactly as usual though. She could not have been so quiet if she had known." —

"How's that?" said the doctor, — "Miss Button coming out of the store just as you went in, and the faint, or whatever it was, going on at the same time inside?"

"Yes."

"Whew!" whistled the physician to himself, softly.

"What is it?" asked Adrian.

"Oh — only — the fact of a man's

being struck down in that way within reach of his own daughter's hand — under her very eyes, apparently, — and her knowing nothing of it. Were they not together? If they were, how was it possible for her not to know it?"

Adrian was startled, partly by this way of putting the case, but much more by the increasing seriousness and even gloom, which grew upon the physician's manner with every word he uttered.

"I don't think they went together," Adrian observed. "He drove straight up, — at least I suppose so, — from his office. Ann often goes shopping in the mornings; of course Jenks & Trainor's is one place to go to; she used to take Civille with her — Civille's taste is worth using, you know — By George!" exclaimed the young man, stopping short, coloring high, and looking straight into the doctor's eyes.

"Hush!" said Dr. Veroil, lifting a warning finger, and speaking very low, — "You've thought of it, I see. But not a word! Even you and I won't say it to each other, at present! We'll try to get Civille out all safe and clear, and if we can do that, we'll prevent all the further scandal we can, all round. There's sorrow enough in the world, — there's a full share in this house. As for this miserable boy, he'll be dead in a year if they don't lock him up in some inebriate asylum. And besides this matter that we are thinking about, here's the father. — Why, it's the annihilation of a family! It's astonishing how the strongest men go all to pieces in an instant! Their fibre is so dense that they seem perfectly well outside until they are all mined away within, like a hard wood tree; and then down they go, with one

single crash, and you see how thin the shell of life was. I've been expecting something like this. His complaints about the back of his head — about being dizzy — that means a pretty severe drain of the nervous energy, at its very fountain. What you said this morning about his feeling so remarkably well startled me at the moment — I was too busy to pay much attention however — you know it is often the case that for a short time before a stroke of palsy or apoplexy, the patient feels so much brighter and stronger than usual, that he often speaks of it himself."

"No, I did not. That is as if the disease retired to put one off his guard and so be sure to get a good hit at him."

"Somewhat so."

"Well, doctor, what is the real state of Mr. Button's case?"

"Impossible to tell definitely at present. Requires some days to take stock of such attacks. The stroke was a very severe one, for a hemiplegia — worst I ever saw, I think — right side completely paralyzed, and the left side much affected sympathetically. He has rallied somewhat; his life is probably safe for the immediate present; they are almost always very irritable after such attacks, and he is extremely so. But he has a tremendous constitution, and a tremendous will, and that makes a vast difference. He don't mean to die, this bout, — I can see that. He is excessively anxious to do something, I can't say exactly what, and he can't speak or move yet. I've told him to be patient until to-morrow, and he is trying to be; but it's a strange state! His command of his body is gone, and he has no feeling, or hardly any, anywhere; and yet his nerves are thrilling and thrilling like telegraph wires in the wind, and I suppose he never felt so perfectly and uncontrollably cross in his life, while he is utterly without power of expression or motion."

"Well," said Adrian, "if it rested with me, Mr. Button should be up again quick enough. He's rough, but there's much to admire in power like his. I wish I could cure him! I can't ask him about the old house, either; he was to let me know about that this evening."

"House? What's that?"

Upon Adrian's explaining, the doctor promptly promised to see to that matter also, by deputing his man, a trusty and efficient person, to go over and negotiate a further delay in the work of destruction.

"You're very good, doctor," said Adrian, "to take all this trouble."

"Nonsense," said the physician, rather shortly; "you'd do as much for me; so would Civille; and if I don't see her through this pinch, who will? But, young man, you may be looking out, if you choose, for somebody to take charge of her in future. I can't have everybody on my hands."

"What do you mean, doctor?" said Adrian, blushing — "She's my cousin and I like her."

"Situation vacant for a young man, that's all," said the doctor, with a very intelligent look. "Apply at once."

"Well, doctor," rejoined Adrian, "if you meet the employer, have the goodness to put in a word for me, and perhaps I'll apply."

"Very good. Now go off and go to bed; you've done a very fair day's work, and we must be on hand bright and early to-morrow morning. I must stay here a while longer. Stop for me and we'll go to the police court together."

The two men parted, with a hearty hand-shake, and good wishes, for they suited each other well.

CHAPTER XXXV.

THE usual morning jail-delivery of a New York police court is a humiliating spectacle; one cannot feel very proud of belonging to a race off which is incessantly rising so very foul a scum. Adrian and Dr. Veroil, for fear of accidents, were punctually present at the Jefferson Market court-room when its doors were thrown open at seven o'clock next morning. Although his honor the judge did not appear for more than an hour, it would have been perfectly unsafe for them to do otherwise. The judge does not usually appear at one of these courts until nearly nine o'clock, sometimes still later; but in cases where influence is used, it might easily happen that one party in interest, coming to court at a usual hour, should find that the honorable court had been hurried by somebody; and that court had been opened promptly at seven A.M., the evil human harvest of the night swiftly marshalled before the bar, and the particular object of solicitude hastened off to prison before the intended help could be given, or hastened off to liberty before proof could be made of crime to be punished.

So the doctor and Adrian had a good long hour and a quarter to wait, and they occupied the beginning of it by a careful and conscientious scrutiny of the morning papers.

"Hallo! here we are!" said Adrian suddenly, in the midst of their reading; and he added, as his companion looked up, the words of the caption of a local item:

"DANGEROUS FIRE! NEW YORK

HOTEL IN PERIL! AWFUL DEATH OF A WELL-KNOWN DETECTIVE! STRANGE PHENOMENON CONNECTED WITH THE REMAINS!"

The report, which was written in that vociferous and perturbed dialect which may be called newspaper English, or perhaps, to use a diabolic adjective, — a very Caliban of an adjective, — of its own spawning to describe it, REPORTORIAL English, — went on to give an account of the fire, which it called "the devouring element;" of the efforts, which it called "the heroic, devoted and self-sacrificing struggles" of the firemen, and so on, — all which is natural enough for people whose work is often paid for by the yard instead of the merit. Filtered, this turbid mess afforded the statement that the building which had been burnt had been burnt, which was true; that the New York Hotel had been in great danger, which was false; that the fire had been subdued, which was true again; that a man had been rescued from the building, which was true; and lastly, that the well-known detective Mr. Amos Olds, had been burned alive in his rooms there, nothing being left of him except a very small shrivelled heap of animal matter partly transformed into a substance resembling gutta-percha, and which had been found among the half-consumed *débris* of the room, after the fire had been stayed at that very place. All this last, Adrian read for what it might fetch; he could not know whether it was true or false, however vivid was his recollection of the horror he had felt at handling the ghastly relics on the bed. And there was a short paragraph about the professional abilities of the deceased, his remarkable personal appearance, and his eccentric fancy of being seen abroad only in the evening.

In another local item the name of Betsy Jones, charged with shoplifting, duly appeared, in sufficiently bad company. On these and divers other topics suggested by the "mighty engine," the two men talked; and they succeeded in passing away the time without much difficulty until a small bustle near a door at one end of that side of the room on which the judge's desk was railed off, gave token that the great man would shortly issue forth with his ermine on. On the appearance of this phenomenon, Dr. Veroil and Adrian, who had been sitting on one of the front benches of those that filled the main body of the room, arose, and stepped up to the persons at the side-door. The doctor, sending in a card, requested a moment's interview with the judge, for self and companion. This was granted, and they were admitted to the judge's private room, a rather bare little den, with a stove, a table, a few chairs, a book-case, and a worn and dirty red ingrain carpet. The dignitary was talking with a police captain, and meanwhile brushing up forward past his ears two locks of hair, one each side of his shiny bald head. He was a rather angry looking man, trig of costume, erect of carriage, alert and quick of movement, so that he made Adrian think of a boxing-master. He had an intelligent face, whose decided forms were enhanced by a thin high nose, heavy mustache, and heavy black eyebrows, whose level line strongly accented his keen dark eyes.

"Wish to see me, Doctor?" he asked at once, quickly but politely. "How can I serve you, sir?"

Dr. Veroil briefly explained that one Betsy Jones, held for shoplifting, was known to him as a perfectly respectable young lady, arrested under a complete misunderstanding; that he wanted his honor to permit her not to be arraigned, but to be privately examined, and dismissed on bail, which he, Doctor Veroil, would give or secure to any required amount; he added that Olds, the complainant in the case, was stated to be dead, and he laid before the judge the papers which Adrian had shown to the police lieutenant the evening before.

"Olds dead!" exclaimed his honor, — "oh, well, this memorandum of Bird's and Mr. Jenks' noté will do well enough, I guess: where's Bird himself? Can't he come into court?"

"No; he would have been dead too," said Veroil, "if it hadn't been for my young friend here; as it is he is hurt, and is in the hospital."

"Ah," said his honor, looking at Adrian: "you're the man that got him out, are you? Good thing to do. Dorr told MacMurdo here about it this morning. Well, I think, doctor, we can arrange it for you. Will you take seats here, gentlemen, until I am through with these poor creatures, or will you have a look at the operations of the machine?"

They preferred the latter, and resumed their seats before the bar. The judge took his seat, the clerk of the court established himself at a lower desk at one side of him, court was duly opened, and Captain MacMurdo, after receiving the judge's directions about Betsy Jones in No. 8, left the court by another door, with three or four officers. In about five minutes they returned, marshalling the contents of the cells of the station house, a frowsy and horrible crew; an officer at their head opened the gate of a stout square pen at the side of the room, and the prisoners huddled into it, seating themselves in a promiscuous crowd upon the benches inside. One of the policemen now took charge of the gate of this pen; and as one name after another was called, he or she was let out by the gatekeeper, the officer who had made the arrest led the prisoner by the arm up opposite the judge; a few questions were asked, the officer made a statement, the judge said a few words, the clerk made an entry in his book, the case was judged, and the prisoner was led off. Adrian studied intently, meanwhile, the herd of objects in the pen. He had never before examined such a sight. There were some twenty-five or thirty of them; not far from an average day's arrests in one city police-court jurisdiction. There were some old men, some old women; a number of streetwalkers; some "drunks and disorderlies" and some "assaults." Adrian, studying the group — he was near enough to see the details of faces and clothes, — was struck, first by the general lowness of the heads, shallowness and scantiness of the foreheads, roundness and fulness of the back heads, and the high cheekbones. Then he saw the sensual and sullen expression of the mouths, and the less frequent, but still too frequent scowl of eyebrow and furtiveness of glance. Only one or two of the whole had good heads, and these had either silly faces or angry if not malignant ones. All these evil favors were greatly enhanced by the toilets of the company, which were in such a state as if they had all been furiously shaken up in a bag along with a cartload of mud. Torn and dirty garments, daubed sometimes with the thick whitewash of the cells, gaudy finery all soiled and broken, smashed hats, bare heads with indescribably tormented hair, dirty faces, red eyes, with a few black ones, and bloody noses, dry and cracked lips, a general condition of sleeplessness, haggardness, and abject noisome musty misery, made out the picture. Almost all the voices were either husky or rasping and coarse. One or two, apparently decent persons overtaken for once by liquor, were overwhelmed with pitiable shame; but most of them were either obsequious to servility, brazen and impudent, or sullen and obstinate. In the judge, Adrian noticed a swift and business-like efficiency which he admired, and he was especially surprised at the accurate promptitude with which from his personal recollections he detected the attempts of several culprits to impose upon him a false name or to lie about their criminal antecedents.

"What's your name?" said he to one of these quirkish evaders, after the officer had made his charge.

"Mary Orton." Adrian thought he recognized the voice that had jeered him last night from the next cell.

"Ever here before?"

"No, your honor."

"What's your business?"

"Sewing-girl."

"Mr. Clerk, enter her name Sabina Allen; been sentenced already three times by me. Business, landlady of a panel-house. Thirty days — ten of them for lying. Next time tell the truth, Sabina."

"Yes, your honor," said the woman with a courtesy and a grin, as the officer carried her off.

Mrs. Barnes, the best looking of the whole collection, was also perhaps the most dangerous looking, to one who could read faces. As she came forward to the bar walking with natural grace, but with a stubborn lowering look upon her rather handsome features, she espied Adrian and the doctor. She gave a start, and flushed deeply. The officer who was leading her looked round with surprise. When placed before the judge, she compressed her lips, and would not answer a question nor say a word.

"Very hard case," said the officer.

"I'm afraid so," said his honor.

Adrian, without exactly meaning to, arose and stepped up before Mrs. Barnes, to the judge's desk.

"May I say a word to your honor about this case?" he said, in a low voice. There were tears in his eyes, and the judge, looking at him with some surprise, said, Yes, certainly.

Adrian simply said that the woman had a young child, of which she was very fond; that she was known to the young lady mentioned before the opening of court and was to some extent under her influence; that she had by accident been locked up in the same cell with her; that to his knowledge the young lady was engaged about some charities connected with Dr. Toomston's church, and was desirous of trying to reform Mrs. Barnes; that he thought he could promise that she would try to keep out of difficulty herself; and that he wished respectfully to suggest to the court whether under the circumstances judgment might be suspended?

The judge nodded assent; Adrian returned to his seat;

"The gentleman has spoken for you, Mrs. Barnes," said the judge, seriously, but not unkindly; "he promises for you that if I suspend judgment you will do your best not to come here again; and the lady you have been with will try to help you. Will you try to keep straight?"

Not a word. After a pause, the judge added,

"It would be the best thing you could do. You may not care what happens to yourself; but what right have you to ruin your baby's chance of doing well?"

With a shiver, the poor woman, in a smothered voice, said,

"I'll try," and turning to Adrian she nodded to him, the tears running down her face; and the officer led her sobbing away.

"That's right, Adrian," whispered Veroil; "she may not stick to it — those impulsive fiery subjects don't often — but she'll try hard this time."

It took not very long to clear the docket, and when this was done, the judge, beckoning to Veroil and Adrian, went into his private room again, and sent for Civille, who was brought in by a side door. She looked pale, fatigued, worn; but as she entered, the judge, after one keen glance, arose and bowed, as a gentleman bows to a lady. She bowed in return, and smiled brightly to Adrian and the doctor, with both of whom she shook hands.

"Please to be seated, Miss"—

"Miss Van Braam," said the doctor; "this is Judge Flynn, Civille, who is kind enough to see us here instead of in court."

Civille expressed her thanks, and took the chair which was offered her. The judge now asked her a few questions, and then put a few to the officer who had arrested her. The answers were only as Adrian already knew.

"I think there need be no hesitation," said his honor. "I will accept your bail, Doctor, for Miss Van Braam's appearance before me when required; but I apprehend it will be a matter of form merely. I think we shall hear no more of this charge."

The proper papers were made out and signed, and the judge, with considerable grace, expressed his regrets for the annoyance that Civille had undergone, and his happiness at having been able to prevent further inconvenience, as well as to promote her views about "her friend Mrs. Barnes," as he said with a smile. Civille looked puzzled, but on Adrian's explaining, she thanked the judge with so much enthusiasm that he laughed.

"You don't seem to care so much about your own case, as about hers," he said.

"Poor thing!" said Civille, in her solemn introverted way — "poor thing! she needs care a great deal more than I do. The prison don't hurt me, — it will destroy her. We must try to take care of her."

The kind hearted judge — for he was kind hearted and considerate in spite of his angry black eyebrows, and did as much good, or rather as little harm, as he could, in his official position, — now took his leave of them and went back to his courtroom. In a few moments Civille and her escort were whirling rapidly homeward in Veroil's coupé, which was made to hold three inside passengers on this occasion by main strength and some management.

"Dr. Johnson said," observed Adrian, when they were well wedged in, "that a ship was simply a jail, with a chance of drowning. A coupé is simply a police-station cell, with a chance of upsetting."

"Less the whitewash and the smell and plus freedom and motion and sunshine, you grumbling fellow," said the doctor.

"How is father?" said Civille.

"Nicely," said the doctor, (who hadn't seen him since the day before)

— "nicely. — He don't know you've had any trouble, and you are not to tell him at present. I gave him a light dose of opium last night to quiet him, and left orders with Katy to say this morning in case of inquiry that you had just gone out and would be back in a little while."

And so they were. They found Mr. Van Braam awake, though a little dreamy, and the situation was easily re-established. When the doctor had examined his patient and received Katy's report, he insisted on some breakfast for himself and Adrian, on the wonderful pretence that bail were always treated by their principals. While they were eating and talking over their affairs, two letters were brought in, both for Adrian, and both from Hartford. He opened and read them, and looked grave, for a moment; and then with a quiet smile he said to Civille,

"We are all to be turned out of house and home at once, it seems — let's all be unhappy together, will you? They have finally made an ordinance to cut their new street through the old house, my aunt says. And here's my friend Stone who complains and informs, as the lawyers say, that my resignation of my assistant librarianship is accepted."

"Resignation!" exclaimed Civille, making great eyes, "what made you resign?"

"Wouldn't have let me come any other way, Civille; at any rate they would have dismissed me if I had, and I preferred to dismiss them."

"Perfectly right," remarked the doctor.

"Well," said Civille, looking in her unconscious way right into Adrian's eyes — in fact right into his heart, and thinking aloud rather than

talking, — "it's right, — I would have done so for him."

"That would be an immense compliment," said Adrian to the doctor, "only that she would do it for you either, or for anybody. — But I must remember to go and see Purvis to-day — he spoke about some business; who knows but he has a large salary waiting for me?"

"I must go and see Mr. Button," remarked the doctor, — "and you may come too, if you wish, Adrian; if he can see you this morning we'll arrange about the house."

"Very good — but I must go down to the New York Hospital first and see if poor Bird is alive or dead."

Katy, who was passing behind Adrian at the moment, in some service of dish or pitcher, stopped short. "Is he hurt?" she exclaimed, in an excited way. They all looked at her in astonishment.

"Let me go and see him!" said Katy. "I must be with him!"

"I dare say he may be better this morning" said Adrian, kindly, in spite of his surprise; "you shall go down with me if you like."

"Wait a moment, please," said Katy, eagerly — "I'll get my hat." And she darted out of the room.

"She's talking English!" said the doctor. "She's no Irish girl! Some deviltry!"

It was true, and Civille and the doctor looked puzzled enough. Adrian remembered his having seen her and Bird in communication on the night of the party at Mr. Button's, and also her insolent speech to Civille at the door of the supper-room, and a theory popped into his mind. "I guess" he said, "I can" —

In darted Katy again, like a small whirlwind, with her hat on, a pair of thread gloves on her hands.

"You've no shawl," said Civille.

"No matter," said the girl, "I couldn't find it; I couldn't wait."

"Here," said Civille, "take this;" and she gave her Mrs. Barnes' shawl, which lay on the sofa. "Bring it back, please; it isn't mine."

"I'll go right down, doctor," said Adrian, "and I'll come back to your office and report progress; and if you are not there I'll try Mr. Button's."

"Do so," said Veroil; "and if Bird needs me I'll go down right after dinner." And leaving Civille to take care of her father, the party broke up, Adrian taking a note from Dr. Veroil to the house surgeon at the hospital, by way of introduction.

PART XIV.

CHAPTER XXXVI.

THE New York Hospital is now so called because it is not in New York City. It is hardly connected with the accidents and miseries which it was meant to help. That help is nominally given by means of a few beds put up in an old building in one corner of the City Hall Park. When Adrian however went thither to see Mr. Bird, the tall roomy gray stone buildings of the old Hospital were still standing in the middle of their quiet square, and the two high iron fences, one at the street, usually ornamented with a beggar or two, a seller of ballads, or a peanut stand, and an inner one, garnished with the porter's lodge, between the outer and inner courtyards, still protected the institution from the intrusions of mere curiosity or idleness. But the estate thus devoted to the uses of the sick poor was too valuable. There is not humanity enough in an American city to devote property when it becomes very valuable indeed, to God, kindness or beauty. The church is made into a livery-stable. The hospital square is covered with stores. Even in the comparatively Christian city of Boston, the advanced skirmishers of the money Huns have cut off the outposts of the ancient Common, and over the corpses of half a dozen centennial elms, the victorious and guzzling aldermen and their allies the real estate speculators are planning the campaign which shall cover the whole of the Common with stores. The fate of the Central Park in New York is only a question of time. It will be cut up and sold for building lots whenever the land becomes so valuable for business purposes that the New Yorker cannot bear it any longer.

Adrian and his companion were admitted without difficulty, and were shown into the convalescent ward, where to the great relief of both of them, they found Mr. Bird, not even in bed, but comfortably established in an easy chair, and reading a newspaper. He had a white bandage round his head, it is true; but the white fillet is of old a symbol of royalty; and observance, if not authority, is an attribute of invalids which may liken them to the ancient kings.

Adrian, with several suspicions contending in his mind, watched Bird's face very closely, as they entered. He had barely time however to see him look up astonished and displeased; for Katy quickly ran up to him and kissed him.

"All right, Kate, as long as you're here," he said, his expression changing to one of amused resignation ; — "I'm all correct except a cut on my head — but let me see that shawl though," he added, his face lighting up with a sudden interest.

She took it off and handed it to him ; it was an imitation camel's hair shawl, with some white along the margin, of good quality and size, a good deal soiled, but not particularly remarkable. Bird inspected it deliberately, one side and edge after another, as one looks for the initials on a handkerchief, but with a peculiarly persistent and almost microscopic scrutiny. As he came to the last corner, his countenance lighted up. "Kate, where did you get that ?"

"Miss Van Braam let me take it," said the girl, readily, still speaking without the least shade of brogue.

"She did !" exclaimed Bird, — "Is it possible !" And he looked uncertain, as one does who reflects upon news that is good and bad at once.

"Mrs. Barnes gave it to Civille in the station-house," observed Adrian. "And Miss Button gave it to Mrs. Barnes."

"Ah !" said Bird, with obvious relief — "Mrs. Barnes whose baby was turned out of that charitable thing, isn't it ?"

"Yes."

"Allow me to make you acquainted with my sister, Miss Catherine Bird," said he, as one who takes a sudden resolution, and with a sufficiently good manner ; "Kate, my friend Mr. Adrian Chester."

Adrian, after a moment's look at Bird's face, which wore an expression of "It's so, — the cat's out of the bag !" and another at the young lady, who blushed a little, but not much, made his manners, not without a shade of embarrassment or rather sense of queerness, and bowed to his new acquaintance.

"I have had the pleasure of seeing Miss Bird already," he said, "but have not had the honor of an introduction."

"Come," said Bird, "get chairs and sit here ; there's nobody in the ward" — he glanced round the room — "who will pay any attention. There's been more trouble than I meant, and your friends sha'n't have any more at any rate, Mr. Chester. As for Mr. Button, he may do the best he can" —

"He has enough trouble already," said Adrian, gravely.

"What do you mean ?" asked Bird. Adrian hereupon told him the story of his yesterday's experience after their meeting in Washington Place, including his seeing Ann Button coming out of the store, his passing the place where at the same moment Mr. Button had been struck down with palsy, and not omitting his experience in the burning building. When he came to this place, Bird and his sister interrupted him to thank him ; the latter with tears, both of them, after their manner, without many words. But there was more in Bird's steady look at Adrian's eyes, the firm grasp of his hand, and his brief "I won't forget it, Chester," than in a whole sensation sermon on Thankfulness. When Adrian had ended, which he did by continuing his account through his visit to the police court and to the present moment, he began to state his theory of the charge of shoplifting.

"Now as to this criminal charge," he said, "I was at first a little afraid that my cousin Civille might have furnished some ground for it, particularly after you assured me that stolen goods had been found in her possession. But" — he glanced at Katy Bird — "I don't care who found them there, I've learned what sort of a woman she is since these two visits of mine to New York. People think she's queer — I thought so. It's because she's too good for practical purposes, that's all. If a ton of stolen goods were found in her room — if she hadn't a garment on her that wasn't stolen — she did not steal them, whoever did." Here Bird smiled and nodded, as much as to say, "That's right." Adrian resumed: "But now I say the facts are these" — and he stopped. He would not say it of the woman to whom he had been betrothed, and whom he had believed a kinswoman, though she was relative and betrothed no longer.

"Well?" said Bird.

"No," said Adrian; "I won't state my opinion. But I think if Civille chooses she can make Jenks & Trainor pay pretty heavy damages for her arrest and imprisonment; and if Olds hadn't been burnt up in his room, I would make him clear up the whole thing, if I had to murder him."

"Poor Olds!" said Bird, "he's dead then." And he looked at his sister in a dubious kind of way. She looked as if she wanted to laugh; a grim display from a young lady about a death by fire.

"Remains turned into gutta-percha, I observe by the paper," continued the police reporter, in the same queer mixed manner — "sad business! But after all, Chester, Miss Van Braam won't want to sue Jenks & Trainor, for they have been the means of furnishing evidence that amounts almost to proof, that she did not do the stealing, and that somebody else did."

Adrian looked puzzled.

"It's the same view that's in your mind," said Bird, with decision: "only, as I was saying, it's proved, or nearly so. It's easy to see that you can't like to speak out about it.

Now I'll make a clean breast of it. First of all, I'm Olds."

"What do you mean by that?" said Adrian, with entire incredulity.

"The lamented deceased, you remember, had the eccentricity of only being seen in the evening. It's easy to vary one's voice. The stuffed suit and soft gutta-percha mask that you found on the bed were safe enough to wear then; in the day-time they wouldn't 'wash.' And a man can disguise himself to be bigger than he is; not so easily to be smaller."

"Bird," interrupted Adrian, "why did you have Civille locked up over night? That was not the right thing to do."

"I couldn't help it after I was knocked in the head, could I?" said Bird, coolly. "And she wouldn't have been put into a cell at all if the officers had done as I told them. It was no part of my plan, Chester. But let me tell you; it's a straight story. I was Amos Olds in the evening, and Mr. Bird the police reporter all day. Jenks & Trainor employed me to work up this case some time ago, and it was a long time before I could find any clew at all. At last I settled on our two lady friends, but I couldn't tell which. Then I got Katy to go and live in their houses at different times."

"And you had the face to make love to her yourself, you scamp!" said Adrian, half amused and half disposed to be angry.

"All in the way of business," answered Mr. Bird, with calmness. "Besides, it's a free country. A cat may look at a king. I couldn't tell what means would prevail. And I confess that it would have been foolish for me to try it in earnest. And least of all, *you* needn't complain, I reckon!" concluded the detective, significantly.

"But do you mean to say that

you really suspected Civille?" said Adrian, rather hotly, but blushing.

"Weren't you half afraid or more that it might be she yourself?"

Adrian was silent. "Besides," resumed Bird, "in such a case one must proceed by the facts. If you allow yourself to believe to begin with, that anybody — anybody, I don't care who, — my own sister; the worst thief in the city, — either is guilty or is not, you are pretty sure to blunder. There's only one line to follow: keep your eyes wide open; find out every thing you can; reason as you go along; but be ready to throw away all your conclusions at the very last moment if the facts balance the other way."

"I should kill myself, I think," said Adrian, "rather than to follow a business where I had to be ready to think ill of everybody."

"Oh, you must be equally ready to think *well* of *anybody*," answered the detective, with an emphasis that doubled his meaning; "and I guess you'd find *that* the most surprising part. But I think what I enjoy is, *getting at the facts.*"

"Then you do really enjoy the business?"

"You couldn't coax me to follow any other," was the reply; "I love it so that I perfectly understand why a thief won't stop stealing. Katy is about as fond of it as I am. — Well; the person I have been shadowing is as cunning as the Old Scratch, and in spite of us we couldn't make our arrangements fetch. Now the characters of these two young ladies are very different, and I reasoned that while Mr. Van Braam was so ill, if I had his daughter locked up, she was a person who would tell a perfectly straight story one way or another, in order to get back to the old gentleman, and so I tried it. I don't know of any thing,

at present, that would make the other open that tight mouth of hers. But Miss Van Braam was to have been detained with the matron at head-quarters, not locked up in a cell at the station, and I should have talked with her and made every thing right that afternoon if I had not been hurt."

"How came you in that room, any how?" asked Adrian.

"Oh, I had a little money and some papers that I couldn't very well lose," answered Bird, with a smile and a gesture to his breast pocket, — "I came along after the fire had got well agoing, and slid up by the side door. I was getting out all right when something hit me a tremendous bang on the head, and I didn't know any thing more until I woke up in the bed here. Slight concussion of the brain, they said; a very dangerous blow."

"Well, what struck you?"

"I can't think of any thing except this: I was passing before that tall wardrobe of mine, and I remember that just before I was hit, a second stream of water came flying bang through the window. It must have hit my big plaster Shakspeare on top of the wardrobe and upset it on me. It wasn't convenient to investigate, but that's my theory. — So now, last of all, here come you and Katy, who got excited and dropped her Irish, and I had to explain. And as you were so good as to get me out of that furnace, I can't very well do less than to help you out of your annoyance, so far as necessary. You and the doctor have done it already though, for what I see. There's no danger except whatever risk there is of the newspapers getting hold of it. I see no names in the police reports this morning; and I guess we can manage it now, without exposing anybody."

" But the proof you spoke of ? " said Adrian.

" Oh, yes. — This shawl has the private mark that Jenks & Trainor have had stitched into an immense quantity of their fine goods, this six months. When a purchase is made, the cash boy goes to the cashier with the money and a ticket, and the goods are taken at the same time to be checked off and tied up. They took out the private mark when they did up the goods, so that if an article from their store has the mark on it, it's almost certain that it was stolen. They can tell what invoice the shawl was from, and nearly when it was taken, too. I have studied all their fine goods this good while ; I recognized that cashmere the moment I saw it. When Katy said that Miss Van Braam gave it to her, I couldn't help my thoughts, though I wondered at it's being so dirty ; but when you explained that it came to Miss Van Braam from that Barnes woman and to her from Miss Button — why, I guess it's a pretty clear case."

" But consider the situation, won't you ? " remonstrated Adrian. " Mr. Button may be dying this moment ; he's effectually broken down, the doctor says, even if he lives. As for his son, you know what's the matter with him. — Are you really going to try to make the family any more trouble ? "

" Oh no, — make yourself easy. Mr. Button must pay Jenks & Trainor's bill, and the young lady must keep her fingers to herself in future, that's all. Nobody wants to make any scandal."

" What about the lace ? " asked Adrian.

" I've no doubt in my own mind," said the detective, " that the thief put that in among Miss Van Braam's parcels — You said she had a good many that day, Katy ? "

" Yes," was the reply ; " six or eight at least ; the lace was rolled up small amongst them, but not papered."

Adrian now remembered the suggestion that Katy had made to Civille at Mr. Button's, viz., that if Civille had missed any thing, she, Katy, could account for it.

" So you found this among Civille's parcels," he said, " and you were hinting it to her in Mr. Button's supper-room that evening ? — But I remember her answering very quietly that she hadn't missed any thing ; what did you conclude from that ? "

" We thought," said the young lady, " that either she knew nothing about the lace, or that she knew how to appear exactly as if she did not."

" It was a sharp dodge," said Bird ; " and it would leave me doubtful now if it wasn't for this shawl."

" Well," remarked Adrian reflectively ; " I suppose that when you spoke to Katy on the stairs at Mr. Button's on the evening of the party, it was to arrange about the supper-room question ? "

They laughed. " Yes," said Bird. " I didn't think anybody would see that, Chester. You have a quick eye and a quick wit. You'd do well in our business."

" No," said Adrian, " I'd as soon live in the sewers. — Beg pardon, I didn't mean any thing against those that like it."

" A difference of opinion makes horse-races," answered Bird, " as they say in Kentucky. No harm."

There was a little further conversation, during which it was arranged that Bird should see the police authorities and other parties in interest, so as to give an official and final character to the provisional arrangements which had been already effected about the charge of theft.

Bird said he should stay one day more at the hospital, as the physician recommended a day's quiet; but that he was promised that he should be all right next morning. It was further agreed that Katy should at once make some further researches which she said had occurred to her as worth trying. "What are they?" asked Adrian. Katy shook her head. "I don't know that it will amount to any thing," she said; "if it does,"—

Bird smiled. "I'm a phrenologist," he observed, "thoroughly for the inside of the head, and a good deal for the outside."

"I am too," said Adrian; "but what is the point?"

"Oh, only this: secretiveness is even more important for a detective than for a criminal, because he has the criminal's secretiveness to overcome. Now no secretive person likes to tell what he *is going to do;* it's all he can bear to tell what he *has done.* That's all; so Katy's shaking her head is a kind of official announcement. Besides, I sometimes almost think that it kills the life of a plan to name it."

"That's very true," commented Adrian, as he got up; "a purpose is like an egg; if you break the shell, it spoils very quickly; if there isn't a chicken then, there never will be."

"Correct," said Bird: "good morning—by-bye, Katy; see you to-morrow at nine o'clock, at the other place." And off they went.

Adrian accompanied Katy nearly home, and then leaving her to go and report to Civille,—but borrowing the shawl,—went to Dr. Veroil's, and not finding him, to Mr. Button's. Here he asked for the doctor, and was shown into the parlor, where in a few moments Veroil came down to him.

"How is he?" asked Adrian.

"Has rather more command of the left side, according to the usual rule of re-actions in such cases," said the physician. "The first shock of the attack disarranges the whole system; then there is a partial recovery—if any—as far as the vital forces of the patient can repair the evil; the extent of this recovery measures the real violence of the attack; and then the system waits for the next assault, like a besieged fort for the opening of the second parallel, after it has been unable to prevent the establishment of the first."

"Is there never any recovery?"

"I have never known a complete recovery. Quiet and trifling occupations, comfort, the diet almost of a baby, have often prolonged life; but a stroke ends the furious activities of the Man.—But have you seen Bird?"

Adrian, in reply gave a brief summary of the interview. The doctor listened with much interest, nodding at the revelation of the complicity of Katy, as much as to say, "I said so this morning"—but staring with amused surprise at the account of the gutta-percha remains of the supposed Olds.

"Why," he said, "this Bird's a perfect Phœnix; he rises out of the ashes of his predecessor younger and handsomer!"

"Here's the shawl," said Adrian. The doctor's face grew serious, as he examined the soiled cashmere with that interest which attaches to things, as well as to persons, that have been significant instruments. A servant entered the room, and said to Adrian, "If you please, Mr. Button says he must see you."

"Very well," said the young man.

"I don't know whether it is very well," said the doctor, discontentedly, "but I suppose it must be so. He is so excessively irritable that it will be worse to say no than yes, probably. He can speak this morning, but very indistinctly. And Adrian, don't be startled at his looks. And whatever he wants to know, we'll let him know it. It can't make much difference, — he may as well have his own way, as far as we can make it so. He won't find he'll have much of it, at the hands of those two ladies, I guess!"

And the two men went up stairs to the sick-room.

CHAPTER XXXVII.

A CERTAIN horror is a just conclusion by logic of facts, at all suffering or misfortune whatever. No death is strictly appropriate, according to perfect humanity, except the quiet and welcome death of old age. Accordingly, what we feel at knowing or witnessing such a death, has nothing of horror, but only a natural apprehension at the transition into a new state of existence. Every other death is violent, because it is premature ; it is the failure of an organism to complete its full cycle; the extinction of an immature life; the hurrying of a soul into a new phase before it has duly ripened in the experiences of the previous one. This disappointment corresponds to, and renders natural, the startled feeling, the horror, which is more or less experienced, at violent deaths, at deaths of young persons, of the strong and active.

The like truth is involved in the horror which is felt at witnessing the sufferings or sickness of others; suffering and sickness are violations of the natural state of man, who was meant to be well and happy. As grown persons can reason and resist and endure, we are less agonized at their suffering. But the sickness of infants impresses us with a peculiar pain, almost as if the soft helpless little things were wantonly tortured. In the next degree to this sympathetic pain over infants who suffer, comes that which is felt from the sufferings of strong or healthy people whose life is yet unexpended in them, and who are therefore in some obscure way felt to have some title of some kind to the enjoyment of their natural activities.

Without any articulate statement or distinct consciousness of all this, it was such an instinctive pain which quietly settled upon Adrian as he followed Dr. Veroil to the bedside. Although he carefully set his countenance to look cheerful, in accordance with the spirit of the physician's caution, he could scarcely help a shiver as he saw the distorted features of the man whom he had left the day before so powerful, so active, so resolute, so full of purpose and of multiplied plans, of conscious abounding ability to execute them all. — One side of the bluff, broad face was sunk and blighted by the frightful half-death of the disease ; the eye was shut, the mouth drawn down. The other eye was open, and moved restlessly ; tremors of nervous irritation flitted now and then across the visage ; the left hand, lying outside the bed-clothes, moved uneasily. As Adrian came up to the bedside, the sick man, looking up to him, uttered thick and indistinct sounds, which only an ear as quick as Adrian's, or as experienced as the physician's, could understand to be a greeting; what he tried to say was,

"Glad to see you, Adrian. Didn't expect this. Last of me, I guess." And the enfeebled left hand dragged towards him over the bed-clothes. Adrian pressed it gently, and held it a few moments; and then he exchanged salutations with Mrs. Button and with Ann, who sat in gloomy grandeur at the further side of the bed.

"Send away the women," said the sick man, in the same painful struggling imperfect way.

Mrs. Button remonstrated, with a good deal of sharpness. "I don't choose to be absent from my husband's bedside at such a time," she said. "It's my right and my duty to be here. Besides, I expect Dr. Toomston every moment, to pray with us."

"And anint me with ile?" said the sick man, indistinctly. "Let 'em stay then. Worse for them. Doctor, got a little while?"

Dr. Veroil nodded.

"Writing things," said Mr. Button.

"Oh, he is certainly quite incompetent to make a will," said Mrs. Button, who was not very profound on the subject of medical jurisprudence. It was evident that the patient was irritated at this resistance to his wish, for his face flushed, and he repeated with more distinctness, as if his passion almost subdued his disease,

"Writing things."

"Be quiet," said the doctor — "be quiet, or you'll put yourself where you can't do any thing. You shall have it just as you like, but don't you get excited, — And ladies, you will resist Mr. Button's wishes at your peril," he continued, with that prompt sternness of his which seemed so out of harmony with his ordinary genial and jovial ways — "Let us have the writing things instantly. If not," —

With a most bitter bad grace, Mrs. Button brought a writing desk. Doctor Veroil made ready to write.

"Write after me, doctor," said Mr. Button; and he dictated, two or three words at a time, as follows:

DEAR CIVILLE: I got you into the trouble at Jenks & Trainor's. It was I who did it all. My father saw me at it. It brought on his attack. I ask your pardon.

"Oh, he's quite out of his head," said Mrs. Button, impatiently; "that's all nonsense. His father! he died forty years ago! he's perfectly demented!"

"All down?" said the sick man. Either the continuous exercise of his faculties and his organs was making it easier to use them, or else the leaden hand of the disease was relaxing its hold, or else the steady powerful will of the man, intensifying and multiplying its force with the consciousness of an important occasion, was fighting its way up against the awful burden of paralysis: at any rate, he spoke with greater clearness.

"All down," responded the writer.

"Ann, copy that and sign it," said Mr. Button.

Ann Button gave a start; rose from her chair; sat down again; cast down her eyes, set her lips together, and was silent.

"Ann, copy that and sign it," repeated her father.

"Anjesinthy Button," said her mother, "I forbid your doing any such thing."

The girl neither spoke nor moved.

"All right," said Mr. Button: "take another sheet." The doctor did so. "Write again." And he dictated again:

To all whom it may concern: I hereby constitute and appoint Adrian Scrope

Chester of Hartford, State of Connecticut, my general agent and attorney, with full powers —

There was a start of surprise by all the company. "He can't execute any thing," said Mrs. Button, in a moment, with decision, — "he can't sign any thing, anyhow."

Adrian was about to speak, but Mr. Button cast towards him a look of indescribable anxiety and beseeching.

"Don't fail me, Adrian," he said.

"Wait a little, at any rate," remarked the doctor. Adrian felt the force both of the patient's imploring look, and of Mrs. Button's grimly practical comment; and he nodded assent. Mr. Button resumed:

—full powers to take charge of all my property and business of every kind, and to consult with me and report to me exclusively but no further than his own discretion may suggest; and to and with no one else unless he wishes, and to make for me all purchases and sales; and to execute and sign for me all deeds, agreements and instruments necessary for managing my said property and for acting with as full authority as I could have in and about my said business. Said Chester to sign as such attorney as follows: T. Button, by Chester atty. And my first purpose in this appointment is that said Chester shall as soon as possible dispose of my publishing business to the best advantage and invest the proceeds in a safe and permanent manner, and to pay over quarterly one half the net income of my said business or property to the order of my wife, and to invest the other half at his discretion as my said attorney, in the manner aforesaid. And I hereby declare in case of my death that I make and proclaim this as my last will and testament; and in particular I declare that my daughter Ann has this day in my presence refused to write and sign as I required, and that I therefore will and direct that my wife shall receive from my estate after my death only what the law would give her as dower if I died intestate, and that I leave nothing to my children, expecting their mother to support them; and I give and bequeath in consequence of my said daughter's said refusal, one half of all the rest of my property real and personal over and above such legal dower to the Eleventh Presbyterian Church, now known as Dr. Toomston's church, as a fund for the maintenance of said church and its charities, to be held and administered like the other property of said church; and the other half of said property over and above said dower I give and bequeath in consequence of my said daughter's said refusal, to Civille Van Braam, daughter of Adrian Scrope Van Braam of New York City, in token of my belief in her goodness. But if my said daughter had obeyed me, then my will would have been to leave my whole estate in three equal parts; one third part to my said wife for herself; one third part to my said wife in trust to be used at her discretion for the support of my son William; and one third part to my said daughter Ann for herself. And said Chester is to receive nothing for services as executor in case of my death; and for services as my said agent and attorney he is to receive one tenth of the net income of my property and business, to be paid quarterly upon a quarterly balance-sheet. And I will and request that in case of his acting as such executor, no bonds be required of him as such executor.

The sick man paused, and appeared to reflect. Having done so, he said,

"Read."

Dr. Veroil read the whole instrument, deliberately and distinctly.

The listening of the two women was a phenomenon of intensity. At the clauses which were to give the young attorney such absolute and uncontrolled authority — uncontrolled even by the owner himself — of the great possessions of the capitalist, an expression of contemptuous anger crossed Mrs. Button's face; and this was repeated more plainly at the provisions respecting the alternative testamentary dispositions of the estate. And at these last, Miss Ann Button, looking up from the floor for the first time since her silent disobedience to her father's command, showed full as angry an interest as her mother. An unlovely pair of faces!

"Anjesinthy, step this way," said Mrs. Button, and the two women went to the window and consulted in whispers.

"Ring bell," said Mr. Button. A servant came.

"Bring another," said the sick man. "Witnesses," he added. Two of the servants were soon at hand.

"Put seal," said Mr. Button. Dr. Veroil affixed opposite the place for signing, the usual representative of the ancient seal.

"Lift me up," said Mr. Button. They did so. "Put the desk here," he said. The writing desk, with the paper on it was laid upon his knees as he sat up among the pillows.

"Pen," he said. Veroil looked surprised. "Left hand," said Button, with inexpressible resolution in his voice and his face. Without a word, Dr. Veroil dipped the pen in the ink, placed it in the trembling left hand of the sick man, laid the hand upon the paper, and was going to guide it.

"No. Alone. My act and deed." said Mr. Button; and with an effort concentrated and intense far beyond the steady resolution which had enabled him to dictate the instrument itself, he traced upon the paper, slowly, awkwardly, but without stopping once, a tangle of heavy, shaken, spattery lines, in which could nevertheless be recognized the signature of "Tarbox Button."

"I declare this to be my free act and deed," he said, "and I execute and deliver it as my last will and testament;" and he fell back, silent and exhausted. The servants signed as witnesses, as Dr. Veroil directed them, and the doctor himself signed after them. Mrs. Button and Ann were meanwhile absorbed in their discussion; Doctor Veroil, having folded the paper, gave it to Adrian.

"The power is executed, ladies,"

said the doctor. "Permit me to urge you to comply with Mr. Button's wish in regard to this note."

He spoke with emphasis, and even the two angry foolish women were startled into attention.

"He can't write a word," said Mrs. Button. "What do you mean, doctor?"

"Perhaps he could not at this moment," said Dr. Veroil, with a compassionate glance at the distorted face on the pillow. "But he has will enough for ten men. He signed with the left hand. It's the greatest triumph of mind over matter that I ever saw. If he could only inject it into the nerves of the right side again! But I fear the bridge is broken down that way. See here, madam. Look, Miss Button."

And taking the document from Adrian, he stepped round and showed the signature, the witnesses' names, the seal, to the astonished women; and with intelligent adaptation, he read aloud the part calculated to impress them most, the caption over the witnesses' names, with its legal verbosity: "Signed, sealed and delivered as his free act and deed and as his last will and testament, in the presence of the following witnesses, who have signed their names as such witnesses in the presence of the said Tarbox Button."

Mrs. Button and her daughter examined in silence the inky tangle of shaking sprawling lines. But the tremendous will of the sick man, shattered as was its bodily tabernacle and instrument, had too plainly delineated the letters of his name, even amidst the darkness and weakness of his overmastering disease, to permit the shadow of a real doubt or contradiction, however mutinous the disposition might be. But neither of the women was deficient in obstinacy nor in cunning.

"I'll consider upon it, doctor," said Mrs. Button; "I'll give you an answer to-morrow. You'll leave the paper for me to examine at leisure, won't you?"

"A copy, certainly, madam," was the polite — and prudent — reply, and a copy was made in a few minutes, and with a grave bow was handed to Mrs. Button. This done, the doctor made a careful and detailed examination of his patient; gave explicit directions not to have him disturbed; arranged to send proper nurses; and was taking leave, when the sick man, opening the one eye that he could move, muttered something.

"What is it?" said the physician, bending over him.

"I've got 'em, — they'll come to it," said Mr. Button, feebly.

"Yes, they will," said the doctor.

"I want the Van Braams to stay in the old house," continued Button.

"Well, I guess we can arrange it," said the doctor; and with a kind farewell to the patient and a polite one to the ladies, he turned to leave the room. "I'll come in one moment, doctor," said Adrian. He stepped round the bed to where Mrs. Button and Ann were still talking in whispers. They both looked at him with a sullen anger, hateful enough to see. "Ann," said he, handing her the parcel which he had kept with him, — "there's the shawl which you gave Mrs. Barnes" —

"I don't want it," said the girl, sourly.

"But Mrs. Barnes gave it to Civille, and Civille to Katy, that lived here with you for a while; and Katy is a detective, and the shawl has Jenks & Trainor's private mark on it" —

She seized it promptly enough now. And Adrian, bowing, followed the physician, for he expected that this glimpse of her position would have more influence upon the young woman than a fuller explanation of it; and he was not unwilling that she should be able to destroy this material proof against herself. He did not much consider, nor care, whether he had a strictly legal right to give her the shawl, and he meant the gift to be a hint of his own good will.

CHAPTER XXXVIII.

"FEAR is moral rum," remarked Veroil, as the two men walked away from Mr. Button's. "I bullied those women. I've done it before. But you whip an ugly boy who is poisoning your school, if you cannot wait for more healthy moral regimen. Once well stimulated into obedience, the diet of health will probably serve. If he falls into another moral collapse, intoxicate him again, if necessary. Fear is prompt. Love is gradual. For barbarians, for brutes two-legged or four-legged, fear may be absolutely indispensable. Wisdom requires, not the absolute disuse of it, but the substitution of higher motives as soon as possible. These fellows who want the rowdy boys of the public schools of a great city like New York to know that there will be no whipping, are offering a little sweet oil to an ugly beast. Very likely a white hot poker to sear his nose will hardly keep him off you."

Adrian, assenting to the doctrine, further expressed his surprise at the readiness and efficiency of the physician in taking charge not only of the person but of the family and business of the patient all together.

"Oh," said Veroil, "it was rather

irregular, no doubt. But a doctor might as well be ready to be clergyman and lawyer, in a case like this, where he is a kind of personal friend also, and where the questions are so mixed. It wouldn't do, in this case, for instance, to send for a lawyer; that —— Mrs. Button, I mean, — would have made trouble; the patient was very irritable and weak; and the sudden way I guess was the only way to do it. I believe those women would have committed any crime necessary — on the spur of the moment at any rate — to prevent executing that paper in your pocket."

" I don't like to think that," said Adrian : " is that all their religion can do for them ? "

" Their religion is perfectly genuine and sincere," said the physician. " But religion does not necessarily imply intelligence, however useful the two are to each other. And these women, having feeble intellects and enormous selfish instincts, are liable to be carried to any extreme by an evil impulse that pushes them in the right time and place. Under advice, possibly on reflection alone, their case might be different. I used promptness and sternness, and forestalled them. Or rather I helped do so. Button is the man who has effectually beaten them. Wonderful! wonderful ! "

The doctor's admiration was perfectly just. A physician is of small account unless he is a psychologist; and Veroil was an ardent lover of his profession, and by that and by instinct also, a student of souls. Adrian was almost equally fond of mental philosophy. Knowing the helplessness of the bodiless metaphysics — that mere ghost that turns somersets on a trapeze in the clouds — he had studied the physical emplacement of the soul as well as he could. So the two men, though from different sides, were almost equally enthusiastic over the marvellous power of mind which Mr. Button had shown.

" See," said the admiring doctor : " could there be a more volcanic explosion of that idiotic doctrine that the soul is only a phase of matter! Here the man's matter is smashed. For what I know he has a second stroke at this very moment ! " — Veroil spoke with so much earnestness, and stopped short on the sidewalk and faced round on Adrian so suddenly, that the young man actually thought Mr. Button had the stroke — " at this very moment, and the second or third will make a dead certainty of him — and just see what he laid out in his mind. The key to it all is a sense of justice. Nobody could have imagined — at least I didn't, that the rough fellow had so much nobility in him. He has planned out, *first* to do complete justice to Civille at the expense of his own child ; *second*, to do complete justice to you ; he must think very highly of your business abilities and morals too, young man, to give you such a power as that — and *thirdly*, to do complete justice to his own family ; for if they do what is right, they are to have the whole estate. And consider the shrewdness of the means. Those two women are as ugly and selfish and obstinate and cunning, — well, as beasts. So he fights them with their own natures. The girl has stolen and borne false witness; if she confesses it she will be rich and independent ; if she refuses she will be poor, and wholly dependent upon her mother, and the woman she tried to ruin will have her money. And if Mrs. Button does not succeed in inducing Ann to do right, she loses more than half her fortune. And both of them, by obeying orders, and doing justice, will secure their own wealth, and will reduce your authority to the minimum. I confess that I doubt whether you and I together could have contrived so efficient a machine, all alive and well as we are, as that poor fellow with his half-dead brain! And he knew that talking wouldn't do any good; so he wasted no time in that; he just *did* the *thing*. Why, it was a manœuvre as masterly as Austerlitz or Salamanca! And then what a clean piece of work! Not very technical in form, but that instrument will stand, I tell you! I know enough of such things to see that. It's a *very* neatly worded paper!"

"I only observed one thing to add," said Adrian; "there is no clear provision for terminating my authority. But I shall not do any thing without consulting Mr. Button, and his lawyer too; and if the business is settled and the women do as he says, I can transfer the property to them and surrender the trust. But doctor, one question: — How came Mr. Button to know about Civille?"

"Oh, Ann had hinted something to him on her side of the question; and when he caught her at the store, he saw the rest of it plain enough. He knew she was arrested, because I told him this morning."

By this time they had reached Veroil's office, where a company of patients — impatients, perhaps, they should be called by this time — were waiting in the anteroom. In a few moments' further consultation it was decided that Adrian should take no steps under his power of attorney until after a definite reply from Mrs. Button and Ann. It was obvious enough that he must proceed, when he

did so, upon full consultation with Mr. Button's own confidential legal adviser; and these points having been agreed on, the doctor went in to his prescriptions, and Adrian hastened to Mr. Van Braam's.

He found the old gentleman quite cheerful, and evidently on the way to a complete recovery. A full and explicit conversation with Civille had relieved the poor old gentleman of the terrors and pains which had done so much to throw him into what the doctor called a typhoid fever; although he cried a little over her account of her experience at the hands of the law, lightly as she touched it. Probably his sojourn in the upper room had done him good, by the mere substitution of a somewhat purer air for the close and vitiated air of his parlor. Probably the opportune delinquency of Adrian in respect of his duties as nurse had contributed somewhat to the convalescence. At the moment when Adrian came in, the work of nature was being assisted by some cream toast, cold roast lamb and black tea, which Civille was ministering, as Miss Katy Bird had left them bright and early that morning; and of which Adrian, on invitation, partook with a fine appetite, for it was late dinner-time. While they ate, Adrian supplied his contribution to their knowledge of the situation, "exchanging wisdom for refreshment," remarked Mr. Van Braam, "like the angel Raphael at Adam and Eve's lunch in Paradise."

"Giving orations for rations," said Adrian.

"He o'd the balance," said Civille. The two men reproached her for following their example.

When Adrian, in his recital, came to the description of the relics which he had found on the bed in Olds' room, Mr. Van Braam, though struck with the intensity of the situation, remarked with coolness, " I'm glad he's dead ; " and when in the progress of the story it turned out that he was not, he was rather discontented.

Adrian doubted somewhat in his mind what to say about the scene at Mr. Button's; but on the whole he thought best to tell it all; for he knew very well that he was talking to a safe audience. The picture which Adrian described was a striking one, for he possessed a very fair talent for describing. The summary analysis which he subjoined of the evident object of Mr. Button, was even more effective, and it prevailed even over the obstinate and constitutional dislike of Mr. Van Braam, to some extent.

"I don't like him," he said, "and I never shall; I can't; and I won't stay in his house a day after I have a hole to hide in. But he has done a just and manly action. I like *that.*"

Civille agreed to the admiration, and she added her love. " He always liked me," she said — " I know it : I'm so sorry for him ! I wish so I could make him well again ! " But she was as anxious as her father to get away from the house. And they united in an absolute and almost angry refusal to receive any portion whatever of Mr. Button's estate on any terms. This, Adrian said, was right, but he reminded them that the gift could only take effect after Mr. Button's death; that it was only a contingent one, conditioned upon Ann's obstinacy in disobedience; and that being by will, it was revocable at any time during the testator's life, if he retained his mind. Thus, he convinced them, silence for the present might do good and could not do harm.

This point thus decided, Civille and her father were the more anxious to escape from their present domicile; and the general question of ways and means was almost of necessity brought (so to speak) before the house.

"Well, my boy," said the old gentleman, "I have almost always contrived to have a hundred or two in the bank, but that won't go far in New York; and besides, I haven't got it, at present. — We can sell the furniture."

" I can raise money enough to last us a while," said Adrian — " the old house at Hartford is done for, you know, — there'll be something paid for that. Then I suppose I must have a pretty handsome income from this trusteeship, unless I should destroy the property " —

" All that's none of my business," said Mr. Van Braam with one sort of gruffness.

" Won't you let it be my pleasure then ? " said Adrian — " you know you would do so for my aunt and me. Let us have our turn first, that's all."

Civille, who sat near Adrian, quietly put out her little hand and clasped it upon his. He started, and looked at her with shining eyes.

" That's different," replied the old man. " Oh, — it's a horrible thing to have to be helped ! " And he groaned and twisted himself in the bed. It is true; it is frightful, for a man, to be helped instead of helping himself.

" At any rate," concluded Adrian, after considerable discussion, — " at any rate, my dear sir, you can't go quite yet; and if you allow me, I'll look you up a place." As he spoke, an idea arose in his mind which he almost uttered on the spot. It made him give Civille's hand a sudden little squeeze, which puzzled her, for she thought it meant "You understand!" and she did not understand. But it meant only itself. It was agreed accordingly that the young man should try his luck at house-hunting.

"Besides," said Mr. Van Braam, all at once, hitching the conjunction however to a link some little ways back in the chain of conversation, — "it would take some time to raise money on real estate, even if we could give security for it. And we want some at once. Rent must be paid in advance in this city. It costs terribly to move, Adrian; — I know I could be carried — at any rate, to-day, if I had a place to go to. And I don't believe that we three have twenty-five dollars in cash, available at this moment."

It was true. The habitual indifference of Mr. Van Braam to money considerations, the exhaustion by his illness of the trifling savings he might have put aside, the loss of his secretaryship, left him almost penniless. On Adrian's part the loss of his position, the narrowness of his own means, the amount, considerable for him, which he had been expending right and left during his few but sufficiently busy days in New York, had almost emptied his pockets. As for Civille, the dear child had nothing. "I have some rich relations," said the old gentleman, after a rather disagreeable pause — "and Adrian, I'll tell you what; if you'll undertake to get them to do something for Civille and me now, I'll let you repay them if we can't, when the time comes. That would do, perhaps."

"Oh, father, you mean over at Belleville?" said the young lady.

"Yes. Old Philipp Van Booraem has kept his Dutch name and his Dutch nature too, better than I. I'm Scrope. He's Van Booraem. I haven't communicated with him nor his wife this fifty years," continued the old gentleman. "I know they're alive, that's all; and they are rich."

"Oh, I'll try it," said Adrian, cheerfully. "I'm not afraid to have a man say no to me," he added. "I must try to see Bird at once, too; he's likely to know of some house or some real estate agency; and by the way I agreed to call at Purvis's to-day. I'll go over to Belleville to-morrow morning, and I'll see you as soon as I get back."

CHAPTER XXXIX.

THE ten days next following the day of Civille's release and of Mr. Button's *coup d'état*, were to a certain extent days of suspense to Mr. Van Braam and to Civille. Adrian returned the next day from his expedition to Belleville, and reported with the grave brevity of one who makes the best of a defeat that old Mr. Van Booraem had refused, not obligingly, to advance any money whatever. This report Mr. Van Braam received with much equanimity, saying that it was like the old gentleman. Adrian went on to observe that he was in hopes he had heard of a nice place for them already, but that he must wait a while, and as the dictionary men advertise, "get the best."

"Well," said Mr. Van Braam, "when you find a place you and Civille may go and consult over it; if it suits you it will suit me."

Adrian reported further that he had made an arrangement of a strictly business nature with Mr. Purvis, which would enable him to provide for the expenses of removing and re-establishing the household gods without any inconvenience. "You shall owe it and pay it, interest and all," he said, "just as extortionately as you like; you won't refuse me that, I am sure?"

This was all correct and reasonable; but still, thought Civille — However, she did not quite think it, either; it was one of those faint, faint impressions that are only remembered afterwards, like those paths across the Scottish moors which can only be seen from the distance, so imperceptibly do their color and surface differ from the rest of the expanse. So she said nothing, but with a curious serious smile, offered Adrian an envelope. "I got it this noon," she said; "read it." He did so. It was the note from Ann Button. "I kept it to show you," said she; "now I will burn it."

"Wait," said Adrian — "I don't know. Burning would not be so good a plan as to return it to her to be destroyed. She would be certain then. But even then, she might fancy that you had kept a copy. And besides — On the whole, Civille, it will be safest for yourself to keep it for the present." Mr. Van Braam was of the same opinion; and the note was kept.

Apropos of Ann Button's note, two other pieces of information were forthcoming. Civille told Adrian that she had learned that morning from Dr. Veroil that Jenks & Trainor had sent in a bill to Mr. Button "for sundries supplied at sundry dates," which Mr. Button had ordered paid. And Adrian told Civille that he had met Katy Bird in the street — somewhat, he added, as if she had been waiting for him, — and had learned from her that her plan of campaign had been altogether successful. Her idea had been suggested to her by the shawl of Mrs. Barnes. She had ascertained from some of the church officers the names of all the children of Ann's Sunday School class, and of a considerable number of the parents of infants accommodated at the Shadowing Wings. Amongst these honest folks the detective lady had found a great harvest of gifts, all proceeding from Miss Ann Button; being divers sorts of goods from Jenks & Trainor's, and some books, probably selected on similar principles at bookstores. This system of gifts Miss Bird had concluded, explained the circumstance which had so thoroughly puzzled herself and her brother; to wit that while a stolen article had absolutely been found in Civille's possession, not the least trace of any such thing could be discovered at Mr. Button's, "though" Miss Bird had remarked with graphic energy "I raked every inch of that house from garret to cellar with a fine-tooth comb." The same cunning which had served to escape so long the eager watchfulness of merchants and police, had suggested the effective method of promptly dispersing all acquisitions among the obscure and unsuspected multitude of church beneficiaries, whose shiftless habits and rough usage would rapidly destroy them. Thus the stream of these unsanctified benefactions had been sinking silently into the desert of poverty, as some desert rivers spread and disappear into the sandy wastes, without leaving any mark of life, unless it be the coarse, rank and worthless sedges and reeds generated by the salt and barren ground. Had it not been for the accidental discovery of the shawl which Mrs. Barnes had given Civille, the balance of evidence would in a certain sense have inclined against Civille herself. And as Bird had remarked at the hospital, it was

Jenks & Trainor's own act in causing Civille's arrest, that had brought the shawl into the case, and had at once liberated the innocent and convicted the guilty. For it was the sight of the shawl, the knowledge of its transfers, and the consciousness of so many other existing proofs of the same kind, which had vanquished even so obstinate a will, so limited an intelligence, as those of Ann Button. Accomplished facts may tell on such minds; they certainly do not feel statements nor arguments nor beseechings. The fact of the shawl not mentioned but shown — the fact of the disinheriting, not threatened but executed — had prevailed to extort the written confession from a mind obstinate as glass, bending only under an intensity of heat that would destroy most metals into vapor. The very distortion or defect of this unhappy child of two strong parents was a union of their faults; their obstinacy, their secretiveness, and above all their love of gain, had in their daughter intensified beyond a healthy power and tone, and had become that species of silent fury, which is called monomania.

Mr. Button continued in about the same state. Adrian consulted fully with his lawyer, a dusty-looking and dried up person, who shook his head a good deal over the power of attorney, complaining particularly of the unlimited trust it conferred, and of its duplicate nature as power and as will. But after having himself seen Mr. Button, and also the doctor; and after being a good deal consoled by Adrian's request that he should supervise all transactions under the power, and should charge accordingly, that it would be safe for Adrian to execute his trust so far at least as related to the publishing business; that is, to exercise a general supervision over it,

and to dispose of it in case of a good opportunity. The nomination to Congress was of necessity made over again, "the candidate, our well known, popular and energetic fellow-citizen, T. Button Esq., having been obliged" — as the papers delicately observed, "in consequence of a somewhat serious illness, to withdraw his acceptance. All parties and persons," the paper added, "join in hoping for a gentleman so useful and public-spirited, a speedy and complete recovery." And thus the political career of the publisher died before it was born.

———

Upon the morning of the tenth day, came Adrian to say that at last he thought he had found exactly the place; and would Civille be pleased to go and inspect it?

Yes, she would. She was quickly ready, and the young man escorted her to one of those neighborhoods which are as if somebody had planted a few clean streets for a specimen in the middle of the careless dirt of New York. It was on the "west side," so called, pretty well up town. As they went, Adrian began to entertain Civille with a few conundrums and other nonsenses, and was merry before her, insomuch that the young lady inquired what he had had for breakfast, and recited to him with a grave smile,

"Woe to that land whose princes are drunk in the morning."

"Wrong, oh princess," said he with glee. "There's no such saying. There's a verse in Ecclesiastes, 'Woe to thee, O land, when thy king is a child, and thy princes *eat* in the morning.' This would seem to show that in Palestine under the Mosaic dispensation breakfast was an immorality. But as the poet observes, a better lot has been planned for me.

Coffee is a glory and a beauty that not even the Preacher ever dreamed of; and so is a good United States breakfast, oh princess. But Civille, why are you so sober?"

"I don't know exactly," said she; "I don't like to go away from that solitary old house, and yet I know I shall be glad when I have got away. —I guess it must be the mere fact of the change. Besides, you know I am a serious person."

"Yes, I do," said Adrian, "you are. But yet I always have an idea that you are conscious of the funny side of things, under your grave face. I am very often perfectly conscious of the serious side of things when I am perhaps making fun about them outside."

"Then, Mr. Button's illness, and his family — I'm so sorry for them!"

"Why, so am I," said Adrian; "that is, I would do any thing I could — conveniently — to help them — not so much as you, Civille, for I'm not so good; but still, a little. But all the same, I can't see why I should be unhappy over them myself. If I should do a little bit of misery over every misfortune, I should go hang in a week. It's not because I'm insensible, Civille; it's because I'm so uncommonly delicate and sympathetic, and I have to guard myself against it."

She looked at him in her grave sweet way, with her peculiar introverted expression, and said, as if she were reflecting, rather than speaking,

"You think you are joking, but it is more like the truth, Adrian."

"Well," said he, "I don't want to cry this forenoon, any way. I sha'n't do that unless you dislike the house, Civille."

"I guess I shall like it, Adrian," she said; "I almost always like what you do."

"Then, dear, please to promise to like all that you find out to-day I have done, and all I do to-day too — will you?"

The tone, light as he tried to make it, was shaded with earnestness; if he had quite succeeded, she might perhaps have promised; but with a feeling not of doubt, not amounting to shyness — an undefined hesitation, she looked up at him — saw something a little eager and anxious in his eyes, and looked down again, silent. They walked on, chatting as before, but with a little less frivolity on the young man's part. As they approached the place, Adrian explained that it was the second floor of one of those houses built in separate tenements, of late years becoming so common in New York; and that he was afraid she would find the rooms very scanty and cramped after their whole house.

"Oh, I don't mind," said she — "you know we don't give many very large dancing-parties!"

The house was of brick, and looked new and clean. It was on a corner, and the entrance was on the side street, on the north side.

"The windows look south, east and west," said Adrian. "The flats lie cross-ways, through and through the block, and the party-wall naturally shuts in the north side of all the rooms." He opened the outer door with a pass-key, and showed her upstairs. The tenement was soon inspected; it was perfectly clean and new, none of the floors in that house having in fact been occupied at all, Adrian said, except the fourth or uppermost. There was a parlor, with a little bedroom off it; three other rooms; and a cosy little kitchen. All these, by ingenious management, were lighted from the outside air; the closets and store-rooms being arranged to occupy the darkest part. "All the modern improvements" were provided; gas, water, a snug bath-room even.

Civille, as they went from one room to another, expressed a reasonable de-gree of satisfaction. "You don't like it quite well enough to suit me," said Adrian. "Bare walls and floors always look dreary; it is like trying to tell by a skeleton whether it be-longed to a handsome person. I knew that would be so, and I hap-pened to find out that the people in the floor above have just got it fitted up and are to move in to-morrow, and so I got the agent to get me leave to go in there this morning. We'll go up and see how the rooms look fur-nished."

They went up accordingly, and be-ginning at the kitchen, examined the whole, in the reverse order from the floor below. The clean stove, the new tables, a good ingrain carpet, pantry and dish closets well fur-nished, gave the kitchen a look of comfort. There were beds in the bed-rooms; floors were carpeted and windows were curtained; the dra-peries and furniture were not new, but were in that comely, comfortable, *tamed* condition, that tells of skilful and careful use.

"It is almost as if I had been vis-iting here before," said Civille; "it wouldn't surprise me to have the lady of the house open the parlor door and ask me how I did."

They came to the little parlor that overlooked the avenue.

"Oh, what a delightful room!" said Civille. It was carpeted with a Brussels carpet, mostly in cool gray, with some green, and a few lit-tle sprigs of clear red and spots of warm brown. The walls were in a paper of similar tone; plain dark shades, with neat lace curtains be-hind them, were at the windows. There was a fire in the stove, and the room was summery and pleasant. A book-case rather too large for the room crossed one end of it, and there was a piano and a little sofa. The tables and some of the chairs were noticeable; they were very old solid mahogany or cherry, almost black, and the backs of the chairs were pierced and carved in elaborate grace-ful designs. Some modern ones of a more luxurious if less majestic char-acter, were however interspersed.

"Sit down and rest you a little, Civille," said Adrian; and he led her to the sofa. — "Well?"

She looked all around the room: "How pleasant it is!" she said.

"Will the rooms down stairs do, then, when they are furnished, do you think?" said he, with some anxiety.

"Why, it's lovely, Adrian, — they will be lovely," said Civille, and she blushed with pleasure, and the tears stood in her eyes. "It's just perfect. Every thing's so snug and nice! I half grudge to have the people come."

"They won't until afternoon," said the young man, well pleased. "Now you can tell how differently it will look down stairs when you get all your things in there. — Then you are sure it will do?"

"Indeed I am, Adrian. Why?"

"Why, the fact is, — I've hired it. You see, the agent wouldn't give me much of a refusal, and I consulted my judgment and decided to run the risk. But it's a great relief — though I felt pretty sure. — I'm going to try the piano, — if they've only been sen-sible enough to leave it unlocked."

They had; and he sat down and struck a few notes. It was not a pow-erful instrument, but full and sweet-toned. He played a waltz or two.

"Sing," said Civille; and Adrian sang her "Bessie."

BESSIE.

Bessie wears a gown of red; A home - spun gown, and an
a - pron blue. She has no hat up - on her head, And her
wee brown feet are without a shoe. Bes - sie's hair is like
sun - set's gold, And her eyes are born of the deep blue sea.

BESSIE—Concluded.

In their depths is a sto - ry told— I love Bes - sie, and

she loves me, I.... love Bessie, and she loves me.

Bessie's hands are hard with toil,
  And her cheeks are dark with the wind
    and rain;
But her lips are rich with the rosy spoil
  That if once I taste I must taste again.
Bessie has never a silken gown,
  Nor a crimson hat, nor a necklace fine;
But she wears of cowslips a golden crown
  That I'd rather than any queen's were
    mine.

Bessie's step is light like the fawn's,
  And her voice like the chiming of silver
    bells.
I hear it oft in the summer morns,
  But I dare not whisper what it tells,
Lingering and dying around my heart,
  Ever and ever, its echoes be.
Who shall divide us, or what shall part ?
  I love Bessie, and she loves me.[1]

  "Ah, it's good," said Civille.

  "But is it true, Bessie?" asked Adrian.

  "Love is always true," said she. — "I wonder what old box that is, Adrian? And where's the clock that I've heard ticking ever since we came in?"

  She had been studying the room and its appointments with a sort of pre-occupation ever since she came in; walking round to chair and table and stopping to inspect and as if to dream, or rather as if each of the wooden antiquities in its turn whis-pered to her a profound secret. Once or twice she jumped up from the sofa to go and look at the old-fashioned mirror over the mantle-piece, — a noble plate of heavy old French glass, — or at a picture or two on the wall.

  "Oh, some old family chest or other," said Adrian, smiling; "what makes you so uneasy? You hop like a hen on a hot griddle."

[1] These pretty and musical words appeared almost twenty years ago in Putnam's Monthly. If the author's name was forthcoming it would be acknowledged; and if there is any wrong in repeating three stanzas of them here, pardon is asked, and on notice right will be done.

"I don't know," she said; "it's like those sudden sensations the books tell of, that flit across your mind with a feeling that it has all happened once already. — It hasn't. — I didn't know the house was here."

"Oh," said Adrian, "it's prophetic; it's because you're going to be here again — in the house I mean; "Coming events cast their shadows before."

"It's so queer to leave that old thing in this pretty room!" said she, — and yet it's a nice old chest!" —

"The draymen might have left it by mistake," said Adrian; "they couldn't help making some blunder or other."

But Civille arose and stepped toward the chest; stopped short and turned toward the side of the room:

"There!" she cried, — "I knew it was one of those old hall clocks! Why, you old beauty!" And she clapped her hands, applauding. Well she might. Behind the door, so that she had not seen it, was one of those ancient columnar clocks whose stately heavy deliberate beat seems to tell only patriarchal time. The hurried fussy tick of the petty clock of to-day is a suitable memento of our over-driven state. "Everysecondeverysecondeverysecond!" chatters the tormenting thing. But the calm old hall clock quietly says, "AN, HOUR; AN, HOUR; AN, HOUR."

This clock-case was a wonder. It was of a polished fine-grained red wood, apparently one of the rare dense African sorts; and was inlaid throughout with many curling abundant wreaths of leaves and flowers in a wood of very white color and close satiny surface. These wreaths trailed and waved in sweet easy curves all over the panels, and around the fanciful inlaid arabesques that centred each panel. Elaborately ornamented slender columns finished the edges of the case; delicate little carved rails and pinnacles, fine and graceful as old lace, set off the ledge below the face, and the edges and summit of the gabled top. The bright silvered face told hours, minutes and seconds, and a mysterious opening further displayed the days of the week and of the month.

Civille looked over to Adrian with a puzzled air; "It's so long since I was in Hartford," she said, — "but I thought your aunt had a clock like this."

"She did," said Adrian, — "but it was not quite so old as this one is."

Civille turned about, stepped back to the old chest, which stood just in front of the book-case, and knelt down to look at it. She sprang up instantly and cried out,

"Adrian Chester, what does it mean? This is the Scrope Chest! See there!" And sure enough she pointed to the elaborately floriated old English letters of the word "Scroope" and the familiar old arms, carved on the front. She tried the lid, but it was locked.

She rose and came back towards him, flushed, perplexed, the great gray eyes shining, the white teeth just glancing through the parted red lips.

"Sit down again, Civille," said Adrian; "I'll 'fess.' Yes, it is the Scrope Chest. The things are ours; that is what puzzled you so; that is our clock; it wasn't as old when you saw it as it is now. — I could hardly keep my face straight to see you go dreaming round and asking questions of every old chair. I was waiting to have you remember."

"Why, I never saw them but once, and then I was a little bit of a girl. But — tell me?"

"The rooms are ours," said Adrian. "So you see I ran a double risk in hiring those below for you. Come — sit down." So he seated her again at his side on the sofa.

"I knew there was something familiar the instant I came into this room," said she. — "You secret man!"

"Family failing," said Adrian. "Do you tell all that is in your heart, Civille?"

She smiled. "Come; tell me," said she; "What a vision it is!" And she gazed all about the room again with affectionate delight.

"Well," began Adrian; "The chief idea of all came into my head while I was arranging with you and your father to find you a house. I mean the idea of having my aunt come here. Apparently I shall have to stay in New York for a while, and the old house in Hartford has got to go; so I wrote that very day to tell aunty all about it, and I exhorted her to have every thing packed and sent here that we wanted to keep, and to have every thing else sold, and to come. Isn't she a splendid old lady? She did it, and she's here — stopped with an old friend of hers in Brooklyn until we could get in some supplies, and she and I will sleep here to-night.

"When I had posted that letter, next I went to see Purvis; he had asked me the day before to come, you know. He said there was a librarian wanted, for a new library, here in New York, just begun; one of the reference kind, where steady attendance is required, and gentlemanly manners; and he was so good as to say he thought I should do. So I thanked him, and explained my situation, and said, Can't it be had for my old friend and relative Mr. Van

Braam? So he said perhaps yes, but he didn't know him, and could we give any references? I thought a while, and mentioned Mr. Stanley. Purvis said that would do, if Stanley would write one; for, you know, Stanley is very famous in a whole world of about two dozen antiquarians and book collectors, and the man who is founding this library is one of that kind. Stanley was to be in New York in a few days, Purvis said, and he would see what could be done. I don't doubt we shall arrange it, nor does he. Then I went over to Belleville. Oh, Civille, they've got such a pearl of an old Dutch palace there! a great square stone mansion down by the river, all hidden in old trees, and so stately! And they are delicious old people. The old gentleman is a great big heavy old fellow, more than six feet high, with a broad fat face and two light greenish eyes that positively project beyond his face; the only real boiled-onion eyes I ever saw. And his wife, a perfectly wonderful person, ancient and prim beyond all description, and with a prodigious lace cap. They were very courteous and magnificent, and ordered in cake and wine in a delightful old fashioned way, and I bowed and drank a solemn health to Mrs. Van Booraem, which they approved. I opened the business as delicately as I could, and they heard me gravely through. Then the old gentleman proceeded to answer on hereditary principles, as it might have been during some unfriendly negotiations between the authorities of New Amsterdam and the Colony on the Great River. His kinsman, he said, had married into some Connecticut family — please to remember, Civille, this ill-assorted marriage was that of your great-great-great-grandfather! — had married into a Connecticut family; and as he had made his bed, so he must lie in it. And he declined positively to advance any money either by way of loan or gift, either with security or without.

"So I had to fall back on my friend Purvis and myself. I have made all the arrangements, Civille, that I could; Mrs. Barnes is going to do our work for us; she will do yours too if you like; she says she would rather work for you, Civille, for nothing and find herself, — and you too, she said — than to get double wages anywhere else. May she?"

Civille looked at Adrian; with tears in her eyes, but with a quiet look of gladness, very serious, very deep, very sweet.

"But, Civille, so would I. — May I?"

———

— "Love," said Adrian, interrupting himself, "why did you never write me all those reasons you promised for refusing me? Tell me what they were."

"I don't know," said she, reflectively, always with her penetrating steady serious gaze, as if it was the soul only she spoke to, and with that introverted manner, as if her utterances were half unconscious, — "I don't know. I guess I didn't want to. But I meant to."

"Well; what were they?"

She blushed, very deeply; "Perhaps I had not quite escaped from some influences of — of the *Solidarité* people. And I didn't know — I mean I could not leave father. And I was afraid — Adrian, perhaps it was silly, but I have not been very strong the last year or two, while we have been in that old house — I was afraid I should always be sick. — I

don't like sick women. — And I didn't know how much — you must guess it, Adrian," she whispered.

"Yes, dear. — You are myself. — Now, Civille; do you remember about the things you told me at Mrs. Babbles's room that night? — I think you just reflected back to me the thoughts in my mind. Do you remember? There were four things; and what you said was my own meaning. Only, I did not know it so distinctly then as I did afterwards when the time came for the things to happen. I asked you — though it was in a roundabout way, — these four questions: Whether I should accept the offer that Mr. Button had made me; whether the Scrope Estate would be recovered; whether I should marry Ann; and whether it was you or she who had been stealing. So you answerd to the four: No; no; no; she. It was as if those four judgments were four buds in my mind, and you could see them before they were open; I had to wait for the blossoms."

She mused a little; "Very likely," she said, simply. "I don't understand it. But if I am yourself, that's the reason. I don't think I feel quite so wise, since I've been away from all those philosophers. I don't care, though. You may see all my thoughts, dear, if you want to; but if I have to be asleep before I can see yours, you'll tell me afterwards?"

He promised.

"But," she resumed, "what made you think of that evening just now?"

"I think it was my meditating over those questions and answers that gave me the habitual feeling that we are the same person," said he.

"You said that just like me," answered Civille. "But how fortunate that I did not write you all my wise reasons. If I had," she said, laying her two hands in his, and looking at him with a lovely perfect trust, " if I had, think of all the revenges you would have wreaked on us — by letting us alone."

" Oh, certainly !" said he; " but only think how such a sentence would look if you wrote it ! I think I like it though, when you give me an interlinear translation with your eyes and your hands, Civille."

———

— " Don't, please — that's enough," said she.

— " I was punctuating the translation," said Adrian.

— There was a peremptory rap at the door. The young people gave a great jump, but before Adrian could open it, Miss Chester entered.

" Where are your ears ? " said the old lady, sharply. — " Civille, my dear, kiss me. How you have grown ! How nice and rosy you are ! What's the matter ? I knocked twice, and then pounded, before I came in. Am I late enough ? Was I discreet ? "

" Yes, aunty," said Adrian ; " All the arrangements are approved."

" Very good," said Miss Chester, whose remarks might imply some previous understanding with Adrian, unless indeed they implied a wondrous present insight. " She would have been a silly thing not to approve them all. You are good enough for anybody."

" It's well she isn't a Hartford girl," said Adrian ; " you know they always say there ' He isn't half good enough for her.' "

" Every man is a fool that doesn't marry," answered Miss Chester, sententiously ; " and every woman's a fool that does."

" So you are willing to have a fool in the family ? " asked Civille.

" We shall hardly make it out this time, my dear," said the old lady, kissing her.

" Well," said Civille, " I must go back to father."

CHAPTER XL.

" My wedding gift to you, father," said Adrian, and he held out to Mr. Van Braam an old fashioned key, with intricate wards, a steel barrel, and having, in place of the modern ring, a handle curiously and elegantly worked in brass.

" But isn't it a barbarian custom, my boy, to buy one's wife ? "

" Oh, this is only a civilized memorial of it, just as shaking hands is what remains of the ancient surety of disarming. It is not an equivalent ; it's a compliment."

The key was that of the Scrope Chest. The chest itself had that day been brought down from the floor above, and was placed on two chairs before Mr. Van Braam's easy chair, in his new quarters. He had some days before been moved over from the old home, having recovered sufficiently, and the two little households had in the most natural manner in the world been fused into one joint and several family. They ate together at most meals, and sat together most evenings ; but each of the four could be alone at will. Enforced society is next in discomfort to enforced solitude — next either way, according to the tastes of sufferers.

This evening they were together ; Adrian and Civille were to be married next day. The few and simple arrangements and formalities had been provided for. Civille, Miss Chester and Adrian sat by. The old gentleman took the key.

" What is it, Adrian ? "

"Open it, father, open it," said Civille: "we all know except you. Adrian didn't mean to tell me, and he did not at first; but — he says — he couldn't help it. It's something you'll like."

Mr. Van Braam looked at the three happy faces, and with a funny affectation of excitement, he unlocked the Scrope Chest and threw back the oaken lid.

"Books, hey?" he said. Then he looked suddenly at Adrian; his pale face flushed quickly: —

"Is it — is it" —

"Yes, father," said Adrian: "it is the Lost Library. Not over thirty volumes; but look at them."

The affectation of excitement gave way to a real one. The old man's hands trembled so that he could not hold any thing. Adrian lifted out the largest volume, a good-sized folio, bound in rough looking blackened leather, and opening it to the title-page, laid it in Mr. Van Braam's lap, so as to lean against the chest.

"Sixteen hundred and twenty-three," said the old gentleman. "Printed by Isaac Jaggard and Ed Blount! What business had Adrian Scroope with Shakspeare? The First Folio! Why, Adrian! — is that what you call only a compliment?"

"But look at them all," said Adrian; "See," — and he took up another black-looking old thing, a small thick quarto, and opened that. "Mamusse Wunneetupanatamwe up-Biblum God," he read, — "Eliot's Indian Bible, first edition!"

"I won't look, I won't hear, I won't have a thing, you sha'n't have Civille, if you don't tell me this instant, how you got them, Adrian!" said Mr. Van Braam, desperately.

So Adrian, recapitulating the account he had given Civille of old Philipp Van Booraem's refusal, went on with a chapter which he had omitted on the morning when Civille had recognized the chest:

"Mr. Van Booraem refused in the point-blankest manner. When he was through, the old lady said the family had had a similar experience before. 'You remember, Philipp,' she said to her husband, 'that that very Philipp who married the Hartford person, borrowed some money of your great-grandfather? There was some security — an old box of goods, I believe. That is up in the store-room now. Suppose we return this to our kinsman? If it was good for money then, it is good for money now.' 'My dear,' said the old gentleman solemnly, 'a just thought. We will do so.' Then they sent up-stairs, and finally went themselves; and had a long hunt and at last dug out an old red cedar chest all locked and marked 'Philipp Van Booraem, 1698,' which they formally made over to me. I accepted it with equal formality, and got it over here as fast as I could without opening it, for I had a presentiment; and I did not choose to let them see what the contents were, if I should be right. And I found the books, and put them in here; and you are as welcome to them as the roses are welcome in June."

"And *now* will you look at your Shakspeare?" asked Adrian, as he took out a pocket rule; "The celebrated Scrope Shakspeare of the future. There isn't such a copy in the country! There isn't a leaf missing nor imperfect, nor a repaired leaf in it; it's a tenth of an inch taller than the Roxburghe copy, and it's full a sixteenth of an inch broader than the broad Lenox copy. There's just one single stain, — a mark of four fingers, in the middle of 'Troilus and Cressida.' And for my part I'd rather have those old thick bevelled English oak boards and that curly broken black leather grinning open at the corner, than risk having the book pared in binding by Roger Payne himself, — if the old cheese-eating artist were alive! Just see how bright Droeshout's engraving is! You couldn't improve that copy, humanly speaking, unless you could get Shakspeare's autograph on it!"

"As he died seven years before Heminge & Condell published the edition, that would be too much to expect," answered Mr. Van Braam; "I think we may be contented with the best copy — for if you are right, this is the best copy known."

"I collated every folio of it," said Adrian, with the certainty of a bibliographer, "by Bohn's Lowndes, and by Mr. Barton's privately printed account of his copy. This has not Mr. Barton's two cancels, it is true; nor any cancels; but what are cancels to that extra white paper? Toads to a phœnix!"

"What had Adrian Scroope to do with Shakspeare, I want to know?" repeated Mr. Van Braam, after laughing at Adrian's Dibdinity; "I should have thought him much more likely to groan with Prynne in the Histriomastix over the horrid superiority in style of manufacture and extent of sale, of play-books over bibles. Above 40,000 play-books sold in two years, Prynne says, and he cannot but with grief relate it."

"I imagine that Puritan or not, Adrian Scroope knew good literature when he saw it," said Adrian, — "or he wouldn't have been a Scroope. Scholarly Puritans liked Shakspeare well enough. Read Milton's sonnet on him, full of admiration and reverence. Prynne was a bigot and a pedant; not a scholar. Our friend had to keep his play-book pretty quiet though, in Old Hartford. That accounts for its being in such prime order. And the fact that all the books have lain in pawn for a century and a half accounts for all of them being in such extraordinary condition."

The whole collection was taken out and laid on the table. There were about thirty items; but thirty books may represent a comfortable little fortune, if each volume will bring $17,-000 like the Perkins Bible, or even $11,000 like the vellum Boccacio, or even $3,580 like the Daniel Shakspeare, or even $1,100 like the Rice Indian Bible. Besides these two books, there was a copy of the Bay Psalm book; several of the rarest of the Mather publications; a perfectly clean copy of the Indian Primer of 1684; —

But those who wish the details may apply to Mr. Van Braam for a copy of his little privately printed list; a marvel of bibliographical fulness and care, and in which the zealous old gentleman has introduced a number of terms of enthusiasm which — incredible as it may seem, Mr. Dibdin did not know of.

As for Mr. Van Braam's happiness, it was such that his three companions just sat and laughed, for pure sympathy of enjoyment — and cried a little too. He laughed himself, and then he stopped short and looked as if he was afraid they were laughing at him instead of with him.

"No, it's because we are as glad as you are, father," said Civille, who saw what he was thinking.

A ring at the door. Mrs. Barnes brought up the cards of Dr. Veroil and Mr. Stanley.

"Show them up," said Mr. Van Braam — "Adrian" (in a low tone) — "my boy, have you a list of the books?"

"Yes," said Adrian, laughing; "and we'll watch Stanley with all our eyes, too."

"I declare I've half a mind to lock 'em up and not say a word," said Mr. Van Braam, with a sort of half genuine anxiety.

The gentlemen came in.

"A last professional call," said the doctor, pleasantly; "not to appear in the bill, but to be the thirteenth of a good honest dozen."

"I staid a few days longer in the city than I expected," said Mr. Stanley, "and hearing from Mr. Purvis of the great good fortune of Mr. Chester, I could not resist the double temptation to call on my kinsfolk and to see the treasure."

The treasure was shown. Probably no man in America could so fully appreciate it or could be so intensely unhappy at not having it, as Mr. Stanley. He opened and scrutinized book after book, in silence, pale, and with a face like a gravestone. For a collector feels quite as much anguish over what another man gets, as if he himself had lost it. Meanwhile Mr. Van Braam, watching him sharply, also thanked him for his kindness in helping him to obtain the place of librarian.

"No kindness at all," said Stanley, with his cold dry smile. "Pure matter of business. Mr. Chester gave me the Scrope Genealogy, and I gave him my influence."

"You did!" exclaimed Mr. Van Braam, in distress, to Adrian.

"I did," said the young man, with a smile, "and would again if it were to do now."

"I wouldn't have parted with that pamphlet to get librarianships for all the twelve apostles, and Moses, and the prophets besides," said Stanley, exalting the value of what he had, to comfort himself before the sight of what he had not.

"Oh, I've got another," said Adrian, in the quietest manner in the world.

Everybody started and stared. Stanley looked as if he was going to faint. "What do you mean?" he said.

"Just that," said Adrian. "You have your copy, haven't you?"

Stanley felt in his pocket, and found the precious pamphlet. Adrian drew forth from his pocket another, which he compared with it. It was true; print, signatures, sketch of Scrope arms, and all. Doctor Veroil gave a great laugh.

"Found it with the books, I suppose," he said.

"Yes," said Adrian.

"But it's not according to agreement" said Stanley, his face white, and his voice trembling, with his concentrated anger.

"Yes 'tis," said Adrian a little gleefully: "You said 'Give me your Scrope Genealogy, and I'll get him the librarianship.' And I said Done: and done it was. I didn't covenant that there wasn't another. Ask Purvis; it was in his shop, and he stood by. I gave you *my* Scrope Genealogy. This one is not mine; it is Mr. Van Braam's. Adrian Scroope must have kept two copies, marked alike, by way of making sure of the evidence of his identity; and instead of one, it was thus two that were preserved when the edition was destroyed."

"Good enough for you, Stanley," said Dr. Veroil, with satisfaction.

The unhappy East Hartford antiquary cast a look of the profoundest scorn upon his copy of the Scrope Genealogy, and slapped it down vengefully upon the table, as if to knock its brains out. "I'd burn the rascally thing," he exclaimed, "if 'twasn't for making yours worth more, Adrian Chester! But you've got five hundred of them, probably — the whole edition!"

Nobody thought it worth while to answer this taunt of the infuriated Stanley; and Adrian said, taking a few old yellow documents from his pocket,

"There was a small file of papers too; and a couple of those are particularly interesting. This" — he unfolded a ragged-edged strip of coarse paper — "is the other half of the Scroope Will. I don't know how the Will should have come to be written on this leaf of an old book, unless paper happened to be scarce at the moment; nor have I the least idea how one half should have strayed out of the old box and the rest staid in. There are accidents enough, however — At any rate here it is, with the rest of Adrian Scroope's name at top and in the signature. I meant to offer it to my friend Mr. Stanley, but I'm afraid to do so at present."

"Pass it over," said the antiquary, gruffly, and yet making a great effort even so, — "least you can do, I think. You can't have a second original of *that*, at any rate!"

Adrian handed it to him, and Stanley at once subjected it to a searching scrutiny. Adrian continued: "And here finally, is the explanation of the career of the books, and of the Throop question too." —

Everybody looked up, even Stanley himself:

"Of course it was plain enough that the books had come to Belleville from the Van Booraem side; but as the will shows that they were expressly given to Deidamia, it remained to discover how Adriana's husband, Philipp Van Booraem should have made use of them as a pledge to borrow money on. So here is a letter that tells this story; it's a nice letter, and a credit to the family."

Adrian read it; it was a formal, old fashioned, elaborate composition, such as the cultivated ladies of the time used to write, but through the flourishes and periods there penetrated a very lovely sisterly affection. In it, Deidamia Chester explained that she had received all their deceased father's property of every kind according to the tenor of the will; that she was moreover fully possessed of his personal wishes, which the document did not clearly explain. According to these, she continued, she had conveyed to "our dear Brother Adrian or Adeodatus Throop, presently a Minister in Norwich" (Bozrah was not set off from Norwich as New Concord until 1737, explained Adrian) "his full share and rightful inheritance," viz., the real estate' left by the deceased, and sundry books of divinity. The personal property, "and amongst it the rest of the books, and even a Bible or two," the writer had kept; and then she added that she loved her sister as much as her brother; that she knew their father would at this moment (viz. of her writing) choose that she should follow her own heart rather than the recollections of his displeasure while alive; and that therefore she should insist that Adriana should accept a full and just half of the personal estate referred to; "and," pursued the kindhearted woman, "inasmuch as my deare Husband is a man of activitie and publique trusts, and whereas your Philipp is a Student, doubtlesse hee may preferr to his share (which is yours) in part all the Bookes which I have kept, and indeed, deare Sister, I did perhaps keepe them to that end." And so, with many expressions of affection, the quaint old document ended.

"There is an indorsement," concluded Adrian, "which notes that books and money and furniture were received accordingly. Now this letter tells the whole story, you see. The Reverend Mr. Throop remained Throop in Bozrah. Very likely his old father went and lived there quietly with him, and died and was buried there. I shall search the old burying-ground when I go there for an ancient gravestone with A. T., or A. S., or both, on it. It was the son, however, not the father, who was *the* Reverend Adeodatus Throop of Bozrah. Deidamia kept the Scrope Chest, which staid at Hartford. As for the student Philipp Van Booraem, he wanted money, and pledged the books to his grouty Dutch cousins, and the ill-conditioned creatures kept them safe for us; I'm under obligations to them."

"Well," said Civille, "it was quite right in Deidamia to do that."

"Certainly," said her father, "any of us would have done it, I hope."

"It would have been a struggle for some of you," observed Dr. Veroil with a funny look at Stanley; "as for the rest, the question might have served to test the blood, for what I know, I don't imagine Mr. Button would have thought it necessary."

"How is Mr. Button?" asked Mr. Van Braam.

"About the same," said the physician; "he may live twenty years in this state; or he may go off to-morrow. His active life is ended, however, at any rate."

"And his Theological Seminary, and the Scrope Association, are ended too, I guess," said the old gentleman, with sympathy that had a faint color of amusement.

"All buttoned up together," said Stanley, with a grim cold satisfaction not tinged at all with sympathy. "How is it, Chester?"

"One is as dead as a herring, and the other as Julius Cæsar, Mr. Stanley," said Adrian — "as you seem to fancy figures of speech in the matter. In fact, I got a most enthusiastic letter two days ago addressed to Mr. Button, from Mr. Aymar Brabazon de Vere Scrope of Scrope" —

"Mr. Bird called him 'Brab,'" interrupted Civille, smiling.

"Oh, let him have his name," said Stanley, "he hasn't much else, I guess" —

"Agent of the Scrope Association, to say that legal proceedings had been set on foot with every hope and almost a certainty of success; that this was the more evident from the active opposition already set up by certain wealthy parties now in possession of some of the Scrope lands in Buckinghamshire; that the prize was magnificent; that law expenses were heavy" —

"There it comes!" said Stanley with a grin.

"Yes," said Adrian — "it does —; in fact, unexpectedly heavy, he admits; but he appeals to Mr. Button's family pride and enterprise and decision of character and so on, and wants a remittance of a thousand dollars, say £200 gold, at once."

"I wish he may get it!" said Stanley, — "what did you reply?"

"I wrote him a formal business letter as attorney for Mr. Button, to explain that he was not of the family after all, and to request repayment of the sum of $500, cash advanced, or a note of hand satisfactorily indorsed, for the same with interest."

"Why," said Stanley, "Button didn't expect repayment, and you can't enforce it, even if Scrope were here."

"I know that," said Adrian; "but we sha'n't hear from him any more."

"Chester," said Dr. Veroil, "you were telling me one day about that devilish cellar saloon place in one of Mr. Button's houses where you and Bird and Scrope went one night" —

"I know, doctor," said Adrian — "I warned the fellow out the very day I saw the lawyer, I found the attorney didn't much like to have the estate lose the rent, but I told him at once that if any such questions were made I should drop the whole business, and he held his tongue. They offered to add fifty per cent to the rent; but I don't agree with Vespasian; I think such money *does* smell bad. So out they go, Paradise, devils, fig-leaves and all."

The visitors soon took leave, Stanley somewhat mollified by his manuscript. It was growing late.

"It's time to go to bed," said Miss Chester.

"Sing us one song first, Adrian," said Civille.

He sang Tennyson's "Bugle Song."

BUGLE SONG.

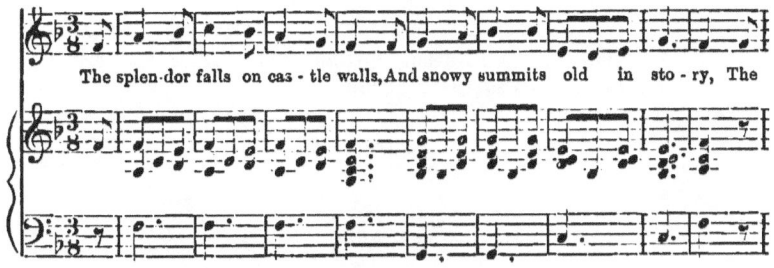

The splen-dor falls on cas-tle walls, And snowy summits old in sto-ry, The

long light breaks across the lakes, And fall and cat-a-ract leap in glo-ry, Blow,

BUGLE SONG. — Continued.

bu - gle, blow, Set the wild ech - oes fly - - - - ing! Blow,

bu - gle, an - swer, ech - oes, dy - ing, dy - ing, dy - - ing.

"Is it true, Civille?" said Adrian, turning to her as he finished the last of the three sweet stanzas.

She only blushed and looked at him.

THE END.